Advance Praise for *Resting Places*

"This is a beautifully crafted novel of unbearable loss and earned forgiveness. Elizabeth, a middle-aged lawyer, crosses the country in search of her son's final resting place. Along the way, she uncovers the best and the worst of herself. Michael C. White has wrought a remarkably moving tale of love and redemption."
— Anita Shreve, author of *The Pilot's Wife* and *Rescue*

"*Resting Places* takes readers into that most feared of landscapes: the difficult terrain where a parent must grieve the loss of a child. But Michael C. White is a masterful storyteller and a deft tour guide who interfaces this meditation on sorrow and death with a classic but contemporary quest story. Traveling alongside the author's complex, sympathetic, but not always likable protagonist as she searched for the meaning of her son's life and death, I read compulsively and voraciously. Elizabeth Gerlacher is a character I will long remember and Resting Places is a story I will not soon forget."
— Wally Lamb, author of *She's Come Undone* and *I Know This Much Is True*

"This is a lovely, searing book. A son dies in a baffling car smashup, and circumstances hint at the even-worse agony of a suicide. With consummate skill and tenderness, Michael C. White follows his parents onto the broken ground of the unbearable hereafter."
— Jacquelyn Mitchard, author of *The Deep End of the Ocean*

"*Resting Places* is no restful terrain for Elizabeth, the heroine, in White's deeply soulful and brilliantly mythical novel. It is a masterful summation of all life's possibilities and its ultimate triumph. The ending made me weep with joy; the grace of this masterful novel still lingers deep inside my soul long after I grudgingly laid this book down."
— Da Chen, author of *Colors of Mountain* and *My Last Empress*

"In *Resting Places*, Michael C. White takes on that most daunting of challenges: excavating the grief of a mother who has lost her only son. While her husband Zack attends support groups, Elizabeth isolates herself emotionally until a chance encounter of a rainy highway sets her on an unexpected path toward salvation. Haunted by the makeshift roadside crosses commemorating lost souls, Elizabeth searches for answers, and for a resting place of her own. The story is a masterful exploration of the guilt, the anguish, and the mystery of catastrophic loss. Michael C. White is one of our most gifted authors, and he is at his best in this profoundly moving and brilliantly written book."
— Clint McCown

Resting Places

Michael C. White

Open Books Press
Bloomington, Indiana

Published by Open Books Press, USA

www.OpenBooksPress.com
info@OpenBooksPress.com

An imprint of Pen & Publish, Inc.
www.PenandPublish.com
Bloomington, Indiana
(314) 827-6567

Print ISBN: 978-1-941799-23-9
eBook ISBN: 978-1-941799-19-2

Library of Congress Control Number: 2015955821

Printed on acid-free paper

Cover artwork by Ali Reynolds
Cover design by Jennifer Geist

For Reni,

With love,
in our season of mists

And my people shall dwell in a peaceable habitation,
and in sure dwellings, and in quiet resting places.

—*Isaiah*

Prologue

The summer Luke was five, they had gone on vacation to the British Isles. After spending a week touring London, they'd taken the train to Fishguard, Wales, for a night-time ferry crossing to Rosslare, Ireland. During the train ride the three of them had played games, like rock, paper, scissors and the find-it game, where the first person to spot something passing by in the countryside—a cow, a steeple, one of those red phone booths—won. They were going to spend another week traveling around Ireland, stopping along the way in Tralee, where Elizabeth's father had been born. Her father had passed away a few years before, and his death had left Elizabeth with a jagged hole in her heart. Suddenly she felt herself drawn to her roots, and she wanted Luke to remember his grandfather.

"That's Poppy," she explained to her son, showing him the black-and-white photo in her purse. It was of a tall, good-looking, raven-haired young man in a seersucker suit standing in front of Sean Og's Pub in Tralee. Elizabeth had always been told she was the spitting image of her father, tall, with that dark hair and broad mouth.

"He's dead," her son said.

"Yes, sweetie, Poppy's dead. But we're going to see where he was born."

"Was he little like me?"

"At one time, yes."

Weary as they got off the train well past midnight, they lugged their suitcases through a cool, oddly bluish drizzle toward a small café and gift shop along the wharf to await the boarding.

Inside, they dropped their bags, and Zack leaned in and kissed her. "This is going to be fun."

Glancing over Zack's shoulder, she asked, "Where's Luke?"

"He was just right here."

They hurried back to the train and began searching up and down the aisle of the car they'd been in. Trying to reassure her, Zack touched her shoulder and with that engineer's pragmatic approach to any problem, he calmly said, "Don't worry. We'll find him." Of course, they would, she told herself. Wasn't this just like Luke to wander off when she turned her head for a moment—in the mall, a crowded airport, at the beach. Sometimes she thought Luke did it on purpose, an only child vying for the attention of his busy, professional mother.

"Luke," Elizabeth called in a fluttery voice, at first mimicking those restrained British tones. But then, as the seconds ticked by, louder, more urgently, she cried out, "Luke, honey! Luke!" When he didn't turn up on the train, they hurried outside, searching among the growing crowd of people assembling for the ferry crossing. As the uneasy seconds spiraled quickly into terrifying minutes, Elizabeth kept telling herself that Luke would show up any second, as he always did; she told herself that everything would return to normal and they'd board the ferry and continue on with their vacation. *Wait till I get ahold of that little stinker*, she even said to herself, trying to make light of the whole thing. But then she happened to catch the expression on the face of her normally unflappable husband. It was a stiff mask of barely withheld dread. That startled her. If Zack was scared, then it must really be serious.

At that point there was an announcement over the loudspeaker telling people they could begin boarding the ferry. This was followed by a sudden surge of damp bodies *en masse* toward the ramp. Elizabeth and Zack felt themselves being lifted up as if on a wave and carried along toward the ship. In such chaos, she thought, how could they ever hope to find Luke? Her mind quickly bounded over all the other possibilities and went straight for the worst, the blackest prospect. What if at that moment their son was being abducted and whisked away. Or what if he had fallen into the murky sea, his little body floating face down in the harbor. This line of thinking carried its own inexorable and brutal logic. A lawyer used to arranging facts in a line of causation, she began working out the implications of Luke's disappearance. Having to describe her son to the local authorities: age, height, weight, the color of his eyes (a grayish blue, sort of), what he was wearing (she couldn't remember), the tiny scar beneath his chin he'd gotten from a fall when he was two (her fault, as well). Canceling the rest of their vacation. After a certain interim, having to imagine the unimaginable plane ride home, just her and Zack, the empty seat between them mocking their loss. Followed eventually by wondering what she'd do with Luke's things back in Connecticut, his clothes, his toys, his entire bedroom. And finally picturing the interminable days that would stretch out in front of her and Zack to the end of time, and all without their little Lukey. One moment they were a happy little family and the next everything had been ruined. Like *that*!

But suddenly her mood changed from fear to anger. She'd be damned if she was going to let this happen. No, she was Luke's mother and she'd move heaven and earth to find him. She would do anything.

"Luke!" she cried out with renewed vigor, abandoning finally the last vestiges of restraint or dignity, no longer caring in the least how absurd she must have appeared to those around her—this loud-mouth, hysterical American parent. She left Zack and ran through the crowd, jostling people, shoving her way past them, all the while crying out her son's name. Nearly knocking down one man with a cane ("What in the bloody hell, lady!"), she frantically made her way through the crowded wharf. Finally she stopped, spun around, her eyes darting this way and that, the pulse pounding in her neck. Then, beginning as a frail, almost inaudible whisper, a voice rose in her head, a voice that was both hers and that of a complete stranger. It was something she hadn't done, not in years anyway, something that wasn't part of her normally pragmatic, rational makeup. Elizabeth was thirty-six years old, someone who hadn't been to church since she'd gone off to college, who hadn't spoken a word to God once in all that time. Yet she now found herself offering up a plea somewhere within the darkened corridors of her mind: Please God, don't let anything happen to my baby.

Seconds passed.

Finally, Zack was at her side, his arm around her shoulder.

"It'll be okay," he said, squeezing her.

Later, she wouldn't be able to explain why or how, what made her think of it, but she took Zack's hand and rushed with him toward the café. Inside, standing in front of a display of touristy trinkets was Luke. He was completely mesmerized by some toy he was playing with, twirling the thing back and forth in front of his face. Seeing him, alive and whole and unhurt, Elizabeth felt herself finally exhale the breath she hadn't known she was holding, the sour feeling of dread passing from her lungs. The entire ordeal lasted perhaps only ten minutes, but it was the most frightening, most defining ten minutes of Elizabeth's life.

When he saw his parents, Luke came rushing up. "Can I get this, Mom?" He was holding out a small toy in his hand.

Squatting, Elizabeth grabbed her son roughly by his narrow shoulders and had to fight the urge to shake him silly.

"Don't ever do that again," she yelled, tears springing to her face. "You scared mommy."

As tears welled up in Luke's eyes as well, she came to her senses, and hugged him, desperately, fiercely, squeezing him so hard he cried out, "Mom, geez! You're hurting!" After a while, she saw what it was that Luke held: in his palm sat a tiny toy airplane, a die-cast model of a British Spitfire, so small it could fit in the palm of his hand. Taking after his father the engineer, Luke had developed a obsession for model airplanes. He loved collecting them, displaying them on his shelf, hanging them by string from the ceiling. Of course, she bought the thing for him—she'd have bought him a thousand toys, anything to show her gratitude. Zack bent down and wrapped his arms around his wife and son.

"Didn't I tell you it would be all right?"

Feeling suddenly grateful, as if they'd been granted a second chance at happiness, Elizabeth grasped Zack's face and kissed him. "I love you," she said.

"I love you, too. But we'd better get a move on or we'll miss the boat."

They hurried out and boarded the ferry and carried on with their vacation. Elizabeth tried hard to push the near-tragedy of that moment from her thoughts. As they toured Ireland, with Zack stressing out every time they came to a roundabout and Luke in the back making *zzzzzzouuu* flying noises with his toy airplane, she tried to enjoy herself, tried to forget what "might" have been. But she couldn't, not completely, not in Ireland nor later on the plane ride home, nor in fact, in all their subsequent years together; in fact, she couldn't hear the word "Wales" or see that airplane on Luke's shelf back home without it conjuring up that dark memory, that moment of unholy terror of a mother facing the loss of her child. Nor could she avoid the nagging vulnerability that would plague the rest of her days, knowing as she did that in the blink of an eye everything could change. Like *that*.

Chapter 1

Elizabeth had just gotten off the phone when a timid knock sounded on her office door. She'd hoped to have a little time to collect her thoughts but before she could answer, the door opened a crack and a slight, haggard-looking woman—more girl than woman—poked her head in. Her blackened eyes reminded Elizabeth of a raccoon.

"*Perdone usted, señora Elizabeth,*" the woman asked meekly. "Ese time now?"

"*Un momento, por favor,*" she said to the woman.

The woman withdrew and shut the door. Elizabeth sat there for a moment, trying to regulate her breathing, hoping to get herself together enough to deal with someone else's problems. Sometimes she felt like an actor who had to put aside her own life to assume that of the character she was playing. She'd sensed a growing annoyance on the part of Sheriff Crowder, the man with whom she'd just gotten off the phone. "I *told* you ma'am, we already sent you all his personal effects."

"But I'm sure he had it with him."

"It's not here."

"Could you just humor me and look again?"

"We don't have it, Mrs. Gerlacher," the sheriff said flatly.

"Did you even—" but before she could finish he cut her off.

"I have to go, ma'am. Goodbye."

"Fuck," she cursed, slamming her palm so hard on the flimsy dinette table that it spilled some of the coffee from her cup. This made the fifth or sixth time she'd called the Marrizozo, New Mexico Sheriff's Department in the past few months. Not only about the missing diary but to discuss other things in the police report. Things that didn't make sense. That didn't add up. Each time she called, the sheriff seemed to get more defensive, and each time, growing increasingly desperate for answers, Elizabeth had become more pugnacious, allowing her cross-examination behavior to leach into her normally civil demeanor.

Finally she got up and went to the door and opened it. Peering out into the hallway of the annex of the small chapel, Elizabeth saw the woman sitting on the floor, her feet curled up Buddha-style beneath her. She appeared as anxious-looking as an eighth-grader waiting to speak to a teacher about a bad grade. The last time Elizabeth had seen her, nearly a week before, the rawness of her bruised, swollen eyes had taken Elizabeth's breath away. But the swelling had gone down considerably, and now the gaudy yellows and purples looked more like some teenager's idea of a makeup statement.

"Please come in, Fabiana," Elizabeth said.

The young woman entered and sat down opposite Elizabeth. She was wearing a Mets baseball cap, a flannel shirt that hadn't been washed in a while, and torn, loose-fitting jeans. She kept both hands over her distended belly, holding it like a football player guarding against a fumble in the last minutes of a game.

"*Cómo estás?*" asked Elizabeth, opening her file on the desk.

"*Bien.* Good."

"And your eyes? *Ojos*," Elizabeth said, touching her own eyes.

Nodding, the woman replied, "Better. No hurt."

"And how is . . ." Elizabeth asked, patting her own flat stomach, "the baby?"

"*Sí. El bebé está bien.* Kicking," she said with a smile.

For the past several years, Elizabeth had been doing pro bono work at the Mystic Women's Shelter, a couple of afternoons a week and sometimes on Saturdays. The shelter was part of a Catholic retreat on a small island off the coast of eastern Connecticut. The cramped space Father Paul, the director, provided Elizabeth as a part-time office was actually an all-purpose room, containing the copier, a coffee machine, an apartment-sized refrigerator, a tag-sale kitchen set with cracked vinyl seats. It was also where Father Paul— or simply Paul, as he preferred—hung his vestments in the corner. On one wall was a picture of John Lee Hooker, Father Paul's favorite blues guitarist, while on the opposite wall was one of Jesus feeding the five thousand. Loaves of bread and fishes appeared to fall from the sky, a downpour of food. Elizabeth helped women with legal matters—began divorce proceedings, sued for child support or alimony, or sometimes defended them against crimes like theft or drug possession. Or like now, to guide them through the intricacies of filling out a restraining order. Unlike in her law firm where she worked mostly with affluent middle-class people, her clients at the shelter were mostly poor white or women of color, or, like Fabiana, recent immigrants. Fabiana journeyed from Honduras two years earlier and when she related the complex story of how she got to the US, Elizabeth could only shake her head and say, "Jesus." There were no translators so Elizabeth had to rely on her rusty high school Spanish and hand gestures to communicate.

Elizabeth began helping the woman fill out the restraining order, which was intended to keep her boyfriend from beating her up again.

"What that mean?" Fabiana asked Elizabeth.

"*Ex parte.* That means we're asking the court for immediate relief from the respondent."

"*Qué es* . . . respondent?"

"That's your boyfriend. Jorge."

Fabiana stared down at her lap. Elizabeth felt that if not for the fading bruises around her eyes and a depleted look that belied her nineteen years, Fabiana would have been pretty. She had lucid, acorn-colored eyes, a generous mouth, lustrous skin the hue of burnished leather, and long, auburn hair she kept in a tight braid down her back. Her fingernails were chipped and dirty from the per-diem work Father Paul had arranged for her on a local farm sorting carrots and potatoes. Even from across the table Elizabeth could smell the sour sweat and farm odor on her body. The woman's son, Esteban, two, was at that moment playing with the half dozen other kids in the shelter's nursery, several doors down. Occasionally, Elizabeth could hear a gleeful cry or a wail of disappointment emanating from down the hall. Sometimes, when Elizabeth wasn't busy, she'd go down to the nursery and get down on the floor and play with the kids. Fabiana's Esteban was adorable.

"I no can see him?" the woman asked. Against the brown skin of her neck Elizabeth spotted a silver crucifix.

"*He* no can see *you*," Elizabeth replied, almost harshly.

"*Cuánto tiempo?*"

"That will depend."

"On what?"

"On a lot of things. Mostly what the court decides in his case."

"Will he go to *la cárcel?*" Prison, Elizabeth knew.

"Yes. But only if you testify. *Comprendes? Testificar.*"

The woman shook her head vigorously.

"What do you mean? You have to testify. Look what he did to you."

"I no want him go away to *la cárcel.*"

"Next time it might be worse. You have to think of your unborn child. *Su bebé,*" she said, patting her own stomach again.

"Jorge, *ese* good man. He just get *un poco loco* when he drink."

"But you have to press charges and you have to take out this restraining order. We need to make sure he stays away from you. If you don't want to do it for yourself, do it for Esteban. For your baby."

"Jorge love Esteban. And he *es padre del bebé,*" the woman said, pointing at her stomach. "He no hurt them."

Elizabeth stared at her. "But he's capable of that. You must do this, Fabiana."

"*Lo siento.*" I'm sorry. The woman waved her hand in front of her face as if she were brushing away a bad smell.

"I can't help you if you don't let me," Elizabeth said, her anger and frustration slipping into her voice.

Elizabeth didn't understand such women. Women who were abused, who were used as punching bags for their husbands' or boyfriends' frustrations and angers, and who still somehow loved them. But that wasn't really love, she thought. That was need or fear or guilt or something else entirely, but not love. Love couldn't grow in such unfertile soil.

"I know, I know," Fabiana said, tears beginning to run down her bruised cheeks. "You so good to me, *señora Elizabeth. Lo siento.*"

Despite being annoyed with her, Elizabeth got up and went around the table. She squatted down and put her arms around the woman. Fabiana's sobs convulsed her small body. She clutched onto Elizabeth like a frightened child.

"It's all right, Fabiana," Elizabeth said, rubbing the woman's back in small circles. She was so skinny, Elizabeth could feel the vertebrae along the woman's spine. As she stroked her, she recalled when Luke was small and crying about something or other, her holding him and quieting his fears. *It's all right, sweetie. Everything's all right.*

"At least promise me you'll think about filling out the restraining order. You at least have to do that."

"*Sí, sí,*" the woman said. "I think about it."

Elizabeth stood, suggesting to the woman it was time to leave, that she had done all she could for her. The rest would be up to her. At the door she turned and said, "*Señora Elizabeth, usted es una buena mujer.*" You are a good woman.

"*Gracias.* You think about it, Fabiana. For both your children."

She was sitting at the table, doing some paperwork and imagining how sweet that first scotch was going to taste, when Father Paul stuck his bald, narrow head in the door.

"How's Perry Mason today? I guess I'm dating myself with that?" he said with a boyish grin.

"You're not that much older than me. When I was a little girl I used to watch the reruns with my father."

"The Irishman?"

"As Irish as Paddy's Pig," she said with a laugh. She'd told Paul about her father. Though she didn't go to church herself any more, she'd had Paul say a Mass for the man. It was something her father would have appreciated.

"He loved how Raymond Burr always got the bad guys in the last two minutes," she explained.

"Virtue always rewarded, sin punished. What a perfect world."

Father Paul was thin, with a shaved head and the sharp, lupine face of a fox. His countenance was softened a bit by sad-looking Bassett hound eyes, eyes that were perpetually pink from his doing laps without goggles in the overly chlorinated YMCA pool in town. As usual he wasn't wearing a collar, but rather cargo pants and a ratty old sweater he'd bought when he was in the Aran islands on an archaeological dig involving the ancient church Na Seacht Teampaill. Elizabeth and Paul would talk about Ireland, the places Elizabeth's father had gone. A brilliant man, Father Paul possessed a bushel-full of advanced degrees and spoke a dozen languages.

"Unfortunately, we don't always get the bad guys, Paul," she said, rolling her eyes conspiratorially at the priest.

"You mean, Fabiana's boyfriend?"

"Ah huh. She wouldn't sign the restraining order and now she's not sure she wants to testify against our boy Jorge. She doesn't want him to go to *la cárcel.*"

"She's a very feeling woman."

"Or a very foolish one."

"It's not always a bad thing to turn the other cheek."

"It is when you know the other cheek is going to get itself smacked."

Father Paul came in and sat down across from her. He ran his hand over the top of his shiny, bald skull. His shaved head reminded Elizabeth of a newborn's, soft and vulnerable.

"You don't know that for sure."

"I'm willing to bet on it."

"All right, what?" he asked, extending his hand across the table.

"What do you mean, 'what?'"

"I'm willing to bet he's learned his lesson."

"All right. How about a bottle of scotch?"

"I'm not much of a scotch man. How about if I lose, I buy you a bottle. But if you lose, you come to work here."

Elizabeth let out with a chuckle. "Now *that* seems like a fair deal."

"I can't match your salary. But you'd get this nice plush office with an ocean view," he said, grinning. When he grinned he looked even more like a fox. The first couple of times he'd asked her to come work here, his tone had been almost playful, and each time she treated it as the joke that she thought it was. But recently he'd told her the shelter had gotten a large federal grant and that he actually had the money to pay her, though far from what she was currently making. Of course she already had a job, a junior partner in a small law firm twenty miles away. She liked Father Paul. He was smart and worldly, well-educated, with a good sense of humor. And she liked that he wasn't preachy. His faith wasn't a Sunday-morning spiel, but rather a way of life. He talked like a regular guy, about jazz or sports, history or politics, but he let his actions speak for him. He'd set up this island retreat for battered woman and their children, raising money by the seat of his pants, twisting the arms of donors, cajoling or embarrassing them, and often spending his own money on food and toys for the kids. He was a good salesmen, too, getting people to donate their money or time or expertise to the cause. Like with Elizabeth.

"You're so good with women like Fabiana," Paul said.

"Now you're giving me a snowjob. What's next, you're going to try to sell me some indulgences? Then again, I could probably use some."

"No, you are. You obviously have a gift."

"The only gift I have is that I'm a lawyer. And I don't think some dirtbag ought be able to beat her around whenever he feels like it."

"It's more than that with you. You get satisfaction from working here."

It was true, though. She did enjoy working with these women, seeing that they got at least a semblance of legal representation. Despite the annoyances and frustrations, like with Fabiana, she felt that her time and effort here made a difference. Sometimes a big one. It was, in fact, one of the few things which gave meaning to her life lately. She not only provided legal counsel but also helped women get social services, food stamps, day care. Sometimes she even sat with them and helped them learn to read and write. At the same time she'd begun to find the work at her law firm increasingly tedious: wills and divorces, pre-nups and LLCs, defending spoiled little rich kids against DUIs and possession charges. In fact, she'd been spending so much time at the shelter lately she'd let her regular job slide, so much so that Warren Fuller, the senior partner, had had to call her into his office on a couple of occasions to speak to her.

"And how are you, Elizabeth?" Father Paul asked, his expression what she could imagine it to be in the confessional: thoughtful, considerate, patient.

She looked across at him. "Fine."

"That's your default reply. How are you really?"

"What do you want me to say?"

Paul sat there for a moment, his fingertips forming a little tepee that he tapped against his nose. "It takes time," he offered.

"As in, 'time heals all wounds'?"

"Something like that." He continued staring at her, his pink eyes slick and painful looking.

Elizabeth stood, started to pack her briefcase.

"Getting over something like this does take time, Elizabeth."

"No offense, Father, but how the hell would you know about *something like this*?" she said more harshly than she had intended. She was obviously still annoyed by the phone call earlier. When she looked over at him she saw the effect it had. He looked snubbed. "Forgive me, Father. I had no right to say that."

"No, no, it's all right. Besides, I have the hide of a rhino," he said with a smile. "With this job you have to be thick-skinned. And you're right. I can't possibly know what it is to lose a child. But I have suffered loss. You can't be human without suffering loss, Elizabeth."

She was going to say this was different, that there was no loss in the world like this, but decided not to say anything.

"If you'd ever like to pray with me, Elizabeth?"

"Thanks for the offer. But I don't think so."

"Well, I'll pray for you and your son anyway. Is there anything new in your son's case?"

"I guess nobody but me thinks it's a 'case,'" Elizabeth said, using her fingers to make quotation marks around the word. "I don't know if I told you this before. But Luke had a diary."

"Really?"

"I think it was with him. When he was killed."

"And you believe that's relevant?"

"It wasn't among his things they sent us later. I've called the sheriff down in New Mexico several times asking for it but he says they never had it."

"How would that be important?"

"Who knows?"

"You're thinking it might give you some insight into what he was feeling then?"

"It couldn't hurt."

She finished packing her briefcase and snapped it shut. Then she grabbed her umbrella and started for the door.

"Well, keep my suggestion in mind."

"Which one?" Elizabeth said with a smile.

"The job. We couldn't pay nearly what you're making, but what a view, huh?" he said, looking out at the ocean. The day was rainy and blustery, the sound full of angry whitecaps. Only a single lobster boat braved the rough waters. "Drive carefully. It's pretty bad out there," Father Paul said.

As she headed out she saw Fabiana at the back of the small chapel. Elizabeth paused unseen for a moment. The younger woman had lit a candle and was praying. Elizabeth hadn't been to church since her college days. Yet as she watched Fabiana, her head bowed and her eyes tightly shut, Elizabeth found herself longing for such simplicity. She thought of Father Paul's offer to pray with her. She thought, too, of how fervently her own father used to pray in church, his head bowed, his knuckles white from his tightly folded hands. As well she thought of that time in Wales, when they'd "lost" Luke, of the prayer she had offered to God. She had prayed that time and like some sort of magic trick her son had reappeared. If only it were that easy.

Chapter 2

Elizabeth was heading home through a driving rain. Sheets of water coated the windshield, even with the wipers on high. Since it was already after five, she'd decided to skip going back to the office and go straight home. She had to prepare for a contentious divorce hearing the next day, but she was exhausted and figured she could go in early and review her notes. She'd taken a shortcut along a divided turnpike that wound its way through the rolling hills and apple orchards and rock-strewn dairy farms of Eastern Connecticut. Normally a pleasant drive, today the rain had pooled in spots along the road, and Elizabeth found herself occasionally jolted and having to fight the steering wheel to keep the car going straight. Besides, the Saab was getting a bit long in the tooth, and didn't handle well in bad weather. Zack was always on her to trade it in and get a new car. He preferred she get a four-wheel-drive, something substantial for the New England winters, something she'd be "safe" in, as if she had to negotiate the mountainous terrain of the Andes instead of suburban Connecticut. Lately he was unusually concerned about her safety. She both appreciated and understood his concern but at the same time found it a little claustrophobic. Besides, she liked her old Saab, the hand-worn steering wheel and the cracks in the leather seats, its familiar old car smell. She'd had the thing for fourteen years. She'd taught Luke how to drive on the car, along the curvy road that skirted the lake they lived on. The thought of getting rid of it caused an actual physical ache beneath the angle of her jaw.

She leaned to her right and opened the glove compartment and removed the small pint of Cutty Sark she kept stashed there. All day long she'd been yearning for that first drink. How it seemed to release some pressure valve inside of her. She opened the bottle and took a sip, feeling the sweet, hot, almost tender rush of the booze, first at the back of her throat, then in her stomach, before slowly radiating out through her body like liquid smoke. She felt her shoulders, unknowingly tense, begin to relax. It had been a long day, first at her law office and then at the women's shelter. The memory of her conversation with the sheriff from New Mexico still rankled her. *We don't have it, Mrs. Gerlacher.*

She was about to take another sip from the bottle when she saw it, an old green pickup, pulled way over onto the shoulder of the highway as if broken down. As she approached it, she happened to spot a figure to the right, in the high grass off the road, just at the edge of some woods. Coming abreast of him, she slowed and gave a quick sideways glance. Through the distortion of rain on the glass she thought she saw a man on his knees seeming to peer at something before him on the ground. Elizabeth continued on a short ways, then, on an impulse she would later wonder about, pulled sharply over and hit the brakes, the car skidding to a halt on the wet, loose gravel. She glanced back over her shoulder at the man. What on earth was he doing, she wondered. Perhaps something was wrong.

She thought of calling 911, but instead she did an odd thing: she put her car in reverse and backed up until she came within a few feet of the truck's bumper. She stopped there and, angling the rearview mirror, she was able to spy on the man. Yet even this close she still couldn't quite make out what he was doing. Maybe he'd hit an animal that lay in the high grass, perhaps a deer he'd stopped to tend to. The man was so preoccupied with whatever it was, he didn't seem to have noticed that a car had stopped. Dropping the pint on the passenger seat and grabbing her umbrella from in back, she got out of her car and trudged along the shoulder of the highway. The rain was driving hard, and even with the umbrella she felt water striking her legs, dampening the hem of her skirt, soaking the toes of her high heels. As she passed the truck she saw that it was battered and rotted out, with a make-shift plywood frame set onto the bed for loading things into it. On the door were painted the words *Georges Dump Run's, No Job Too Big or Too Small.* A stickler for language, Elizabeth couldn't help noticing the apostrophe was in the wrong place. The law, she felt, had to be precise, its language clean and clear and unequivocal, avoiding the hazy possibilities of the metaphorical or the sloppiness of the emotional. The law helped to give order to a chaotic world. In her expensive Anne Klein pumps, Elizabeth cut across the sodden, grassy area toward the man.

She stopped a dozen feet away and called. "Excuse me." However, with the downpour he didn't seem to hear her. So she tried again, louder this time. "Hello!"

The man suddenly shot up and whirled around.

"Jesus!" he cried, one hand clutching his chest. "You wanna give me a heart attack, lady?"

"I'm sorry. It's just—"

That's when she saw it, the object of the man's attention. It was composed of two pieces of wood, a vertical and a horizontal slat, joined at right angles. A cross. That's what it was, what he was looking at. One of those roadside things marking the spot where someone had died in an automobile accident. Elizabeth had seen them before, of course—they were everywhere—but it had always been in passing, from a distance. She'd never viewed one up this close, had never paid them much mind. And she'd never actually seen anyone there before, visiting one.

Embarrassed, she mumbled, "I thought . . ." But she didn't know what to say. It seemed perfectly obvious now what the man had been doing: he was praying and she'd interrupted him.

He was an old man, perhaps seventy, with a ruddy complexion and thinning, stringy white hair the rain had plastered to his uncovered and balding skull. His eyes had a strange glow to them; she couldn't tell whether he'd been drinking or if it was just the rain. Thick-necked, burly as an ex-football player gone to seed, he wore a plaid flannel shirt unbuttoned over a black t-shirt bulging over a prominent belly. He was soaked through, the water running down the sleeves of his shirt and spilling in torrents from the deep creases in his lined face, dropping from his bushy eyebrows. His wet jeans clung to his squat, heavy thighs.

They stared at each other for a moment, unsure who should speak next, like a pair of actors who'd bungled their lines. Finally, Elizabeth said, "I thought something was the matter."

He didn't respond immediately, but instead glanced over his shoulder at the cross. It was about two feet high, the white paint faded now almost to gray. Elizabeth noticed along the horizontal bar there was some writing in black lettering: "RIP Hannah. All my love, G." Elizabeth wondered if this man was "G" and if it was the same one as the "George" painted on the truck. Along the vertical bar there was more writing, though it was smaller and faded so badly and she couldn't make it out from this distance. At the base lay a fresh bouquet of white roses wrapped in clear plastic, the sort bought at convenience stores as a last-minute gift, as well as assorted other items—a crucifix, a couple of melted candles, dried flowers, various things she couldn't put a name to.

The man turned back to Elizabeth. "No, nothing's the matter," he replied.

"Well. I guess I'll be going then," she offered with a glibness that tried to belie the awkwardness of the situation. But she remained rooted there, gazing at the cross.

"Why'd you stop?" the man asked.

"I thought you might need help."

"No."

The man held one hand up to shield his face against the driving rain. His eyes, she saw, had a peculiar intensity to them, like someone gazing into a fire, lost in thought or like someone with a fever.

"Well, goodbye then," she said as she turned to leave.

She'd only taken a couple of steps toward her car when he called after her.

"How long's it been?"

The question stopped her in her tracks. She turned and stared at him. "Pardon me?"

"I said, how long has it been?"

"How long has what been?"

"Since your loss?" His voice was flat, the vowels nasally and mashed to hell, a Northern New England accent. Maine perhaps, she thought.

What did he mean: *since her loss*? And yet, somehow, she *knew* exactly what he meant. The question was, *how* did he know? Just a wild guess? Or was it something deeper, more fundamental? Something in her look perhaps? That something she herself would occasionally glean in the mirror, the look of one holding grief so tightly in her eyes, clenched in her mouth like a bitter pill she couldn't bring herself either to spit out or swallow. Or perhaps it was the fact that she had stopped in the first place. Maybe that's what these *sorts* of people did, people who put up these ridiculous roadside crosses. Like a little club. Maybe they had their own rituals and stopping like this meant one was expected to commiserate, to share one's own tragedy. The way it was assumed that people at AA meetings were expected to stand up in front of complete strangers and admit they were drunks. In any event, she wasn't sure she wanted to share anything with this man. This stranger. Still, she had to admit his question had piqued her interest.

"What are you talking about?" she asked, deciding to play dumb.

He wagged his large head. "You've lost someone, haven't you?"

"Why . . . yes," she replied. "How did you know?"

The man shrugged his broad shoulders, turning one palm skyward, so that the rain immediately formed a small puddle in the center of it. She could actually see the drops splattering there.

Instead of answering, he asked, "How long's it been for you?"

She sucked in a breath before replying. "A while," she replied. "More than a year."

"A year, huh?" he offered, with what seemed to Elizabeth a condescending smile. "Why, you're still a newbie."

"Newbie?" she said, the word jabbing her in the throat like a needle. She hardly felt like a newbie, whatever the hell that was. In fact, she felt as if she'd been grieving all her life, as if she'd been born grieving. It was almost as if she'd never known what it was like *not* to grieve, *not* to be in pain, *not* to ache. Like a chronic physical ailment that was always there, reminding you daily. "You don't know anything about me, mister," she said, the acrimony in her tone surprising even herself.

"Listen, I'm sorry," the man conceded, throwing his hands up in the air. "I didn't mean that the way it sounded. Hell, we're all newbies. You never get to be an old hand at this business."

"Business?"

"Losing somebody. For me, it's been six years since Hannah passed." With his thumb he made a blunt gesture toward the cross behind him.

"Hannah?"

"My wife," he replied. "And who did you lose?"

She just stared at him for a moment, wondering why on earth she should be standing in the rain having this conversation with a stranger, why she wasn't in her warm car heading home to one of several glasses of scotch that would slowly deaden her nerve endings and permit her the solace of a few hours of sleep.

But instead she said, "My son. He was killed."

The words seemed to hang in the air, sodden, weighty. There was something astonishing about them, perhaps their stark, unadorned plainness or the exhausted finality of them. They were a kind of irrefutable acknowledgment of Luke's passing, one that she had fought so hard and so long to deny. Ironically this kind of finality hadn't happened that night over a year ago during the phone call from the sheriff down in New Mexico. Nor later, seeing Luke's body lying on the table in a back room of Weldon's Funeral Home. Nor reading the police report months later when she'd finally worked up the courage to open the imposing envelope from the Marrizozo Sheriff's Department. And not even all the times in the past twelve months when she couldn't sleep and would creep into his bedroom and lie on his bed. No, none of those other occasions seemed as irrefutable, as irrevocable as her saying,

My son. He was killed. The words seemed to drive home the fact, like nails into a piece of wood. She coughed, then gulped a damp mouthful of cool air and felt her lungs burn as if she had tried to breathe underwater.

"You okay?" the old man asked.

"Yeah . . . it's . . ."

And just like that she was sobbing. Ragged gasps tore from her lungs and her eyes stung with sudden tears. She hadn't cried for a long time and had even thought her grief had evolved into some more nuanced form, distant and impervious, hard and smooth as polished stone. Unlike those first months after the accident, when she'd start crying like this over anything. A smell. A sound. Some fleeting memory. Such moments would creep up on her, catching her unawares. Once a piece of junk mail addressed to Luke had lured her into tears out at the mailbox. Another time in the car a Bee Gees song had come on and she recalled how she and Luke driving home from his guitar lessons at Mrs. Crossetti's used to sing a parody of "Stayin' Alive." In a moment the tears were so fierce and blinding she had to pull over to the side of the road. And then there was the time sitting in the waiting room at her gynecologist's office. Seated across from her were two women blabbing about bringing their children to college. It made Elizabeth remember the time they'd driven Luke up to St. Anselm College for his freshman year, and how during the drive she and her son had gotten into an argument. She couldn't even recall what had caused it. Those college years were tough ones for her and Luke; almost anything would set them off. Zack used to joke they were like a pair of cats with their tails tied together. According to Luke she was too demanding, a perfectionist, that nothing he ever did—his music, his grades, his friends—was good enough for her. She'd even thought he'd settled on St. Anselm when, with just a little more effort, he could have gotten into an Ivy League school (as she had). When it was time to leave Luke, Elizabeth went to hug him but he actually spurned her embrace, right in front of his new roommate. Hearing the women in the waiting room talk about bringing their kids to college suddenly made Elizabeth start sobbing so that she had to get up and leave.

The old man remained silent, just letting her cry. After a while he said, "Sometimes it sneaks up on you, doesn't it? The pain."

"Y-yes," she replied between sobs, wiping her eyes with the back of her hand, which was soaking from the rain. "I'm sorry for your loss, too."

"Thanks. That's gotta be rough though, losing a kid. I got three and I can't imagine them dying before me. How old was he?"

She looked across at him. "Twenty-one."

The man winced, baring stumpy, yellowish teeth. One was missing behind the right incisor, giving to his face a feral look. "Just coming into his own," he said. "How?"

"A car accident." He stood there looking at her, waiting for more. Then, as if his question had punctured something swollen inside her, words came spilling out, one after the other. "They don't know how it happened. He just went off the road. Straight off. His car flipped over and he was thrown from it. At first they said he was wearing his seat belt, and then they told us he wasn't." Elizabeth shook her head at the sheer inexplicability of such a thing. "He always wore his seat belt. Always. We were really strict about that. They think maybe he fell asleep. There was no other explanation for it. It was a clear evening and he wasn't drinking. The autopsy said he didn't have alcohol in his system. Nothing was wrong, except that he ended up dead. But really, nobody knows how it happened. My husband prefers to say it was just one of those things." She took a breath and when she blew it out, it condensed in a gray cloud in front of her. "How can you lose a child and chalk it up to 'just one of those things'?"

"What's your boy's name?"

She caught how he used the present tense, as if Luke were waiting for her in the car.

"It *was* Luke," she replied. "Listen, I should be running along. I didn't mean to disturb you."

"You're not disturbing me," the man continued. "Did you name him after Luke in the Bible?"

She thought that an odd comment. "No, I just liked the sound of it."

"That's my favorite gospel, you know."

"I can't say I've read it," Elizabeth conceded. "I'm not really into all that."

"All what?"

"Reading the Bible. Going to church."

Her father had gone to church every Sunday, dragging along his two daughters, Elizabeth and her younger sister Suzanne, and their older brother Danny. Mr. Moran, Elizabeth's father, had attended Mass and gone to confession and received communion, all with a seriousness that bordered on the maniacal. Elizabeth's mother, on the other hand, went only occasionally, when she didn't have, as their father explained to them, her sick headaches. When Elizabeth was older she realized it meant her mother was hung over. After college Elizabeth gradually stopped going to church. Later, when she had Luke, she would go for Christmas Mass or Easter service, for the pageantry, for the music, but not much else. She didn't "buy" all that, as if religion were a tag sale whose oft-used items she wasn't particularly interested in purchasing.

Her husband Zack had always been the more religious of the two. Like her father, Zack had gone to church most Sundays, even bringing Luke along. It was something that the two shared. A few months after Luke's death, Zack joined a grief support group that met the first Wednesday of every month in the basement of St. Catherine's in town. He talked her into going once, where they sat around in a circle and, as Elizabeth put it, "spilled their guts in front of strangers." "But we know some of those people," Zack had argued. "The Eversons lost their son in Iraq. And you know Tammy Gracetti's daughter died of leukemia." It didn't matter to Elizabeth. She wasn't about to take a knife and cut out her heart and pass it around for everyone's inspection. Her grief was something private, intimate, not to be shared. In addition to attending the monthly grief support sessions, Zack was now going to Mass every Sunday, sometimes for meetings during the week, working on fundraising projects, getting more and more involved. His latest project was helping organize a candlelight vigil for parents who'd lost children. When he came home from those grief support sessions, Elizabeth thought she noticed a change in him. He seemed oddly relaxed and up-beat, this slightly spacey expression on his face, almost as if he'd taken a Zoloft. Sometimes he'd even whistle around the house as he cooked dinner. Elizabeth couldn't say why exactly, but his attitude bugged her a little. Whistling after what had happened to their son.

"Maybe you ought to read *Luke*," the man offered. "It has some good advice for somebody in your shoes."

"My shoes?"

"For someone who's suffered."

"I'm not into all that Bible stuff."

"*Luke* is different. It has . . ." The man thought for a moment and what he said next surprised her, that is, coming from someone who made a living hauling away people's trash. "Human empathy."

"I'll have to take your word on that," Elizabeth said, not even trying to feign interest.

"'*To give light to them that sit in darkness and in the shadow of death.*' Know where that's from?"

Elizabeth smiled. "It wouldn't be *Luke*, would it?"

"Bingo," the man said, grinning from ear to ear. "And here you say you don't know your Bible."

"A lucky guess."

"Sometimes we need a little light in the darkness."

"How often do you come here?" she asked, hoping to change the subject.

"Used to come all the time. Now I get over here a couple times a year. For her birthday or our anniversary. And of course on the anniversary of the accident."

Elizabeth wasn't sure she wanted to know, but she gave into her curiosity: "Which one is it today?"

He stared at her, his face pale and blank as a peeled potato. "Six years ago today she was killed here. At this very spot. A drunk driver crossed the median over there," he said, pointing out at the highway, "and plowed into her. Killed her instantly. At least she didn't suffer."

Elizabeth felt her heart contract. She imagined the horrific screech of tires, the crash of metal, the breaking of glass, followed by a stone-like silence, one in which all the noise seemed sucked out of the universe. She often imagined those circumstances surrounding Luke's accident. The Honda going off the road, rolling over, Luke being thrown from the car, then the hissing of the radiator, followed at last by that terrible stillness that she imagined spreading out over the desert night. Her child lying there, helpless and alone, looking up at the desert sky while his life slowly leached out of him into the sand. Of course, she didn't know any of that from the police report, except for the fact that it said he'd been DOA at the hospital. But it was how she *imagined* it to have happened. Filling in the blank mystery of Luke's last moments, even if only with her imagination, was preferable to the baffling enigma of his end.

"I'm so sorry," she said to the man. "It must be a hard day for you."

"Ey-ah, in some ways," he said, that Maine accent slipping into his voice. "But I'd rather spend it with her." He drew a hand across his meaty face again, then grimaced up at the sky, as if he'd only just then noticed the rain. "Boy, it's really coming down."

"Aren't you cold?" Elizabeth asked. Even with the umbrella she was wet and beginning to shiver. "Here. Get under," she offered, holding out the umbrella.

He hesitated, then ambled over, ducking his head under the umbrella. Up close she could see that he was shorter than she by several inches, especially with her heels. Nonetheless he gave the impression of being substantial, imposing in the manner of an unpolished block of granite. He hadn't shaved for a while, and the stubble was coming in white against his ruddy complexion. She noticed he had wild, gray eyebrows and deep-set eyes the color of hazelnuts.

"By the way, I'm George," he said, offering his hand to her. She took it, a large, powerful hand, that of someone who did very physical things for a living. Though she had large hands herself, his dwarfed hers, made her feel like a little girl holding an adult's hand.

"Hi, George. I'm Elizabeth," she replied.

"A pleasure to meet you, Elizabeth," he said with a slight bow of his head, a formality that made both of them smile. "Look, your nice shoes are getting all wet."

They both looked down at her feet, which made Elizabeth blush a little. She had big feet. At five-eleven, Elizabeth had spent a lifetime trying to get used to her height, the length of bone she possessed in superfluity. Her mother, for whom she could do nothing right, used to call her Bean Pole or Big Bird or even Olive Oyl. "At least slump your shoulders a little," the woman used to advise Elizabeth. "So you don't look so *big*."

"What do you do for a living, Elizabeth?" he asked.

"I'm a lawyer."

"Ah, a lawyer," he said. He appeared as if he were going to make a comment but then seemed to think better of it.

"I see you do . . . " Elizabeth began, glancing over at the truck. But then she felt more than a little foolish saying "dump runs," and was glad the man finished her sentence for her.

"I'm a handy-man. Clean out basements. Backyards. Take care of other people's messes," he said with a practiced laugh. "You got stuff you want hauled away, I'm your man."

"Well, if I need someone, I'll let you know," she replied, smiling.

"I'm retired. I just do this on the side to supplement my retirement," he said. He took out his wallet and handed her a business card. "Just in case something comes up."

"Thank you. What did you do before?"

"Taught high school social studies for thirty-nine years. Coached wrestling, too."

"That's a long time."

"When I finished college, there were no teaching jobs up in Maine so we moved down here. Bought a house. Raised a family. We always talked about going back up, but one thing led to another. When she was killed, I didn't see any reason to go back."

"May I ask you a question?" Elizabeth asked. "Why'd you put it up? The cross."

He rubbed the stubble of his beard. "As a remembrance, I suppose."

"But I assume her remains are buried some place."

The man gave a cynical laugh. "I get a kick out of that word, *remains*. Like leftovers."

"I only meant—"

"I know what you meant," the man said, though he didn't sound angry, just weary of having to explain himself. "Yeah, her remains are buried in a cemetery. But this is where I can feel her."

"Feel her?"

"This is where Hannah was last alive in the world. So this is where I have the strongest connection to her."

"You don't feel a connection at the cemetery?"

He shook his head. "Cemeteries are cold. If I want to feel close to her I come here. Pray a little. Talk to her."

"What do you talk about?"

He smiled, catching the note of condescension in her voice.

"The usual. What I made for supper. The grandkids. This and that. Everyday stuff."

Elizabeth didn't know how to reply.

"You're probably thinking this guy's some kind of nutjob. Talking to the dead."

"I didn't say that."

"It's what you're thinking though—am I right? I don't blame you. This must look pretty weird. The Spanish call them *descansos*," the man explained. "It means 'resting places.'"

"For the dead?"

"No. Actually for the living. Way back when, before hearses, before wagons even, it was where the pall bearers rested on their way to the grave site. Sometimes they had to carry a body some distance, so they had to stop several times along the route and set their burden down. Wherever they stopped, they would mark the spots with stones. When you think about it, it's the living who carry the load of the dead on their shoulders."

"I guess I never thought of it like that. Did you bring all that stuff?" Elizabeth asked, with a nod toward the cross.

"The flowers, yeah. The other stuff people just leave here."

"People leave stuff?"

"You wouldn't believe what I find here sometimes. Crucifixes. Prayer cards. Flowers. Once I found a picture of a little girl."

"Who was she?"

He shrugged. "My guess is somebody had lost that child. So they left a picture of her."

"Why would they do that?" she asked.

"I think they find a connection."

"You keep using that word. What do you mean by it?"

"Some people say there's an energy they can feel where someone died violently."

"Like a ghost?" Elizabeth said, holding back a smile.

"Not a ghost. More soul or spirit or whatever you want to call it. You ever stop at one of these roadside memorials?"

"Can't say that I have."

"I never used to before either. I was too busy rushing here, rushing there. Too busy with living. But now, sometimes when I see one of these memorials I'll stop."

"What do you do there?"

"All depends. I might say a prayer. Maybe light a candle. I keep some in the truck. Or maybe I'll just sit there and not say a word. Just keep 'em company for a while. If I'm really quiet sometimes I can feel them."

"Come on," Elizabeth said, incredulous.

"You'd be surprised. And every one of these is different somehow. Every one has its own story. At some *descansos* I can feel a lot of sadness. At others I feel anger. Or regrets. I feel that a lot. But always when I stop, I feel somehow closer to Hannah."

A shudder ran through Elizabeth. This was all getting way too weird for her.

"You're cold," the man said to her. "I got an extra jacket in the truck."

"I'm all right," she replied. She just wanted to leave now, to get out of there. She'd had about enough of this sort of talk.

"Ever pay a visit to your son?" he asked.

"I've been to his grave a few times."

"No. I meant where the accident happened."

Elizabeth shook her head.

"It might give you some peace of mind."

"Who says I need peace of mind?" she countered, a sudden edge to her voice. "Besides, he was killed out in New Mexico."

"What was he doing out there?"

"He was driving cross country," she explained, with a contemptuous roll of her eyes. "This big trip before his senior year. To tell you the truth, I wasn't thrilled with the idea."

"No?"

"I thought it was dangerous. Driving all the way across the country by himself."

"Young fellow like that gets it in his head he wants to see some of the country, there's no stopping him."

"That's what my husband said. Listen, it's getting late. I really should be running along."

She started to turn away once more, but she felt his hand on the sleeve of her jacket.

"Elizabeth, if I can give you one piece of advice. And please don't take this the wrong way."

She stared at the man, waiting. His eyes held hers with their gleaming intensity.

"We all got regrets."

"Regrets?" she said.

"I mean, when we lose a loved one. There's not a single day goes by I don't regret something or other regarding my wife."

Elizabeth frowned. "I don't know what you're talking about."

"I'm just saying, it wouldn't be unusual for you to have regrets concerning your son. Don't beat yourself up too much over it."

"Well, it was nice talking to you."

She turned and walked swiftly to her car, got in and took off. Her jacket and shoes were soaked. Chilled to the bone, she turned the heat on full blast. As she drove off, in the rearview mirror she could see the man squatting once more beside the cross, becoming smaller and fainter until he disappeared behind the water cascading over the back window.

Chapter 3

On the ride home, Elizabeth kept thinking about the strange meeting. The odd things the old man had told her. How the spirits of the dead remained where they died. How he spoke to his wife, the connection he felt at, what were they called? *Descansos*. Resting places. Of course, it was all utter nonsense. Even a little creepy, what she imagined a séance being like. What unnerved her most, perhaps, was how he'd known she had lost someone. She supposed it could have been just a lucky guess, but it felt as if he *knew* her son had died. How weird was that? Despite all this, some part of her had responded to the old man, had felt a genuine sympathy for him. Here he was visiting his wife on the anniversary of her death. Kneeling there in the pouring rain. Bringing her roses. Talking to her as if she were still among the living. Though weird, it was also touching.

Elizabeth then thought of what he'd said about cemeteries. How he didn't feel any connection to his wife's grave. It made her think of the cemetery where her son was buried. They'd had to do so much in those Valium-filled days following the accident—buying a cemetery plot, making funeral arrangements, a thousand other trivial details. It was Zack who had flown out to New Mexico to take care of returning Luke's remains (there was that word again), while Elizabeth had stayed behind and arranged the funeral and took sympathy calls from friends. She'd had to pick out a coffin, write an obituary for the local paper, even buy a suit (Luke hadn't owned one). She had to go into a men's store in New Haven and pick one out. For some reason she hadn't told the salesman it was for her dead son. At one point he'd said to her, "It might be easier if your son just came in to be measured." In the past year, she had gone to the cemetery three, maybe four times, dutifully carrying flowers, as well as her dual burdens of sadness and guilt. She would kneel at the grave site, staring at the letters carved into the cold granite as if they were some strange hieroglyphic whose meaning she couldn't decipher: *Luke James Gerlacher, July 16, 1992–August 12, 2013*. The stone and the grave site seemed to have nothing whatsoever to do with her son. Even less with herself. She was never quite sure what she was supposed to *feel* there, but she certainly didn't feel anything as tangible as Luke's spirit, didn't feel the slightest "connection" to him. Mostly what she felt was a generalized numbness, an odd distance, almost as if she'd left her body and was hovering a few feet above watching this other woman go through the motions of grief. She would hear her say, *Hi, Sweetheart. It's Mommy.* Or, *I miss you so much.* Or, *Are you all right, dear?*

Regrets—she recalled the old man saying that to her. What was he implying? Had it just been one of those general statements one offered to a person who'd suffered a great loss, something as vague and applicable and ultimately meaningless as a fortune cookie saying "You will receive good news soon"? Still, his comment had struck a nerve and even now seemed to reverberate in her mind.

Despite having the heat on full blast, Elizabeth still felt chilled to the core. She reached across and picked up the pint and took another sip. She sometimes didn't know how she would get through each day without a few drinks. A glass of wine or two with a client over lunch. After an appearance in court, pulling over to the side of the road and taking a quick nip from the bottle. Another glass of wine with dinner followed by a few more, when Zack's eagle eye wasn't watching. Otherwise how could she sleep? She didn't see it as a problem, no more so than a life jacket was a problem to a drowning person: something to keep her from going under. Zack, however, thought it was an issue. He'd stare disapprovingly when she poured a third or fourth or fifth glass of wine. She could recall the Fourth of July party they'd gone to at the house of one of Zack's colleagues. She hadn't wanted to go in the first place, but Zack insisted; he said they needed to get back into "living their life," making it sound as if they were bronco riders who'd been bucked off their mount and had to get back on. At one point when she'd refilled her glass with scotch, Zack had leaned over to her and whispered, "You might want to go a little easy on that, honey." She turned on him viciously and said, loud enough to draw the attention of several others standing nearby, "No, I *don't* want to go easy."

Perhaps it was the old man's comments about regrets or the sheriff blowing her off again about Luke's diary, or maybe it was the second nip of booze. Then again, it could have been anything. Her thoughts were so easily drawn to that night. *That night.* It sat in her mind as a moment insulated, hermetically sealed as a snow globe. Elizabeth had gone down to Washington for a legal conference. Mostly, though, the conference was just a subterfuge to be with Peter, her lover. The affair had started out innocently enough, as affairs go—a few drinks, a stray touch, a lingering glance, a double entendre that proved to be not so double. One minute she'd have told herself she was happily married, and the next she was in bed with a man she'd not even known a few days before. It had been so out of character for Elizabeth, too. In twenty-six years of marriage she'd never cheated on Zack, not once. She loved her husband, she told herself. If not with the passion they'd once had at least with a sense of loyalty and the intimacy that came with time and shared memories.

But their life together had become not only boring and predictable, it had grown cold. She often felt as if Zack didn't appreciate her, didn't find her attractive or desirable. Over the past few years, they seldom made love, or if they did the perfunctory nature of it was in some ways even worse than celibacy. They seldom spoke of anything beyond the prosaic concerns of daily life. They seldom surprised the other with gifts or impromptu kisses or expressions of affection, beyond the most mundane and obvious ("I love you, goodnight"). When Elizabeth gazed across the breakfast table at Zack eating his yogurt with granola and checking his emails on his phone, she was struck by the absolute certainty that she knew everything there was to know about this man, that she had already plumbed the depths of his soul and theirs, and there was no territory left to be discovered. Still, she preferred to consider the affair merely a hiatus from her *real* life, a momentary and completely irrational diversion from what *was*, and from what assuredly *would be*, her life. After all, she wasn't in love with Peter. It was . . . what? A distraction? A temporary bout of insanity? She even told herself a short affair might do their marriage good, though couldn't have said how. By the time they went to Washington, she and Peter had been lovers for several months. Already, however, she was tiring of it, regretting having allowed herself to become enmeshed in it; the excitement, the heady exhilaration of illicit love had begun to wane while her own guilt had grown proportionately. Each time she returned home to Zack she felt her shame as a burning along her cheeks. She was certain Zack could see her infidelity in her countenance, her eyes. How could she do this to the man she loved, the father of her child, her best friend? Whenever the affair came to an end, she felt she'd return, gladly and with due contrition, to her "real" life, to her husband, to her family, to her other self, and continue on as if nothing had ever happened. And she *knew* that it had to end.

That day, they'd skipped out of a tedious session on "Mediation," and strolled along the Washington Mall. Peter appeared animated and boyishly handsome, and for a moment she could see why she had been originally so charmed by him. As they passed the Lincoln Memorial, she'd wanted to tell him right then and there that she thought they should end it. She was afraid that if they went back to their room, she wouldn't be able to do it. Yet he suddenly took hold of her hand and led her up the steps and recited from memory the Gettysburg Address, something he told her he'd had to do in fifth grade. Several other times that day she felt on the verge of saying something, but each time the right moment never seemed to present itself. She liked Peter, didn't want to hurt him needlessly. That evening they were tired and decided to stay in and order room service. Peter had opened a bottle of champagne and poured them a glass.

"To us," he offered as a toast.

"Peter," she began, determined to get it over with. "We should talk."

Instead, he interrupted to say, "I'm falling in love with you, Beth."

The comment not only took the wind out of her sails, it startled her. "You mustn't say that, Peter."

"What do you mean, 'I mustn't'? It's true."

"You can't fall in love with me."

"And you can't tell me how I feel."

"But too many people will be hurt," she'd said.

Peter, a few years younger than Elizabeth, was married with two little kids. Once when he happened to leave his cell phone on the nightstand of some motel at which they had rendezvoused, she was startled to see a picture of his family. A pretty wife, two blonde adorable daughters. Before, she'd only had to deal with the guilt she felt regarding her own family. Now she had to deal with hurting his family, too.

That's when her phone rang on the bureau across the room. She assumed it was Zack calling to "check in" with her, as he liked to put it. She felt a fresh wave of remorse strike her face, stinging like a hot wind filled with bits of sand. She started to get up.

"Don't answer it." Peter leaned into her and tried to kiss her but she turned away.

"What's the matter?" he asked.

"We need to talk."

The phone rang again but she didn't want to interrupt what she'd started, afraid that if she did she couldn't say what she needed to. She was able to summon up the courage to tell Peter that it was over, that she liked him but that she loved her husband, was committed to making her marriage work. He stared at her, shocked and hurt.

"I'm sorry, Peter. It was a mistake."

"That's all I am to you, a mistake?" he cried.

"I didn't mean it like that. I only meant that I can't keep doing this. Sneaking around. I don't feel right about it."

"But you felt right when we started."

"I know. But it was wrong then, too."

"I love you, Beth," he blurted out.

"I'm sorry, Peter. I really am."

When it finally sunk in that she wasn't going to change her mind, he angrily began throwing his things into his suitcase.

"Where are you going?" she asked.

"Well, I'm sure the hell not going to stay here."

Then he stormed out of the room. She couldn't blame him for being angry. She felt horrible for how things had turned out, but what could she expect? As a lawyer, she handled divorces. She knew how affairs almost always ended badly, with all parties feeling broken, damaged. At the same time though, she felt as if this terrible burden had been lifted off her shoulders. She was ready to try harder to make things work with Zack. She also felt suddenly very lonely, and she wanted now to talk to her husband, the way they used to back when they were first dating and they'd chat well into the night. She considered whether or not she should confess to Zack, make a clean breast of things, tell him she loved him and ask for his forgiveness. Or would her betrayal only push them further apart, ruin any chance of their marriage surviving?

When she picked up her phone, though, it came as something of a surprise to see the two calls weren't from her Zack, but rather from her son. That summer Luke had driven cross country. He'd told them he was heading out to visit some friends in San Francisco, and then they were going to drive down the coast together. The mere fact that he'd called surprised her. While on his month-long trip, he hardly ever called, despite her constant reminders. If he called once a week they were lucky. He was, Elizabeth felt, in his own little world, testing out the heady waters of adulthood, pulling away from his parents—especially from *her*—as fast as he could. She hadn't been in favor of this trip, didn't like the fact that he was driving across country all by himself. But now that he was twenty-one, they couldn't really stop him anyway. Of course, she could have cut his purse-strings—the credit cards, the cell phone—but she didn't want to resort to such hardball tactics and alienate her son any more than he already was. For her part, Elizabeth called him daily, leaving him doting messages, little maternal texts: *Hey, Lukey. Where are you? Are you eating enough? Be safe. Please call when you get a chance.* Of course, she worried about him. How could she not? He was her son, her only son, all alone out there, an entire continent separating them.

Lately more than a continent seemed to have come between them. She missed how things had once been, the closeness, the easy intimacies they shared. Giving him a bath when he was little. Later, lying in bed and reading a story to him. When he was twelve, a movie and pizza on a Friday night, just the two of them. Even when he was in his early teens, he used to share everything with her: his fears, his joys, questions about growing up, about dating, girls. Unlike most teenage boys, he even used to talk to her about sex. *What does it feel like, Mom?* he'd once asked her, smiling awkwardly. But all that had changed. *Luke* had changed. He'd become this moody stranger, sometimes silently distant, other times in-her-face confrontational. Home for the summer after his junior year at college, Luke no longer wanted her opinions on anything. He communicated curtly with her in passing, as he was rushing somewhere far more important than being in her company, often in one-word answers (*uh-huh, sure, whatever*). Or in business-like text messages: *Mom, could u wash my white shirt?* Or, *Won't be home tonight.* Sometimes he'd snap at her, lose his temper. *Where the hell is my iPad, Mom?* he'd once screamed at her from the top of the stairs. To which she yelled back, *Watch your mouth, mister. And I didn't touch your damn iPad.*

The change in Luke had seemed to start after he went away to college, but accelerated the last year of his life. He had become, to Elizabeth's mind, too thin, almost gaunt. Yet he hardly touched anything the few times the three would sit down for dinner. Like a lot of parents, Elizabeth blamed it on the usual suspects: drugs, psychological problems, the new kids he'd started hanging around with in college, girlfriend issues. The latter, Luke's sudden and inexplicable break-up during his junior year in college from his long-time girlfriend TJ, was Elizabeth's prime suspect. Luke and TJ had gone out since sophomore year in high school. They'd seemed inseparable, joined at the hip. In fact, Elizabeth, perhaps foolishly, she later realized, thought they'd eventually get married. Such a sweet girl, someone who seemed perfect for her introverted son. It was after their break-up that Luke really seemed to act differently, to become withdrawn, distant. Yet he wouldn't even talk about the break-up, except to say that TJ didn't want to see him any more that she wanted to date other people.

Elizabeth took the phone and lay down on the bed. Still upset from the business with Peter, she hadn't noticed at first that her son had left a message.

"Mom, you there?" came Luke's voice, slightly annoyed, but filled, too, with an almost childlike need that immediately set off some red flags in Elizabeth. There followed a long pause, scratchy, as if he'd had the window open and air was rushing past the phone. "I'm in New Mexico." *New Mexico?* she wondered. What on earth was he doing there? He'd told them he was headed out to San Francisco to stay with friends. "There's something I really need to talk to you about, Mom." Yet his voice trailed off once more, a long, brooding silence that segued into that scratchy sound again. Finally he said, "Whatever. I guess it'll have to wait till morning."

She played the message again, Luke's words leaving her even more uneasy the second time. *There's something I really need to talk to you about, Mom.* And: *I guess it'll have to wait till morning. It,* she thought. What was the *it* he needed to speak to her about? What had made his voice so insistent, so needy? Lately her son had expressed little need for her.

She immediately called him back. Glancing at the bedside clock, she saw that it almost midnight. Which meant it would have been near ten o'clock in New Mexico, and that it was two hours after he'd first called. The phone rang until Luke's voice message kicked in: *I'm not here but you probably guessed that by now. Leave a message, etc. Luke.* Where was he, especially after his message which seemed so urgent? Maybe he'd stopped to get some food. Maybe he'd forgotten to charge his cell phone. Maybe he was tired and had pulled over to the side of the road for the night. She'd warned him such a practice was dangerous, that you never knew who you might run into. But he wasn't about to listen to her. He was a big boy now and big boys didn't listen to their mothers. She thought again of the message he'd left: *There's something I really needed to talk to you about, Mom.*

So she left a message of her own.

"Hi, Sweetie. It's Mom. Sorry I missed your call earlier. Is everything okay? You sounded a little, I don't know . . . funny. I'm here if you need to talk."

She got under the covers and tried to sleep. Yet her mind was abuzz with all that had happened: the business with Peter, the issue of whether or not she should confess the affair to Zack, the odd phone call from Luke. The funny thing was that Luke had grown so distant lately, so *unknowable*, she couldn't even venture a guess about what he needed to talk about. Then something occurred to her that made the breath catch in her chest: *what if he had known?* About the affair, that is. Of course, she and Peter had been careful, discreet, had only met at out-of-the-way places. Still, what if someone had seen them together? Kissing as they left a motel room, holding hands in a darkened corner of some restaurant. One of Luke's friends, say? It was possible. She recalled a time once at the beginning of that summer, right after Luke had gotten home from college. Elizabeth had just returned home one evening after being with Peter. Zack was working late at the office. She happened to bump into Luke in the kitchen, who was looking for something in the refrigerator.

"Oh, hi," she said, startled to see him home. He was usually out, with his friends, she'd assumed, and didn't get home until late. "Where have you been?"

He looked up at her and smiled conspiratorially.

"Where have *you* been?" he challenged.

"Out," she managed to say.

"Out?"

"Yes. Out."

She told herself he meant nothing by it, that he was just being his usual contrary self with her, but his question seemed to imply something, some intimate knowledge. Could he have known? Could that have been what he wanted to talk to her about?

She finally dozed off. In the middle of the night she was awakened by another call. She naturally assumed it was Luke, that whatever it was he couldn't wait till morning to talk about it.

"Luke!" she cried, expecting his voice.

Instead, her ear was assaulted by an unfamiliar male voice on the other end, a voice at once deferential and yet authoritarian, polite but bearing the full weight of nothing less than doom itself. Immediately the backs of her arms sprouted goose-bumps and she shivered. Something terrible had happened. She could feel in her bones.

"Is this Elizabeth Gerlacher?" the man asked formally.

"Why, yes," she replied, trying to keep her heart from leaping into her mouth.

"I'm Sheriff Crowder. I'm calling from the Marrizozo Sheriff's Department."

"Where? Who are you?" she stuttered, her mind trying to take in the facts.

He repeated himself. Then he said, "Do you have a son named Luke, ma'am?"

Please, she thought. This was the middle-of-the-night call that was every parent's nightmare, the conversation every parent dreaded yet had secretly rehearsed. She had a wild, irrational urge to deny she had a son named Luke, figuring that if she denied it then whoever this Sheriff Crowder was wouldn't be able to tell her the rest.

"I do," she conceded finally.

"Ma'am," he said. "I'm afraid I have some bad news."

In the split second before the officer spoke again, she found herself thinking back to that other time in Wales so long ago, the first time she'd lost Luke. But that time she'd gotten him back. She had prayed and been granted a second chance. A miracle. That's what it was. Maybe this time it would work too. *Please*, she entreated again. She was ready to bargain, to give anything. *I'll go to church again. I'll pray. I'll do anything You want. Just make him be all right. Please, God.*

And then that voice of authority told her, politely but unequivocally, that her son had been killed. Just like that. One minute Luke was alive, not only possessing a present, but a future, an expansive, yet-to-be-lived time that included a woman that he'd meet and marry, children he would father, Thanksgivings and Christmases for which he'd bring the grandkids to Zack and Elizabeth's. Everything waited out in that golden future, brimming with potential. And in the next moment, her son, as well as the entire entourage of that future, was gone. Vanished. Whisked away. She didn't recall much after that. Just miscellaneous bits and pieces, unconnected as beads from a broken necklace spilling on the floor. Later, picking those pieces up, she would remember things like *thrown from the vehicle, cardiac arrest, air-lifted*, things that seemed to have no connection to her son. To her Lukey.

"Ma'am?" the Sheriff said. "Are you there?"

"Yes," she replied, waiting for him to say something that could still change things, undo what he'd just told her.

"Let me give you my number. In these situations, people usually have questions later on." On the motel stationery, she mechanically copied his name and number. "I'm sorry for your loss, ma'am."

When she got off the phone she tried calling Zack but there was no answer. She tried again and again. She sat up in bed, asking questions that had no answers. *What was he even doing in New Mexico? How could he be thrown from the vehicle? Luke was a careful driver. He always wore his seat belt. Maybe they had the wrong kid. Maybe it was some other Luke. Another mother's son. Please,* she pleaded, *let it be some other mother's son.*

Finally she got dressed, took a taxi to Dulles, and decided to try to catch the first flight home. While waiting stand-by to board a plane, she was finally able to get hold of Zack.

"Where have you been?" she asked, almost a challenge, as if *she* had any right to question where *he'd* been.

She heard his yawn. "I was sleeping," he explained. "What's the matter?" Then she told him.

On the flight back to Hartford, as a fiery sun burst through the ragged cloud-cover over the ocean, she remembered her son's voice message. She picked up her phone and played it, again and again, hoping to find some hidden clue as to his intent: *There's something I really needed to talk to you about, Mom.* What did that mean? What was the something he needed to talk to her about? Had his mind been preoccupied and he wasn't paying attention to the road? If only she'd answered when he'd first called. If only she hadn't been with her lover. Maybe her son would still be alive. And as she stared out the window at the clouds, she thought to herself, *Damn You.*

Chapter 4

When she finally arrived home, the house seemed strangely unfamiliar, almost as if she'd entered the wrong home by mistake. Right in the entryway, she began peeling off her sodden things: shoes, skirt, pantyhose, jacket, even her blouse had gotten wet. Water formed a dark pool on the floor around her as she stripped down to her underwear, goose bumps rippling her long bare limbs. She grabbed an old flannel shirt from the hall closet, one she used to garden in. It smelled of sweat and deodorant, earth and roots, a not unpleasant odor that brought back a different time in her life. A happier time.

"Boy, you're drenched," Zack's voice sprung from behind her.

She turned to see her husband standing in the hallway. Tall and lean, still handsome, he wore a full-length apron with ducks on it—a birthday present she'd given him. He leaned in to kiss her but she turned to offer her cheek. She didn't want him to catch the booze odor on her breath.

"It's really coming down out there," she offered.

They both turned to look out the window, as if they'd never seen rain before. In the gathering darkness, the lake appeared like a shiny black piece of metal, lights from cars inching along Lake Drive shimmering off its riffled surface. Leaves scurried past the window in the downpour. Though only late September, fall was intractably upon them.

She saw him staring at her. In the past few years, they so seldom glimpsed each other without clothes. Not long ago she had caught Zack stepping out of the shower. He hadn't seen her at first and she was able to scrutinize his naked body. He appeared older, tired—the graying hair of his chest, the sagging flesh of his butt, in the mirror the sad-looking genitals. She felt both a tenderness for him as well as a vague sense of arousal. They hadn't made love in months. She longed for that clear, uncomplicated passion they'd once had for each other, even more for the simple desire of his touch. But she was usually too tired, he too busy with his work or with stuff at the church. Besides, sex seemed too intimate, too private and thorny a region for them to enter right now. Sex, she felt, implied a certain trust, a willingness to allow oneself to be vulnerable, and that they hadn't had with each other since Luke's death. Pleasure felt almost obscene since the death of their son.

"You've lost weight," he said.

She glanced down at her stomach, her legs, the skin pale and puckered with goosebumps, the flesh slack and untoned from lack of exercise. She'd always been in good shape, do yoga and work out at the gym, ran several times a week around the lake. Now she hadn't exercised in months. Exercise suggested a future, the will of one preparing for a long marathon.

"Actually, I've gained a few pounds."

"Let me get your robe before you catch cold."

Zack bounded up the stairs and returned in a moment carrying a towel and her maroon terry-cloth bathrobe, a gift he'd gotten her from LL Bean a few Christmases before. Like the apron, they were the functional sort of presents they had begun to get for each other—fluffy robes and warm wool socks, a GPS for her car, a tennis racket for him. Practical, useful gifts. Safe gifts. Things they would open on Christmas morning without the least surprise and say, "Boy, I really needed this."

"Let me dry you," he said.

"No, it's okay," she replied, reaching for the towel.

"Just hold still." With the towel, he dried her hair, then went down her body, along her back and buttocks, circling over her breasts, bending finally to dry her thighs, even between her legs. Then he held the robe for her to step into. For just a moment, she felt his arms around her. For that moment things between them almost seemed as they once had. As if she could fall into his arms, open herself to him, allow herself to be warmed, to be comforted. To be loved. In a moment though, she twirled out of his embrace and cinched the belt around her waist.

"I was getting a little worried," he said.

All the way home, she wondered if she would tell her husband of the meeting she'd had with the old man. It was all so very bizarre. She didn't know what to make of it herself, let alone try to explain it to someone else, especially someone like Zack. An engineer, someone both hyper-literal and linear in his thinking, someone who didn't like metaphors, who eschewed problems that didn't have clear, finite solutions. And yet, she wanted to tell someone, to share the peculiar story of her meeting.

"You wouldn't believe what just happened to me. Let me get a drink first."

She headed down the hall and into the kitchen. From the refrigerator, she removed an open bottle of Chardonnay and poured herself a hefty glass. This, she felt, was different from drinking secretly from a bottle hidden in a glove compartment. This sort of drinking, out in the open, from a glass instead of a bottle, with someone as a witness, was sanctioned. Zack may not like it but he couldn't really complain. It was just a glass of wine to relax after work. Normal.

"Boy, something smells great," she said.

"Hope you're hungry," Zack said, coming into the kitchen. "I made beef *bourguignon.*"

Zack, a superb cook, made most of the their meals, had done so ever since they were first married. Elizabeth didn't mind. She took after her mother, had neither interest in nor much of a talent for cooking. Luke used to come home from school and say, "What's Dad cooking?" On the rare occasion that his mother cooked, Luke would wrinkle his nose at her. Tonight, she hadn't much of an appetite. Often lately she had none. She used to love to eat, to go to fancy restaurants in New York City with Zack—Bâtard or Le Bernardin. Yet food now was only a means of dampening a physical ache. She could easily have survived on spoonfuls of peanut butter eaten straight from the jar every night.

She worked up enough enthusiasm, however, to say, "That sounds wonderful."

The conversation, as did most of theirs lately, struck her as artificial, as if they were trying too hard to sound normal, to sound as if nothing was the matter. To sound as if they were still a family, intact, happy, moving together toward some mutually agreed-on future.

"So tell me what happened?" asked Zack, who went over to the stove to check on dinner. Elizabeth took a seat on one of the barstools at the counter. The three of them used to eat breakfast there in the morning, looking out at the lake. Sometimes when Luke was little, he'd be doing last-minute homework, his head bent low over some assignment, his tongue jammed into the corner of his mouth the way he did when concentrating on something. *You should have done that last night, Mister,* she would say to him. She, always the task-master, the stickler for rules and deadlines and good grades, the bad cop to Zack's easygoing good cop.

"I met this old guy on the side of the road," she began.

Despite her hesitation, she went ahead and told Zack about the meeting, how the man would visit the spot where his wife had died six years before.

She found herself, though, unconsciously editing certain parts, cleaning up sections, leaving others out altogether. Trimming and shaping it like a story, making it more palatable, more plausible, too, she supposed, instead of just something random that had happened. Like leaving out the part about the man talking to his dead wife, or how he said spirits hovered near where they died. Those seemed a little too "bizarre" even for her. They would have made the old man appear to be a weirdo, which perhaps he was, but Elizabeth didn't see any need to get Zack all worked up. And of course she didn't say anything about the man referring to her "regrets." When she'd finished, her husband remained silent, stirring the contents of the pot.

"Well?" she said.

"What do you want me to say?"

"Isn't that strange?" she offered with a little laugh.

Zack turned to face her. A three-lined vertical frown fanned out over his brow, one that had deepened over the years. When they were younger it had given to his demeanor a certain *gravitas*, a sign that he had character, that weighty thoughts went on behind the frown. Now it was his normal expression, one that made him look overly cautious, judgmental, pedantic in the manner of a smug professor who thought all of his students' questions were dumb.

"What's strange is why you stopped," he said.

"What do you mean?"

"Why on earth would you stop for some guy you didn't even know?"

"I told you, I thought he might need some help."

"Help?"

"Maybe he'd been in an accident or something."

"That wasn't very smart, Elizabeth."

"It didn't have anything to do with being smart," she countered, her tone already tending toward prickly. "I thought he needed help so I stopped."

"If you thought he needed help, why didn't you just call nine-one-one?"

"I don't know. I just didn't."

Elizabeth was already regretting she'd brought any of this up. Lately, they got into arguments over the least little thing, with her more often than not to blame. As a diversionary tactic, she went over and dipped a spoon into the pot of stew and tasted it.

"*Uhm*," she said. "Yummy."

"He could have been some nutjob for all you knew," Zack stated.

"Oh, come on. He was just a sweet old man."

"But you didn't know that when you stopped."

"I could tell pretty quickly he meant no harm."

"You ask me, he sounds weird."

"Zack, you weren't there. Besides, he seemed pretty religious. He was quoting the Bible."

He let out a sarcastic chuckle, one that set her teeth on edge. "And that makes him safe, because he quotes the Bible?"

"You go to church. I thought *you* of all people would appreciate that."

"I go to *church*. I don't pray along the side of the road." Zack shook his head.

"So prayers in church are the only ones that count?"

"Elizabeth, I don't understand. What on earth would possess you to stop like that?"

"The poor guy lost his wife. He goes there to grieve for her. It was really quite sad."

"That still doesn't explain why you'd stop in the first place."

"All right, let's just forget it," she said, annoyed.

The tension she'd felt in her neck and shoulders all day began to return. She took a big gulp of her wine. She realized now why she hadn't wanted to tell Zack about the old man. She felt, for reasons she couldn't quite explain, somehow protective of the experience. The meeting had stirred something in her, something raw and powerful, and while she was still trying to understand it, she'd sensed that Zack wouldn't "get" it. Despite all of her own reservations, she felt some strong affinity to the man, a strange fascination with what he'd told her, and she knew Zack would press her on it—exactly as he had—until she got flustered for not quite understanding her own motives for stopping. And then she'd get angry at him for having to justify herself.

Those were the complicated mechanics lately of their conversations. They argued over anything. And when they weren't arguing, they were silent, moving about the house as if walking on eggshells, wary of saying or doing anything that would provoke a disagreement. Elizabeth felt that despite everything—the affair, Luke's death, the difficulty of the past year, the growing distance that had formed between them—she still loved Zack, still wanted their marriage to work. She told herself they just needed time. Time to heal. To get to some other, better place. But instead of healing, instead of arriving at that better place, things only seemed to go from bad to worse. She drank more and more. Only when she was a couple of sheets to the wind, as her father used to say of her mother, were the sharp edges of her life blunted enough for her to not feel their sting. The other thing that seemed to help was keeping busy. She spent more and more time at the women's shelter, throwing herself into dealing with other people's problems. It kept her from dwelling too much on her own—her loss, her guilt, on the nagging mystery that was at the center of Luke's death. As long as she kept busy doing things, moving about, she felt that life was tolerable.

Even the way she and Zack handled their loss was as different as night and day. He went to church and to his support group, shared his suffering openly, sought to move on with their life, while she stayed by herself and drank and plunged deeper into her dark, solitary grief, into trying to find answers to a past she couldn't hope to explicate. To Elizabeth, it seemed that Zack had made some sort of peace with their son's death. He was ready to move on, to carry his grief with him like a small overnight bag into some form of future life, while she could barely stir under the burden she lugged into each day like a millstone around her neck. Yet a burden she'd gotten so used to she almost couldn't bear the thought of parting with it. How many times had she thought of telling Zack about Luke's phone call that night. But she feared if she told him that part, she would have to tell him the rest, *everything*—about the affair, about being with Peter on the night their son had died. She feared that if Zack found out now, it would finish whatever little was left of their marriage. That thought scared her more than anything.

"I have the right to know why you'd stop like that," he said. "After what happened."

"What do you mean, 'after what happened'?" she repeated.

"You know what I mean."

Of course, she did. He meant that they had only each other now and if one were to die, the other would be completely alone. He was afraid of losing her, afraid she'd slip away as Luke had. That she'd drive off one day and not come back.

"Look, I didn't mean to worry you. I'm sorry. I guess I wasn't thinking."

He came over to the counter and put his arms around her. "Sweetheart, it's just that I don't know what I'd do if anything happened to you."

She felt a hot rush of tenderness for him. The way she used to feel about him. He was a good man, kind and tender and thoughtful, and he didn't deserve any of this. Not her affair, not Luke's death, not the way she'd been treating him, not the distance at which she'd kept him. "I know, Zack."

He kissed the top of her head.

"So what else did this guy say?"

"Funny thing is he knew."

"Knew what?"

"When I first got there, he said, 'You've lost somebody, haven't you?'"

"How did he know that?"

"I don't know."

Zack pursed his lips but didn't say anything. Instead, he went back over to the stove. With his back to her he said, "Oh, that sheriff called you again."

"Crowder?"

"I don't know his name. The one from New Mexico. He left a message. He said he looked again."

"That was all?"

"Yes. He seemed annoyed."

"He's always annoyed, that guy."

Elizabeth got up and went over and poured the rest of the wine into her glass. She felt a couple of drinks away from that tingling looseness in her jaw, the one that made things all right.

"What's this about?" Zack asked, turning to face her.

"I told you already. Luke's diary. I'm sure he had it with him."

"And you think they're hiding it?"

"Maybe they're just too lazy to look for it. Or maybe they misplaced it. Stuff like this happens with police departments all the time. Frankly, I don't like the guy's attitude. Every time I've asked him anything he blows me off. Maybe they just don't want to admit they screwed up."

"What did they screw up, Elizabeth?"

"What *didn't* they screw up? Remember they first told us they couldn't find Luke's cell phone? Until I made a big stink and suddenly it shows up."

"But what difference did that make?" Zack asked.

Not much as it turned out. The phone had been so damaged in the accident that even with Elizabeth bringing it to a computer specialist, no data could be retrieved from the SIM card, which meant no revealing texts, no incriminating pictures or illuminating voice mails. Nothing that would have given Elizabeth the slightest clue into her son's state of mind.

"That's not the point," Elizabeth said. "What about the business with the seat belt? First they tell us Luke's seat belt was buckled but then the police report says he wasn't wearing one."

For months after the police report arrived in the mail, it had sat unopened in her desk drawer. She couldn't bring herself to open it, couldn't bear to read the ugly facts of their son's death. But when she finally did, some of those facts surprised her. Like the seat belt issue. Or the fact that they found cigarette butts on the floor despite the fact that Luke had never smoked. Or the fact that the night had been clear, the road conditions perfect, and that Luke just seemed to swerve off the road into eternity. Or the half dozen other things that didn't quite fit together, that didn't make sense. It was sometime after reading the police report that she filed legal motions to get hold of Luke's credit card bills, his phone records.

"What's so important about the damn seat belt?" Zack asked.

"Luke always wore one. You know that."

"Maybe he didn't this time."

"Or what about the fact that they weren't sure which direction he was driving."

"How does that matter in the least?"

"That's basic stuff, Zack. Police investigation 101, for crying out loud. If they screw that up, who knows what else they might have screwed up."

"Sweetheart, what difference does *any* of this make?"

"Maybe nothing. Then again, maybe everything. The police report says it was a clear evening, the road was straight and Luke just went off and flipped over? You buy that? You know Luke was a good driver."

"Even good drivers have accidents."

"But there are all these unanswered questions."

"They're only questions to you."

"They're questions any reasonable person might have. Can you tell me what he was even doing in New Mexico in the first place? He was supposed to be driving out to San Francisco."

"Maybe he decided to take a detour. Maybe he wanted to see the Grand Canyon. Who knows?"

"The Grand Canyon's in *Arizona*," Elizabeth said with a scornful laugh. "Not northeastern New Mexico. Besides, his credit card bills tell a different story."

"What story? Luke's death wasn't a story, Elizabeth."

"But it is. Don't you see?"

"No, I don't. It was an accident. You're the one making it into a story."

"There's too much that doesn't make sense about it."

"Accidents don't make sense. That's why they're called accidents. Besides, none of this will bring him back."

"Don't you think I know that?" she snapped at him. Then softening, she added, "Zack, I just want some peace of mind."

He looked at her for a moment, then averted his gaze.

"What?" she said.

"Do you really think all this is giving you peace of mind?" Before she could reply, he added, "Listen, we'd better eat. I have to be at a planning meeting at the church at eight."

During dinner they made small-talk so the awkward silence wouldn't consume them, mostly about the change in weather, the fact that they had to get some potted plants on the deck in before the first hard frost arrived, what they needed from the store. Safe topics. Pedestrian topics. They spoke to each other as polite strangers. Through their awkward smiles and overly hearty nods, though, each could tell that the other felt uncomfortable, as they often did after talking about Luke or the accident.

At one point Zack glanced at his watch and said, "Oh, shoot, I'd better get running."

"Go ahead."

"I hate to leave you with the mess."

"Don't worry, I'll clean up."

"I might be late. Don't bother waiting up."

As Elizabeth washed the dishes, she thought about her earlier conversation with Zack. For her husband it was simple—their son's death was an accident. Merely a random confluence of albeit deadly forces that took their son's life. Elizabeth, on the other hand, didn't see it that way. It wasn't so much that she was convinced it *wasn't* an accident, as it was that she felt there were too many things that simply didn't add up, too many loose ends, too many questions—like the seat belt or that it was a clear night, or what was their son even doing in New Mexico? Maybe it was just the skeptical lawyer in her, the training that made her question facts, simple narratives, peoples' motives, but too much didn't make sense. At night she'd stay up late in her study, rereading the police report, going over Luke's emails, sifting through the phone calls he had made during his trip, reviewing his credit card bills, trying to figure out where he'd been, what he was doing, to whom he was talking. In short, where his head was at the time of his death. His hundreds of emails oddly enough turned up virtually nothing out of the ordinary. Though one did catch her eye. It was to a monastery in New Mexico, Blessed Mother of the Redeemer, which proved to be just a few hundred miles from where Luke's accident happened. Yet it turned out to be a false alarm. Luke had ordered some coffee from the monastery to be delivered to his advisor at St. Anselm, Father Jerome in the Theology Department. From his credit card bills, Elizabeth was able to pinpoint where Luke had stopped along his trip—to buy gas or to eat, or to stay over at a motel; at each one she'd place a black magic marker dot on a large AAA map of the United States. She hoped in this way to link them into a picture, to piece together a story of her son's last days on earth, at least a story that made more sense to her than Luke simply driving out into the desert and getting himself killed. Once she'd received his phone records, she began calling the numbers that had either called Luke or to whom he had made calls during the days leading up to the accident. Most were to her son's friends back in Garth's Point or schoolmates up at St. Anselm in New Hampshire. "Hi, I'm Luke's mom," Elizabeth would begin what usually proved to be an awkward and pointless conversation. She'd state her reason for calling, ask what her son and the person had talked about, if they'd noticed anything out of the ordinary regarding Luke. No, he seemed regular, most replied. When Elizabeth would ask what they meant by regular, they would say, "I don't know. Just regular Luke."

Elizabeth wasn't sure if her questioning put them on their guard, made them fear saying something damaging about a friend, especially now that that friend was dead, but with one or two of Luke's friends she couldn't help feeling the way she did sometimes with a client she sensed wasn't telling her the complete truth; she felt something being left unstated, some equivocation. Other calls Luke had made simply didn't make any sense, including one to a late-night right-wing talk radio station in Virginia. Why would Luke, a self-professed liberal, call a right-wing radio station? Two calls were to a number in Pennsylvania that had since been disconnected. Another was to the number of his old girlfriend TJ. Elizabeth thought this odd, since Luke had said the two no longer spoke. However, the call lasted only thirty-seven seconds, so Elizabeth assumed he'd only called her by accident, a pocket call. And there was no return call. So there was nothing to ask TJ about. Which was, she felt, for the better as she didn't really want to talk to Luke's old girlfriend. It would only bring back painful memories, for both.

One phone call Luke had made just two days before the accident was to a kid named Sam Rosello, a former roommate of Luke's at St. Anselm. She'd met Sam once when she drove Luke back to school. A tanned, blond kid who was, according to Luke, a ski bum and a big pothead. When Elizabeth asked Sam if he thought anything had been bothering her son, he replied, "Some of the guys thought he was acting weird."

"Did you think he was acting weird?"

"A little."

"How?"

"He didn't like to party like he used to," Sam explained. "He got all serious on us."

"What does that mean?"

"He was always going to the student Mass on Wednesday nights. And helping out at the soup kitchen."

"And is that so weird?"

"It was for Luke. He used to be a regular guy."

A regular guy, Elizabeth thought when she got off the phone.

She decided not to put much credence in what someone her son described as a pothead had to offer. She didn't find anything all that odd in Luke going to Mass. Sometimes when he came home from school he'd attend St. Catherine's in town with his father or even by himself. And Luke was always doing social-justice sorts of things like working at soup kitchens, donating his time reading to patients in nursing homes, or going on a spring-break service-learning trip organized by Father Jerome. Luke and a dozen other students went out to the Rosebud Indian Reservation in South Dakota to help build houses, while most of his friends were headed off to party at some beach in Florida. Her son had certainly seen his parents' social conscience in action: his father helping out at the church, organizing can drives and collecting blankets for poor kids in Guatemala, while his mother did her pro bono work at the women's shelter.

What did strike her as a little odd though was the fact that Luke had begun wearing a crucifix around his neck.

"What do you make of that?" she has asked Zack one night as they were getting ready for bed.

"He goes to a Catholic college, doesn't he?"

"I know, but still. I'd hate to have him become some sort of Jesus freak on us."

"A lot of young kids wear them. It must be cool," Zack said.

Then there was the issue of the diary. She'd bought it as a Christmas present for Luke his junior year in college. He'd told her he needed something for a weekly planner, and to jot "down his thoughts," and so she'd bought him a small, black, Moleskine diary at the card shop in town, with his initials monogrammed in gold in the lower right corner: *LJG.* The summer after his junior year, Luke was living at home, and his behavior had struck Elizabeth as odd and distant, or as she'd told Zack one evening, "He's acting weird." Luke, she felt, seemed preoccupied, absorbed in his own little world. One day she happened to be in Luke's room changing his sheets when, lifting the mattress, she happened to spot the black leather diary lying there. The lawyer in her mustered all the usual arguments why she should leave the thing untouched—it would be wrong, she'd be violating some sacred parental trust, she might see something she really shouldn't. She might get caught. Opposed to those arguments was a single one: this was her son and she wanted to make sure he was all right. So she went ahead and picked the thing up and started reading it anyway. Mostly the entries reassured her: they were surprisingly mundane, pedestrian observations about the life and times of Luke Gerlacher. *Need to buy some razorblades.* Or: *Had the dream again about being on the train?* Or: *Sat, Sun—work at the soup kitchen.* There were entries about upcoming tests, laundry lists of things he had to finish, ramblings about grad school applications, friends, parties. There was one reference to helping Father Jerome on some project at the church up in Manchester. Others were to things he wanted to do, places he wanted to see. *Tibet would be cool to visit.* A couple of entries included inexplicable numbers, a name of someone Elizabeth was certain Luke had never mentioned to her, the random angst of a college kid. An occasional line from a poem:

> *To see a World in a Grain of Sand*
> *And a Heaven in a Wild Flower*

Sometimes there were entries that gave Elizabeth pause, that suggested the still waters of the young man that was her son ran very deep indeed. *The heart is deceitful above all things, and desperately wicked*, he wrote once that spring. And then there was the quote from Camus: *I would rather live my life as if there is a god and die to find out there isn't, than live my life as if there isn't and die to find out there is.*

She'd only been reading for a short time when she heard Luke's car pull into the driveway. She quickly closed the book and placed it back under the mattress and, feeling a little like a criminal, scurried out of his room.

Don't do that again, she chastised herself.

Yet at some point later that summer, curiosity got the better of her and she checked under the mattress again. Flipping through the pages, she came across the same sort of mundane entries, about appointments and "things-to-do" notes to himself, such as, *Need to get winter coat* or *Have mom make me a dentist's apt.* Or *Call Griff.* In one, however, dated just that June, Luke had written three words: *Duc in altum.* She wasn't surprised by the Latin; after all, he'd taken four years in high school and had continued it as a minor in college. Later when she looked it up on the internet, she found that it meant "to put out into the deep." The deep of what, she wondered. A few entries later, she came upon the word *discernment*, set off all by itself, not in any context, but underlined several times. She knew, of course, what it meant in law; it had to do with whether or not a person had the judgment to know his actions and be held responsible for them. But she didn't know what Luke had meant by it. In any case, though, she decided it wasn't her business. She slipped the book under the mattress and never spied on her son again.

In fact she'd forgotten all about the diary until several months after Luke's death. Something spurred her memory about the book, so she went upstairs and into his room and looked for it. To her surprise it wasn't under the mattress. And after searching the room from top to bottom, she didn't find it anywhere. What became of it, she wondered. Standing there in her son's room, it came to her; first as a vague possibility, then as a distinct probability, and finally, as an utter certainty—he had taken it with him on his trip. That was the only logical conclusion. Otherwise, where was it? And yet, it hadn't been returned with the rest of Luke's effects—his clothes, class ring, the crucifix, wallet, a few other personal items he'd had with him at the time of his death, the small die-cast model of a WWII Mustang fighter. That's when she decided to call the Sheriff's office and ask if they had overlooked it, that perhaps it was sitting somewhere in their evidence room. The Sheriff already knew Elizabeth Gerlacher. She'd pestered them before this, calling several times about the missing phone, the discrepancies between what she and Zack had been told about the seat belt and what the police report said, even the direction the car was headed. Each time this Sheriff Crowder told her, in a tone so excessively polite and monotone she felt he had to be mocking her, "I don't know what-all you're talking about, ma'am. We sent you all of your son's effects." Perhaps, she liked to think, the diary might hold some key to the "accident," or at the very least to what he'd wanted to talk to her about that night.

Of course that last part was the one fact about Luke's case that her husband didn't know. She hadn't told Zack their son had called that night. Yet to Elizabeth it seemed much too coincidental that on the same night Luke would die in an "accident," he would want to talk to her about something of significance, the same child who called so seldom, who was normally so reticent to speak about his feelings, would want to talk to her about something important.

Tonight, she brought a bottle of scotch and a glass into her study and sat at her desk. Outside, the rain continued to drive across the deck, tipping over the lawn furniture. On the far side of the lake she could see headlights inching slowly along the road. She told herself she probably should spend some time on the divorce meeting she had the next day, but instead, she got out her notebook on her son's "case." It was a spiral-ring affair with white lined paper and pockets on the inside, and on whose cover she had attached a label with the single word "Luke" written in black Magic Marker. As she would for a legal case, she had been jotting down notes regarding Luke's phone calls, his credit card bills, where he'd stopped for gas, where he'd eaten or stayed overnight. As if she were mustering evidence for a court case, she'd begun to piece together an argument, a narrative of her son's movements. She looked at one credit card bill, from a place in West Memphis, Arkansas, called Lil' Sonny's, where Luke had stopped and spent $122.69. The amount had caught her eye. She Googled the place, found it was a barbecue restaurant. How could he have spent that much on lunch? Though it was, like all the others, a long shot, she decided to call.

"Lil' Sonny's. Can I hep you?" an older woman answered in a syrupy Southern drawl. There was noise in the background, voices, people yelling, the slamming of metal pans, music blaring. Elizabeth had a hard time hearing her.

"Hi, my name is Elizabeth Gerlacher. My son stopped in your restaurant a while back."

"Say again."

She repeated what she'd said, louder this time.

"How long ago we talking?"

"It was a year ago August."

The woman let out with a sardonic whistle. "That's a long time ago. Is he a regular here?"

"No. He was just passing through."

"I doubt anybody's gonna remember him from that long ago."

"But he spent a lot of money for a single meal. A hundred and twelve dollars."

"People come in here and drop that much all the time. It's really good food."

"But I think it was just himself for lunch."

"You say 'lunch'?"

"Yes."

"You oughta call back during the day shift. We got a different crew on during the day. Maybe someone there remembers him. Why, did somebody screw up the bill?"

"No. I don't think so anyway. I'm just . . . Never mind. Thank you," Elizabeth said and hung up.

She grabbed ahold of the bottle and headed upstairs to Luke's room. They usually kept the door shut, as guarded and off-limits as a police crime scene. Inside, the air was stuffy, a lingering odor of foot powder and deodorant, of old socks and cologne hanging there, the room as quiet and formal and forbidding as a shrine. Whenever she entered, it was like stepping into a past that was as palpable, as visceral as a draft of cold air. Here were his books, his memorabilia, the Springsteen and Clapton posters still on the walls, his guitar propped in the corner, waiting like some fiercely loyal dog for its master's return. She would sometimes touch his things, those possessions of Luke's that were now like a raw wound for Elizabeth; she'd open his bureau drawers and lift his perfectly folded T-shirts or sweaters and place them to her nose, inhaling deeply, trying to breath in his odor, trying to rekindle his Luke-ness. Tonight she picked up a framed photo on the bookshelf, the one of Luke and his girlfriend TJ at their senior prom, the one Elizabeth had taken. They were down at the dock, the lake shimmering in the background. TJ looked lovely in a long, red gown while Luke, tanned and glowing, wore a powder-blue tux with a red carnation. "Say cheese," Elizabeth had said to them. The young couple beamed with youthful exuberance, glowing like a pair of movie stars on the red carpet. Next to the picture on the shelf was the miniature collection of model planes, including the one that she'd bought Luke in Wales, a British Spitfire. Also among them was a silver airplane with a shark's teeth painted on the nose, something Zack had said was a World War II Mustang. It was yet another one of those odd things about Luke's death. It had been returned along with the rest of Luke's effects by the Marrizozo Sheriff's Department. The only logical conclusion was that Luke had bought it on his trip out west.

Sometimes, like tonight, she would lie on his bed. Fully dressed, on top of the covers. She would try to allow the fading musk of Luke—from the pillowcase and sheets she hadn't washed—drift over her senses like sunlight breaking through on an overcast day. Some nights she could almost do it. Some nights she convinced herself she could actually smell Luke. And sometimes for the briefest moment, he seemed just a little closer, close enough in fact that she could almost reach out and touch him. As she lay there this night, the bottle resting on her sternum, she thought again of all the strange things the old man had told her. About *descansos* and the spirits of the dead lingering where they had died and being able to talk to them, feel their energy. It was all so very odd. Disturbing actually. And just before she fell asleep, she thought how the old man had asked her if she ever paid a visit to her son.

Chapter 5

Don't go. Not yet.
I have to.
Please. Just five minutes.
Mom, I have to go.
When will I see you again?
I don't know.

The dream had several variations. Sometimes Luke was a little boy in the dream. Other times a gawky teenager with suddenly elongated limbs and a pimply face, while still other times he was college-aged with a growth of beard on his chin and a sullen look in his eyes. But in every version Elizabeth seemed to wake up and there he was sitting in the corner of her bedroom. Just sitting there. Each dream seemed so real, so life-like, Elizabeth felt if she could only reach out and touch her son, her fingers would contact solid, living flesh. Not a dream. Not a phantasm of longing. In some of the versions, Elizabeth found herself pleading with her son to stay a little longer. Five minutes. Just five. In the dream she always had the unmistakable sense that the leave-taking was both imminent and irrevocable. Not death so much as an action unalterable, a final act, and that this was the last time she'd ever see him. She usually woke with a clawing pain in her throat.

"Elizabeth." An arm nudged her. "Elizabeth."

Opening one eye, she saw Zack standing in the doorway, already dressed for work. She opened the other eye and followed his gaze toward the half empty bottle of scotch on the nightstand. Glancing around, she was disoriented for a moment. Where was she? Then it came to her: *Luke's room.* She was in her son's room. Vaguely, she recalled shuffling into his room and curling up on his bed the previous night. She didn't remember much beyond that.

"What time is it?" she asked, swallowing something dry, a lump of sawdust.

"Almost eight," replied her husband, holding up his watch as if for proof. "Damn it."

She was going to be late for work—again. And this morning she had that divorce meeting at nine, with a client she'd already had problems with and this would only make things worse. Swinging her legs off the bed, she stood too quickly, so that her head swirled with a dizzying lightness. Bright flares went off in her brain, forcing her to sit back down on the bed. Her stomach churned, and she felt on the verge of being sick.

"What are you doing?" Zack asked.

"I overslept."

"No, I mean *this*," he said, pointing toward the bottle. Then, holding both hands out in an expansive gesture that took in the entire room, he added, "Coming in here. Sleeping in his bed. For God's sake, Elizabeth."

Sometimes in the morning when she woke here, she'd have this intense, if fleeting sensation that she was a young mother again, waking in her son's room after a night when he couldn't sleep. Luke often had bad dreams, of monsters and wolves, of things lurking under the bed. In the moment before the painful realization hit her, she could almost feel the warmth of Luke's body against hers, the sweetish scent of his hair and breath, the vague urine odor.

"This isn't healthy, Elizabeth," Zack said.

"Just stop. Please."

"You have a problem, Elizabeth."

"I'm not in the mood for a lecture right now. I don't feel so hot."

"Is it any wonder?" he said, his gaze landing on the bottle again. "You have a problem."

"My problem is I'm late," she explained, rising unsteadily and making for the door. However, Zack, all six-four, two-hundred pounds of him, stood there blocking her way.

"Zack, please," she said. "Don't do this. I'm already late."

"You need to see somebody."

"We've been over this already."

"But you don't *do* anything about it."

"There's nothing *to* do."

"Of course, there is. You could go and talk to somebody."

Zack had made it perfectly clear he felt she needed professional help. That her grief was eating her up, that she was probably suffering from depression—the drinking, her coming into Luke's room and falling asleep. Several times he'd suggested they make an appointment to go see a therapist together. He'd even found the names of a couple of shrinks and jotted them down on a Post-it note he placed at eye-level on the fridge. But Elizabeth didn't see the point. As if talking to someone for an hour a week and downing some Paxils would make her feel any better. As if it would bring Luke back.

"Honey," he said to her, reaching out and placing his hand tenderly against her cheek. "I know you miss him. I miss him, too. Not a day goes by that I don't. But we have to think about us."

"Us?"

"Yes. Me and you. This isn't . . ."

"What? Normal?" she said, suddenly angry.

"Yes."

Staring up into his eyes, she said bitterly, "So why don't you tell me what's normal, Zachary. Because I really don't have a fucking clue. This is all virgin territory to me."

"Stop it."

"No. Maybe you can act as if nothing happened, but I can't." She could see the immediate effect her words had on him. He couldn't have been any more startled if she'd slapped him. He gazed down at her, wounded into silence, then removed the hand from her cheek and brought it to the bridge of his nose. She noticed his tie was askew and she reached out and straightened it, an act of past intimacy.

"I'm sorry, Zack."

"We need to talk."

"Tonight, okay?"

"I can't tonight. I have my group meeting." He paused, then offered tentatively, "You could come with me."

"That's your thing, Zack."

"Why's it *my* thing?"

"Talking to a bunch of other depressed people isn't my idea of help."

He leaned back and she used the occasion to slip by him into the hall and hurry toward the bathroom.

"Then when?" he called after her.

Instead of replying she slipped into the bathroom, shut the door, and got into the shower. As the Water Pik punished her throbbing head, she thought about how Zack wanted to move on, to go forward with their lives. Once he'd even mentioned the possibility of their having another child.

"Are you crazy?" she'd cried. "I'm fifty-one, for heaven's sake."

"We could adopt. Not now. I'm talking down the road."

"There is no 'down the road,' Zack. Besides, I don't *want* another child. I just want the one we had back."

"He's gone, Elizabeth. And he's not coming back."

She thought of the dream again: *Don't go. Not yet . . .*

* * *

By the time Elizabeth got to work, she was a half hour late. She rushed past the office of her colleague Joan Lanzetti and down the hall and into her own. She shut the door and tried to compose herself. Her hair was still wet, and she'd hastily applied her makeup on the twenty-minute car ride to work. Her head continued to pound, her stomach churning, filled with something like battery acid.

"Where the fuck is the Healey file?" she muttered to herself as she rifled through the mess on her desk.

Knuckles sounded on the door; before she could respond the door opened and Joan poked her head in.

"Where've you been? They've been waiting for you in the conference room."

"I got hung up," Elizabeth replied.

"Is everything all right?"

"Yeah, everything's just great."

"That Healey woman is fuming," said Joan.

A contemptuous little laugh slipped from Elizabeth's mouth. "Let her fume. That's what she does, fume."

"You know she's going to bitch to Warren about this." Warren Fuller was the senior partner of the law firm. A crotchety old man who wore rumpled suits and who sometimes snored through meetings, he still ran the firm with an iron hand, as if it was a small third-world country of which he'd been made dictator for life. Warren and Daphne Healey's father were old golf pals. It was Warren who'd given Elizabeth the case, with the caveat that the woman might need some TLC. That was an understatement.

"If she wasn't so goddamned unreasonable, we'd have settled this already," Elizabeth said.

"By the way, you look like crap," Joan offered.

"Thanks."

Joan paused in the doorway for a moment.

Elizabeth looked at her and raised one hand, palm up, as if to say, "What?"

"Are you all right, kiddo?"

"I'm fine. I'm just playing catch up here," Elizabeth said.

"All right, we'll talk later."

Fuller and Fuller was a small law firm housed in a restored Victorian that looked out onto the Garth Point village green, a town along the eastern Connecticut shore. Elizabeth, a junior partner, had worked here for nearly ten years. She liked Joan and her other colleagues, and for the most part, tolerated Warren. When she'd first moved to Garth's Point, after having spent a dozen years working in a large firm in New York, she enjoyed the slower, small-town pace. She'd wanted to have a normal life—which meant a family, time to travel, to pursue her other interests, her *pro bono* work. But in the past few years, she'd gradually become disillusioned by her job in the firm, by the fact that her work here didn't seem all that meaningful to her any longer.

Finally, she found the file she was looking for and hurried into the conference room.

"Sorry, I'm late," Elizabeth offered to everyone seated there.

Staring at her were Josh Healey, the husband of Elizabeth's client, and his attorney Adam Goldstein, a local lawyer Elizabeth knew and didn't particularly like. Across from them was her own client Daphne Healey, who stared at Elizabeth with the cold, venomous eyes of a cobra.

"I'm glad you could make it," Daphne offered sarcastically.

"Can I have a moment with my client?" Elizabeth said to Goldstein.

"I'm already running late for court as it is, counselor," Goldstein said to her.

"Just five minutes. Please."

The words from the dream echoed in her mind.

Elizabeth led Mrs. Healey into her office. Before she had a chance to say a word, the woman launched into one of her usual tirades. "That son of a bitch wants Kate every other weekend."

Daphne Healey was about forty, anorexic-thin, with dark eyes and a frizzy blonde perm, a severe-looking woman whose body had been tortured by numerous plastic surgeries and Botox injections and a Barbie-doll boob job. Her maiden name had been Abernathy, one of *the* Abernathys, a clan that could trace its roots back to the original settlers of Garth's Point.

"Mrs. Healey, no court is going to grant you sole custody based on your husband's extramarital affair," Elizabeth explained. "What you're asking for isn't reasonable."

"Don't tell me what's reasonable. I love my daughter."

"I don't doubt that you do, but what about your husband?"

"What about that prick?"

Elizabeth thought how different it was to deal with someone like Fabiana, someone humble and polite, who had nothing and yet who was willing to forgive a man who had beaten her up. And here was this woman who'd been born with a silver spoon in her mouth, and still it wasn't enough.

"I'm sure your husband loves her, too," Elizabeth lectured. "And he has parental rights."

"Screw his rights," she cried, pounding Elizabeth's desk with her bony, heavily bejeweled fist. "It's your job to get me full custody."

"No, it's my job to explain the law to you and then do the best I can."

"Then do your best. That's what I'm paying you for."

Elizabeth's head throbbed, and her stomach suddenly felt even more queasy, as if she were on a small boat in the sound on a day when the water was choppy. She took a deep breath and exhaled, trying to calm her belly.

"It's obvious you have your daughter's welfare utmost in mind, Mrs. Healey." The woman didn't seem to catch Elizabeth's thinly disguised sarcasm. "But as a mother, you have to understand that she's going to need a father too."

"*You* don't understand," said the woman, pointing an accusatory finger at Elizabeth. "I'm the aggrieved party here. That son of bitch was screwing his bimbo of a hygienist."

"But right now we're focusing on what's best for your daughter."

"*I'm* what's best for my daughter. Kate needs me."

"I'm sure she does, Mrs. Healey." Elizabeth thought then of her own father. She was in her thirties when he died yet it still seemed as if the rug had been pulled out from under her, as if she were suddenly orphaned. "But she's also going to need her father, too."

"I don't need a lecture on parenting," the woman exclaimed.

"I'm just pointing out the legal parameters."

"Do you have children, Mrs. Gerlacher?"

The question set Elizabeth back on her heels. She usually tried to avoid getting into her private life with clients. It was better to keep them at a distance. Still, Garth's Point was a small town. News got around. For a moment she thought the woman was toying with her, playing some sort of perverse mind game. Surely, she would have heard about Elizabeth's son. It was in the local paper, the scuttlebutt around town. In any case, Elizabeth wasn't quite sure how to respond to the woman's question: *Do you have children?* Since her son's death, she'd been asked this once or twice. The first time was only a couple of months after Luke died. She was on the train to New York for a meeting in the city, when a young mother with an infant in a Snugli sat down across from her. They struck up a conversation, Elizabeth asking the usual questions about the baby—her name, age, was she sleeping through the night. At some point, the young woman asked Elizabeth if *she* had children. Though she later realized she should have seen it coming, the question nonetheless took her a little by surprise. Beyond the fact that she didn't want to throw a pall over an otherwise pleasant conversation, she wasn't sure what the answer was. How *does* a parent whose only child has died reply to such a thing? Should she say she *didn't* have a child? Simple math: one minus one equals zero? Or does having a child imply that you *always* have one, that no matter what happened you were *always* a parent and therefore you *always* had a child?

"No," Elizabeth replied to Mrs. Healey.

"I didn't think so."

"Really? Why is that?"

"You don't look the type."

"What type would that be?" Elizabeth threw back at her, her annoyance barely restrained.

"The maternal type. That's why you can't possibly imagine what you're asking me to do."

"I can certainly empathize with your position."

"No, I don't think you can, Mrs. Gerlacher," the woman said.

Elizabeth felt her head swoon with a dizzying rush of anger and outrage. She actually saw spots floating before her eyes. She'd gotten annoyed with clients before but she'd never experienced this visceral urge to lean across her desk and slap the woman's face.

"It seems to me, Mrs. Healey, if you cared half as much about your daughter's welfare as you do for your own revenge, we'd have settled this already."

"How dare you!" She paused, then muttered something under her breath, something that sounded suspiciously like "Bitch."

"What did you say?"

"Nothing," the woman replied.

"To tell you the truth, Mrs. Healey, I can't blame your husband for running off."

Elizabeth would have smiled at this retort, except for the fact that the sour feeling in the pit of her stomach lurched up into the back of her throat right at that moment. She had to put her hand to her mouth, as she tasted something vile as warm vinegar. She had all she could do not to retch then and there.

"You'll have to excuse me," she managed to get out, as she stood and hurried around the desk and past her client into the hall.

"Jesus, where are you going now? I want to talk to Warren," she heard Daphne Healey call after her. "Do you hear me?"

Elizabeth barely had time to close the bathroom door behind her before she bent over the toilet bowl and vomited violently. Not once but again and again, as if she were trying to eject something foul and toxic from her stomach, as if the poison of the past year was something she could expel and rid herself of. As she paused, her head over the bowl, waiting, she heard her son's voice, the words she'd heard playing in her head a thousand, ten thousand times before: *There's something I really needed to talk to you about, Mom.*

* * *

A little after noon, Elizabeth was in her office working. Her stomach had settled down a little but her hangover throbbed dully behind her eyes. She looked forward to going out to the car and having a little nip. That always helped settle things.

Her door opened suddenly, and Joan entered. "You want to grab some lunch?"

"My stomach's not feeling so hot."

"Then take a walk with me. Some fresh air will do you good."

The afternoon was sunny, with an autumnal crispness in the air as they walked down the street toward The Coffee Clutch, a little café on the green. The downtown of Garth's Point resembled a setting for a 1940s Frank Capra movie about small-town America. The town green was surrounded by no less than four churches, each facing the other and seeming to represent one point of the town's moral compass. One of the churches was St. Catherine's, where Zack met his grief support group. On the green, people walked their dogs and read on the benches; in summer there was Shakespeare in the Park and a huge craft show, while in winter there was the Christmas tree lighting.

In The Coffee Clutch, Joan ordered a Cobb salad and a mocha latte to satisfy, as she put it, her afternoon chocolate craving. Elizabeth got only a bottle of water. They sat at a table near the window, which looked diagonally across the street at an up-scale women's boutique called Greta's Garb. It had its "Summer Clearance" items on a rack out on the sidewalk, hoping to catch the eye of the last of the summer tourists.

Short and curvy, Joan had red hair which fell in a wild, bushy perm and large espresso-colored eyes that always seemed on the verge of breaking into laughter. She was feisty and outspoken, and shared with Elizabeth the most intimate details of her and her husband Ray's sex life. Elizabeth, on the other hand, never divulged anything about her and Zack in that way. She was way too private a person. Though Joan was her oldest and closest friend, Elizabeth had never told her about the affair. She thought Joan would look down on her for it.

"Brianna decide on a major yet?" Elizabeth asked.

Joan looked surprised. Funny, but lately she never talked about her kids to Elizabeth. It was almost as if, since Luke's death, it had become an unspoken rule not to bring up the subject of kids, as if the general topic of children was taboo.

"She's doing gender studies," Joan replied with a roll of her eyes. "I mean, what does one do with a gender studies major? I could see if she were a lesbian or something."

Both women chuckled at that, a nervous laughter that seemed mostly intended to dissipate the tension over talking about their kids.

"Same with Luke going into theology," Elizabeth offered.

"Theology? I thought he'd been pre-law," Joan said.

"He was. But since *I* was the one who suggested pre-law, of course he wanted nothing to do with it."

"Isn't that always the way? If we say up, they say down."

Joan had two daughters; the older one, Allison, had been in Luke's grade, while Brianna was two years behind. When their kids were little, Joan and Elizabeth used to get them together for play dates. The three kids would play house, with Luke and Allison as the stern parents to poor little Brianna, who always got stuck as the baby even when she was five. In fact, Luke and Allison had been quite close until high school when the changing social currents had swept them into separate groups. Elizabeth and Zack used to get together often with Joan and Ray socially, and when the kids were little on several occasions the two families had rented a summer place out on Wellfleet. Even before the accident, though, the four had started to drift apart. They blamed it on their hectic schedules, their kids' routines, spouses' work, life. But especially in the past year, her friendship with Joan had ceased to be as close. Though unspoken, Luke's death had made things uncomfortable for both of them.

Joan fell silent, eating her salad and not making eye contact. Elizabeth had a feeling something was on her mind.

"So what's up?" Elizabeth finally asked. "Why did you want to talk?"

Joan raised her eyebrows. "What on earth were you trying to do with Daphne Healey today?"

"What was *I* trying to do with *her*?" Elizabeth scoffed.

"She told Warren you said her husband was right to run off with his girlfriend."

"She called me a bitch."

"I know she can be difficult."

"Difficult? The woman's a royal pain in the ass," Elizabeth cried.

"Agreed. But she's our client. You can't speak to her like that."

"You know what else she said to me? That I wasn't the maternal type."

Joan reached across and patted Elizabeth's hand. "She had no right to say that. But she's still our client."

Elizabeth shook her head. "All she wants to do is make her husband pay for cheating on her. She doesn't give a damn about her kid's welfare."

"I don't doubt that's true but it's not our business."

"But it *is* my business to lay out what's legally possible. There's no way in hell she's getting full custody. You know that as well as I do."

"I know. But it's the *way* you deal with her," cautioned Joan.

"So I'm supposed to handle her with kid gloves just because her father's a big muckety-muck in town? And he's pals with Warren? The hell with her."

"You can't take that attitude with her."

"Really?"

"Unless you want to make trouble for yourself. Listen, I could care less about that woman," Joan said. "It's you I'm worried about. You can't behave like that. It's not professional. And besides, you were late again."

"Don't—" she began but Joan held up a hand to stop her.

"Warren called me into his office. He told me he smelled booze on your breath one day last week."

"What?"

"He said you'd been drinking."

"That's crazy."

"Is it?"

"*Yes*, it is!"

Joan glanced out the window, then back at Elizabeth. "I've noticed it, too."

"You've noticed what?"

"When it looks like you've been drinking."

"Like when?" Elizabeth challenged.

"Like this morning."

"I told you, I wasn't feeling well. I have this stomach thing."

"Come on, it's me, kiddo. It's getting pretty obvious. You go out to your car and when you come in your eyes are all screwed up."

"They are not."

"Besides that, Warren thinks you've been spending too much time doing your pro bono work."

"What I do on my own time is my own damn business," Elizabeth snapped.

"But not when it's affecting your work here. You've fallen behind on several cases. And there've been other complaints. On the Lavigne closing, you had the figures all screwed up."

"So I mess up one time and everybody's on my case."

"It's not just one time," Joan said. She paused and took a sip of her coffee. "Zack told me what's going on at home."

"What do you mean, 'what's going on at home'?"

"He said you haven't been sleeping well. That you've been, well, drinking too much."

"That's bullshit. I mean, I have a drink or two in the evening. To relax and unwind. But I don't have a problem," she said.

"He's concerned about you. We all are."

Elizabeth could just picture the two of them—Zack and Joan—talking about her behind her back, arranging an intervention strategy. Planning ways to get her to go to a therapist, join Zack's support group, confess to having issues.

"Well, I'm glad everyone is so damn concerned about me."

"Elizabeth, come on. Don't take it that way."

"How am I supposed to take it? The two of you going behind my back."

"We're not going behind your back. We love you. We're trying to help."

"It doesn't sound like help."

Elizabeth felt her face growing hot.

"How bad is it? The drinking."

"I told you. I have one or two. To relax."

"Zack said you go into Luke's room at night and pass out."

"I don't pass out," said Elizabeth, shaking her head. "Jesus. You guys are unbelievable."

"He's just worried about you."

"Maybe I went into Luke's room once or twice. So what? It's nobody's goddamned business but my own."

Elizabeth had raised her voice, so that several customers looked over at them.

"Easy," Joan said, trying to calm her. "Do you think it's a good idea though? Sleeping in his room."

"If it helps me to get through this, what's so bad about it?"

"But *are* you getting through this?" Joan asked.

"What's that supposed to mean?"

"Do you feel you're getting any better, kiddo?"

"You tell me what 'better' means," said Elizabeth. "I get up, I go to work. I put one foot in front of the other. That's all I can do right now."

"Have you thought about taking some time off?"

"Geez Louise. We've been over this before."

"You could go away. Just the two of you. Have some fun."

Fun, Elizabeth thought. What was that? Several times Joan had suggested she take some time off, go away on a vacation. Get her head straight. Yet the thought of having nothing to do, nothing to structure her days scared the hell out of her. Just this gaping expanse of time to fill up, like being stuck in a doctor's waiting room without a magazine in sight. What would she and Zack do, just the two of them? What would they talk about? How could they possibly pretend to be enjoying themselves when Luke was gone from the world?

"Trust me, a vacation is the last thing I need. I need to keep busy," Elizabeth retorted.

"But you came back *two* days after the funeral," Joan said, holding up a pair of accusatory fingers.

"So?"

"You didn't give yourself a chance to grieve properly."

Elizabeth let out a fluttery laugh of exasperation. "I didn't know there was a *proper* way to grieve. You sound like Zack now."

"Come on, Elizabeth. You know what I mean."

"No, I don't. Since when did you become a shrink?"

Joan sucked on a piece of lettuce caught in her teeth. "Maybe you ought to see one."

"Did Zack tell you that, too?"

"I'm just trying to be your friend."

"Then be my friend. Stay out of my damn business," she said harshly. "You don't know what it's like. Every day I get up, I think it's all just a bad dream. It's like I'm waiting for him. Waiting for him to come slouching down to breakfast with that sour puss of his. Or when I set the table at night, I'll hesitate for just a moment, wondering if I should set it for three as if I expect him to come home. It's been a whole year and I still can't really believe he's gone."

They stared at each other from across the table. But it might as well have been from across opposite sides of the Grand Canyon. For what divided the two was the great chasm that separated one parent whose children were alive from another whose child was dead. They both sensed it, too, and knew nothing could bridge that divide, not friendship or love or empathy, not even the bond that mothers shared.

"Listen, kiddo," Joan said, reaching across and taking her hand. "You're right. I don't know. But as your friend, I have to tell you that you need to get a hold of things. You can't keep coming in late, and you gotta cut out the booze. If you keep on like this you're going to endanger your position with the firm."

"What's Warren going to do? Fire me? I'm a partner. He can't fire me."

"I wouldn't push that, Elizabeth. If things don't change, Warren's ready to call a meeting of the board and have you suspended."

"He wouldn't dare."

"Yes. He would. Trust me. You don't want to force his hand, Elizabeth."

She suddenly felt defensive, alone, attacked from all sides. Even her best friend was turning on her.

"Listen, kiddo," Joan said. "Why don't you take the rest of the day off and go home and get some sleep? And think about taking some time off. A few days. A week. It might do you good."

Chapter 6

Elizabeth didn't take any time off from work, but she decided she'd better heed Joan's warning and cut out the booze, get to the office on time, focus more on her responsibilities. At the same time, she found herself—at work, driving somewhere in the car, standing in line at the grocery store—replaying the chance meeting she'd had with the old man. The things he'd said seemed to strike a chord in her, a low vibration at the base of her skull that seemed to grow in volume each day. How he'd told her he felt a connection with his dead wife at the roadside memorial. How the spirits of the dead often stayed near where they had perished. She remembered, too, how he'd laid his hand on her arm and said, *We all got regrets.* He seemed to have some intimate knowledge regarding the intricacies of grief and guilt.

In the evenings after she and Zack ate a quiet dinner, she would excuse herself, saying she had work to catch up on, and head down into her study. There she would take out her notebook on Luke, go over once more his credit card bills and phone records, scanning the dots on her map, trying to connect them, trying to see if some picture might emerge, a portrait of her son's final journey on earth. One evening she decided to call a place in central Texas called Ned's Landing, where Luke had charged $93.67. Was it a gas station? It seemed an awful lot just for gas. It was the day before the accident. Three hundred-odd miles before he arrived in Marrizozo, New Mexico.

An old man answered, a voice so dusty and parched she had to listen carefully in order to understand. She explained that her son had stopped there to buy something.

"He spent over ninety dollars. That seems a lot for gas."

"Gas?" the man said. "We don't sell gas."

"You don't?"

"No, ma'am. We run a museum."

"A museum?"

"Aircraft. We have vintage World War II planes. A little gift shop out front."

Then it hit her: *That's where Luke had bought the plane.*

"Do you sell a P-51 Mustang model?" Elizabeth asked.

"Ah huh. Mustangs, Hellcats, Black Widows, Thunderbolts. You name it, we got it."

"My son bought a Mustang from you. I wonder if you remember him."

"We sell a good many P-51s. They're the most popular."

"He was tall. Thin. Twenty-one years old. Dirty blond hair," Elizabeth recited as if she were describing a suspect in a crime.

"Don't ring a bell, ma'am," the man said. "When you say he was here?"

"A year ago August."

"That's a long while back," the man said with a laugh. "My memory ain't what it used to be. What was he doing here in Haslitt?"

"I think he was just passing through. He was driving out to the West Coast."

"Maybe if I saw his picture."

"Thank you," Elizabeth said and hung up.

* * *

During lunch one day, she left her office and stopped at Tully's Florist Shop just off the green to buy some flowers. The place smelled pungently of mortality, like a funeral home.

"What are they for?" asked Jocelyn, the owner, a red-haired woman in her mid-forties.

"For a friend."

The woman picked out a bunch of lilies and chrysanthemums.

"Do you want a card?" she asked Elizabeth.

"No. That won't be necessary."

She drove over to the cemetery, parked, and got out. The fall had grown suddenly colder, a sharp wind slicing in off the sound like a serrated blade. The cemetery sat on a small rise overlooking an apple orchard, and beyond that was a bluish-gray sliver of ocean. She hadn't been here in a while. Perhaps May or June. The last time she came was in the evening, and she'd been a little drunk and had trouble finding Luke's stone. When she finally found it, she curled up on his grave only to wake in the middle of the night, cold and damp and disoriented. Whenever she visited she always left more frustrated and confused than before she'd come. And of course she never felt in the least any connection to her son, never felt his spirit or whatever it was she was supposed to feel here. George Doucette was right about that. Cemeteries were merely filing cabinets for the dead.

This day she knelt and put the lilies and chrysanthemums at the base of the headstone. She did some minor housekeeping, mostly nervous energy—ripping up weeds and brushing away a few stray leaves that had been blown here from the woods at the back of the cemetery.

She recalled the day of the funeral. Her son's casket lay suspended over the astroturf-covered hole in the ground. Father Jerome had come down from New Hampshire to give the eulogy. A tall, slender, athletic-looking man with a neatly trimmed goatee that reminded Elizabeth of some TV soap opera actor, he spoke about how Luke's remarkable promise had been on the verge of being fulfilled, about faith, about a loving God, none of which Elizabeth could understand in the least. A loving God could take her son? After the ceremony, the priest had come up to her and Zack, his eyes misted over, and taking Elizabeth's hand, he said how he felt a certain measure of responsibility for having supported Luke's decision to go on this trip.

Elizabeth didn't know what he was talking about.

"It wasn't your fault, Father," Zack replied, glancing sheepishly at Elizabeth. "I thought it was a good idea, too."

It appeared for a moment he would say more, but instead, he offered his apologies for not being able to stay for the reception and turned and left.

Today, glancing at the words cut into the polished marble, she whispered softly, "Luke," the way she'd first uttered his name when the nurse in the hospital had placed him in her arms, as if testing the name out for size. She could still remember the sweet smell of his jaundiced skin, the bruises along his temples from the forceps delivery. Her Lukey had not come into the world willingly, had to be dragged, kicking and screaming, perhaps a metaphor for the man he was to become—stubborn, prickly, often difficult. Perhaps like his mother. She smiled though at the memory of his pale pink eyelids, those incredibly delicate, frog-like fingers as they groped tentatively at this strange new world he'd entered. She got out her cell phone and scrolled through the pictures she had of Luke. Sometimes she did that, as if to rekindle her memory of him. There was one in particular she was fond of. It was one of the last photos she'd taken of him. It was down at the lake, on a bright summer's day that last summer. He was sitting on a lounge chair on the dock, in his bathing suit, reading. His hair was sun-bleached, his face tanned, handsome, serious. She could still recall the book he had with him most of that summer: *Siddhartha*.

Somewhere along the line Luke had changed. Especially in the last year of his life, he'd grown distant and withdrawn, become this stranger who could have called her on the night of his death to say he needed to talk and she hadn't the slightest idea what it might be. She could remember one particularly dreadful incident that happened when Luke was a junior. He'd come home from college one weekend, and the three of them had gone out to celebrate Zack's fiftieth birthday in New York. She'd wanted the evening to be special. She'd planned a lovely dinner at a posh restaurant and splurged and bought Zack a Rolex, perhaps because she felt guilty about the affair she'd only recently become involved in. Their waiter, a young, overtly gay man, had given them, Elizabeth thought, poor service. Their food was cold, he'd mixed up one of their orders, didn't refill their water glasses, mostly ignored them. When he brought their bill, Elizabeth had reprimanded him, embarrassing him publicly. Luke as usual—whether it was simple contrariness on his part or his natural affinity for the underdog—had come to the waiter's defense. "Why are you making such a big deal out of it, Mom?" he'd said.

"If I'm paying good money, I expect good service."

"Maybe the poor guy was busy. Or just having a bad day. Can't you cut him a little slack?"

"His bad day isn't my concern. If I'm having a bad day, my clients shouldn't have to pay for it."

"Why do you always have to be so hard on people?"

On the way home, she and Luke continued their argument, with Zack performing his usual role as referee, which only infuriated Elizabeth all the more.

"Just stay out of it," she'd snapped at her husband. Then to her son in the backseat, she'd said, "You can be forgiving when it doesn't come out of your pocket."

"You just didn't like him because he was gay," Luke accused.

The comment took her by surprise. "What! Don't be ridiculous."

"It's true. You pretend to be this big liberal, doing all your women's shelter work, but you're just an elitist snob."

The accusation was like a slap in her progressive face. Was she an elitist snob? Had she been hard on the waiter because he was gay? Was she always so hard on people, as Luke had alleged?

She knelt on the damp earth, feeling the moisture leaching through her nylons. She remained silent, waiting, though for what, she hadn't the faintest idea. She remembered how George Doucette had scoffed at the word *remains*. He'd been right, of course: it was a vile term for somebody's loved one. What lay there in the ground below her wasn't her son, her Lukey. So where was he then? At one time, when she was little, like her father she'd believed in the whole nine yards, in a heaven, in forgiveness, in the grace of a loving God. But what sort of loving God could have stolen a mother's child like this, for no reason, a pointless accident in the desert? Even after all these many months, Elizabeth couldn't reconcile herself to the fact of his absence. How could he be gone when she could *feel* him still, in her heart, in her fingers, recall the touch of his skin, the lemony tang of his hair? Or the sound of his voice that, from time to time, sounded so real, so close. Though the actuality of Luke may have dimmed, she felt him still. As she knelt there, she closed her eyes and said something she had given voice to several times before, usually when she lay half drunk in the dark on Luke's bed: *What did you want to tell me, sweetheart?* She waited for several seconds, but save for the wind rubbing against the headstones, a silken sound, there was only the pulse beating in her throat. That and silence. Instead, she thought of a line she'd once glimpsed in Luke's diary: *He is no fool who gives up what he cannot keep to gain that which he cannot lose.* She knew what she had lost. What she wasn't sure about was what she had gained.

* * *

After the meeting with George Doucette, she'd begun to see those crosses, those *descansos*, everywhere. In the past week she must have spotted a dozen. As she drove around town or up to Hartford for a court case, there they were suddenly. They seemed to appear out of nowhere. Along the sides of roads, at intersections, in the center median of highways. One overlooked a bridge that crossed the Connecticut River. Another was nailed to a sycamore tree. Still another she spotted before a pasture filled with cows that stared at her with curiosity when she stopped the car to look at the cross. All the places where people had died suddenly, unexpectedly, and where other people, their loved ones, had put up crosses to their memory.

She spotted three in Garth's Point alone. One was just south of the green, on the way to the shore. She'd been by this section of road countless times, and had never really noticed it before. This time, she slowed the car as she went by it but didn't get out. The cross was a small, simple thing, with a plastic wreath of faded flowers draped around it. She spotted another heading west past Bartlett's Orchards. This one had been the scene of a notorious crime in town. A dozen years earlier a man walking his dog at night had been struck and killed by a hit-and-run driver, whom they'd never caught. And just before the high school, in a swampy area on the west side of Great Hill Road, she came upon a large cross nailed directly to a fence post. The kid who died at that spot, Joey Parsons, was from one the oldest families in town. Elizabeth knew the mother and had gone to the funeral, which brought out half of Garth's Point. It occurred to her that these memorials had been there, in some cases for decades, and she'd never noticed them before, at least not on a conscious level. Since meeting the old man, however, the crosses seemed to leap out at her, crying *Look at me!* And each time she saw one, she couldn't help but imagine a barren section of desert, Luke's battered Accord tipped over, steam rising from the radiator, broken glass and twisted metal, her son lying on the ground looking up at the sky.

One day during her lunch hour she drove out to the women's shelter. She hadn't had a drink in nearly a week. She was trying really hard to get a handle on things, trying to take it one day at a time. Searching online she'd also picked out a couple of names of therapists. She hadn't called any of them yet to make an appointment but she felt a little better for having simply looked. It was, she felt, just a matter of willpower. Of willing yourself to get better. Just like Zack had said. You needed to *choose* to move on, to get on with your life, rather than wallowing in grief and self-pity. Who knows, she might even go along with Zack to his grief support group? What could it hurt? Besides, it would please him.

"I guess I owe you that bottle after all," Father Paul said to her when she stopped by his office.

For a moment she'd forgotten their wager, thought it was merely some perverse attempt at humor by Father Paul directed at her effort to stay on the wagon.

"Fabiana. She ended up in the emergency room."

"Oh, no!" cried Elizabeth. "What happened?"

"She's got a broken arm. Some bruises."

"That son of a bitch. Where is she now?"

"With her son in the play room."

Fabiana was on the floor playing with Esteban. Elizabeth took a quick breath when she saw the cast on her left arm. When the woman spotted Elizabeth she got up and came over to her.

"*Hola, señora,*" she said. She held up her arm, gave Elizabeth a you-were-right nod.

"Oh, Fabiana, I'm so sorry."

"*Debería haber escuchado a usted.* I so *estúpida.*"

"It's all right. How are you?"

"Better."

"Will you sign the restraining order now?"

"*Sí, sí.* I sign," she said, pantomiming signing with the hand that was in a cast.

After she'd finished at the shelter, Elizabeth was driving back to work along the interstate, her thoughts on Fabiana, when she saw it up ahead. *Two* actually. A matching set, like salt and pepper shakers. A pair of crosses just off the highway, between the shoulder and a service road that ran parallel to the interstate, halfway up a little rise. They stood side by side facing west. How many times had she driven this stretch of road without ever noticing them before? On something more conscious than a whim, she pulled off at the next exit, crossed over the highway, and drove back along the service road until she figured she'd reached the spot. She stopped and got out of her car. She walked over to the edge of the road, where a six-foot-high chain-link fence separated the road from the highway. The crosses were just on the other side of that hill, she thought. She cautioned herself: *Just what the hell do you think you're doing?* But she disregarded the warning and went ahead and awkwardly clambered up the fence in her high heels and skirt. If anyone saw her, they'd think she was nuts. And maybe she was. As she lifted her back leg awkwardly over the fence, her nylons snagged on a sharp edge; she heard a tearing sound and felt a sudden sharp burning sensation along her calf.

"*Fuck!*" she cried.

She continued over and clambered down the other side. She saw that her nylons were shredded and that she had a cut running crosswise along her Achilles. A trickle of blood had already formed against her pale skin. About halfway down the steep, grassy embankment were the crosses. She used her high heels like crampons to dig into the side of the hill, and she had to keep one hand near to the ground so as not to slip. The crosses were about twenty feet above the pavement. Below, cars and trucks roared by with a brutal ferocity, their occupants' eyes, Elizabeth felt, locked on this strange scene unfolding before them. It occurred to her that someone might actually call the police and then how would she explain what she was doing? Warren would think she'd completely lost it and fire her. Yet once more she ignored her own warnings and continued down.

Reaching the spot, Elizabeth squatted in front of the two white crosses. From the looks of them, they'd been put there ages ago. They were wooden, painted white, with dark lettering. Only part of one name was legible—Anthony Something. However, it was obvious that whoever put them here had taken meticulous care in their arrangement. Someone had used a level and had taken his time. Perfectly aligned, same height and angle, they could have been crosses at Arlington National Cemetery. The horizontal sections had been attached with screws and the bases had been secured into the ground with cement. When she touched them, they didn't budge at all, felt as solid, as immovable, as marble headstones. The area immediately around the crosses was set apart from the surrounding hillside by stones laid out in a crude circle. Inside the circle was an odd array of junk: several melted candles, cigarette butts, an empty tequila bottle, a browned Christmas wreath, a ribbon with an attached bronze medal that was for second place for some unspecified competition, a plastic doll with straw-like hair and lusterless black eyes staring unblinking at the sky, ashes where a small fire had been built. Despite the crosses, the disparate items conjured up a scene that was slightly pagan.

Elizabeth guessed it had been a couple of high school kids who had died here, a boy and a girl. Maybe sweethearts. She pictured their friends coming here, lighting candles one night, singing, laughing, crying, drinking booze, carrying on as if at an Irish wake. Did other people, strangers, stop here as she did, and leave something behind, some sort of memento? She recalled how George had said people sometimes did that. Left things. As if to make a connection with the unknown dead. She also remembered how he had said that each place, each *descanso*, had a certain story to tell. Though she couldn't quite say that she felt anything, this place, she reasoned, had to have been a sad story. Two kids dying here.

As she was staring down at the debris, something glittering in the long grass caught her attention. She reached down and picked it up. It was a small heart-shaped locket on a chain, the gold-plating tarnished by the weather. When she pried it opened with a nail, she saw a picture on one side. The rain had all but obliterated the features, but from the outline of the hair Elizabeth could tell it was a young girl. On the facing side was an inscription: *Erin, forever in our hearts.*

Elizabeth glanced at the locket in her hand, then at the two crosses. She wondered if the families or loved ones who visited here could feel the spirits of the two kids. But how exactly did one go about feeling the spirit of some-one who'd passed on? Was there a particular technique, a conscious applica-tion of will, like with meditation or hypnosis? Did they offer up prayers, light a candle, as the old man said he sometimes did? Or as in a séance, was there a specified set of incantations or a particular chant to summon up the un-willing dead? Or did all of it presuppose a certain level of faith, that you had to *believe* in things unseen before you could ever hope to feel their presence? Elizabeth had never even remotely had that sort of feeling at a grave. Not at the grave of her father, whom she'd loved very much, nor at that of her son.

She sat down, then lay back, resting her head fully on the ground, the sun-warmed, sweet smell of grass in her nose. She closed her eyes. Behind her lids she could see red insect-like things rising and falling. She tried con-centrating, tried forcing herself to block out the deafening roar of the high-way below. As when she used to meditate, she tried both to empty herself of thoughts and sensations, and yet at the same time to be more open, more re-ceptive to whatever might play across her mind. A heightened awareness. She could hear the pulse in her temples—*dfff, dfff . . . dfff, dfff.* After a while the car noises did seem to recede to some middle ground. *Luke,* she said to her-self, the way she did sometimes at night while lying in the dark of his room.

She said his name again. *Luke, sweetie.*

Mom.

Startled, Elizabeth opened her eyes and sat bolt upright. Of course, she knew it was just her own inner voice replying. Or a memory of his voice. Either way, it wasn't *really* him. Just her mind playing tricks on her. Still, it made her heart ratchet up a couple of notches. It almost felt as if Luke were nearby. Glancing down at the highway, she could imagine it all unfolding. The accident, that is. The two kids driving along, maybe drunk, perhaps just merely careless as teens can be. Talking and laughing, holding hands, flirting, not paying the slightest attention to the relentless laws of physics, the cruel mechanics of the world. Then in an instant everything changed, the car sud-denly careening off the highway, airborne for a chaotic moment. There might have been time for a single, *Oh, my God!* before the car slammed into the side of the hill. Then there was the breaking of steel and glass and bone. And after that silence. Just silence.

And then she imagined, weeks, months after the funeral, the father of one of the two kids, down in his basement one evening, methodically cut-ting the boards, screwing them together, carefully painting them white, then stenciling in the children's names and dates of birth and death, maybe an inscription of love: *To my darling daughter. To my beloved son. Erin, forever in our hearts.* What would have gone through his head, she wondered, as he made them? Did the ritual of constructing the crosses give him any sort of solace? Did it lighten his burden? Did he drive out and put them up all by himself? Or did his family accompany him? Or perhaps, both families, as in some odd posthumous wedding ritual. And what did they *feel* when they drove out here again, months or years later to this site where death had stolen their children? Did they, like the old man she had met, feel their loved ones' spirits floating here like bright mobiles over an infant's crib? In one sense she could imagine all this. It seemed now a perfectly acceptable means of dealing with loss. Of making a connection with their departed loved ones. Of fathoming the unfathomable. But in another way, it was still a complete and utter mystery to her, something beyond her grasp. These crosses, finally, were just pieces of wood and paint stuck there in the side of the hill.

Chapter 7

A couple of days later, Elizabeth found herself sitting in her car in the parking lot of an office building. She was early for a five o'clock appointment. It was with a woman therapist, someone Joan had recommended: a Dr. Hotchkiss. Elizabeth figured it couldn't hurt, seeing someone. The truth was, she'd never been to a therapist before. She'd always taken a smug pride in being able to manage her own problems, at telling herself things were fine, that it didn't hurt, that she just needed to work harder, buckle down. But after a year of trying to deal with Luke's death on her own, she had to admit she'd not done a very good job. She'd been drinking too much, not sleeping well, her job was suffering, and her marriage was falling apart. When she'd informed Zack that she'd made an appointment to see a therapist he was delighted.

"That's great, sweetheart," he'd said to her. "Maybe I could come along, too."

"Let me go by myself. At least this first time."

As she waited in the car, she felt nervous. What would the therapist ask her? Would she finally have to share with someone that the guilt she felt over her son's death had a great deal to do with where she was that night? Would she finally have to confess to her own terrible sin? Out of habit she opened the glove compartment but realized she'd already thrown the bottle out. She rifled through her pocketbook, looking for mints, gum, something to put in her mouth. That's when she saw it: the small business card. *Georges Dump Run's, No Job Too Big or Too Small.* She thought perhaps she'd thrown it out; now wished she had. She saw that his address was a town some half hour away to the northeast. Looking at the card, she recalled that odd meeting a few weeks before. It seemed almost something imagined, something she'd only dreamed of. Yet in the past week she'd stopped at several more roadside crosses—*descansos*—drawn to them as if by some magnetic force. At each one she got out, knelt down to read the inscriptions, touched the objects people had left. At each one she pondered the dead person's circumstances, tried to imagine how they had died, what their final thoughts were, and why the person or persons who'd put up the cross had arrived at that decision. After each visit she felt a distinct light-headedness on rising, and as she glanced at herself in the mirror she couldn't say she recognized the woman she'd become. Who was this person? It was all just nonsense, she told herself. When someone died, that was it. End of story. There were no second chances. No lingering spirits. No saying what had been left unsaid in life. But each time she left a memorial, she felt burdened somehow, with an indefinite but no less real feeling of anguish, of personal loss, as if the people who had died at those places were not strangers, but intimates, loved ones, and their deaths touched her in some palpable way. She wondered how she would tell the therapist about all this, if the woman would think that she was crazy.

She waited until it was a minute before five. Then, suddenly, she turned on the ignition, put the car in drive, and slipped out of the lot, with the distinct feeling that she was a criminal fleeing the scene of a crime. On her GPS she keyed in George Doucette's address.

* * *

The last rays of sunlight were fading in the west as she pulled up in front of a house on a hardscrabble rural road way out in the boonies. She spotted the familiar truck in the driveway. The small brown Cape was peeling badly, and the yard a complete disaster. A massive oak dominated the front, spilling leaves and limbs below. A tire lay beneath the tree, a frayed rope still attached from where it had once been a swing. The gutters, half rotted, were chock full of leaves spilling over the edges. Along the side of the yard were garbage bags and piles of junk, presumably waiting to be hauled away by George.

Before she could talk herself out of doing whatever it was she'd come here to do, she got out of the car and marched up to the porch. She stood before a screen door that didn't quite shut flush, the screen partially kicked out. From inside she could hear a TV blaring. She paused for a moment, then knocked on the screen, which rattled loosely. Immediately, a dog commenced barking. A big one by the sounds of it. *This was crazy*, she thought. However, before she could retreat, the storm door creaked open and there behind the screen stood George.

He was wearing a ratty t-shirt and his gray, uncombed hair looked as if she'd just awakened him. He had on a pair of glasses, black-rimmed, thick, which made his eyes appear wide and distorted. He stared at her blankly for a moment, his bushy white brows furrowed in confusion. Slowly, though, a smile carved his broad face into something resembling recognition. He snapped his fingers and pointed at her. "Elizabeth, right?"

"You've got a good memory. Am I interrupting anything?"

"Are you kiddin'? Come on in," he said, almost as if he'd been expecting her.

The dog, a large black Lab, was on her in a moment—barging into her legs, jumping up on her, trying to lick her hands.

"Get down, you," Doucette warned the dog. "You hear me?" The man tried to swat the dog on the muzzle, but the dog was obviously used to this game and like a skilled fighter dodged each blow. "This is Tucker. He's friendly to a fault. I could put him in the other room if you want."

"That's all right. I like dogs."

"Let's go in here."

She followed him into a small living room where the TV was on, turned up way too loud. A local female news anchor was on. Like the yard, the inside was equally messy, littered with newspapers and magazines, dirty dishes on the coffee table, laundry scattered about as if a miniature tornado had hit his hamper. And everywhere there was black dog hair collecting in hairballs. On the couch, there were more newspapers, a reusable ice pack, a laundry basket with more clothes Elizabeth wasn't sure were in need of folding or washing.

"Pardon the pigsty," George Doucette said, clearing a space on the couch by simply shoving it onto the floor. "Please, sit. Can I get you something to drink?"

"I don't want to put you to any trouble."

"No trouble. You want water? Some orange juice. Coffee? If you want something stronger, I think I still got some Jack Daniels squirreled away somewhere. From my wilder days," he said with a roll of his eyes.

"I'd better not. I'm trying to be good."

"Aren't we all?" the man said with a laugh. "How about some coffee then?"

"That sounds good."

"I'll be right back. Tucker, you want a treat?" he said to the dog, tempting the animal away from the visitor.

She could hear him back there turning on the water, getting cups, silverware. While he was gone, she had a chance to glance around. The room was dark and it took her a moment for her eyes to adjust. She felt a little odd being in some stranger's house, somebody she'd met once on the side of the road, and then under circumstances that were, to say the least, peculiar. She could only imagine what Zack would say if he knew: *Have you completely lost your mind, Elizabeth?* Who knows? Maybe she had. Instead of a therapy meeting she'd come here. That said plenty about her mental state. Dark wood paneling covered the room's walls, and what little light permeated the gauzy curtains seemed absorbed by it. Against one wall was a bookshelf, with knick-knacks and pictures of kids at various ages. There were a couple of pictures of a younger George standing with a team of boys in wrestling uniforms. Elizabeth's gaze was attracted to one picture of a young woman with a big bouffant hairdo and cat eye glasses. A black-and-white fifties high school graduation portrait. Another showed the same woman and a young slender man dressed up, the woman in what appeared to be a wedding gown. His wife, Elizabeth thought. What was her name? Hannah.

From the kitchen the man called out, "How do you take your coffee?"

"Black is fine," she replied.

"Do you really take it black or you just being polite?"

"No really, black is fine."

She got up and went over to the shelf. She picked up the photo of the newlyweds and looked closely at it. The bride and groom were standing in what looked like a park, with trees and a pond in the background. The groom, Elizabeth could tell, was a much younger, thinner version of George. He was beaming at the camera, as if he couldn't believe his good fortune. The bride wasn't wearing glasses in this one and her light brown hair was piled on top of her head like a shaggy crown. The wedding dress bared her broad shoulders and her neck was long and sinuous, her skin pale in contrast to the dark, full mouth. She was lovely, Elizabeth thought. The young couple looked happy, bursting with excitement to be on the verge of starting a life together.

"That's Hannah and me," explained Doucette, as he entered the room carrying two steaming mugs of coffee. "Hell, we were just kids there."

"She was pretty," Elizabeth said.

"She was a *knockout*," Doucette corrected. "All the boys of Rumford, Maine, were after her. She could've had her pick. I still don't know why she chose me. Probably musta been my charm," he added with a wink. "What's your husband's name?"

"Zack."

"Do you have children?" He caught himself and quickly added, "I mean, *other* children."

She shook her head. "No. Luke was an only child. We thought about having more but . . ." She left the thought unfinished, almost the way she and Zack had left the decision of having other children unfinished, too. There had been their careers to think about, then the fact that she'd had problems even getting pregnant to begin with. A couple of miscarriages before Luke. Another one after. At some point, almost unstated, they decided to cut their losses, count their blessings, and settle for being a one-child couple. She'd always pictured having two kids. She told herself that they would just have to love Luke twice as much.

Doucette took a seat across from her in a lounge chair where the foot rest was already raised up. Tucker came up to her again and began to lick her hands. He was so black his coat had a bluish tinge to it, except around the muzzle where it was starting to turn gray.

"Hey, I warned you," the man yelled at the dog. "Don't let him spill your coffee."

"He's fine, really."

George Doucette picked up the remote and turned the TV off. Elizabeth noticed that on the end table was a tattered copy of what appeared to be the Bible. It was black leather with gilt-edged pages.

"By the way, how'd you find me?" he asked.

"You gave me your business card."

Elizabeth scratched the dog behind its ear. The animal stared up at her with eyes the color of dark chocolate, savoring her touch. When she stopped scratching him for a moment, the dog put its muzzle under her hand and forcibly lifted it up, wanting her to continue.

"I assume you didn't come here to ask me to do some clean-up work for you," he said, grinning.

"Actually, I was curious about something you said to me the other day, Mr. Doucette."

"Please. George," he corrected. "What was it?"

"About your wife, George. You said you can feel her there, where she died."

"Ah huh."

"I'm not very religious. I mean, I'm not somebody who normally believes in that sort of stuff."

"What sort of stuff would that be?"

"You know. Spirits. Talking to the dead."

"Haven't you ever talked to your son since his death?"

"Yes. But only in my head. I can't really *talk* to him." Yet she couldn't help but think of that time. Those two crosses off the highway, when she'd have sworn she heard Luke say, *Mom.*

"Why not?" replied George.

Elizabeth smiled awkwardly. "Because . . . well, he's dead."

"If you already knew the answer to that, why'd you come here then?"

"To tell you the truth, I don't really know."

He stared across at her, his gaze unrelenting. "I think you do. I think you know exactly why you came, Elizabeth."

He continued staring until she had to look away. Why *did* she come, she wondered. Why wasn't she spilling her guts to some therapist, someone trained to work with issues like hers. And not talking to some guy who hauled people's garbage away.

"Was it always like that for you?" she asked. "I mean, the first time you went there you could feel your wife's . . ." She hesitated then said, "Presence?"

The man ran a hand over his jaw. She could hear his beard bristling against his fingers from across the room.

"No. For a long time I had too much noise in my head."

"Noise?"

"Self-pity. Guilt. Mostly anger. All that stuff gets in your head and you can't hear a thing."

"Who were you angry at?" Elizabeth asked.

"Who wasn't I angry at? The whole damn world. Especially the son of a bitch who killed her. I used to contemplate how I was going to track him down and make him pay. Hell, I used to picture strangling him with my bare hands." He glanced down at the big, gnarled hands in his lap, blunt weapons ready for retribution. "Angry at Hannah, too, for leaving me. At the man upstairs," he explained, pointing upwards with his thumb. For a brief moment Elizabeth took him literally, that there was someone upstairs he was mad at. "You know, for letting it happen."

"I don't even know if I believe in Him and I was mad at Him, too," Elizabeth offered with a hollow laugh.

"If you're angry at Him, that means you believe in Him," George Doucette said. "Mostly, I guess I was angry at myself."

"Why? You didn't do anything."

"Of course, I did. Remember I told you about regrets. When somebody dies there's always something we can blame ourselves for."

"What was it in your case? If you don't mind my asking."

"For one thing, not loving her enough."

"I don't really know you, George, but just the way you speak about her it seems as if you really loved her."

"Not as much as I should have. As much as she *deserved* to be loved." Doucette took a breath and held it, so that his cheeks were puffed out like those of a trumpet player about to hit a high note. He glanced over at the pictures on the shelf, breathing heavily through his open mouth. "I did something once I felt ashamed of. Even to this day.

"You see, my wife had a kid before we were married. Out of wedlock, as they used to say. Someone else's. She was just a kid herself so marriage wasn't an option, and abortion wasn't either, her parents being Catholic as the pope. So they convinced her to have the child and give it up for adoption. The hospital never even let her hold her baby. They just whisked the child away and she never saw it. She always regretted it. It was something that would make her cry now and then out of the blue. Then we got married and had children of our own. That's when we got the news that the baby my wife had hadn't been placed, that the adoption fell through or something and that the child—a daughter, we'd heard—was in an institution. One of those places they used to call an institution for the mentally retarded."

George paused to take a sip of his coffee.

"Evidently, her little girl had Down's. And Hannah wanted to get her back."

He stopped then, nodded to himself.

"What happened?" Elizabeth asked.

"I didn't want it. I even thought of the child as an 'it.' Not a baby. I thought it would've been too much. Taking on a handicapped child like that. And if truth be told, I didn't like the idea of adopting some other man's child. Another man's mistake, is how I thought of it then."

"So that's what you regret?" Elizabeth asked.

"It's *one* of the things. One of the many. Another is that I never got to say goodbye to her before she died. You think your loved ones are always going to be there, that you'll always have another chance to say what you wanted to say, another chance to do what you've been putting off. You never think they'll leave one the morning and that's it—*pfff*," he said, snapping his fingers to suggest the ephemeral nature of life. "You must know about that though."

Elizabeth nodded. "Boy, do I ever."

"Want to know what the very last thing I said to Hannah was? I was running late for school and I called out to her, 'Honey, I think the milk is sour. Can you get some on the way home from work?' Imagine that. Of all the things I could have told her, that's what I said. The last thing she heard from my mouth was about sour milk. But here's the best part." He smiled wistfully and shook his head. "They found a half gallon of milk splattered in her car after the crash. Evidently on the way home from work Hannah stopped to get some."

Elizabeth tried, as she had countless times before, to recall what the last words were that she'd spoken to Luke. Probably something as prosaic as *Don't forget your seat belt* or *Pay attention to the speed limit*. It'd be just like her to say something like that.

"Hannah was always thinking about me, the kids. I guess you could say I took her for granted."

A remarkable thing happened then. At the sound of the woman's name, the dog's ears seemed to perk up and he left Elizabeth and ambled over and stood in front of his master, expectant, his tail wagging, his gaze shifting rapidly about as if looking for something.

"You still remember her, don't you, boy?" he said to the dog. "Where's Hannah?" The poor creature whimpered excitedly, then trotted to the front door and glanced out. "Been six years, and he still thinks she's coming home. For the longest time afterwards, Tucker'd catch her scent, from her clothes or something, and he'd go crazy, barking and carrying on. Even now, after all these years, he hears her name and he runs to the front door."

George shook his head and stared vacantly toward the front of the house. He then glanced over at her.

"So what about you?" he asked.

"What do you mean?"

"What do you regret, Elizabeth?"

"Me?" she said, in a way stalling for time, so as to decide what if anything she wanted to tell him. "I guess I regret I wasn't always the best mother."

"You seem like a pretty concerned mother to me."

"I could be selfish. I had my career. And according to my son, I could be pretty demanding. He thought nothing he did was good enough in my eyes. Maybe he was right. I don't know. In the last couple of years, he and I fought a lot." Elizabeth hesitated for a moment, wondering if she really wanted to get into this. "And like you, I regret I didn't get to say goodbye to him. Though he did call the night he died."

"What did you two talk about?"

"That's just it. We didn't. I was too busy to take his call. So he left a message on my phone. Said he needed to talk to me about something."

"What was it?" George asked.

"I never found out. Whatever it was it seemed important though."

George nodded. "And you blame yourself for not taking his call?"

"I suppose so." Elizabeth took a sip of her coffee, which was now cool and bitter tasting. "There's something else. Something I've not told anyone."

The man looked at her, waiting.

"I wasn't alone that night. The night he called. I was with somebody. Somebody not my husband."

It struck her as odd that the first person she told this to was a complete stranger. Perhaps ten full seconds slid by before anyone spoke again. She could feel the pulse in her neck. Finally Doucette said, "Like I told you, there's not one of us who doesn't have regrets in these situations. Thing is, Elizabeth, you have to learn to forgive."

"Forgive?"

"Ah huh. I had to learn to forgive the guy who killed her. To forgive God. Mostly I had to learn to forgive myself."

"I guess I find it hardest to forgive myself."

"Like they say, charity begins at home," Doucette offered. "It's not easy forgiving yourself."

Elizabeth almost wished she'd taken him up on his offer of booze. She could almost taste the hot sweetness sliding down her throat, embracing her, loosening the knot in her neck.

Darkness had fallen outside, and the metallic sound of crickets sawed through the night.

"I guess what's bothered me most are all the questions," she explained.

"Questions?"

"All the things that just didn't add up. Like what he wanted to talk to me about. Or why he was in New Mexico when he was supposed to be driving out to San Francisco to meet some friends. Or why he wasn't wearing a seat belt. Or . . ." But she fell silent.

"The thing about death, Elizabeth, is that it doesn't make much sense. At least not to the living."

"Is that saying God works in mysterious ways or some such crap?" she said bitterly.

"No, not at all. I only mean that we're so wrapped up in our daily lives that we can't see the forest for the trees. Of course, death doesn't make much sense to us if we think it's the end."

Elizabeth didn't know what to say to that. Death *was* the end.

"Have you thought about going out there?" George asked.

"Out where?"

"Where he died."

"New Mexico?" she said incredulously, her voice rising.

"That's what I'd do."

"And just say for a moment, I did go. What would I do out there?"

"I guess that would be up to you. But seeing where your boy passed on just might lift some of that burden you're carrying around. It might just be your *descanso*."

The dog returned then, slowly padding into the room, his nails clicking on the wooden floor. It sat down next to his master, his brown eyes frustrated.

"It's okay, boy," Doucette said to the animal, stroking its broad head. "I miss her, too."

After a while, Elizabeth stood. "Well, I should be going. Thanks for the coffee. And the advice."

"You're welcome. Come any time. I like the company."

He got up and walked her to the door, where they shook hands.

"Goodbye, George," she said.

"Goodbye, Elizabeth." As she was heading out to her car, he called after her. "And good luck."

* * *

All the way home Elizabeth's mind kept returning to her conversation with Doucette. The regrets he'd had. The child he hadn't wanted to accept. The noise that had dominated his head. Hadn't her own head been filled with noise for the past year? She thought, too, how he'd said, *Have you thought about going out there?* As she drove along, she felt something stirring in her, some nascent feeling gathering momentum, forming and taking shape, a feeling that was disquieting, even a little terrifying. Whatever it was, she sensed she wouldn't be able to stop it, that she wouldn't *want* to stop it even if she could. That whatever it was, she was going to surrender herself to it wholly and completely.

When she arrived home, Zack was in the den, watching something on the History Channel that involved knights in armor.

"Hi," she said, poking her head in the doorway.

"Oh, hi. Did you eat yet?" he asked. "I kept something in the oven for you."

"Thanks. But I had a late lunch. I'm not that hungry."

"How was your session?"

"Oh," she replied, feeling herself caught in a lie, even though she hadn't lied yet. Recovering quickly, however, she said, "Good. It was good."

For a while she didn't move from the doorway. *Maybe,* she thought. Maybe this could be the moment. The one where she told Zack the truth for once. Maybe she could share with him the conversation she'd had with George Doucette, try to make him understand what it all meant to her, how important it was, what she'd been feeling about Luke, about her stopping at various *descansos,* about the fact that their son had wanted to talk to her the night he died. Maybe she could even confess that she'd been with another man. Why not? She could throw herself on her knees, beg his forgiveness. Tell him she loved him and was sorry. Sorry about everything. But she was afraid. Afraid Zack wouldn't understand. Afraid that when she told him about the affair he would leave her. And then what would she do?

"I'm proud of you," he said.

"For what?"

"For going to see someone."

Instead of saying anything, she walked over and kissed Zack on the cheek. He looked up at her, surprised.

"Goodnight," she said. She paused for a moment, then added, "I love you." She hadn't said that in a while.

"I love you, too."

Upstairs, she went into the bathroom and brushed her teeth, scrubbed her face hard. After she dried her face, she glanced at herself in the mirror. *This is crazy,* she told herself. Then she headed into the bedroom and got under the covers. She curled up on her side and lay very still for a long while. She felt her heart beating faster, felt that odd sensation again, growing in her belly, felt it swelling upwards into her chest and arms, into her head, taking over her spine, and moving down into her legs, all the way to her feet, spreading like a fever. It seemed as if she was on the threshold of something, as if a door was about to open for her but a door she wasn't sure she wanted to step through. After lying there for a long time, she finally lost hold of consciousness and felt herself falling, plunging into sleep, like down a long, dark tunnel.

She had the dream again, the one where Luke had returned home for a short time but was now preparing to leave once more. He sat on a chair in the corner of the room, staring across at her, his packed bags on the floor between his feet.

> *Please, just a little while longer, Luke.*
> *I can't, Mom. I have to go.*
> *I miss you. Will you come back?*
> *He shrugged.*
> *Call me. Please.*
> *Goodbye, he said.*

She woke in the middle of the night and lay very still in the dark. Next to her she heard the soft, raspy sounds of Zack's breathing. She knew what she was going to do. What she *had* to do. It was as if her sleeping mind had been working on it, figuring it out, making plans.

Carefully getting out of bed so as not to wake Zack, Elizabeth quietly grabbed some clothes from her closet, her running shoes, a pair of jeans, a t-shirt, and slipped out of the room. She dressed in the bathroom without the light on. She thought of leaving a note for Zack, but worried if she delayed even for a moment the plan would disintegrate, crumble like a sand castle before a wave. She would lose this precious momentum she felt swelling in her chest. No, she'd call when she got far enough away. Downstairs, from her study she got the map she'd made of Luke's journey and the notebook she'd been keeping of his phone calls and credit card receipts. She was about to head out the front door when she thought of it. She turned and tip-toed back up the stairs and headed down the hall to Luke's room. She closed the door and turned on the light. Glancing around the room, she tried to decide, to se-lect something she would take. One of the posters on the wall? His guitar? A favorite article of clothing? The picture of him and TJ? *What*, she wondered. Finally, almost inevitably, she moved over to his model airplane collection. They were aligned on the shelf just as he had left them, in a formation as if for some unspecified battle. She picked up the miniature Spitfire that she had bought for Luke that time in Wales, and then the P-51 Mustang that he had purchased at that place in Texas, and slipped the toys into her jean's pocket, turned off the light, and headed downstairs.

The night was chilly but clear as she got into her car and pulled out of the driveway. The stars hung in the sky like scattered grains of salt on a dark table cloth. The lake glimmered coldly. The world was quiet, expectant, as if waiting for a voice to fill it. Without being fully aware of it, a single thought flickered through her head: *I'm coming, sweetheart. I'm coming.*

Chapter 8

The lights of the oncoming vehicles along the highway nearly blinded her. Ill-tempered semis patrolled the night highway like vicious Dobermans, growling and snarling, blasting their horns, zooming right up on her rear end as if she were an unwanted interloper in their private domain. She stopped once at a convenience store just past New Haven, filled up the Saab with gas and bought one of those energy drinks to stay awake. Before she pulled back on the highway, she got out her notebook and looked at the map she'd made of Luke's journey. She didn't quite have a plan. Rather, she'd simply follow in her son's footsteps, as much as she knew of them, and hope for something. Perhaps to meet someone Luke had spoken to during his trip. Someone who might offer her some glimmer of what he was feeling in those last days. It was a long shot, she knew. But what else did she have? After leaving home her son had first used his credit card in a small eastern Pennsylvania town, at a restaurant called The Sandlot, so she set her GPS for there.

For now she wanted to keep things simple—her mantra was, *don't think, just drive.* She hoped to put as much distance between herself and Garth's Point as she could by first light: sort of like an escaped convict trying to get as far away as possible before anyone noticed she was gone. She felt two contradictory emotions. On the one hand, being in motion was oddly liberating; she felt unencumbered, light, filled with some indefinable potential. For the first time in months she sensed herself directed by some inner purpose, liminal and unshaped though it might have been. Still, it was as if she were consciously and willfully moving *toward* something rather than *avoiding* things, as she had been during the past year. At the same time, she felt anxious, filled with a vague apprehension, as if she was headed for some unknown disaster. Partly it had to do with this sweeping sensation of isolation that had come over her since leaving her house, abandoning her normal life. Here she was on the road, in the middle of the night, heading off to God knows where, and no one, not a single soul in the world, knew where she was. Something could happen to her, one of those horrid semis could run her off the highway and down into some ravine, and she'd be like one of those people you read about dead in a car for days before someone found her decomposing body. She thought of Luke, after his car went off the road, alone in the desert night. All by himself. Not a soul had known he was there. The accident report had said he'd lain there for several hours, alive, bleeding, in shock, before help arrived. She hated to think of her son so vulnerable, so alone like that in the universe. She wished now she had the bottle in the glove compartment, something to bolster her courage.

Stop it, she told herself.

She tried to give herself over to the simple rhythm of the road slipping beneath her, the purely mechanical reactions of her body as she steered the car, sped up or slowed down. For background noise, she had the radio tuned to the Albany public station playing classical music to insomniacs. Yet despite her attempts to avoid thinking, to keep her mind at bay, she couldn't *not* think. Thoughts flew at her like bats at twilight, swooping around her head. She pictured Zack sound asleep, that innocent but equally determined way he had of surrendering so completely to sleep, on his back, his mouth slightly agape, his hands locked over his chest like someone resting in a coffin. If it was true that a sound sleep was the sign of someone with a clean conscience, then Zack was innocent as a child. She had a powerful desire to curl up beside him and hold him while he slept, to protect and comfort him. When he woke to find her gone, it would confuse him. The engineer in him would want to *do* something. Fix it. He'd call her, and when she told him what she was planning, he'd try to talk some "sense" into her, which would mean getting her to turn around and come back home. When he couldn't do that, would he get in his car and come after her? Would he call the police? She had no idea what he was capable of in this situation. No more, in fact, than she had of herself. She'd entered some alien and unpredictable region, where it was impossible to base anything on what had gone before. From now on, she'd be making up the rules as she went along, reinventing her life. Reinventing herself.

Then again, how would Zack know she'd taken off, that she hadn't just gone in to work early? She pictured how her "disappearance" would unfold. When she didn't show up for work (she had a closing that morning), someone from the office would call her cell, several times probably, more and more anxious with each passing hour she failed to show up. Prior to the past year she had always been so reliable, so conscientious. In fact, she hadn't taken a sick day in years. But recently she'd grown slack in her duties, arriving to the office late, calling in sick, missing court appearances and meetings and dead-lines. When she didn't answer her phone, Joan would probably call Zack. She could picture her friend saying something like, *She can't keep doing this, Zack.* But then he'd tell her that she wasn't home "sick" and their annoyance with her would quickly turn to worry, that something had happened to her. Some-thing serious. That she'd been arrested for drunk driving, or that she'd been in an accident. Perhaps she ought to text him, she thought. Leave a note telling him she was fine. But what did "fine" mean? He'd want to know where she was and she couldn't very well type with one hand the necessarily complex plan she was enacting, while driving a busy interstate at night with the other. And she didn't want to stop and lose her momentum. Besides, what could she say in such crude shorthand, how would she describe what she couldn't even describe to herself? *Going out to see where our son died.* Or, *Trying to find out what he wanted to tell me.* That would make no sense at all to Zack, and in fact would probably only serve to heighten his alarm. She could stop and call him later, before he left for work. Yet she was reluctant to engage him in direct conversation, fearing that he would try to talk her out of this. Her commitment to this course of action, she sensed, was fragile, in its embryonic form and therefore easily shattered. No, she wanted to get far enough away before the various "authorities"—Zack, Joan, the police, the rational part of her own brain—were alerted.

She thought of the house closing she was supposed to be at the next morning, now, in fact, just a few hours away. Of all her duties as a lawyer in the firm, this simple, mundane aspect perhaps gave her the most satisfac-tion. She liked helping people get their house, their home, especially young, first-time buyers. After leading them through all the perplexing hurdles and the arcane legalese, she savored watching as the happy couple left her office feeling they were about to head off into their "New Life," one which she had played a small role in fashioning. She considered calling Joan and leaving a message that she wouldn't be in, make up some excuse—say that she was feel-ing sick to her stomach, or that she needed to take some time off. But if Joan answered the phone, Elizabeth knew she'd wiggle the truth out of her one way or another. And if Warren got wind of it, who knows what he'd do? *She what?* he'd cry. Elizabeth feared, too, that if she tried to explain what she was doing out loud to someone else, attempted to give it a shape and meaning, it might appear for what she sensed it was—preposterous. Insane. The work of a mind that had completely unraveled. Perhaps only in the forgiving darkness of the night, with the motion of the car lulling her into a state of resigned acquiescence, did any of this make sense.

So she didn't call—not Zack, not anyone. Not yet. She just drove on, speeding westward into the night.

As she crested a hill, a sign along the highway caught her attention. Brightly lit, it showed a father tucking his small daughter into bed. The caption below the two said, "If something were to happen to you, who would take care of her?" Some insurance company shamelessly playing upon a parent's desire to protect his child. The sign, however, evoked a vivid memory in Elizabeth. In it, Luke was four or five, and she'd just finished reading him his favorite story, *Hamilton*, about an obese, voracious pig who foils a wolf from taking over the barnyard. The book was dog-eared, and she must have read it to him a hundred times. Her son couldn't hear it enough. She could still remember a line from it: *"For a pig is just downright supposed to be big."* This one night she had just tucked Luke in and was about to turn off the light when he told her he was afraid. She assumed it was the usual, run-of-the-mill fear of "monsters" or after reading about Hamilton, the occasional "wolf." Elizabeth would make an exaggerated, comical show of looking under his bed, in the closet, checking to see that the window was locked. "See," she'd say. "Nothing."

But this time, he surprised her. "No, not monsters."

"Then what, sweetie?"

"Will I die?"

"Don't be silly," she scoffed, trying to make light of it. Then seeing how his light-blue eyes had darkened with an apprehension she hadn't seen before, she added, "You're not going to die, sweetie."

"What about grandma?"

Shortly before this, Elizabeth's mother had passed away from a stroke. Elizabeth, who had always had a troubled relationship with her mother, felt mostly guilt that she didn't feel more at the woman's passing. Luke, too, hadn't seemed particularly affected by his grandmother's death. And yet, obviously it had taken more of a toll than she'd imagined.

"Grammy was old," she comforted, cradling his head against her shoulder.

He seemed to chew on that thought for a moment. Then he said, "But everybody has to die someday, right?"

"Someday. But not for a long, long time."

Her son seemed to chew on that answer for a moment. "But I'll die someday. And you and dad, too. Everybody."

She'd had no answer for that. Elizabeth would come to realize that her son, slow when it came to things like learning to throw a baseball or dating a girl, was precocious regarding more adult subjects like mortality, the suffering of others, simple kindness. For example, once they were walking the streets of New York when seven-year-old Luke ran over to a homeless person and put a dollar of his allowance money into the man's can. Or another time when the mother of a fourth-grade classmate of his had died, Luke had asked Elizabeth to make a second lunch so that he could bring it in to school and give it to the boy. "He won't have anybody to make his lunch now, Mom."

Zack used to say that Luke had an old soul.

* * *

She drove into Pennsylvania, sunlight just beginning to spill over the humpbacked mounds of coal culm bordering the highway. An hour south of Scranton, she spotted the first one—the first *descanso* of her trip. She was heading down a steep incline hacked into the side of a mountain when she saw the cross, small and starkly white against the black background. It stood not far from the entrance of one of those runaway truck ramps. She slowed and pulled over to the side of the highway. She got out and stretched, her legs and back stiff from having driven hunched over for nearly four hours. The morning was chilly, and with just the t-shirt she'd worn to bed she shivered in the brisk autumn air of the Pennsylvania mountains.

She walked over to the memorial, squatted, and read the faded lettering written on the horizontal section of the cross: *Ray Zimmerman, 1949–1991.* Forty-two, Elizabeth calculated. She wondered if he'd been driving a truck when his brakes gave out on him and he tried to slow down on the runaway ramp. Below his name and attached to the cross was a small metal plaque covered with patina, which made the inscription on it hard to read. She had to lick her index finger and wipe it across the engraved lettering to be able to read it. *My Dearest, I miss you so much. Until we meet again. Love, Ginny.* She found intriguing the image of Ray Zimmerman's wife coming out here by herself and digging a hole and putting up the cross. Arrayed on the ground about the cross was what she had come to know as the usual collection of junk, though in this case it had a particular theme: fishing rod and reel, waders, a fishing hat with all those little lures attached to it. Nearby rested a small St. Christopher's medal. They were supposed to keep travelers safe. Evidently it hadn't worked very well in this case. Everything looked weathered from the elements and undisturbed for ages, as if no one had come here for a very long time. As she squatted there, her bare arms rippled with goosebumps, she thought of the things George Doucette had told her. How the spirit of the dead person hovered near where he died. How sometimes one could feel a connection to that spirit. How each resting place had its own story to tell. She somehow didn't feel sadness or anger or regret here. Instead, Elizabeth pictured a man on a quiet, early morning stream, mist hovering above the water, casting toward a deep pool, waiting for an unseen trout to strike. Would that be his version of heaven? The place where he came to rest?

Raymond, she thought to herself. *Raymond, can you hear me?*

Behind her, semis roared by, their exhaust pipes clattering away as they geared down for the steep grade. After a while she became adjusted to the noise and mostly what she heard was her own pulse sounding in her temples, beating in her neck. It was in that moment that she became aware of it. At first barely audible, then from somewhere up in the woods, she heard a faint, fluttery cry, haunting and melodious. *Oo-wah-hooo, hoo-hoo.* She recognized it as a mourning dove. She used to hear them down at the lake early in the morning. She loved lying in bed listening to the bird's cry. The sound so beautiful, so poignant. So other-worldly.

Oo-wah-hooo, hoo-hoo.

* * *

Around mid-morning, a half hour past Harrisburg, she arrived at the place called The Sandlot. It turned out to be a small diner in a Quonset hut that sat adjacent to a large stone and gravel operation. Several dump trucks zoomed past the diner, trailing a cloud of reddish dust in their wake. As she entered the restaurant, half a dozen burly, baseball-capped men seated on stools at the counter stopped in mid-sentence, turned, and stared at her. She felt as if she'd entered someone's private kitchen. A young, thin, hard-looking girl who wore a lot of metal in her face and black lipstick seated her in a booth over near a window. Her hair was hacked off on one side, while the other had gaudy streaks of pink and green in it. The girl wore a white polyester uniform that had her name tag pinned to her breast pocket: *Nadine.*

"You want coffee?" she asked almost impatiently, as if Elizabeth were interrupting her from something much more important. Her voice was scratchy and frail, like someone with laryngitis.

"Please."

Finding herself suddenly famished, Elizabeth ordered the breakfast special—two eggs over easy, bacon, homefries, toast, and a glass of milk. Outside the window, a steady procession of dump trucks rumbled past, shaking the table, swirling up a cloud of dust. Even in the diner, Elizabeth could taste it, a sweet, burnt odor like incense. As she sat there, she decided it was time to make some calls, now that she was far enough away from the gravitational pull of her obligations. She called Zack first. In some ways she was relieved that he didn't answer. She'd eventually have to talk to him, but the delay was appreciated. "It's me," she said. "Don't worry, I'm all right. I . . ." She paused then, not quite knowing what to say. "I'll call you later. Okay."

Next she called the office. She got Amy Roorsbach, the paralegal.

"They're all here for the closing, Elizabeth," Amy said anxiously to her. "What should I tell them?"

"Let me talk to Joan."

In a moment Joan came on.

"Elizabeth," her friend cried, "where the hell are you?"

"I'm not feeling well. The file's on my desk. Everything should be in order. Could you handle it for me?"

"No, I can't. I have to be in court." Then in a whisper, Joan said, "Are you drinking again?"

"No, I . . . I told you, I'm not feeling well."

"Well, why didn't you call earlier?"

"I'm sorry. Really," she said.

"Warren's going to hit the roof on this. I don't—" But before Joan could continue hectoring her, Elizabeth hung up. The phone rang again but she didn't answer it. In fact, she silenced it, though she did hear it buzzing on the table, like some sort of angry wasp.

When her food came, she put the phone into her pocketbook. She decided not to think about her job, the trouble she was making for herself. Instead, she dug in, eating ravenously, for the first time in memory. The eggs done just the way she liked them, the bacon nice and crispy. She happened to spot the young waitress seated diagonally across from her in a booth. She was facing Elizabeth, head down, appearing to count her tip money; it was spread out over the table, and, like a child after having broken her piggy bank, she was putting like coins together in small piles. As Elizabeth watched the young waitress, she happened to notice something she hadn't before. The subtle swelling just above her lap. *Pregnant.* Just a few months but definitely pregnant. Elizabeth didn't see a wedding ring though. This girl wasn't much older than Fabiana.

The waitress noticed her staring. Getting up, she went over behind the counter, got the coffee pot, and returned.

"You need a refill?" she asked almost curtly.

"No, I think I'm all set." Elizabeth hesitated, then asked, "How far along are you?"

The girl screwed up her mouth, gave Elizabeth a look that was part surprise, part annoyance, as if to say, *It's none of your damn business, lady.* Elizabeth couldn't get over all the metal sticking out of the girl's nose and eyebrows, her lower lip and ears. Her face looked mutilated, tortured, as if held together by nuts and bolts. And that hair. If she were her kid, Elizabeth wouldn't let her leave the house looking like that. But up close Elizabeth could see that beneath it all she was kind of pretty, with dark, almond-shaped eyes, and a soft, full mouth that made her appear vulnerable when she pursed her lips. Though she looked nothing at all like TJ, Elizabeth was reminded of Luke's former girlfriend for some reason. Something about her mouth.

"Four months," she finally confessed. "It's a girl. I didn't want to be surprised. I had enough surprises already."

"You must be so excited."

"Thrilled," she said, lifting the metal in one eyebrow so that Elizabeth couldn't tell whether she was being sarcastic or not.

"Have you picked out names?"

This question seemed to open up something in the girl. "I'm leaning toward Amber Moon. Howard's not so hot on it though."

"Is that your husband?"

"He's the father. But I figure he doesn't get to have a say."

"Oh. Why's that?"

"He keeps saying we'll get married just as soon as his divorce is finalized. But I've heard that line before. He's still living with his wife."

"Must be hard. Being a single mom, I mean."

"I'm doing fine. It's my parents that are freakin' out. To hear them, you'd think I killed somebody or something."

"You hang in there," Elizabeth said, hoping to put a period to the conversation. Instead, the girl stood there, coffee pot in hand.

"This isn't how I planned for things to go."

"Life never goes how you plan, believe me. Just don't give up."

"Hell, no. I got plans, Howard or not. I'm saving up to go back to school."

"What do you want to be?"

"I'm going into medical billing. So I can take care of Amber Moon by myself, if I have to."

"Good for you. Mind if I ask you a question?"

"Sure, I guess so," the girl replied, sliding into the booth and sitting down.

Elizabeth took her phone out and scrolled through her pictures until she came to one of Luke. It was of him sitting at the dock reading.

"Do you recognize him?"

The girl stared at Elizabeth suspiciously, hardly glancing at the photo. "Should I?"

"He came in here. About a year ago."

"A lot of people come in here."

"Could you take a closer look?"

The girl leaned forward, staring at the photo.

"Boy, he's cute. Is he single?" she asked with a girlish smile.

"Was."

"Now why couldn't I find some guy like that. Who is he?"

"My son. Do you recognize him?"

She shook her head. "I don't think so."

"His name was Luke."

The girl looked from Elizabeth to the picture and back again. "You keep saying 'was.'"

"He died. A few days after he stopped here, he was in a car accident."

"Geez! That really sucks," the girl said, wrinkling her nose as if she caught a whiff of a bad smell. "Why do you want to know if he was in here?"

"I'm trying to find out what his last few days were like. Where he stopped. Who he might have talked to."

"Can I see his photo again?" the girl asked. Elizabeth slid her phone across the table. "If I'd talked to him, I would've remembered. He's not one of our regulars," she offered, with a sardonic flick of her head toward the men sitting at the counter. "I'm real sorry."

"Thank you, Nadine," Elizabeth said, reaching across and patting the girl's hand. "You take care of Amber Moon, okay?"

"I will."

"By the way, here's my card," Elizabeth said.

The girl took it, frowned as she looked at it.

"I'm a lawyer. I work with single moms. If you ever just need to talk, call me."

"Sure."

"No, I mean it."

The girl nodded, slipped out of the booth and walked back over to her table. She quickly swept the small piles of money into her hand and dropped the coins into a pocket on the front of her apron, just in front of where her baby lay.

When Elizabeth finished eating, she placed three twenty-dollar bills on the table. It was all the cash she had on her. Before she left, she wrote a note on a napkin: *Hold onto your dreams.*

* * *

She drove for a few more hours before growing drowsy. Seeing a rest area up ahead, she decided to pull over and catch a short nap. She locked the doors. She'd read about women getting assaulted on the side of the highway like this. She'd warned Luke about doing this very thing during his cross-country road trip, yet here she was breaking her own rules. Leaning her head back, she closed her eyes and within moments was gripped by a leaden sleep. She had a dream, something about being in a small boat that was taking on water. She tried to bail the water but all she had were her two hands. The boat sunk lower and lower, until finally she had to abandon it and start swimming. The water was cold and viscous, and her arms could barely move through it, as if it wasn't water at all but some other more dense substance.

She woke disoriented, a little anxious, the sun streaming harshly into the car. She could feel traffic *whooshing* past, shaking her. Where the hell was she, she wondered. It took her a moment to get her bearings. She reached over into the passenger's seat and picked up her notebook. The next dot on her map was just outside of Staunton, Virginia. Luke had spent the night at a small hotel there. Before pulling back onto the highway, for some unknown reason, she recalled a visit to the house by Luke's closest friend, a kid named Griff McCoy.

It had been an uncomfortably humid morning near the end of August, not a week after the funeral. Elizabeth was home alone and still in that dazed, post-trauma mode, where the depths of her pain were just being sounded. She moved about the house like an old person with arthritis, each step filled with a new and surprising ache. Everywhere she looked, there were memories that jolted, that seemed to prick her like a hypodermic needle or slam her like a hammer to the chest. When she answered the door, she was surprised to see Griff standing there on the porch. Most of Luke's old friends from town had come to the funeral, as well as several of his St. Anselm classmates and Father Jerome. Even Luke's former girlfriend TJ came. They'd all shown up at the funeral, hugged her and Zack, offered their condolences, and then left. Not a single one had stopped by to visit afterwards, neither for the gathering right after the funeral nor in the days or weeks or months that followed. Elizabeth felt as if they'd abandoned Luke.

"Hi, there, Mrs. G," Griff had said, as she opened the door.

Griff, short for Griffin, was a large, bulky kid, soft around the middle, with a perpetual, ironic-looking smile pasted on his doughy face, which made him look as if he thought everything a big joke. Luke and Griff, along with a couple of other friends, had played in a band together for a while early in high school. Luke was the best musician, the lead guitarist, though truth was he wasn't particularly good either. Of all of Luke's friends, Griff was the one Elizabeth had liked the least. The word that came to mind was *sly*, though Elizabeth had nothing really to go on besides that smile. In all the years she'd known him, she'd never really warmed to him. Luke had sensed it, too, and on at least one occasion had asked her what she had against him. "Does he always have to smile like an idiot?" Luke came to his defense by saying, "Why do you always have to be so hard on people?" But here he was, the only one of Luke's friends who had the decency to stop by and say hello.

"Please, come in, Griff," she said. They sat in the den. "Can I get you something to drink?"

"No, I'm good, Mrs. G," he replied. It even annoyed her the way he called her Mrs. G, as if they were in some dopey sit-com from the seventies.

"You must be getting ready for school."

"I leave day after tomorrow. Figured I'd stop by before then."

Elizabeth and Griff chatted for a while, awkwardly, mostly about college, an internship he was doing at a law firm in New York, his plan to study for the LSATs that fall.

"You're thinking of law?" she asked, a little surprised that he had the drive or smarts to become a lawyer.

"Maybe. It's a possibility."

Elizabeth used to press Luke about what he was going to do after he graduated with a theology major. He didn't seem to have a clue, nor did he seem particularly worried about it. She was more concerned than he was. Several times she suggested he consider going into law.

"Let me know if you need a letter of recommendation," she said to Griff. "Plus I might I have a few contacts."

"Really? That'd be great, Mrs. G."

Griff then stared across at Elizabeth and, without the slightest adornment or preface, said, "Luke was my best friend."

The comment made her throat suddenly ache, it was so simple and pure and genuine. "He always liked you, too," she offered.

"I miss him."

"Me too."

Griff glanced around the room, seemingly confused for a moment, as if trying to remember the purpose for his visit. Then he shrugged his shoulders.

"Well, I should get going."

They stood and she gave him a big hug. Perhaps, she thought, her son had been right; she'd been too hard on him. Too hard on most people. "It was so nice of you to stop by, Griff."

She walked him to the door. She knew they would probably never see each other again, or if they did, that the next time they bumped into the other, say, in town, at the Big Y or some restaurant, she'd be an old lady whose son had died years ago, and he'd be a fat father of three kids and coaching soccer.

"Take care, Mrs. G."

"You, too, Griff. Say hello to your mother for me."

As he started down the steps, she tentatively called out, "Griff?"

He stopped halfway, turned. "Yeah, Mrs. G?"

"Luke called me the night of the accident."

She tossed this information out like a fly fisherman casting a lure, hoping Griff might rise to take the bait. Instead he replied only with, "Really?"

"Yes. He left a message saying he needed to talk to me. But we never got round to it. I think something was bothering him."

Griff nodded noncommittally.

"You wouldn't know anything about that, would you?" she asked.

He shook his head. "No."

"You don't think it could've had anything to do with TJ?"

"TJ?"

"Sometimes I think he still liked her."

"He never said anything about her to me."

"And you have no idea if there was something bothering him?"

Griff sucked in a breath and looked away, out toward the lake. His gaze then returned and held Elizabeth's for the briefest of moments. But in that moment, she thought she saw something, a glimmer just below the surface.

"To be honest, Luke and me sort of drifted apart. We weren't as tight as we used to be."

"Why do you think that was?"

"He changed."

"Really. In what way?"

Of course, Elizabeth had felt it too, but hearing someone else say it made it appear more troubling. She braced herself, both fearing and welcoming whatever Griff might offer. Revelations of drugs, depression, some dark, un-savory side of her son.

Griff shrugged. "He just didn't seem to have fun doing the things he used to. It was like he was in his own little world."

"Really," Elizabeth said, waiting for more.

"I should get running along, Mrs. G."

"Goodbye, Griff."

As she watched him walk to his car, she wondered if he'd known more than he had let on. Or if it was just her suspicious mind working overtime.

Chapter 9

By late afternoon, Elizabeth had reached the hill country of northern Virginia. She felt something of an accomplishment that she'd made it this far, hadn't caved in and turned around as she had feared she might when she'd first set out. The fall afternoon stretched out before her in bold primary colors, as garish as some painting by Gauguin. The Shenandoah Valley rolled by in wave after wave of small farms and graceful hills dotted with red cattle and bay and black horses. In the distance hung the scalloped peaks of the Blue Ridge, while closer to the highway large swathes of hardwood forest were already beginning to turn bright red and orange, russet and yellow. She had always enjoyed the fall. Her early morning run around the lake. The crisp smell of leaves and wood smoke, the sharp clarity of the season. When Luke was little, the three of them would go apple picking at Bartlett's Orchards in town, then buy a dozen of their to-die-for home-made cider donuts and stuff themselves until they were almost sick.

"Can I eat two?" Luke, his eyes bigger than his belly, would always ask.

Just past Staunton, according to her notebook, her son had stopped at a motel called Blue Vistas and spent the night. As the sun was setting over the mountains to the west, her GPS told her to pull off the highway. The place turned out to be a small, one-stoplight town, with a McDonald's and a Pizza Hut and not much else. Elizabeth found herself hungry again, and she stopped at the McDonald's and bought a salad with chicken and two cartons of milk. As she was driving along the main drag, she happened to spot an ABC store. She hadn't had a drink in nearly two weeks, but she worried she might need a little help falling asleep, particularly in a strange bed. However, wanting to limit her "liability," she bought two airline-sized bottles of scotch instead of a pint. It gave her the false sense of confidence that a can of Mace would to one walking through a sketchy section of a city. It was there in case she needed it.

Blue Vistas turned out to be a sad-looking cinder-block affair painted a dull brown, peeling like the shell of a coconut. Below the vacancy sign, the motel boasted "air conditioning" and below that "free in-room movies." Elizabeth could just imagine the sorts of movies that would appeal to traveling businessmen and lonely truckers. As she got out, she thought, *This is where Luke stayed.* It sent an electric vibration between her shoulder blades. She headed up to the front office. The concierge was a striking-looking Indian woman, in her forties, wearing a flowing sari and a red bindi in the center of her dark, lovely forehead.

"How many nights you vish room for?"

"Just the one."

"Smoking or non-smoking?"

"Non-smoking."

After she paid with her charge card, Elizabeth handed the woman her phone with the picture of Luke on it.

"That's my son. He stopped here a year ago. Would you happen to remember him?"

The woman stared at the photo, then shook her head. "No."

"Are you sure?"

"I don't remember. You could ask my uncle Ajit. He is owner."

As she walked toward her room, Elizabeth told herself that the next day she ought to get some cash, as well as a few necessities. The room smelled heavily of Lysol, and beneath that hung the lingering smoke odor of previous deceitful lodgers. In fact, as she opened the drawer of the nightstand, she saw that the top was mutilated from numerous cigarette burns, scarred as a battlefield. There were two twin beds and a single chair in the corner. Elizabeth tossed her keys and pocketbook in the drawer, then grabbed the plastic ice bucket and headed out to get some ice. Back in the room, she turned on the shower, got undressed, and stepped under the steamy water. She made it as hot as she could stand it, then cranked it a little hotter, so that it was actually painful. Her skin tingled and the muscles in her neck began to loosen in the heat. She hoped the hot shower would make her drowsy and she'd be able to fall asleep.

She wrapped one towel around herself, another about her hair, grabbed a plastic cup from the bathroom, and went out and sat on the bed. From her pocketbook she took out one of the little bottles of scotch, cracked it open, and poured some over ice. She smelled it, the heady fragrance making the back of her mouth water. Yet she didn't drink it right away, instead put it on the nightstand to let the ice melt a bit. She opened the first carton of milk and downed it straightaway, then started in on the salad. Though the lettuce was limp and tasteless, the chicken was surprisingly good. She washed it down with the other carton of milk. She was still hungry when she finished. If this journey of hers did nothing else, at least it had restored her appetite. She stretched out on the bed, on top of the slightly damp, cigarette-smelling bedspread, and closed her eyes. While exhausted, her mind continued to spin with a collage of images from her long drive. She could still feel the vibration in her hands from the steering wheel, could still see the road slipping under her, the white lines of the highway flying at her like suicidal birds. She tried to quiet her mind, to slow it down. Yet she found herself thinking, *Right here. Perhaps in this very bed*. She thought how Luke could have slept where she was. As she lay there, she felt the way she did when she would go into Luke's room and lie down at night. Separated only by time.

With her eyes still closed she thought, *Luke*. Then she said the word out loud, the sound seeming to reverberate off the walls of the small room: "Luke."

Her thoughts were interrupted by a faint buzzing sound, something like a fly banging against a window screen—zzzzz . . . zzzzz. It took her a moment to realize it was her phone. She hesitated, then reached over, opened the drawer, and extracted her cell phone from her pocketbook. By then, though, the buzzing had stopped. She saw she'd had a dozen calls that day, as well as two text messages. Two of the calls were from work, the rest, as well as the texts, from Zack. *Where are you?* he said in one. She was struck by the childlike simplicity of the question, as if she'd vanished from the face of the earth and he would never see her again.

She was about to call him when the phone suddenly vibrated in her hand, startling her.

"Zack?" she said.

"Elizabeth. I tried calling you like a dozen times. Where have you been?"

"Sorry. I had my phone on silent."

"Where are you?"

She had to think for a moment. "Virginia."

"Virginia! What the hell are you doing there?"

In his voice she noted both relief at the fact that she was safe, but also annoyance for the concern she'd caused, as well as the confusion prompted by her answer.

"I'm sorry. I should have called earlier," she offered.

"Joan said you'd called in sick. You had us all worried. *Are* you sick, Elizabeth?"

"No. Not physically."

"What does *that* mean?"

"I just feel . . . I don't know. Kind of funny."

"What on earth are you doing in Virginia?"

On the opposite wall hung a painting, the only attempt to soften the room's harsh functionality. A cheap, badly done rip-off of a Remington scene. It was twilight in the mountains, with jagged, snow-capped peaks rising in the moon-lit distance. In the foreground a lone mountain man sat around a frail campfire, his horse tethered to a nearby tree. Elizabeth felt similarly isolated.

"I'm headed out to New Mexico," she said.

"New Mexico! Elizabeth, you're starting to scare me. You're not making any sense."

This is exactly what she'd feared would happen when she finally told Zack what she was doing. She had wanted to talk to him eventually, but only *after* whatever it was she was doing became clearer to herself first. "I know it must sound a little crazy. But I want to see where it happened," she said. The word *it* struck her as odd, as if Luke's death were a thing instead of an action, a pronoun whose antecedent was something unnamed and unnameable.

"Where what happened?" Zack pressed.

"Where Luke died."

Zack fell silent. "What for?"

"Weren't you ever curious to see where he passed away?"

"No," he said flatly.

"Not at all?"

"Why would I want to see where he died? What good would that do?"

"I didn't expect you to understand. That's why I didn't call you right away. But it might help clarify things for me."

"What's there to clarify?"

"Frankly, I have some questions."

"We've been over this before, Elizabeth. There's no mystery to it. He was in an accident. He died. End of story."

"I'm glad it's so cut and dry for you, Zack. For me, it's a little more complicated."

She hadn't wanted the conversation to go this way. She had wanted to be able to explain things clearly and patiently, and for Zack to understand.

"You're making it complicated."

"I need to go out there."

"I don't understand how driving two thousand miles to some spot in the middle of the desert is going to clarify anything for you."

"Never mind," she said, growing annoyed with his questions. "There's no sense trying to explain it to you."

"No, I want to know. I *deserve* to know why you're doing this."

She looked at the drink on the nightstand. She desperately wanted to down it in one sweet gulp, feel the warm confidence wafting through her.

"Do you remember that guy I told you about?" she explained.

"What guy?"

"The old guy I met along the highway. The one who was praying at the roadside memorial for his wife?"

"Oh, yeah. That guy. What does he have to do with this?"

"Well, I drove out to his place . . ." She had to stop and think when it was. Time seemed jumbled to her, as if she'd gone to see him weeks before. It felt as if she'd been on the road not for a mere eighteen hours, but for days, weeks even. "I went out there yesterday."

"Are you kidding? I thought we agreed that sort of thing was dangerous."

"*You* agreed. I didn't."

"God, Elizabeth. You went out to some stranger's house all by yourself?"

"Stop it, Zack. Or I'm going to hang up right now."

Zack was silent for a moment. "All right, go ahead. I'm listening."

"He thought it might do me some good. To see where Luke died."

"You don't go to your therapist, but you listen to some guy you met on the side of the road?"

Somehow he knew she'd missed her appointment. Perhaps the therapist had called, wondering why she hadn't shown up. She felt herself caught in a lie. A string of lies.

"He's been through this," she offered. "He knows about losing a loved one."

"Have you been drinking, Elizabeth?"

"No, for Christ's sake," she snapped at him. "In fact, I haven't had anything in almost two weeks now."

"That's good. That's a start."

His comment struck her as condescending but she decided to let it go. "He thought it might help me if I went out there. *I* think it might help, too."

"What do you expect to find out there?"

"I don't know, Zack. I just know I have to go."

"If you think you're going to find some smoking gun as to why our son died, you're only kidding yourself."

"The night Luke died . . ." she began, not sure where she was going with this, what she hoped to convince Zack of. "He called and left a message on my phone."

"A message?"

"Remember I was down in Washington?"

"At that conference."

Elizabeth wondered if she caught the slightest edge to his voice, the subtlest implication of scorn. Or was it just her guilt making her think that?

"Yes. Well, he called me and said he had something he needed to talk about."

"What was it?"

"I don't know. I was never able to reach him before the accident. But whatever it was, it seemed important."

She could hear Zack breathing on the other end, waiting. "Why didn't you tell me this before?"

"I don't know. I guess it didn't seem that significant," she lied.

"But now it does?"

"Yes."

"I'm still not connecting the dots."

"George thought—"

"Who's George?"

"The old guy I was telling you about. He thought if I went out there it might help me to understand things."

"What things?"

"I don't know. Maybe what Luke was thinking."

Zack made a snorting sound through his nose. "Come on, Elizabeth. This whole thing doesn't make any sense. You know that as well as I do."

"I don't know that."

"Please, just come home. We'll see a therapist together. We should have done that long ago."

"No, Zack. I have to do this first."

"But why?"

"I just do."

"Elizabeth, I get the feeling there's something you're not telling me," he said.

Now, she thought. *The truth for once*. She considered then, as she had so many times before, of telling him. Everything. All of it. Just getting it off her chest. About Peter. About the affair. About the night Luke died. Sometimes though she stopped short because she told herself it would be cruel to tell Zack now. What was the point? First to lose their son, then to find out she'd been with another man the night Luke died. Other times she feared it would shatter their marriage. She loved Zack—at least she thought she still did—and she didn't want to lose him. On the other hand, she sensed they couldn't continue like this, with this terrible secret between them like a metal wedge prying them apart.

Before she was able to say a word though, Zack hurled at her, like a handful of broken glass, "You're just being selfish."

"How am I being selfish?"

"This trip. How you've shut me out since Luke's death."

"I have not," she said, though she suspected he was right.

"Yes, you have. You won't talk about what you're feeling. You won't go to therapy. You'd rather drown yourself in the bottle. In your own self pity. You always thought your pain was so much worse than mine."

"No, I didn't."

"Yes, Elizabeth. You did. We *both* lost a son."

"Don't you think I know that."

"But you act as if I don't miss him. I loved him, too. Just because I want us to move on doesn't mean I don't miss him. There's not a day goes by that my heart doesn't ache because he's gone."

"I know you do, Zack," she said with sudden tenderness. She felt such sympathy for him now, for what he'd lost. "I know you loved him. I can't imagine what you've been going through. It's just that we deal with it differently."

"Then why don't you let me in? Why do you have to keep me so far away?"

"I'm sorry if I have, Zack. Really. I am. But it's the only way I know how to cope."

"Come home, Elizabeth. I love you."

"I love you, too." When she said it like this it sounded natural to her, genuine.

"Then come home. We can work it out."

She took a deep breath. It was tempting. But she felt still she had to go out to New Mexico.

"Goodnight, Zack."

"Elizabeth—" but she'd already hung up. She tossed the phone on the nightstand.

She knew Zack was right. About how she'd kept him at a distance, hadn't let him into her grief. Maybe it was because of the enormous guilt she felt. For the affair. For being with another man the night their son died. For not taking Luke's call. Perhaps for not being a better mother and wife. Sometimes she felt their son's death was all her fault. That it was some kind of retribution, punishment for her sins.

Through the window, she saw that the night had turned the deep blue-black of gun metal, though it was still lighter than the inside of the motel room, which offered the matte darkness of a cave. Elizabeth sat up on the side of the bed. Though exhausted, her head throbbed and she knew sleep would be elusive.

The light from her phone suddenly threw an eerie illumination about the room and she heard once more the insect-like buzzing reverberating on the nightstand. Zack trying to reach her again. She grabbed the phone, thought of answering but didn't know what more she could say to him. So she opened the nightstand drawer, and dropped it in. She was about to shut the drawer, when her eye happened to fall on the black, squarish shape of the Bible lying within. She remembered that line George Doucette had quoted. Something about sitting in darkness.

She picked the book up and turned the bedside light on. She began riffling through the frail, gauzy pages, pages that felt as if they would crumble in her hands like the wings of dried insects. At last she arrived at *The Gospel of Luke*, without really being aware that that was what she had been looking for. *Forasmuch as many have taken in hand to set forth in order a declaration of those things which are most surely believed among us . . .* A declaration of what? It sounds like a contract, she thought. And what was surely believed among us? The language struck her as it had the few times she'd plunged into its bewildering depths—as irritating and confusing, its antique syntax and ancient diction seemingly intent on obfuscation, not clarity; on concealment, not revelation. It reminded her of nothing so much as bad legalese, the sort that tried hard to hedge its bets, to cover all contingencies or worse, to create loopholes for lawyerly wrangling. Why couldn't they just say what they meant without all this bewildering gibberish? But she continued on, pressing forward, skimming the text the way she did at work, looking for the main points of contention. She was able to gather that the child they were referring to wasn't Jesus but rather John the Baptist (the one whose head was later served on a platter by Salome). Finally, she came to the section that read: *And thou, child, shalt be called the prophet of the Highest: for thou shalt go before the face of the Lord to prepare his ways; To give knowledge of salvation unto his people by the remission of their sins, through the tender mercy of our God; whereby the dayspring from on high hath visited us. To give light to them that sit in darkness and in the shadow of death. And the child grew, and waxed strong in spirit, and was in the deserts till the day of his shewing unto Israel.*

Elizabeth reread the line Doucette had quoted to her: *To give light to them that sit in darkness and in the shadow of death.* She reached over and shut off the bedside lamp, and she lay there in her own darkness for a long time. She thought, too, about the tender mercies of God and about a child growing up in the desert. And about the remission of sins. She wasn't sure what any of that meant or what they had to do with her, but the words remained with her, haunting and elusive. Finally, like a warm fog, sleep crept over her.

Chapter 10

Luke was sitting in the corner, smoking a cigarette. His hair was longer than the last time she'd seen it, unwashed, and he appeared tired, his eyes haggard, as if he hadn't been sleeping well.

> *Are you all right, sweetie? she asked.*
> *He took a drag of his cigarette and slowly blew the smoke out.*
> *Are you and Dad going to get a divorce?*
> *Why would you ask that?*
> *Are you?*
> *No. Of course, not.*
> *Are you still seeing that man?*
> *No.*
> *Do you love Dad?*
> *Yes.*
> *Then why did you do that?*

When she woke Luke was gone, though his aura, as always, seemed to linger. She thought she could smell cigarette smoke. While her son never smoked in his life, at least not to her knowledge, he was smoking in the dream. What did that mean? Was it connected somehow to the fact that the police report mentioned cigarette butts on the floor of his car. Had Luke taken up smoking? Or were the cigarettes someone else's? As she lay there, she heard a delicate noise, a whisper, something running along the roof of her room. A squirrel perhaps? A blown leaf? She thought about the time Luke had sprung the idea of his cross-country trip. The three of them were eating a rare dinner together that last summer. Out of the blue Luke said he wanted to visit some college friends out in San Francisco.

"Why not fly then?" Elizabeth had asked.

"I'd like to see some of the country," he replied.

"Well, who's coming with you then?"

"Just by myself."

"You're going alone?" she had asked, looking across the table at Zack for his reaction. He just sat there, silent.

"I'm not a little kid any more, Mom. I can make my own decision about this."

"I still don't think that's such a good idea, Luke," she said. "Zack?"

Yet her husband surprised her by saying, "Why not? He should see some of the country before he settles down."

"Settles down? He just turned twenty-one, for heaven's sake," Elizabeth said mockingly.

"Well, before he goes into his senior year. And he has to start worrying about grad school or jobs. Or whatever."

"*See*, Mom," Luke taunted. "Dad gets it."

Dad gets it. Which meant that she didn't get it.

"Luke and I've talked about it," Zack said.

"Really?" she replied, glaring at her husband. She felt like the odd man out, as if they had teamed up against her behind her back. "And where was I during all this planning?"

"You're never home," Luke threw at her.

"What do you mean, 'I'm never home'?" she countered. Yet her son's gaze suggested that his comment implied something sinister. Were her absences *that* obvious? The times she said she had to work late? Go into the office on a Saturday. The subterfuge of infidelity.

Luke got up and left the table. And with that, his trip was a *fait accompli*. Later in bed that night, she couldn't let it go though.

"I'd have appreciated it if you'd told me about this plan," she said to Zack.

"It wasn't really a plan. Luke mentioned something in passing about driving cross country."

"And you think it's a good idea?"

"Elizabeth, he's twenty-one. We can't really stop him even if we wanted to."

"But we didn't have to make it so easy for him."

"I drove across country when I was in college. What's the big deal?"

She wasn't sure what the big deal was. Perhaps it was that she just felt left out of the decision. Or perhaps it was that her son was growing up and away from her right under her nose. Or that her mind was so occupied by her own secret life that she hadn't been paying enough attention to her son. As she lay in bed now, she thought if only she'd put up more resistance. Maybe Luke wouldn't have gone. Maybe he'd still be alive.

* * *

Elizabeth dressed quickly in the chilly room and then went into the bathroom and brushed her teeth, using only cold water and her finger. She would have to get some things. Outside, the cold Shenandoah Valley morning stretched out with scattered clumps of fog suspended here and there, like tattered clothing hanging out on a line to dry. Shivering, she thought she recalled some article of clothing in the trunk. She opened it and saw an old gray sweatshirt that said *St. Anselm College* across the front in blue lettering. At one time it had been Luke's. She threw it on; the thing smelled of mildew and was two sizes too big for her. Then she headed up to the main office to check out. A gaunt, wizened-looking Indian man was behind the desk this morning. He had streaks of white in his black hair and white eyebrows. He was reading the paper and sipping a cup of tea.

"Checking out?" he asked perfunctorily.

"Yes," she replied. As the man, rang up her charge card, Elizabeth asked, "Are you Ajit?"

"Yes," he said, surprised that she knew.

"May I ask you a question?"

She showed him the photo of her son on her cell phone. She explained to him that he had stayed overnight here last year. She knew the chances of him recognizing Luke were remote. The man knitted his white brows, stared at the photo again, scratched the top of his head.

"Just one moment."

He bent down behind the counter and came up with an old registry book.

"When do you say he stay here?"

"It would have been August seventh or eighth, a year ago."

The old man started thumbing through the pages. He slowed, then asked, "What is his name?"

"Luke Gerlacher." She spelled it for him.

"Ah, yes. Here vee are," he cried, touching a line on the page with a long thin finger. "He stayed one night. A silver Honda. Connecticut plates TXU-684."

"Yes, that was his car."

Elizabeth felt a small thrill at the notion that someone had actually met Luke, had written down his license plate, had taken his credit card. Had spoken to him.

Ajit spun the book around so that she could see Luke's signature. She ran her fingers over her son's name. She felt her throat ache.

"Is there something I can do for you, madam?" the old man asked.

She told him why she was interested, that her son had died just a few days after stopping here, that she was following the route he'd taken hoping to learn whatever she could about his last days.

"Oh, please to accept my deepest sympathies, madam."

"Thank you."

She started to leave, when the man said something in another language. She turned back toward him.

"We having saying in Hindi: *as a man casts off worn-out garments and puts on new ones, so the soul casts off the worn-out body and enters a new one.*"

She stared at the man, not sure how to respond.

"May you have a safe journey." He smiled at her, showing one gold tooth in the front.

* * *

From the highway, she spotted a Wal-Mart and pulled off. She wandered up and down the aisles, tossing things into her cart she thought she would need for the trip—toothpaste and a toothbrush, deodorant, floss, lip balm, a razor, Tylenol, antacids, a hair brush. She didn't buy any makeup, though she had lipstick in her pocketbook. What would she need makeup for? Disinterestedly, she picked out some clothes, a couple pairs of jeans, some socks, several blouses, a flannel shirt, even some underwear. She didn't try anything on, just grabbed something near her size and threw it into the cart. Though Elizabeth was hardly a *fashionista*, she liked dressing well, even expensively, and would never have considered buying clothes from Wal-Mart, and certainly not without first trying them on. Tall, long legged, she found it hard to find things off the rack that fit her anyway. But now it didn't matter. She wanted warm, functional clothes for the trip. Stuff she'd probably donate to the women's shelter after this was over. She felt a strange, almost giddy sense of freedom in this fact. The absence of vanity in shopping for clothes was oddly liberating. As she held up a pair of jeans she thought of what the Indian man had said to her: *as a man casts off worn-out garments and puts on new ones, so the soul casts off the worn-out body and enters a new one.* She was putting on new garments herself.

She bought a simple canvas duffel bag to carry all her stuff in and then she picked up some snacks for the car, a package of trail mix, a half dozen Powerbars, several bottles of Vitamin Water. She also bought a pink scrunch-ie, the sort she used to wear when she went for her run around the lake. Just in case, she bought a flashlight, as well as a charger for her iPhone. In the housewares sections she grabbed a pillow and pillow case, always having dis-liked resting her face on a pillow someone else had slept on.

Getting back onto I-81, she continued south. She pulled her long dark hair off her face, into a ponytail and used the scrunchie to hold it in place. She turned on the radio and listened to country stations. C&W had always been one of her guilty pleasures. She liked the old sort of country music, though, Hank Williams and Tammy Wynette, Johnny Cash and Waylon Jennings, Patsy Cline and Merle Haggard. Her father had liked that sort of music and she could remember him playing it on an old phonograph out in the garage as he worked on their car. She liked listening to it with him. The grit and pathos of lost love, of freight trains and pickup trucks and jail cells, and the boozy attempts at forgetfulness. She missed her father all of a sudden. Unlike her mother, he had always been affectionate, tender, and patient with her and her siblings. A gentle man. Unfortunately, Elizabeth had more of her mother than her father in her.

She got two phone calls about a minute apart, both, she saw, from the of-fice, but she decided to ignore them. Probably Joan warning her that she was on thin ice, that her job was in jeopardy if she didn't stop this nonsense and get back to work. Where was the loyalty? Here she'd worked for the firm for ten years, never called in sick once, had done excellent work, and she has one rough patch, and they were ready to give her the boot. *Fuck 'em*, she thought.

After driving an hour, she spotted two *descansos* within a span of half a mile. She stopped at both. The first was a simple, crudely fashioned affair, made of two sticks tied together with a piece of faded blue cloth that turned out to be a scarf. She thought how very different these roadside memorials were from headstones in cemeteries. You'd never see something like this in a cemetery, she thought. In cemeteries death was expensive and formal and highly ritualized, as much a grand statement of one's social standing as any-thing else. Not only that, cemeteries were meant to segregate the "remains," as George Doucette had mockingly referred to them, to corral them into regulated ghettos of the dead hidden behind ornate fences and well-manicured shrubbery. But these *descansos* were sprinkled among the living, along busy roadways and thoroughfares, forcing themselves upon us in a way that cemeteries didn't. They were a constant reminder, a *memento mori* of just how tenuous our hold on life was. One moment we were riding along, thinking of jobs and dinner and sex, thinking we had all the time in the world, and the next we were in some ditch breathing our last. They made us aware that in a heartbeat everything could change.

As plain and crude as the first memorial was, that's exactly how elaborate the next one was. It stood at the base of a sheer cliff blasted from the side of a mountain when they'd cut the highway through. The shoulder was narrow and Elizabeth barely had room to pull her car safely off the highway. She had to pick her way down a rocky incline before she got to the cross. This one was carefully planned out, constructed of two sections of metal welded together and painted white, with a metal ring surrounding the intersection so that it resembled a Celtic cross. In black gothic lettering along the horizontal section was painted the following: *To our beloved Jack. You are with the angels now, Love, Mom, Dad, and Katie.* On the vertical part it said, *5/13/99– 11/26/08. Nine,* Elizabeth thought. My God! Just a little boy. On the ground surrounding the cross was the usual assortment of mementos: plastic flowers, a Teddy bear, a variety of toys and trinkets, a baseball glove slowly coming apart along the stitching. Also strewn about were random shards of glass and plastic, pieces of black rubber and splinters of chrome, obviously from the crash. Funny, Elizabeth thought, how the objects of life and death commingled there along the highway.

She happened to spot a small recess in the cliff wall just behind the cross. She saw things arranged in the natural grotto and walked over to check it out. Displayed were various religious icons—a small crucifix, rosary beads, some sort of medallion, as well as a dozen plain stones that people who'd stopped had evidently picked up from the base of the cliff and placed there. At the back, Elizabeth noticed something else: a small ceramic figurine. She reached in and picked it up. It was a *pieta,* the cheap sort of icon one could buy in a religious gift shop. The Virgin Mother cradling her dead son, his nearly naked body draped over her lap.

Looking at it, Elizabeth couldn't help but recall the time in the back room of Weldon's Funeral Parlor in Garth's Point. They'd decided to have a closed casket; after all, the injuries had been extensive and with the autopsy and paperwork it had taken nearly two weeks to get the body transported back to Connecticut. Given the circumstances, Kenny Weldon, the owner, suggested a closed casket would definitely be, as he put it, "the way to go." Elizabeth, however, insisted that she see her son one last time, that she be able to place around his neck the crucifix he had started wearing. So Kenny had arranged a private viewing for them. She could remember the man trying to warn her that it "Might be a little upsetting, Mrs. Gerlacher." But, stubbornly, she went ahead with it anyway. Kenny led them into the back room, where, as in some TV crime series, a table rested, upon which was a black plastic bag holding the obvious shape of a body. Before unzipping the bag, he'd looked at Elizabeth one last time, as if to say, "Don't say I didn't warn you." She remembered having the breath suddenly sucked from her lungs and her knees going rubbery when she saw her son, her Lukey, lying there pale and lifeless as some manikin. *Oh my God*, she cried, as she turned and fled the room.

She squatted and picked up a stone from the ground and added it to the collection in the niche. "Rest in peace, Jack," she said.

"Ma'am."

Startled, she turned to see a police officer standing on the shoulder of the highway, his silver Dodge cruiser pulled up behind her car. She hadn't even heard him stop.

"Are you all right, ma'am?" he asked in a slight southern drawl. He was tall, broad-shouldered, with a clipped mustache, his shaved temples below his cap shining an unnatural pink in the morning sunlight.

"Yes," she said.

"What are you doing here?"

Elizabeth realized she must have looked a little out of it, her hair unwashed, no makeup, in the wrinkled clothes she'd slept in the night before.

"I saw the cross."

"You can't park here, ma'am. It's dangerous."

"I was just leaving," she replied, heading up toward him. The cop stood planted there, hands on hips, watching her as if she'd done something criminal.

"Are you sure you're okay?" he asked again, looking her over critically.

"I'm fine, officer," she replied. "You must see a lot of these crosses."

"Too many. If it was up to me, I wouldn't allow them."

"Why not?"

He shrugged. "They can be a distraction. People watching them instead of where they're going."

"I guess people need a place to pay their respects," Elizabeth said.

"That's what they got cemeteries for."

* * *

Over the next couple of hours she spotted a half dozen more *descansos* along the highway. The farther south she went, the more crosses she saw. They popped up everywhere. She wasn't sure if it was that the people down here were just worse drivers, or if they were simply more religious. She spotted a pair of crosses near the base of a sprawling white oak just off the highway. Despite the warning from the state trooper, something about them piqued her interest so she pulled over to take a look. The tree had a deep but fading gash in its bark at about bumper level, which Elizabeth assumed was a healed-over wound from the collision that ended the lives of the two people. She squatted and inspected the crosses. The first was twice as tall as the second. Along the horizontal slat was written "Janet-Marie Holtz" while "Monica Holtz" adorned the smaller one. The two had died at this spot on September 5, 1998. Sisters, Elizabeth wondered. Mother and child? The one named Janet-Marie was only seventeen, Elizabeth calculated from the birth and death dates, but the other one had only a single date written below the name—the date of her death. Written in small letters along the vertical section of the larger cross were the words, "The Kingdom of God is within you." Elizabeth stood there for a moment, pondering the scene before her, recalling that George Doucette had said that every *descanso* had a story to tell. Why did the smaller one have no birth date? Then it came to her in a surge of recognition. Of course. The seventeen-year-old was pregnant when she ran off the road and struck the tree. That's why there was no birth date for Monica, because she had never really been born. She had only died here. The irony of Monica dying before being born somehow struck Elizabeth. She could picture the young mother driving home from work, her thoughts on those things any teenager would be thinking, except for the fact that she was carrying a child already. Or perhaps she was running away, trying to flee from her shame. Elizabeth wondered if she was married. Or if like that waitress back in Pennsylvania was all on her own. Maybe she wasn't paying attention. Maybe she was thinking how screwed up her life was going to be, how everything was going to change for her. No more dating or going to parties. Life for Janet-Marie Holtz was suddenly going to be very serious from that point on. Then again, for all Elizabeth knew the girl was ecstatic to be pregnant, to be carrying life inside her. Maybe she'd just felt the baby move and she was so excited that for a moment she took her eyes off the road to look down at her belly. Maybe to utter the name she was going to give her baby.

Monica.

Elizabeth recalled the first time she'd felt Luke move inside her. She was about five months pregnant, which, after many fruitless years of trying, including a miscarriage, was a shock in itself. She had almost reconciled herself to the fact of her and Zack being childless. She felt she could have adapted to such a life. She had her career, her many interests. Besides, having kids wasn't all it was cracked up to be. Her own mother hadn't seemed all that thrilled to be a parent. Yet Elizabeth was not only shocked to learn she was pregnant, she was, quite frankly, amazed by how much she enjoyed carrying new life within her—the sudden fullness of her breasts, how tender and solicitous Zack had become with her, how incredibly horny her hormones suddenly made her. She and Zack had sex almost every night. And her feelings about having a child changed too. Before, when she'd go to some friend's baby shower and the other women would gush about being pregnant, Elizabeth couldn't understand what the big fuss was. She thought herself odd, lacking some maternal gene other women possessed. Then she became pregnant and overnight it was as if a switch had been flipped inside her. She threw herself into the pregnancy. She fixed up the upstairs study in the old house they lived in in the center of town when they'd first moved to Garth's Point. She reveled in buying maternity clothes, looking for things for the nursery, hunting for cute little items in secondhand gift shops. This one particular day she was pushing a shopping cart down the canned goods aisle of the Stop and Shop in town when suddenly she felt this incredibly strange sensation just behind her navel. It wasn't the "kick" she'd heard others talk about. No, this was a subtle but firm movement, more a shift in things, similar to the minor earthquake she'd once felt while in California, the ground moving under your feet. "Oh," she'd cried out, clutching her stomach with one hand and grasping the cart with the other for balance. "Oh, my!"

An elderly woman nearby turned toward her and said, "Pardon me?"

"I just . . . I felt my baby move," Elizabeth said, with what must have been a dopey grin on her face.

"Good lord, do I remember *that* feeling," the woman replied, retuning the smile. "Do you have names picked out?"

"No, not really. We're thinking of Sarah if it's a girl. After my husband's mother. And if it's a boy we don't know yet."

Only later would she decide on the name Luke. Yet it wasn't so much a decision as it was a revelation. As best she could recall, one morning she woke and the name just appeared in her mind, almost as if someone had whispered it in her ear while she slept. "*Luke. Luke Gerlacher,*" she said, trying the name out for size, like a school girl doodling in the margins of her notebook the names for her boyfriend, her future husband, her first-born. *Luke.*

Elizabeth looked down again at the two crosses, the young mother and her unborn baby. She wondered when the mother had come up with a name for her child and to whom she'd told it. She had to have told somebody, otherwise how had they known to have written Monica on the cross? It struck Elizabeth as terribly sad that the mother had never looked upon the face of her child, never called her by name. Never caressed her or nursed her. Never held her in her arms when she was frightened or heard her laughter. At least she, Elizabeth, had experienced all that. She'd had Luke for twenty-one years. That was something to be grateful for, wasn't it?

Elizabeth touched the smaller of the two crosses. "Monica, sweetheart," she said in a whisper that was barely audible, "can you hear me?"

Cars *whooshed* by. Elizabeth waited.

"Do you know my son?" she asked. "Luke Gerlacher."

She waited some more. Then she turned and got back in the car and continued on her way.

* * *

By late afternoon she had reached eastern Tennessee. She picked up I-40 and turned west, where a dark, impenetrable wall of clouds loomed above the horizon like a tsunami about to strike land. All day long, Elizabeth had been trying to recall the summer before the accident, sifting through her memories like an old Rolodex, hoping to come up with something she might have overlooked, something Luke may have said or done that would shed the faintest light on what he'd wanted to talk to her about. However, she recalled little of importance. In fact, it seemed they'd hardly exchanged more than a few words that summer. Mostly it was a blur of the mundane, pedestrian conversations with her son regarding college bills and dentist appointments, laundry and the need to have the shock absorbers replaced on his Honda. In the few lengthier conversations she could remember, Luke was reticent, seldom offering anything personal. She tried to believe, as Zack did, that their son was only acting the way any college kid did, going through the normal, sometimes unpleasant phase of a son morphing into a young man. But sometimes she suspected it was deeper than that, more profound, something that was troubling her Lukey.

How different things had been just a short time before, when he was with TJ. How happy he'd seemed then. Elizabeth felt she could almost trace the change in her son to the moment when the girl broke up with him. The poor kid seemed devastated. She remembered talking to him by phone one evening at school, right before Christmas break his junior year. When she asked about TJ coming for Christmas dinner, as she often had, he'd told her, with this odd, casual heartlessness it seemed, that TJ and he were done.

"Done?" Elizabeth had cried. "What on earth happened?"

"She wants to date other people."

"She said that?"

"Not in so many words."

"What did she say?" Elizabeth pressed.

"I don't want to talk about it, Mom."

"But—"

"Mom, just stay the hell out of my business, would you?"

It was after that when he seemed to grow more distant—*guarded* was the word that came to Elizabeth, his emotional life something he preferred not to share, or at least not with her. Always a late bloomer, Luke hadn't had much experience with girls nor seemingly much interest. As he hit his teens, on more than one occasion, Elizabeth had expressed her concerns to Zack. "He's so good looking, why doesn't he have any dates?" she'd said. Zack though felt their son was just slow to develop, that he would date in his own good time. Yet in the back of Elizabeth's mind lurked the question all parents ask of a child that was slow to develop an interest in the opposite sex: *Was he gay?* Then TJ came into the picture his sophomore year in high school and overnight Luke changed. He was head over heels about her, his first real girlfriend. She used to come over to the house and hang out with Luke, do homework together, watch a movie, listen to music—their relationship as easy and natural as if she were just another one of his buddies. Elizabeth felt it was wonderful to see her son blossom like this. Sometimes, TJ would sit at the kitchen counter and talk with Elizabeth, while waiting for Luke to get home from some place or other. She was such a sweet kid, smart and funny and pretty, popular but not snooty like a lot of the girls in town. Elizabeth had never had a daughter but TJ obligingly filled that role. She was like a part of their family. They used to invite her for Christmas dinner and to come out to the Cape with them when they went on vacation.

After he'd first started seeing TJ, Luke would come home after a date and want to talk all about it with Elizabeth. When he was a senior, he'd even confided in his mother about the first time they'd had sex. Though shocked by the fact that her little Lukey was being intimate with a girl, she listened carefully, tried not to let on she was secretly aghast. Actually, Elizabeth thought it was cute how he inquired about the "mechanics" of the act, shared with her the fact that he didn't think he'd "been very good," and wanted to know what he could do "better" the next time. And she savored the fact that her son came to her and not his father for such advice.

But after their break-up, he didn't speak to Elizabeth about his love life at all. In fact, about his *life* at all. When she'd inquire if he were dating anyone, he'd snap at her, "Just stay out of my damn business." Elizabeth thought he was still stuck on TJ. Zack, on the other hand, believed it was good that Luke wasn't tying himself to just one girl, that he was "playing the field," as he put it. Though she agreed with Zack in theory, she nonetheless preferred the old Luke to this new version who was so aloof, so distant, so sullen.

* * *

As the skies continued to threaten, Elizabeth got off the highway and followed the GPS to a place called "Cowan's Cherokee Village," a hotel in the eastern mountains of Tennessee where, according to her notebook, Luke had spent the night. She drove along a narrow road that curved between steep, hardwood-covered mountains. After a couple of miles she came upon the place, half a dozen cottages with fake tepee facades squatting in a semicircle around a pool whose water was mold-green. The man who showed Elizabeth to her room must have been ninety, with long white hair pulled back into a single braid (was he trying to pretend he was Cherokee?) and the wild look in his rheumy eyes of a failed prophet. The room turned out to be the size of a death-row prisoner's cell, with a bathroom stuffed into a closet-like space in the corner.

"Hot water might take a spell," the man said. "I got to turn the heater on this time a year."

Elizabeth decided it was pointless to ask the old man if he recalled her son. Instead she inquired about a restaurant called Bart's, where her son had eaten.

"Down thattaway," the man said, pointing a bony finger toward the west. "I think they stay open till eight."

Elizabeth drove down the road about a mile before she reached the restaurant, which was in a small plaza with a couple of other stores. A heavy-set waitress with a cotton-candy swirl of permed-red hair seated her. She had matching red lipstick and nails about an inch long. She called Elizabeth "darlin'" several times. "What y'all gonna have, darlin'?" the woman asked. Elizabeth ordered the baked chicken special with a salad, about the only thing on the menu that wasn't "country fried." Outside the window, she saw that the sky had darkened even more, with clouds boiling into each other, and tinged with those strange yellow and purple tones of a looming storm. A strong wind had kicked up, too, making the tops of the trees quake.

The woman returned after a while with Elizabeth's order. "Looks like we're gonna get us some rain," the woman said to her, standing there and gazing out the window.

"Looks like."

"Where y'all from, darlin'?"

"Connecticut."

"I been to Massachusetts. Ever'body drives a big fancy car up there."

The woman obviously liked to talk.

"What'chall doing way down here?"

"I'm heading out to New Mexico."

"Boy, that's a ways to drive."

While Elizabeth ate her meal she retrieved an earlier voice mail from Joan. "Elizabeth? Are you there? If you are, pick up the damn phone. This is important. Warren's mad as hell. I don't know if I can put him off any longer. Call me, okay. Please."

After a while, the waitress came over.

"You need anything, darlin'?"

"I'm good. May I ask you a favor?" Elizabeth said to the woman. She took out her phone and showed the waitress the picture of Luke. She explained how her son had been in Bart's a year ago for a meal, wondered if anyone remembered him. The woman took the phone and stared at Luke's photo for a while.

"That's one good lookin' young feller. I think he favors you. Cain't say I recall him though. Is it something important?"

"To me, it is," Elizabeth replied. She went on to explain that she was following the trail of her son, that he'd used his charge card here to pay for a meal.

The woman stared at her, waiting. "How come I get the feeling you're gonna tell me something bad?"

"He was killed in a car accident," Elizabeth explained.

"Oh, Lord," the woman exclaimed, her fleshy face grimacing. "I just knew it. That's just terrible."

"It happened a few days after he stopped here. Out in New Mexico."

The woman reached out and put her hand on Elizabeth's shoulder.

"You poor thing. How old was your boy?"

"Twenty-one."

"I swear, sometimes life just ain't fair. Take my son-in-law, Travis. You couldn't ask for a sweeter boy. Like my own flesh and blood. Sang in the church choir. Captain of the football team. Had a full scholarship to play for Appalachian State. Had a smile that was just pure honey. Then Nine-eleven happens and he signs up to go off and fight. Wants to do his *patriotic* duty," she said sarcastically. "Does two tours over in Afghanistan. When he got home, he was changed. He was all messed up," the woman said, tapping a long red nail against her temple. "Drinking, doing drugs. Couldn't hardly sleep at night. Would get in these black moods my daughter didn't even want to be around him. He scared her. It got so bad she took the two kids and moved back in with us."

"What happened to him?" Elizabeth asked hesitantly.

"One night he went out in the truck and put a rifle in his mouth and blew his head off."

"I'm so sorry."

"My daughter said he was never the same. The man who came back was somebody else."

"When my son went away to college, he seemed to change too."

"Ain't that the way. Sometimes I think it's better if people stick close to home. With their family."

Elizabeth nodded.

After eating only a little of her meal, Elizabeth had lost her appetite. She paid the bill and headed out.

"Take care of yourself, darlin'," the waitress called to her.

It was pouring out now. The rain had just commenced, but it came down all at once, without the slightest prelude, like a water balloon punctured by a needle. It quickly turned the parking lot into a churning river, with the occasional clap of lightning followed by the boom of thunder rolling down through the valley. She made a frantic dash to her car but was soaked by the time she got in.

Back in her room, Elizabeth peeled the wet clothes off and climbed into the narrow metal shower. Afterwards, she dressed in some of the new clothes she'd bought. The shirt fit her fine but the jeans were snug through the waist and hips. She left the top button undone. She lay on the bed with the lights out, listening to the rain. Occasionally, the night outside would brighten almost into day from the lightning and moments later the cabin would shudder as thunder rolled past. The bed was saggy and uncomfortable but the new pillow she'd bought felt good beneath her head, clean and fresh and firm. Once again she was struck by a strong craving for a drink and was glad she hadn't bought anything. It would be too tempting now.

As she lay there, something dark rubbed just at the edge of her consciousness, like a feather drawn lightly across skin making her shiver. She pushed it away but it returned. She kept pushing it away, but each time it would return, and each time it would be stronger. She thought of the story the waitress had told her about her son-in-law. How he had been all mixed up, and took his life. It was something that had crossed her mind before but which she had always managed to push away: suicide. What if it had not been an accident? What if he had meant to drive off that road? After all, he hadn't been drinking, and the officer had said that he went off a straight section of highway. According to the police report, the evening had been clear, the road conditions good. And Luke had always been a cautious driver, always wore his seat belt, didn't speed or take chances while behind the wheel. There was nothing to explain why the car just seemed to veer off and carry Luke out of this life, away from her. She recalled, too, Luke's voice on her cell phone earlier that night, how it had sounded "off" to her, as if something was wrong. What if the "something" that had been troubling him was darker than she'd imagined, something so terrible and so private he couldn't tell anyone—or at least hadn't yet been able to tell anyone until he called her. She thought of that line she'd come across in his diary. *Duc in altum.* To put out into the deep end. Perhaps that, too, had darker implications than she'd imagined.

She was lying there in the dark, smoking and listening to the rain assault the roof when her phone rang.

"Elizabeth?"

The connection wasn't very good, but she could tell it was Zack.

"Hi," she said.

"Where are you?" he asked.

"Tennessee."

"Tennessee?" he repeated, his voice rising somewhat incredulously, as if she'd said Siberia. "What's that noise?"

"It's raining."

"Sounds like it's coming down pretty hard."

He said something that she didn't catch.

"What? You're not coming in very clearly," she replied.

"I said, 'you sound better.'" She didn't know what he meant by "better," but she didn't comment on that. "I was kind of hoping you might have reconsidered."

"Reconsidered?" Elizabeth asked.

"This whole thing."

"Zack, I told you I have to do this," she said.

"You don't *have* to do anything, Elizabeth. This is a choice."

"All right. I'm *choosing* to do it."

"Then—maybe I could come with you."

"What?"

"I said, maybe I could come with you. I don't like the idea of you driving all the way out there by yourself. I could fly out and meet you somewhere. Nashville," he tossed out. "Have you reached Nashville yet?"

"No."

"We could go together. Make it into a little vacation."

"It's not a little vacation," she snapped, annoyed that he would even consider what she was doing a form of recreation. "I'm going to see where our son died. I'm not going to Disney World, for heaven's sake."

"Take it easy. I didn't mean it like that," he explained.

She listened to the rain on the roof for moment. It came in waves, driving, pounding rhythmically, like the ocean breaking onto the shore. *Whhhsssh . . . whhhsssh.*

"Are you okay? I'm worried about you."

"Yes. I'm fine. I want to ask you something, Zack," she began. "And I want you to hear me out."

"All right."

"The summer Luke died, did you notice anything wrong with him?"

"How do you mean 'wrong'?"

"Was something bothering him?"

"Does this have anything to do with that call he made to you?"

"It might. When I think about him that last summer, he just seemed so . . . distant."

"He was a college kid. They're off in their own little world."

"This was different. I can't put my finger on it, but I think something was going on with him. Maybe he was depressed. Did you get that sense?"

"No. I don't think so anyway."

Elizabeth paused, wondering if she should just drop it. Wondering if she really wanted to open up this can of worms. And that's what it was, a can of worms. What good would it do either of them now to consider that the accident may not have been an accident? That the randomness of his death perhaps wasn't so random? But she found herself at a place where she felt she didn't have anything to lose. Once she'd decided to get in the car and drive out here, there was no turning back. Whatever happened, whatever she found out, she—they—would just have to deal with it.

"Have you ever thought maybe . . ."

"Maybe what?" Zack asked.

"That it wasn't an accident?"

"What?" he cried. "I can barely hear you."

"Have you ever thought maybe it wasn't an accident?" she repeated, so loudly that the words echoed in the tiny room.

"What do you mean, it wasn't an accident?"

"I mean, Luke was usually a pretty cautious driver. He always wore his seat belt and he didn't this time. And the police report said alcohol wasn't involved. He just went off the road. It doesn't make sense."

"Elizabeth, come on. Think about what you're saying."

"I'm not *saying* anything. I'm just wondering out loud. Maybe there was something bothering him. Something we had no idea of."

"Honey, it was an accident. That's all it was."

"How do you know? How do we know anything?"

"The police didn't suggest it was anything *other* than that. They said he probably just fell asleep at the wheel."

"They don't know that. That's just cops trying to close the books. That's what they do, to make their lives easier."

"And what you're saying, is that any better? Why even think such a thing, Elizabeth? It only makes everything worse."

"I'm just trying to get to the truth."

"Truth? How is what you're implying any more true than what the cops said? They're the professionals."

"Zack, it just doesn't make sense."

"What *you're* saying doesn't make sense."

A flash of light erupted outside, and a few seconds later another *boom* of thunder rattled the cabin. She felt her spine trembling, as if a train had passed nearby. She could still feel the aftershock vibrating the bed.

"I'm only looking for answers," she explained.

"For heaven's sake, Elizabeth. There *are* no answers. It was just something that happened. And we have to deal with it."

"That's what I'm trying to do. Deal with it."

"And you think by going out there you're going to find answers?"

"I don't know," she replied.

"The one answer I can give you is that our son didn't do this on purpose."

"How do you know that?"

"That wasn't Luke. He didn't want to die. He had everything to live for."

"So what do *you* think he wanted to talk about that night?" she asked.

"I have no idea."

"And you don't particularly care to know either."

"Whatever it was, we'll never find out. And even if we could, what good would it do us now?"

"I think it would help if we knew what he was thinking then. Where his head was at."

"You maybe. Not me."

"All right. Me then."

"It could have been anything, Elizabeth. Maybe he wanted to drop out of school. Maybe he wanted to get a tattoo. Who the hell knows?"

"No, it was something important. I could hear it in his voice."

"Maybe he was having girlfriend problems. Something with TJ."

"TJ?" she said, surprised at the mention of her name. "What are you talking about?"

There was a pause, as if Zack was thinking of how he could undo what he'd just said, take it back. "He went out with her a few times that summer."

"What? How do you know that?"

"He told me."

"He *told* you?"

"Yes."

She wondered why Luke hadn't told her about something as important as that. He'd told his father but not her. Could that be what he had wanted to talk to her about, what had seemed so imperative?

"Were they dating again?" Elizabeth asked.

"I don't know. You know kids these days. They don't date any more. He said they got together a few times. Maybe it was nothing."

"Then again, maybe that's what he wanted to talk about."

"You're grasping at straws now."

Perhaps she was. But what else did she have? She wondered why she and Zack had waited all this time to talk about any of this. Instead, they'd both retreated into their own grief, into a marriage of silence and secrets. She more than Zack, but he had done it too, in his own way. Taking his grief not to her but to his damn support group. Wanting to jump so quickly back into a life that no longer existed. To put Luke's death behind them.

"Zack, I have something I need to talk to you about," she began. No sooner were the words out of her mouth than she realized how eerily close they sounded to what Luke had said to her: *Mom, there's something I really needed to talk to you about.*

"Whatever it is, can't it wait till you get back?"

"No, it's important. That night . . ."

"What?" he cried, his voice fading, becoming scratchy, small and insect-like.

"Are you there, Zack? Can you hear me?"

"Barely. I think I'm starting to lose you."

"The night Luke died. I was—"

But the call ended abruptly, their connection broken off by the storm. Or had he hung up on her, not wanting to hear what she might have to tell him? She thought of calling back but she didn't. Instead she crawled under the covers and waited for sleep.

Chapter 11

The storm having spent its fury, the next morning broke still and exhausted, like one waking after a debauched night of revelry. Leaves and branches littered the road, debris was strewn over the parking lot, and up near the motel office, a garbage can lay overturned, a trio of brazen crows picking over its contents. As Elizabeth opened her car door, they took off squawking vociferously. Stuck to her windshield was a newspaper flyer she had to peel off like a sodden bandage.

She picked up the highway and continued west. Her conversation with Zack the previous night returned to her: *You're grasping at straws*, he'd said. Perhaps she was. Perhaps all of this was just grasping at straws. She thought, too, of what he'd told her about Luke seeing TJ that summer. Had her son started dating her again? There was that one brief phone call Luke had made to TJ while he was on his trip. It was odd that these seemingly inconsequential and disparate facts surrounding her son appeared to have such significance now, such import and nuance. Elizabeth warned herself not to do what she was contemplating, but lately she hadn't heeded her own warnings. Lately warnings seemed made for others. She felt reckless and irresponsible; her only law being whatever would illuminate Luke's end. She took out her cell phone and looked up TJ's number, which she'd never bothered to delete. It was as if she'd not quite admitted to herself that they were over.

After several rings, the young woman's familiar voice came on: *Hi, this is Tess. I'm not here right now, but leave a message and I'll call you back. Ciao.* Elizabeth was surprised to hear her use her first name instead of her initials (she wasn't even sure what the *J* stood for). She had always been just TJ. The voice brought back a painful flood of memories of the girl who used to sit in the den with Luke, eating pizza, watching TV or studying for a test with her son, her girlish laughter fluttering in the air, filling the house with joy. She missed TJ, missed even more how her son used to act when he was around her, happy, carefree, vibrant with life. Elizabeth hadn't seen the girl in nearly two years. She'd run into TJ's mother at the dry cleaner's in town a few months before. It was an awkward meeting. They both smiled too much, and Mrs. Pierson acted as if Elizabeth was eighty, and hard of hearing. She spoke too loudly and rested her hand patronizingly on Elizabeth's wrist. When Elizabeth asked how TJ was doing, the woman said her daughter had gotten a job up in Boston, at the Fine Arts Museum. Now, when it came time to leave a message, Elizabeth warned herself, *No, this is all wrong.* Why disturb the poor kid, needlessly bringing up such past sorrow? She hung up, without saying anything.

That day she drove the length of Tennessee, a seemingly endless parallelogram of rolling hills, cattle and horse farms, shimmering lakes dotted with homes, and massive tourist signs advertising the likes of Forbidden Caverns, Opryland, Graceland, Gatlinburg, The Johnny Cash Museum, the Jack Daniels distillery, and Baptist church after Baptist church. One sign in particular caught her attention. Set off the highway along a sloping pasture populated by black Angus cattle, it proclaimed simply, inexplicably, "When you die, you will meet God." Beneath the words appeared what seemed to be a spiky red EKG line, jumping up and down with life until finally flat-lining under God's name, presumably indicating death. Like the life insurance sign she'd seen the first night on the road, this one, too, seemed a hard-sell technique of the most overbearing sort. Though she wasn't sure what was being marketed, other than simple fear.

She passed signs for small towns with hokey-sounding names like Crab Orchard, Helen's Gap, Carthage Junction, Horace Corners, Bear Hollow. She listened to the lulling twang of more country stations, while drinking Red Bull to stay awake and munching on trail mix. Around two she stopped and filled up with gas and bought a dry-as-cardboard sandwich at a convenience store to blunt the dull call of hunger. It was so bad she tossed most of it out the window. The storm ushered in its wake cooler, drier weather. She could smell the change in the air, a clean, sharp odor like ammonia.

Some time later she found herself passing through a broad valley, framed by low, hump-backed hills in the distance, and immediately on either side of the interstate, green pastures, plowed-over fields, an occasional stand of pine woods. Twilight was coming on fast. Some cars in the opposite lane already had their lights on, and she was reminded to turn hers on as well. She thought again of what Zack had told her, how Luke had seen TJ that summer. Maybe the girl had some inkling of where her son's mind was, what he was thinking before he died. Elizabeth decided not to heed her earlier warning. If there was the slightest chance TJ could shed some light on her son, she would take it. She didn't want to leave any stone unturned. So she called again, and again got the recording. This time, though, she left a message. "Hi, TJ," she said. She didn't use "Tess"; that wasn't the girl she knew. "It's Mrs. Gerlacher. Luke's Mom. How are you?" She paused for a moment, then added, "Do you think you could call me when you get a chance?"

Perhaps if she hadn't been on the phone, perhaps if she'd been paying more attention to the present instead of poking around in the cluttered debris of the past, she'd have seen it a second earlier and had a chance to swerve out of the way, to avoid the unavoidable. A sudden streak of brownish-gray appeared just ahead and off to her right, in the headlights' periphery. It had bolted from some woods near the shoulder of the highway and appeared to fly effortlessly into the tunnel of her headlights. It was upon her—or rather, her Saab and the brownish-gray object seemed to meet at the intersection of their respective trajectories, as if there had been some intentionality to their separate movements, an unstated agreement to be joined at exactly that point in time and space. Elizabeth felt helpless, didn't have the slightest chance to do anything—hit the brakes, swerve, tense herself for the impact, utter a sound. There was a nauseating *thwunk* noise, a deep, bone-breaking clatter as the deer's left flank collided with the right front of Elizabeth's car. She felt the jolt in her shoulder blades, then she was being thrown forward and her nose slammed into the steering wheel. She actually saw stars, like in the cartoons, little white pieces of light dancing in front of her eyes. And in the next moment, not so much in slow motion as in a series of distinct still-frames, the animal was first suspended upside down over the hood of her car, antlers pointing earthward, black eyes startled, then flattened against the windshield with an ear-splitting *crrrrk*, and finally, in the rearview, lying crumpled along the shoulder of the road. This all happened so fast Elizabeth hadn't even had time to be frightened.

Looking through a windshield that now appeared as if glazed over with a thick sheet of ice, she instinctively tried to steer the car toward a shoulder of the road she couldn't see. Even then she could tell something was terribly wrong. The steering wheel fought her like some sort of headstrong beast, felt as if it wanted to keep the car going straight on down the highway, and she had use all her strength to bend the wheel to her will. When she'd finally managed to pull the car to a bumpy stop on the shoulder, she sat there for a moment trembling, her heart rapping fiercely in her chest. Now she had time to be afraid.

"Damn!" she cried at last.

Recovering her wits, she got out and stood, her head spinning slightly, then went around to the front of her car. With the light from her phone, she saw that the right front fender was stove in, the bumper and grill crumpled, the headlight smashed and the assembly dangling like an enucleated eye. Her car appeared as if it'd tangled with a Mack truck rather than a single frightened deer.

It was only then that she became aware of a throbbing in her head. She reached up and touched the bridge of her nose. The nose itself was mostly numb but when she removed her hand her fingers were covered with something slippery and dark. She was bleeding.

Walking back to the car, she glanced up the highway and saw in the headlights of the on-coming traffic, the still, lifeless form of the deer lying stretched out along the shoulder. She thought of heading back and seeing to the poor creature. However, viewing its broken and bleeding form up close would probably be the last straw. She couldn't bear that. So instead, she got in her car, avoided looking in the rearview mirror.

She dialed the AAA number.

"I just hit a deer," she explained to the operator.

"First things first," the woman said. She had a high-pitched, twangy accent and a smoker's raspy voice. "Are you all right, ma'am?"

"Mostly, yes"

"Is the vehicle drivable?"

"I don't know. I don't think so."

The operator took Elizabeth's information and where the accident had occurred, and then she told her she'd have someone out to help her as soon as possible.

"But we're awful busy tonight, ma'am. On account of the storm yesterday."

"I'm out in the middle of nowhere," Elizabeth explained to the woman. "And it's going to be dark soon."

"Like I said, we'll have someone out there soon's we can," the woman advised. "In the meantime, y'all want to lock your doors and stay in the car. And don't talk to strangers."

Don't talk to strangers, Elizabeth thought as she hung up. Yet she went ahead and locked the doors and sat way up in the seat, to look formidable to any would-be attacker. For company she listened to the radio. When Freddy

Fender's "Wasted Days and Wasted Nights" came on, Elizabeth couldn't fail to appreciate the irony.

She'd been waiting there for nearly an hour when her cell finally rang.

"Jesus, it's about time!" she cried, ready to give the AAA person a piece of her mind.

"Mrs. Gerlacher?" a hesitant female voice replied.

Immediately she recognized it. "Oh, TJ. I'm sorry. I thought you were someone else."

"How are you, Mrs. Gerlacher?"

"I'm fine," Elizabeth replied. "Well, not so fine actually. I've just been in a car accident."

"My goodness. Are you okay?"

"Yeah. I just hit a deer. I'm waiting for the tow truck."

The conversation struck Elizabeth as decidedly peculiar. Here she'd just killed a deer, was stranded along some highway in Tennessee, and now she was talking to her dead son's girlfriend. Ex-girlfriend.

"Can I do anything?" TJ asked. "Call anybody for you?"

"No, I think I'm all set. The tow truck should be here any minute. Thanks for getting back to me so quickly. Your mom says you're living in Boston now."

"Yes. Working at the Fine Arts Museum."

"That sounds exciting."

"Not really. Not unless you consider leading first-grade tours exciting," she said with a self-deprecating laugh.

The laugh was so familiar Elizabeth had an image of TJ sitting on the couch with her son. Her sandy blonde hair tied in a flattering ponytail, her hand touching Luke's flannel-shirted arm. The first girl her son loved. Perhaps the *only* girl.

"Still, it's a start. And Boston is a great place live," Elizabeth offered.

"It's a lot more exciting than Garth's Point."

Another laugh, to which Elizabeth joined in nervously. Laughing caused her nose to ache.

"You go by Tess now, huh?"

"Yeah, sort of. It sounds more professional. But you can still call me TJ."

"So how are you?"

"I'm good," the young woman replied. "Busy." This was followed by a pause, awkward and weighty, which made Elizabeth wonder if she were debating whether or not to tell her something. Finally, TJ blurted out, "I'm engaged."

"Oh," Elizabeth exclaimed, feeling a shock akin to that she'd felt slamming her nose into the steering wheel. It shouldn't have hurt as much as it did. But it did. Another death, as if yet another part of Luke, a piece of his future, had just been erased. She recalled then how the girl's mother had seemed evasive when TJ's name had been brought up. Had she not wanted to be the one to tell her about the engagement? Elizabeth managed to recover quickly though. "That's wonderful. Anyone from town?"

"No, I met him at college. Greg. That's his name."

"Wow! Congratulations. So when's the big day?"

"We haven't set a date yet. We're not in any rush."

"No sense rushing into things. But that's great news. I'm so happy for you, TJ."

And she was. Happy for her, that is. She'd always loved TJ, like a daughter in fact, the one she'd never had. But in the next moment, Elizabeth found herself wondering just where that had left TJ and her son. Zack had said they'd gotten together several times the summer before their senior year, the summer Luke died. Had this future husband of hers, this Greg, been in the picture then? Had TJ been considering getting back together with Luke and it was only his death that had put an end to their renewed relationship and allowed her to begin another one? Elizabeth could recall how devastated TJ had appeared at the funeral, how much Luke's death seemed to affect her. How tragic that would have been if they'd finally gotten back together again only to be separated by his sudden death. And now TJ, her one-time future daughter-in-law, the potential mother of her grandchildren, was going to marry someone else. Elizabeth had all she could do not to start balling. She clenched her jaw. *Don't! Don't put that on TJ.* It wasn't her fault. God, what was she thinking even contacting the girl?

Elizabeth contemplated making up some excuse for wanting to talk. Perhaps saying she was simply interested in finding out what TJ was doing. After all, the girl had been such a large part of her son's life, not to mention hers and Zack's, for so many years. But then again, Elizabeth had to admit she was curious. If TJ and Luke had started to date again, why hadn't he told his mother? And if something had started up again between the two, perhaps it was somehow related to what he wanted to tell Elizabeth that night. More dots to be connected, more pieces of the puzzle.

"The reason I called, I wanted to ask you something about Luke," Elizabeth said.

"Sure, Mrs. Gerlacher."

"The night he died he called me. He left a message on my phone saying he had something he wanted to talk to me about. But unfortunately we never got the chance to talk."

"That's terrible."

"Yes, it has been. Not knowing what he wanted. That's why I called you. I thought you might have some clue."

Outside on the highway, the traffic roared by, Elizabeth's car shuddering in the wake of every vehicle that passed, the noise making it sometimes difficult to hear TJ's soft voice.

"Me?"

"I mean, you and Luke were so close."

"We were. But not for a while."

"Hadn't the two of you started seeing each other again?"

"What?"

"My husband said Luke told him that the two of you had gone out a few times that summer."

"We didn't really go *out*, Mrs. Gerlacher. We saw each other a few times. Hung out together a little. As friends."

"So you two weren't back together?"

"Me and Luke?" she replied with a fluttery laugh that struck Elizabeth as condescending. "No."

Elizabeth touched her nose and felt blood on her fingers, cool and slippery to the touch.

"May I ask you a personal question?"

"I guess so," TJ said, but her tone was tentative.

"You and Luke always seemed so good together," Elizabeth said. "I even thought you'd get married someday."

"Me, too."

"Then what happened?"

TJ was silent for a moment. Yet over the noise of the highway, Elizabeth thought she caught a faint sniffling sound coming from the other end of the phone.

"I'm sorry, TJ," Elizabeth offered. "I probably shouldn't have brought it up."

"No, it's all right. It's just that I get so sad whenever I think about Luke. I really liked him." Then, like an unwelcome confession for which she felt guilty, she added, "Loved him actually."

"And he really loved you."

"Not really."

"What do you mean, 'not really'?"

"He loved me as a friend."

"A friend? My God, Luke was head over heels about you."

"No, Mrs. Gerlacher. It was the other way around. I was the one crazy about your son. Always was. Ever since like sixth grade."

Right then, Elizabeth heard the intrusive beeping of another phone call. "Could you hold on for a moment, TJ? That's probably the tow truck."

"Of course."

"Hello," Elizabeth said to the other caller.

"Ma'am, our truck is runnin' late," the same woman's voice drawled.

"It's been well over an hour already."

"He'll be there just as soon as he can."

Elizabeth clicked back to TJ. "Sorry about that. I'm a little confused, TJ. If you were so crazy about my son, why did you break up with him?"

"*Me?*" she said, her voice incredulous. "Luke was the one who didn't want to go out any more."

"But . . . I was under the impression you didn't want to go out with him. That you wanted to date other people."

"Who told you that?"

"Luke."

"That's not true, Mrs. Gerlacher. *He* was the one who broke it off with me. God, I cried for weeks."

Elizabeth sat there for a moment, trying to digest this information. She felt the dull throbbing emanating from where she'd hit her nose, radiating back into her skull. It seemed to pulsate there like another heartbeat. Why would Luke have lied to her? Why didn't he want her to know that *he* was the one who'd initiated the break-up? It didn't make sense. She thought of simply dropping the whole thing, saying goodbye to TJ, wishing her luck in her new life, and letting the past just sink down into oblivion.

Instead, though, Elizabeth asked, "Why would he lie about that, TJ?"

"I don't know, Mrs. Gerlacher."

"It's so odd."

"Yes, it is."

"So you're saying Luke ended it?"

"That's right."

Elizabeth's phone rang again, but this time she decided not to get it.

"Why do you think he did that, TJ?"

"I really don't know, Mrs. Gerlacher. But it doesn't matter now, does it?"

Elizabeth knew she was right. It was what Zack had been telling her all along. What good would knowing any of this be now? They were kids and they split up. What was the big deal who broke up with whom? Elizabeth shivered, feeling suddenly cold. It was completely dark out now, and sitting there on the side of the highway, she felt helpless and vulnerable, as if at the mercy of unknown and hostile forces. *Stop*, she warned herself. *Before it's too late.* But something in her, a need both perverse and yet inexorable, compelled her forward.

"It matters to me, TJ."

"I don't think he was interested . . ." she said, pausing, "in having a relationship."

"You mean, with you?"

"With anyone really. I'd felt Luke pulling away for a long while."

"Was it somebody else? Another girl?"

"I don't think so. He didn't seem to be interested in women any longer."

"Not interested in women? What are you talking about?"

"Not in that way."

"In what way?" Elizabeth said, feeling a hot pressure building in her throat.

"Sexually."

"What are you saying, TJ?"

"I'm just saying, he didn't seem to be into the whole dating thing."

"I don't understand." Three cars roared by, one after the other—*whoosh, whoosh, whoosh*—making the car shimmy. "Are you saying that my son was . . . *gay?*"

"I'm not sure."

"What do you mean, 'you're not sure'?" Elizabeth cried, anger and bewilderment leaching into her voice.

Elizabeth thought she heard a voice whisper in the background of the phone, a young man's voice: *Who is it?* Was that her fiancé? The Greg who had replaced her Luke.

"He seemed confused."

"Confused. You mean about his sexual orientation?"

"About a lot of things."

"But you dated him for years," Elizabeth said. "Do *you* think he was gay?"

"I don't know."

"Really?"

"No. In that last year or so I felt there was something different about Luke. Something that had come between us."

Elizabeth recalled what Luke's one-time best friend Griff had told her about Luke changing, being in his own little world.

"How do you mean, 'different'?"

"I don't know how to explain it. I think he was struggling with something. He talked about going away for a while."

"Away?"

"Maybe joining the Peace Corps. And he talked about heading out west."

Peace Corps? Heading out west? All of this came as a surprise to Elizabeth, as if Luke was a complete stranger to her, someone she had never really known. She sucked in a mouthful of air and felt suddenly sick to her stomach. *Enough*, she told herself. She didn't need to hear any more. She didn't need for this to go on. She could pretend this conversation never even took place. And yet, once started, it seemed she couldn't stop, as if her own curiosity had an irresistible momentum that carried her onward even against her will.

"I'm his mother," Elizabeth said defensively. "How come he never said any of this to me?"

"I don't know."

"It just seems odd that he would lie to me like that."

"Mrs. Gerlacher, I don't know how to explain it."

"Do you think he'd lie to me about breaking up with you?"

"I guess he felt he couldn't talk to you."

"What?"

"He thought you wouldn't understand."

Her comment felt like a slap in the face. In fact, Elizabeth felt her cheeks turn hot with embarrassment.

"Really? He said that?"

"Yes."

In a supercilious tone, Elizabeth said, "Frankly, I find all this very hard to believe." Hurt and angered by what TJ had said, Elizabeth wanted to lash out. The lawyer in her seemed to take over. She hardened herself, slipped into her ruthless cross-examination mode. "Are you going to deny the two of you were intimate?" she challenged.

"Mrs. Gerlacher, stop. Please."

"*Were* you?"

"You have no right to ask me that."

"If you're going to accuse my son of being gay, at least you could provide evidence," Elizabeth said, as if this *were* a trial and she was cross-examining a hostile witness.

"I didn't say he was gay. I just said he seemed confused about things."

"And I'm supposed to just take you at your word? And my son not here to defend himself."

"Mrs. Gerlacher, I *loved* Luke," TJ hurled at her.

With that the girl's voice broke and she started sobbing. That was enough to stop Elizabeth dead in her tracks. She realized suddenly she'd overstepped any sort of decency. TJ was right. Whatever her and Luke's relationship was or wasn't, it certainly was none of her business. She took a breath. "I'm so sorry, sweetheart. Please forgive me."

"It's okay," TJ replied between sobs.

"No, it's not okay. You were always a wonderful friend to Luke. And to my husband and me. I had no right to say those things."

"I just wished things turned out differently."

They were silent for a moment.

"Can I ask you one more question?"

"Sure."

"When you met him that summer, do you think whatever he was going through was troubling him then?"

"Yes. Maybe that's why he wanted to get away."

"Really?"

"Yes. He'd talked about driving cross country. To clear his head."

After a while, they said their goodbyes and hung up. Elizabeth sat there, feeling numbed more than anything, a kind of shell-shock as she tried to process all that TJ had said to her. That *Luke* was the one to break off their relationship. That he was confused. That he wasn't interested in women. That the trip had been a means to clear his head. That he was, as TJ put it, "struggling with something." Elizabeth also felt embarrassed for how cruel she'd been to TJ. She'd had no right to say those things to the poor kid. Yet what troubled Elizabeth most perhaps was the fact that Luke felt he couldn't talk to her, couldn't tell her any of this. Of course, if he *had* been gay, she'd have still loved him. She'd have loved him no matter what. That wasn't the issue. But if he *were* gay—and that was still a big "if" to Elizabeth's mind—why hadn't she *known* about it? How could she be so utterly and completely in the dark about her son's sexual orientation. Wouldn't she—*shouldn't* she—have seen the clues strewn along the way? How could a mother have missed such an enormous part of her son's life? And how could Luke have managed to keep something that huge a secret from her and Zack, all those years living under the same roof. If it *were* true, what sort of mother had she been that he didn't trust her enough to place in her care something so essential, so crucial to who he was? At the same time, it would have explained certain things, the distance she felt in her son, that inward turning she had sensed in Luke, the moodiness.

God, she thought. She'd been such a fool for going on this trip, for opening up this Pandora's box of secrets. Why couldn't she have left well enough alone?

Chapter 12

She was still trying to get her mind around all that TJ had told her when a tow truck pulled off the highway in front of her a little ways. It began to back up, its reverse bell clanging loudly like a wounded goose—*awnk, awnk, awnk*. The truck came to rest a few feet in front of her car. A tall, bearded man wearing a baseball cap jumped down from the cab and walked up to her window. He was carrying a flashlight in one hand, a clipboard in the other.

"What's the problem, lady?" he asked, shining the light in her face.

"My problem is I've been waiting here for two hours," she replied icily.

"I tried calling."

"Really?"

"Ah huh. It's been real busy."

Elizabeth wasn't in a forgiving mood. She was pissed at the stupid deer, at herself for having opened a can of worms by calling TJ, at having to wait on the side of the highway all this time.

"What's the point of having Triple A if *you* people are just going to show up whenever it suits you? And get that damn light out of my face."

He averted the light. "Like I said, ma'am, I've been crazy busy tonight."

"And I've been waiting here for two hours. All alone. In the dark. So don't give me any crap about how busy you've been."

"Lady," he said, holding up two hands in surrender, "you just need to take a step back and calm yourself down."

His telling her to calm down hit a raw nerve.

"Don't you tell me to calm down," she cried, pointing a finger at him.

"Suit yourself. Can I see your Triple A membership card, ma'am?" he said, his tone so polite she thought he was making fun of her.

"Two hours and I don't get so much as an 'I'm sorry'?"

He shone the flashlight on his clipboard. "Says here I got the call at seventeen-forty hours, and it's just shy of nineteen hundred now," he said with a smile that made her want to slap him. "According to what Mrs. Pickens taught me in math, that's only an hour and twenty minutes."

"Are you calling me a liar?"

"I'm just giving you the facts, ma'am."

"I want your supervisor's name."

He grinned again and pushed his cap back on his head. "Why that'd be me, ma'am. I'm an independent contractor."

"This is bullshit. Do you hear me—*bullshit*!"

"Whoa, lady," the man said, staring up the highway behind her. "Now we can do this one of two ways. You can calm down and I can try to help you. Or I can get back in my truck and leave your sorry ass here to wait some more. Makes no difference to me."

Elizabeth felt the veins in her neck throb with anger. She wanted to scream, to howl with rage. She wanted to punch her fist through the already-broken windshield. But she got the sense this guy meant business. Finally, she swallowed her pride, took her AAA card out of her wallet and handed it to him without bothering to look at him.

"Now whyn't you tell me what happened?" he said.

"I told them already," she said.

"How about you tell me?"

"I hit a deer."

"Can you start the car?"

"I don't know."

"All right, wait for me to give you the okay." He went around to the front of her car, shone the light at the damage. She heard him let out with a high-pitched whistle.

"Go ahead and crank 'er over."

She turned the ignition and the engine started right up. The man disappeared beneath the front of her car. "Okay," he shouted above the engine noise, "turn the wheel back and forth. Real slow." As she did so, a terrible grinding noise came from underneath the car, like a spoon caught in a garbage disposal, and the steering wheel actually shook in her hands. After a few minutes, he came back around to the driver's side and leaned into the window.

"You can go ahead and turn the engine off."

Up close she saw that he appeared to be in his forties. He didn't have an actual beard but a scraggly goatee combined with the fact that he hadn't shaved for a couple of days. His eyes, of some dusky hue she couldn't make out in the dark, looked glassy, out of focus, heavy lidded. Over the breast pocket of his jacket a name was stitched in white thread: *Stu*, she read from the lights of the on-coming traffic.

"So what's the verdict?"

"Your front end's all busted to hell. Got yourself a broken tie-rod at the very least."

"Is it drivable?"

"Not unless you want to kill yourself."

"Can you fix it then?" she asked.

"There's not much I can't fix, lady. By the way, you got yourself a bloody nose," he said touching his own nose.

"Yeah, I know."

He glanced into the car and frowned.

"For some reason your air bag didn't deploy. Anyways, I'll have to tow it back to my garage."

"How far is that?"

"About thirty miles."

She didn't like the thought of getting stuck at some hick-town service station where it would take forever to fix. She remembered seeing the sign for Memphis earlier.

"Could you tow it to Memphis?"

He snorted at the suggestion. "Memphis is a good two hours. If you want, I could tow it over to Brevard. Save you a trip."

"Save me a trip? What are you talking about?"

"I mean if you got some place over there you'd prefer to work on your car."

She had no idea what he was talking about. "I suppose you should just tow it back to your place and we'll go from there."

"There's not much there for you."

"I won't be staying."

"It's up to you."

He returned to his truck and backed up, then jumped out and began to hook her car up. He walked back to her window.

"It's against the law to sit in a car when it's being towed. You'll need to get in the truck with me."

"Of course," she said, getting out of the car. "What about the deer?"

"Deer?"

"I just thought we should make sure—" she said, turning to look back up the highway. But the animal was nowhere to be seen. "It was right there. Dead."

"Probably just stunned it," the man said. "That happens. I hit one with the wrecker and the thing just bounced off and kept on going. Deer ain't the brightest of God's creatures."

Elizabeth reached back in the car and grabbed her pocketbook and walked up to the tow truck. From the lights over the wrecker she saw "Tidrow's Garage" painted along the door. She climbed into the passenger side. The cab had a certain vaguely familiar aroma to it, a smell which reminded her of one she'd sometimes detect in Luke's room. Then it dawned on her what it was: pot. *Great*, she thought. She was being chauffeured around by some stoned hillbilly. She wondered if she should call AAA back and just tell them to send somebody else. But how much longer would that take? Instead, she just decided to take her chances with this guy. After a while, he climbed into the truck and off they went.

They drove in silence for a while. She glanced over at him once. He had a gold hoop in his right ear and a prominent Adam's apple. She decided to try being friendly. "By the way, Stu, I'm Elizabeth."

He looked over at her and gave her a blank expression.

"Gabe," he said.

"What?"

"Name's Gabe."

"But your jacket—"

"Belonged to a guy used to work for me."

"Well, pleased to meet you, Gabe," she said.

"You're bleeding again. Here," he said, offering her a rag he pulled out from his back pocket. "Put this on your nose and squeeze hard. And tilt your head back."

The rag stank of oil and antifreeze, but she squeezed her nose with it and tilted her head back.

They rode the rest of the way in silence. After half an hour, the man pulled off the highway. He drove though a small town that had a Wendy's and a Pizza Hut and a convenience store, as well as a half dozen other stores that were closed for the night. There was a bar named Sully's that was still open and beside it a dilapidated old mansion called the Fairmont Inn. They continued beyond the town center for a couple miles, out into a mountainous, heavily wooded countryside before pulling into a service station. The man backed her car along the side of the garage, edging it into a chain-link-fenced yard where several other smashed autos rested. A spotlight illuminated the area. He got out, lowered the car, began unhitching the chains, while Elizabeth grabbed her pocketbook and climbed down. From somewhere behind the garage, she heard a high-pitched yelping.

"Now what?" she asked the man when he'd finished unhitching the car.

"I can take a look at it first thing in the morning," he replied.

"No, I mean what do we do now."

"*We?*"

"What am I supposed to do?"

He offered her another one of his blank expressions, which seemed to be his default expression. "Isn't somebody going to drive over to pick you up?" he asked.

"Drive over from where?"

"Brevard."

"What's Brevard?"

"Aren't you from there?"

"No. I'm from Connecticut. Didn't you notice my license plates?"

"The dispatcher told me you were from Brevard."

He headed back over to his tow truck and reached in and picked up his clipboard. "Says right here," he explained, thumping his forefinger on the clipboard, "you were from Brevard. Two towns west of here. I assumed you were going to call and have somebody come and pick you up."

"You've obviously mistaken me for somebody else."

"I didn't make any mistake. I was told there was a vehicle on I-Forty just past exit one-oh-seven heading west. That's where you were, lady."

"Well, obviously *somebody's* made a mistake," Elizabeth said, trying to stand her ground. "So how do you plan to rectify it?"

"Rectify it?" he repeated.

"That means—"

"I know what it means, lady," he snapped. "What would you like me to do?"

"Do you have a loaner car?"

He smirked at that. "No, lady, I don't have any loaners."

"Well, is there a motel in town? Someplace I can stay until I can straighten this out tomorrow."

"There's the Fairmont. But you wouldn't want to stay there."

"Why not?"

"On account of it's a flop house for drunks and dopers."

"Okay. I'll make this as simple as I can for you. Where's the nearest motel that isn't a flop house?"

"Over in Crossville they got a Super Eight."

"How far is that?"

He shrugged. "Maybe an hour."

"An hour! There's nothing closer?"

He wagged his head in a way that suggested he took delight in her situation.

"Could you take me there?"

"Not tonight, I can't. I've been on the road since two yesterday morning and I haven't even eaten yet."

"Far be it from me to spoil your dinner," she said. "So is there a taxi in town?"

He laughed. "Where do you think you are, lady? New York?"

"First of all, enough with the 'lady' business. I told you my name's Elizabeth. And no, I wouldn't mistake this shithole for New York," she sniped. She felt almost as if she'd parachuted into one of those dopey comedies where the city slicker finds herself stranded out in the boonies and at the mercy of yokels who got their kicks toying with them. "So what's Plan B?"

"I don't have a Plan B. Like I said, I thought somebody was picking you up."

"What would you suggest I do?"

He removed his hat and scratched his head furiously. His hair was matted to his skull and thinning in front.

"I got an extra bed," he said, indicating with a nod the double-wide trailer just to the right of the garage. She had a fleeting image of the corpses of women rotting in the crawl space beneath the trailer and untold horrors waiting for her if she set foot inside.

"I wouldn't want to impose on you like that."

"No imposition," he replied.

"How about if I made it worth your while to drive me over to Crossburg?"

He stared at her with a look that made her worry he thought she was offering something other than money.

"What I mean is, I'd pay you to drive me over to Crossburg," she quickly added.

"Crossville," he corrected.

"Whatever. How does a hundred dollars sound?"

"Sounds good. But it'll have to be tomorrow."

"Two hundred then?"

"Listen, la— Sorry, Elizabeth," he said, sarcastically pronouncing her name. "I don't care how much you paid me. I'm dead on my feet and the last thing I want to do is drive an hour over and another back. I have a spare room. You're welcome to it. There's a lock on the door, if that's what you got a hair up your ass about."

"I don't have a *hair* up my ass," she retorted. "I just don't want to put you out."

"I told you, you're not putting me out. It's up to you though," he said with another one of his irritating shrugs. Then he turned and started walking toward his trailer.

"Wait. Where are you going?"

"To make supper," he replied over his shoulder. "Have a drink. Then hit the hay."

He kept walking toward the trailer. Finally she realized he was actually going to leave her standing there in the dark of the parking lot.

"All right, hold your horses," she called after him. "Let me get my things first."

She found the trailer surprisingly neat and clean, with a woman's fastidiousness and attention to detail. There were plastic place mats on the tiny kitchen table, as well as matching hen and rooster salt and pepper shakers. The eat-in kitchen led onto a slightly larger living room with a couch and a couple of chairs, a coffee table, a large-screen HDTV. On the coffee table lay several books, neatly stacked. Everything was picked up, nothing out of place. And there wasn't the least scent of rotting bodies or other depravities.

"Make yourself to home," he said, indicating the couch. "The head's down the hall if you need to use it."

He hung his coat in a small closet to the left of the front door, then went over to the sink and washed his hands. He got out some pans and turned on the gas stove. From the fridge he took out a brown, deli-wrapped package.

"I'm making hot dogs," he called to her. "You want some?"

Only then did she realize she hadn't eaten. "Sure. If it's not too much trouble."

"No trouble at all."

She watched as he threw several hot dogs into a pan. He also got out a Tupperware bowl filled with something which he placed to his nose and sniffed before dumping it into the pan alongside the hot dogs. Then he opened the freezer and took out a tray of ice cubes. He removed a dish towel from one of the drawers, cracked the tray of ice into it, and wrapped the cloth around the ice. He headed down the hall and came back in a second, picked up the cloth and brought it over to her.

"Here. Use this for your nose," he said, handing her the cloth-covered ice.

"I'm all right."

"You'll have a couple of shiners tomorrow if you don't. You probably will in any case. But this will keep the swelling down. And here's a Band-Aid you can put on later. And a couple of Tylenol for the pain."

"Thank you," she offered, almost grudgingly. She took the ice and applied it to her nose, which ached for a while before going numb as the ice started to take effect.

"What would you like to drink?" he asked. "I got some Coke or iced tea. Or do you want a drink-drink?"

"Coke is fine."

He put some of the ice in a glass, poured some soda in, then brought it over to her.

"Thanks," she said, tossing the Tylenol into her mouth and washing it down with the Coke. "You live here all alone?"

He looked at her and smiled.

"Used to have a cat but I think he got eaten," he offered.

"Eaten?"

"We got coyotes around here."

He headed back over to the kitchen and from a cupboard above the sink removed a fifth of Jack Daniels. He poured himself a sizable drink, then topped it off with Coke. He stirred the drink with his index finger, then sucked on the finger. With one hand he tended to the food, while with the other he sipped his drink. Watching him, Elizabeth thought how her strange life had gotten qualitatively stranger in the past few hours. Here she was stranded in the trailer of some guy named Stu or Gabe, in some town in Tennessee she was equally ignorant of, and having just learned that her son might have been gay, or at the very least had ceased being "interested" in women, whatever the hell that meant. The once-familiar lineaments of her life were now completely alien, unrecognizable to her. She'd recently read about a woman in France who'd had a complete face transplant. This is what it must have felt like, Elizabeth thought, for that woman to look in a mirror for the first time. *Who the hell is that?*

"I don't want you to think I don't appreciate this," she called over to him.

"Oh, I can tell you're just brimming with appreciation."

"No, I am. Really. I guess I must have sounded a little bitchy earlier."

"A little?"

"All right, more than a little. It's just that I was frustrated with hitting that deer. And to tell you the truth, I'd just gotten some upsetting news."

She immediately regretted having shared this. Gabe looked over his shoulder at her. She thought he was going to ask her about the upsetting news and she'd decided she wasn't going to get into any of that, that she'd say it was something she didn't want to talk about. She was a little surprised, though, that he just nodded and turned back to the stove without asking a thing.

"I'm used to highway people," he said, over the noise of the sizzling hot dogs.

"Highway people?"

"They're always in such a big rush to get from one place to another and when they break down they think you're supposed to drop everything and come running."

"Isn't that your job, to help them?"

"Yeah, to help them. But I'm not anybody's lackey."

The guy obviously had an attitude problem, Elizabeth felt. She decided not to press the issue. Instead she glanced at the books on the coffee table. There were several glossy ones, including one called *Scenes from the South*, another that was a pictorial history of Tennessee Civil War battlefields. What caught her eye, though, was on the far wall, to the left of the big TV. Three framed charcoal sketches, each about sixteen inches across. Two were of young girls, the older one on the left perhaps fourteen and stunning, the younger seven or eight. The third was of a pretty woman in her thirties, who resembled the girls enough so that Elizabeth assumed it was their mother. The picture had the woman sitting on porch steps, in shorts and a tank-top, knees bent, arms wrapped around her legs, while she stared off into the distance. The woman had long blonde hair.

"Who drew the pictures?" Elizabeth called over to him.

He turned, followed her gaze. "Oh, those," he said, as if he had forgotten about them. "Me."

"They're very good."

"They're strikingly competent," he replied, and went back to fixing dinner.

"Who are they?"

"My family."

"Your wife is lovely," Elizabeth said.

"*Ex*-wife."

"And those are your daughters?"

"Ah huh. The younger one's Jo. She lives over in Nashville with Abby and the proctologist," he said.

"Your older daughter's beautiful. What's her name?"

"Kelly."

"Your ex is married to a proctologist?"

He looked over his shoulder at Elizabeth. "He's not really a proctologist. I call him that on account of him being a royal pain in the ass," he offered straight-faced.

Trying to make conversation, Elizabeth said, "Do you get to see your daughters much?"

"What, are we all buddy-buddy now?"

"I apologized about before. But if you'd rather not talk . . ."

"I get Jo for the summer and one weekend a month. But she's a teenager. Poor kid's bored out of her mind over here. And you?"

"And me what?"

"You got kids?"

She wanted to keep things simple. She didn't want him nosing around in her business or having to explain any of her plans.

"A son," she replied.

"How old is he?"

"Twenty-two," she said without missing a beat.

"And what do you do for a living, Elizabeth?"

"I'm a lawyer."

He grinned at that.

"What?"

"Somehow that doesn't come as a surprise. How many hot dogs you want?"

She told him one was fine. When dinner was ready, he had her sit at the small kitchen table. He served the hot dogs without buns, along with pork and beans and potato salad, Doritos and apple sauce. He refilled her glass with Coke, topped his off with Jack Daniels, then sat down. The table was so small their knees bumped.

"Sorry," he said. "I'm not used to other people's knees. And you're pretty tall. I'm guessing five-ten?"

"Five eleven and three-quarters."

As he took a sip of his drink, Elizabeth noticed his wedding ring.

"Why don't you just round it off to six and be done with it."

"I always felt too big. That quarter of an inch seemed somehow important when I was in high school. My mother used to call me Big Bird."

He stared at her, nodded without commenting, then dug in, wolfing the food down, using the side of his fork to cut his hot dogs and washing it down with big gulps from his Jack and Coke. Elizabeth watched him unawares for a moment. He was obviously used to eating alone. He kept his hat on, a thing frayed and stained with sweat rings, the brim blackened from greasy fingerprints. His cheeks were pitted by old acne scars, and his eyes, a not-un-attractive rust-brown color, were heavy and somnolent, as if he hadn't gotten enough sleep in a long while. His mouth was full and framed by deep fissures like parentheses. He reminded her a little of a young Jeff Bridges.

"How's the nose?" he asked.

"Hurts."

He stared at it, then reached out and put his thumb and forefinger on either side of her nose and tried to wiggle it.

"Ouch," she cried.

"I don't think it's broken."

"Are you a doctor?"

"I broke mine twice and you could feel the bones moving around in there. And I doubt you'll need stitches."

She watched him take a drink of his Jack and Coke and it made her long for a scotch over ice.

He must have noticed her watching him. "You sure you don't want a drink?" he asked. "It might loosen you up."

"Why? Do I look like I need loosening up?"

"So where y'all headed, Elizabeth?"

"New Mexico."

"What for?"

"Business," was all she said.

"Don't business people usually fly?"

"It was a last minute sort of thing."

"And your husband?"

She saw him staring at her wedding ring.

"What about him?"

"He all right with his wife driving out to New Mexico in a car that old?"

"Always been dependable before."

"Car or husband?" he said with a grin. He had this odd habit of staring right at you, without blinking or looking away, so that it was almost like a challenge to see who would blink first. Elizabeth let her gaze drop to her plate.

The conversation seemed to lag after this, and they ate the rest of their meal in silence.

"You want some more?" he asked when they were finished.

"No, I'm good. Thanks."

He got up and served himself another helping.

She took out her cell phone and said, "I probably ought to check in with my husband. Let him know where I am," she explained. "By the way, where am I?"

"Earl's Creek."

She excused herself, and went outside to call her husband. While the phone rang, she realized that whatever animal it was before had now fallen silent.

"Zack, it's me," she said when her husband came on. "Listen, I had an little accident."

"My God!" he cried. "Are you all right?"

"Yes, I'm fine. I hit a deer. But the car is messed up. It had to be towed."

"Jesus, Elizabeth. Are you sure you're all right?"

"I'm fine, really."

"I was worried something like this could happen. And you all alone. Maybe I should fly down."

"No, don't do that. I'm all right. They're going to fix the car tomorrow and I'll be on my way."

"Where are you?"

She knew that if she told him she was staying at a complete stranger's house he'd be worried, so she lied and said she was staying at a Holiday Inn. She realized that in the past few years she'd taken to lying to Zack as a matter of course, that lying—or at least avoiding the truth—had become the norm. At one time in their marriage she had always told the truth. Zack had been her closest confidant, her best friend. What had happened, she wondered. How had they drifted so far apart? They talked for a while, he about his day, her about her travels. She thought about telling him about her conversation with TJ but she didn't have the energy to get into that now.

After a while, she said, "I should go."

"I miss you."

"I miss you, too," she replied. Oddly, she felt closer to Zack now than she had in a long time. Maybe it was the distance, or the fact that she felt so isolated out here. But in any case, she longed to be held by him, to make love to him, and then to fall asleep in his arms. She couldn't recall the last time they had fallen asleep together.

"Be safe. I don't know what I'd do if I something were to happen to you, too."

"Don't worry. I'll be home soon."

Inside she found Gabe doing the dishes.

"Let me give you a hand," she offered.

"You don't have to."

"No, it's the least I could do."

He washed, while she dried.

"Did you always draw?" she asked.

"Since I was a little kid. I wasn't much at sports so I drew and played guitar."

"So how does an artist end up in a place called Earl's Creek, Tennessee, running a garage?"

"I wouldn't exactly call myself an artist. I just dabble. Fool around."

"You seem pretty talented to me."

"I used to think I was. I was even planning on going to art school."

"What happened?"

"A wife and two kids happened. My old man gave me some good advice. He said, 'Gabe, you want to eat, you'd better get your ass out there and get a job.'"

He looked over at her and smiled, one slightly buck tooth catching on his lower lip so that it gave to his face the mischievous look of the kid in school who was always cutting up. The class clown.

"How long have you been divorced?"

"Four years."

"That's a long time to still be wearing your wedding ring," she said.

He stared at it for a moment. Then he finished the rest of his drink with a single gulp and dropped the glass into the soapy water. Instead of answering he said, "So what's this business out in New Mexico?"

"Just some stuff I have to take care of."

"Some stuff?" he said, eying her. "What are you, smuggling dope?"

"Some loose ends I got to see to."

He held her gaze for a moment, then said, "You're probably tired."

He led her down the hall to a small room on the right. From a closet he got her an extra blanket and a towel.

"In case you get cold. Like I said, bathroom's just down on your right. You need anything, give a yell. I'm a light sleeper." He started to turn away, then said, "Oh, like I said, there's a lock on the door. You won't hurt my feelings if you use it."

"That won't be necessary," she said.

The first thing she did once in the room was lock the door as quietly as she could. A tiny window looked out onto a black postage stamp of night. She got into bed fully clothed, including her running shoes just in case she had to make a fast getaway, and she lay there for a moment allowing her body a chance to acclimate. Yet she was no longer as worried about this Gabe as she'd first been. He didn't seem so bad, just quirky, with a chip on his shoulder. Besides, she'd been nasty with him, so what could she expect? She thought again of her conversation with TJ. She shouldn't have called her. She had no right to do that to the poor girl, to say the things she had. More importantly, she didn't know what she was going to do with what she'd told her about Luke.

* * *

Something woke her in the middle of the night. She lay in the stuffy darkness of the tiny room and tried to get her bearings. It was music, the sound coming from just on the other side of the wall. A voice singing *a capella*. After a while she recognized the song as Harry Chapin's "Cat's in the Cradle."

Chapter 13

By the time she woke, the sun was already streaming into her room. Disoriented by the four narrow walls, Elizabeth thought for a moment she was back in her college dorm room, hungover from a night of drinking. Her nose felt tender when she touched it, and her neck was stiff. She made her way into the bathroom and inspected her face in the mirror. There was a small reddish contusion along the bridge of her nose, but no black eyes, thank God. Her hair looked a mess, tangled and unwashed, her eyes blood-shot.

The trailer was silent as she shuffled into the kitchen, still in the clothes she'd worn to bed. Near the coffee pot she spotted a note. *Help yourself. There's milk in the fridge.* She found a cup and poured herself some coffee and walked over to the kitchen window. She peered out, the day offering the unrelenting brightness of an operating room. She heard angry metallic noises (*brrrrp, brrrrp, awwwkk*) coming from the garage next door.

She headed back toward her bedroom, intending to take a shower. As she approached the bathroom, though, she happened to glance into the bedroom at the end of the hall. The door being ajar, she took this as an invitation to poke her head in. The bed was neatly made, the edges tightly tucked in as if this Gabe had been in the military. The room smelled heavily of cigarettes with a sweetish undercurrent of dope permeating the air. On the night stand sat a framed photograph of a woman holding the hand of a little girl. In black and white, the photo showed the two walking along some beach. Elizabeth glanced over her shoulder before going over and picking up the photo and inspecting it. The woman was quite pretty with long blonde hair that fell loosely about her shoulders; she appeared younger than the person Elizabeth had seen in the sketch the previous night, but it obviously was the same woman. The little girl, on the other hand, was four or five and might have been the older daughter, but Elizabeth couldn't really tell.

Right then, Elizabeth heard footsteps on the stairs leading up to the front door, and she had just enough time to put the picture down and hurry out of the bedroom.

"So what's the story?" she asked nervously as Gabe entered the trailer.

He didn't answer but instead headed into the kitchen where he poured himself a cup of coffee. She followed him. She noticed that the goatee had a reddish hue to it, with streaks of gray mixed in, and that the gold hoop in his ear glittered in the sunlight.

"Well, I got good news and bad news," he offered. "What do you want first?"

"How about if you just give it to me all at once."

"I called over to a junkyard in Crossville. They got a ninety-six Saab nine hundred, in good condition. We can get you a quarter panel, bumper, grill, a hood. Even a tie rod that's in serviceable condition, at least so I'm told. Bad news is you got yourself at least one cracked motor mount."

"Is that serious?"

"That's what holds your engine in place. Like so," he explained, making two fists and putting one on top of the other. "Every time you hit the gas, the torque of the crankshaft shifts the motor a little." He turned one fist one way, the other another, as if he were wringing a chicken's neck. "Engine's not stable."

"So what do we do?"

"I'll have to order some. Thing is, Saab's a pain in the ass to get parts for."

"How long are we talking?"

"It'll only take me a day or so to put on the parts we got. But it's all gonna depend on how long it takes to get the motor mounts. You can't light a fire under those damn Swedes."

"Do you think the car's even worth fixing?"

"That's a whole 'nother story," he said, stroking his goatee. "Insurance company's probably gonna declare it a total. Still, your engine seems like it's running okay. And the car looks in decent shape otherwise. But it's your call."

Elizabeth stood there thinking how stupid her plan seemed to her now. Driving that old car across country.

"Tell you what," Gabe said. "Let me make a couple of calls and see how fast I can get the motor mounts. Who knows? Maybe we'll get lucky. How's the beak?" he asked, touching his nose.

"A little sore."

"Put some more ice on it. You hungry? I got cereal. Eggs if you want to make 'em."

"No, I'm good."

"Take a shower. There's the TV. Even got internet. All the amenities of a five-star hotel," he offered with a grin.

She felt better after her shower. She fixed herself a bowl of cereal and then sat in the living room on the couch, facing the sketches on the wall. As she was looking at the woman and her daughters, Elizabeth's phone rang. It was Joan.

"How are you, kiddo," Joan said.

"All right."

"I've managed to work things out with Warren," her friend explained. "If you can get back here tomorrow, he's agreed to let you take a mental health leave and return when you're feeling better."

"Mental health? This isn't about my mental health. I'm trying to find answers about Luke."

"Listen, just get your butt back here and Warren's willing to forgive and forget."

"I can't come back. Not yet anyway."

"Then I can't promise you'll have a job when you do get back. Do you understand what I'm saying, kiddo?"

"I understand."

"What the hell are you doing, Elizabeth? You're throwing away your career. And all for what?"

"I appreciate your going to bat for me, Joan. I really do."

"Where are you, anyway?" her friend asked. "Zack said something about you're going out to see where Luke died?"

"Yes," Elizabeth replied.

"What on earth for?"

"I thought it might give me some answers."

"To what?"

"To Luke's mental state. His death."

"When did you come up with this idea?"

"I don't know. It was brewing for a while."

"How come you didn't tell me?"

"I didn't decide until the night I left."

She glanced at the sketches on the opposite wall again, of the man's ex-wife and his two girls. In the bright daylight, the work didn't seem quite as skillful, the hands now appearing slightly clumsy and inept, the way drawn hands can look when done by someone lacking real talent. The eyes, though, were still quite good; they remained filled with emotion. Especially those of the woman. Elizabeth was struck by this deep reservoir of melancholy in the woman's eyes that the artist had managed to capture.

"Are you sure you ought to be doing this?" Joan asked.

"I'm no longer sure about anything. But I feel I have to do this."

Joan paused, then her voice stiffened as she said, "Zack told me you thought Luke's death wasn't an accident?"

"Jesus!" Elizabeth moaned. "He shouldn't have told you that."

"He was just concerned about you. We all are."

"I didn't say it *wasn't* an accident. I only said that Luke was acting a little weird that summer, that's all. The last thing I want is for people to think . . ."

"You know I wouldn't say anything."

Elizabeth then thought about what she'd heard the previous night from TJ. About Luke. Had there been rumors at school, she wondered. Had other kids known what she was only now coming to realize? Maybe it was common knowledge, and she and Zack were the only ones in the dark. That's, of course, if it were true.

"Joan, did your girls ever hear anything about Luke?" she asked. "You know, rumors. Gossip."

"What kind of rumors?"

"About what girls he liked. Who he was seeing. That sort of thing."

"He didn't give any other girls a chance," Joan said with a laugh. "He was always with TJ."

"But you didn't hear anything?"

"No, I don't think so. What're you getting at, Elizabeth?"

"Nothing."

"Well, obviously, there's something you're not telling me."

Finally she decided she'd just come straight out with it. What did it matter now? What did any of it matter?

"Did your girls ever hear anything about Luke not being interested in girls?"

Joan let out a little cry of astonishment. "You mean like he was *gay?*"

"I spoke to TJ last night. She said Luke was no longer interested in women."

"She said *that?*"

"Yes."

"Jesus. Why would she tell you such a thing?"

"I guess because I pushed her. I called her to ask about her and Luke the summer before he died, if they had started seeing each other again. I asked her why they broke up. I kept pushing her and that's what she ended up telling me."

"That he was gay?"

"She didn't say that exactly. She just said he wasn't interested in girls any more."

"Isn't that the same thing?"

"Did your girls ever hear any rumors? You can be honest with me."

"No, nothing. In fact, Brianna used to say half the girls in school had a crush on him. I'm sure if they'd heard anything they would've told me. Geez, that's strange."

"Yeah, I know."

"Do *you* think it was true?" asked Joan.

"I never would have thought that before."

"Geez, I still can't believe it. Luke, gay?"

"I don't care so much that he might have been gay as I do the fact that I didn't know."

"It doesn't make any difference now, does it?"

"I'm his mother. If he was gay, I should have known."

"Do you think I know everything about my two? They let you know only what they want to. Whatever it is you're trying to find out there," her friend offered, "just forget about it and come on home. I don't know how long I can keep Warren at bay."

"I can't. I'm in this too deep," she replied.

"You ask me, you're in way over your head."

Outside she heard the impact wrench again, tearing things apart, as if it were dismantling her past, moment by moment.

"Listen, I have to be in court in half an hour," Joan said. "Call me if you need to talk. If you need anything at all. Okay?"

"Sure. Thanks, Joan."

"I hope you know what you're doing, Elizabeth."

She didn't know what she was doing. That was the problem. The only thing she was certain of was the fact that she had to keep going. She had to follow Luke's trail. She had to stand over the spot where he'd died. After that, she wasn't sure.

She glanced at the sketches of the two girls again. The eyes of the younger one were innocent, carefree, vibrant. Those of the older one, however, looked like the eyes of the mother, hard and world-weary. Already cynical eyes, though the girl couldn't have been more than fifteen in the picture.

This sense of muted anger, frustration, perhaps even fear haunting them. It seemed obvious to Elizabeth that she had been an unhappy child. Elizabeth wondered why, and if this Gabe, when he drew those eyes, realized he was capturing that unhappiness. Then she thought about whether Luke had been happy. He was when he was little, a happy, untroubled, normal little boy. But somewhere along the line he had morphed into someone who was, if not outright unhappy, at least a brooding, introspective, often distant young man. Was that simply a factor of who he was? Or did his personality change have anything to do with what TJ had said. If he were gay, it would make perfect sense that his moodiness would have had everything to do with the burdensome secret he carried around with him. How could one hide such a fact—from his friends, his girlfriend, his own parents—and not be troubled.

She thought of what Joan had said to her. That she was in this way too deep. Over her head. That line Luke had written in his diary: *duc in altum*. What did he mean by that? What was he thinking when he wrote it? She decided to call Father Paul. He knew Latin. He might know something else.

"Well, hello, stranger," he said.

"How are you, Father Paul?"

"I'm fine. Question is, how are you? We missed seeing you this week."

She didn't want to try to explain the past several days. "I've been busy. How's Fabiana?"

"She's improving. She's asked after you."

"Give her my best."

"I will. Have you thought any more about my offer?"

"I've had other things on my mind. Can I ask you something?"

"Sure."

"What does *duc in altum* mean?"

"It's means 'to put out into the deep.'"

"Is that all?"

"It has a biblical reference. Simon and Peter had been fishing all night and had come up empty-handed. But then Jesus tells them to try again, to put their nets out into the deep. At first Simon was skeptical but he went along with it and this time when they pulled up their nets they were full of fish."

"But what does it *mean*?"

"It means to go deeper. To have faith in something unseen. Why?"

"My son wrote it in his diary."

"When I was in seminary and had doubts about continuing, Father Tom, my spiritual director, used to tell me '*Duc in altum*, Paul.' He wanted me to dig deeper."

"In what way?"

"Into myself. Sometimes we need to be reminded that what we're searching for will be there if only we go deep enough."

"Thanks, Paul. Give my best to Fabiana."

* * *

Around noon, Gabe returned. He went over to the sink and began scrubbing his hands. A bluish-gray lather splattered over the sink.

"So what's the verdict?" asked Elizabeth.

"Is that one of your lawyer jokes?" He dried his hands and went over to the fridge and grabbed a Bud Light, popped the top, and took a long, hungry swig. "We're screwed. That is, *you're* screwed."

"What's the matter?"

"They won't be able to get the parts in for a week," he said. "That's best case scenario."

Elizabeth's heart sank. "So where's the nearest place I could rent a car?"

"Crossville has an Avis. But you're not thinking of driving all the way out there in a rental? Hell, that'll cost you an arm and a leg."

"What other choice do I have?"

"You could fly."

"I'd still have to rent a car once I got out there." Besides, if she flew she couldn't follow Luke's trail.

"But it might be cheaper in the long run."

"Could you give me a lift over to Crossville?"

"I suppose," he replied, tilting his head back and taking another long drink of his beer. His sharp Adam's apple bobbed up and down as he swallowed. He finished the beer and set the empty on the counter. "What are you going to do with your car?"

"I don't know. What's it worth?"

"As is, a coupla hundred for parts maybe. If I fixed it up, I could probably get two grand for it."

"Tell you what. You give me a ride over there and you can keep it."

"Even in the shape it's in, it's got to be worth a hellava lot more than my towing charge."

"We'll call it even. For all your trouble."

"What trouble?"

"For putting me up. And for putting up with me," she said with a smile.

"You weren't so bad."

"For a highway person," she said with a smirk. "When could you drive me over?"

He removed his hat and scratched his head. "Don't have anything pressing right now."

So she gathered her things and tossed them into the duffel bag. Before they left, she went out and got the title out of the glove compartment and signed it over to him. Then they headed out to his Nissan King Cab. He had to clear out a lot of junk from the passenger side, tools and papers and empty fast-food bags, as well as an acoustic guitar, and throw it all into the back.

"Pardon the mess," he said.

"I appreciate your doing this."

The day was awash with light as they drove along the highway, an autumnal crispness making the air thin, almost brittle. They passed stretches of pine forest, long, sloping fields, broad, glimmering lakes, sunlight fracturing off the water into millions of sharp fragments. Her eyes hurt and she wished she'd remembered her sunglasses, another thing she'd forgotten back in her car. She'd have to buy another pair somewhere. The desert would be very bright, and unforgiving she figured.

"Mind if I smoke?" he asked.

"Go ahead."

"I still don't get why you didn't just fly out to New Mexico?"

"I was in a hurry."

"Wouldn't it have been faster to take a plane?"

"Let's put it this way, I had to leave quickly or I wouldn't have gone," she explained.

"The mystery woman," he said, glancing over at her. "You sure do like playing your cards close to the vest."

She thought about just ignoring him or making up some lie. But what difference did it make if she confessed to some stranger she'd never see again?

"My son drove out to New Mexico last year. He was in a car accident. He died."

The matter-of-factness with which she stated this startled not only Gabe but herself. He turned and stared across at her, his cigarette poised about an inch from his lips. He drew his eyebrows together in a "you're kidding me" frown. Then he said, "You're kidding me?"

"I wish I was."

"Jesus. I'm sorry to hear that. How old was he?"

"Twenty-one."

"God, that's terrible."

"Yes, it has been."

"So is this some sort of lawsuit thing? Is that what you're going out there for?"

"No. It's personal."

"How do you mean 'personal'?"

She wondered how to explain things so that it didn't sound quite so weird. So that *she* didn't sound quite so weird. But it *was* weird. All of it. Finally she decided she'd simply tell the truth, as much as she knew of the truth, and let the chips fall where they may. "I wanted to see where he died."

Gabe waited for more and when she didn't say anything, he asked, "Why?"

She reached into the backseat and from her duffel bag she removed her notebook. "I wanted to follow the route he took out there. I made a list of the places he stopped based on his credit card receipts and I'm trying to stop where he stopped."

"Why?" he asked again.

"I guess I thought it might provide some answers."

"But why now? You said it happened last year?"

"It's a long story."

"Crossville," he said, pointing down the highway with his cigarette, "is an hour's drive. I got plenty of time."

"You sure you want to hear this?"

"If you don't mind telling me."

So with that, she launched into telling him how for months she'd had all these questions about her son's death. How she couldn't piece together the facts. What he was doing down in New Mexico in the first place. How she'd called the sheriff's office down in Marrizozo but never got any straight answers. And then how by chance she met George Doucette along the side of the road. How after that she'd begun stopping at roadside memorials—*descansos*, she explained—reading the inscriptions, thinking about the stories of each of the dead, and how the dead person's loved ones had put up a memorial to their memory.

"What do roadside memorials have to do with your son?" Gabe asked.

"George said when he stops at one he feels a connection to his wife."

"A connection?"

"I know it must sound weird. Hell, it even sounds weird to me. But George suggested I go out to see where Luke had died. That it might help somehow."

"So you're doing this because some stranger told you to?"

"No," she replied, thinking it was about what her husband had told her. "I'm doing this because I thought it might help me."

"How?" Gabe asked.

She looked over at him again. He was staring straight ahead now, the brim of his baseball cap pulled down low. He was squinting into the sunlight, the fissures at the corners of his eyes more pronounced in the day. A pair of sunglasses hung over the visor but he seemed to prefer squinting. His eyes reminded Elizabeth of the eyes of his older daughter but without the anger and the fear.

"I suppose I had some crazy notion that it might give me some answers."

"What sort of answers? I thought you said it was an accident?"

"It was. But like I said there were a lot of things that didn't make sense. By the way, could I bum one of those?" she asked, pointing at his cigarette.

"I didn't know you smoked."

"I don't. Haven't since college."

He gave her a cigarette and his lighter. She lit up and took a deep drag, feeling the sweet swirl of nicotine make her head spin, her heart rev up. She hadn't realized how much she missed it. That feeling of her head floating.

"I'm figuring your husband wasn't too keen on you making this trip," Gabe said.

"Why do you say that?"

"Otherwise he'd be here with you, right?"

"No, he doesn't understand why I'm doing this. That's why I left in the middle of the night," she confessed. "Zack—that's my husband—thinks I dwell too much on the past as it is."

"You mean regarding your son?"

"He thinks I should get over it. Move on. As if you can snap your fingers and everything is fine." She glanced over at Gabe again, waiting for him to respond, to ask another question perhaps, but he didn't say anything, just looked straight ahead. He had a way of remaining silent that she found annoying. Here he'd gotten her to open up on the most sensitive of subjects, and now when she was ready to talk a little, he seemed as if he'd completely lost interest. A mile or two of highway slid beneath the truck before either spoke again.

"No comment?" she asked.

"What do you want me to say?"

"I don't know. Something. You're the one asking all the questions."

"I guess it's weird is all."

"What's weird?"

"All of it. You following your son out here. Stopping at roadside memorials. What did you call them again?"

"*Descansos.* Why is it so weird?"

"First of all, I wouldn't want any wife of mine driving cross country by herself. Too many nutcases out there. Not to mention crazy-ass deer." He smiled at his own joke.

"You sound like my husband," Elizabeth said.

"He's just being protective."

"Overly protective. The problem is we handle our grief in different ways. He goes to these grief counseling sessions at his church. For people who've lost children."

"What's wrong with that? If it helps him deal with it."

"Nothing, I suppose. It's just not me."

"So when did you tell your husband about this little trip of yours?"

"Day after I left."

Gabe put his lips together into a mock whistle.

"Seems like something you should've talked over."

"So in addition to being a mechanic and an artist and a doctor, you're a marriage counselor, too?" she chided.

"Just seems like a big decision to make on your own."

"I knew my husband would just try to talk me out of it," she explained. "When I'd first told him about meeting George he thought I was crazy."

"It does sound a little out there," Gabe said with a roll of his eyes.

"It's just that the things George said, they sort of clicked with me. It's hard to explain."

She turned down the window and threw the butt out. "Can I bum another cigarette?"

He handed her another cigarette and his lighter.

"Don't blame me for getting you hooked on cigarettes again. So what's your plan once you get out to New Mexico?"

"I don't *have* a plan," she snapped, a defensive edge slipping into her voice.

All his questions were now starting to get under her skin, and she was regretting that she'd told him anything. It made what she was doing sound foolish, which it probably was. But still. Who was he to question her motives? Elizabeth pursed her lips and glanced out the window. She saw a sign that said, "Memphis, 81 miles." The utter futility of her quest once again struck her. Maybe it was all of Gabe's questions. Maybe it was hitting the deer. In Memphis she could catch a plane home. Cut her losses. Try to patch up her marriage. Get on with her life. In some ways Gabe was right. Why on earth was she going through all this trouble? She'd get all the way out to New Mexico and then what? Mumble some words of prayer, words she wasn't even sure she believed in. Stare at a miserable piece of desert where she could say, *This is where Luke died.* What if she felt the same sort of emptiness and confusion she did when she visited his grave? What answers could she possibly hope to glean from going out there? About whether or not Luke was gay. About why he had gone there. About what he was searching for or what he wanted to tell her that night. Wasn't she doing this as much to mollify her own nagging guilt as anything? Wasn't she really just making a pilgrimage to the shrine of her almighty guilt?

"I'm a little tired. Would you mind just driving?" she said.

"Suit yourself."

* * *

Elizabeth pretended to respond to texts on her phone so she wouldn't have to talk any more. She'd already said way more than she wanted to. Talking about her motives for the trip had done exactly what she feared: it highlighted how ridiculous it was. They'd been driving for half an hour when the truck suddenly slowed as if it had run out of gas, and angled sharply toward the shoulder of the road.

"What's the matter?" she asked, looking over at Gabe.

"Didn't you see it back there?" he said, as the truck slowed to a jouncing stop, dust swirling up around them.

"See what?"

"One of those roadside things."

He opened the door and started to get out.

"Where are you going?"

"Come on."

"I don't want to. Let's get going."

Nonetheless, he got out and started walking back.

She waited in the truck for a good ten seconds, but when she realized that he wasn't returning, she got out and followed him.

"What do you think you're doing?" she called as she approached him. Gabe had stopped and was squatting in front of the cross. When she reached him, she saw that it was a plain white marker, one that had had a recent coat of paint applied to it. There was fresh paint on the ground around the base, too, and the thing gleamed in the sunlight like a piece of gristle. Where the two sections of the cross intersected was written *Anthony "Scooter" Bump*, with the dates, *1983–2001*, contained inside a small heart. At the left edge of the horizontal section, written at a forty-five degree angle, were the words, *Rest in Peace, Scooter*, while on the right, as if to create balance, it said, *Miss you always, Mom and Dad*.

"Is this what you had in mind?" Gabe asked, pointing at the cross.

"What are you talking about?"

"Putting up one of these things for your son."

"I don't know. I hadn't thought that far ahead," replied Elizabeth.

Gabe didn't say anything for a moment, just looked down at the cross. After a while, he said, "If it were my kid, I might do something like this."

"Something like what?"

"Put up one of these things," he said, pointing at the cross. "I'm not all that religious. But I think I'd want to do something like this, too."

"Really?"

"Ah huh. Funny but I never stopped at one of these things before. I've seen plenty, in my line of work and all. But never stopped."

"I hadn't either."

"Hell, he was just a kid," Gabe said, with a nod toward cross. "Wonder how it happened."

As she looked down at the spot where the life of Anthony "Scooter" Bump had come to a sudden and violent end, a memory flickered weakly in her mind, then caught with a *whoosh* like a burner on a gas stove suddenly erupting into flame. It was a few days after the incident in Wales when Luke had momentarily vanished at the train station. They were in the tiny rental car driving through the lush Irish countryside. The day was uncharacteristically sunny, the skies cloudless and blue. A day when it seemed as if nothing bad could happen, when all of life glowed with possibility. She sat in the passenger seat surveying the Fodor's, looking for signs for Cork, while Zack drove with his usual focused intensity. Luke sat in back, occupied by turns with a coloring book he'd brought along or flying the Spitfire, making plane noises. Her husband and her son appeared to have completely forgotten how close they'd come to tragedy. For them it was something that had never happened, or so it seemed. For Elizabeth though, while she tried to shake free of the incident, the near loss of their son continued to cast a pall over her consciousness. She pictured how close, how dangerously close, they'd come to disaster, to their happy little family being torn asunder. Every day she felt a dull ache in the pit of her stomach, what the miscarriage she'd suffered earlier in their marriage had felt like. An emptiness but one filled with pain. And at night she had terrible dreams of something bad happening to Luke.

Out of the blue, her son had asked from the back seat, "Mom?"

"Yes, sweetie?"

"What would have happened?"

She turned and looked at him. "What do you mean?"

"If you hadn't found me? Back there."

So he'd been thinking about it, too, she thought.

"We'd have kept looking until we had."

He stared at her, his small face both serious and innocent. "But what if you *didn't* find me?"

"We wouldn't have given up."

"Never?"

"No. Never," she said exchanging looks with Zack.

Luke appeared to chew on that for a moment. Then he said only, "Okay," and went back to his coloring, as if nothing had happened.

But she could remember thinking, What if they *hadn't* found him? How long *would* they have looked? How long would they have spent searching for him? They couldn't have stayed in Wales forever. When would the unrelenting demands of life, of jobs and responsibilities, of the necessity of returning home, of getting on with "life" have proven too weighty to ignore? She remembered continuing to stare at Luke, trying to burn in her memory everything about him. The exact honey color of his hair, the small cowlick in the front, the scar just under his chin where he'd fallen on the sidewalk at two. The consciously formed picture in her mind of her son was an insurance policy, a guarantee that she would *never* lose him, no matter what. That she would always remember him. As she stood now looking down at the cross along the highway, she could still see that image of Luke in the back seat of the car, head down, coloring. Her little boy. Her little Lukey. She felt a powerful wave of emotion wash over her, felt Luke closer and more real than he had in months, felt him as a palpable ache in her throat.

Her eyes started to tear up. She realized it was the second time in the past few weeks that she found herself crying in front of a complete stranger as they stood by the side of the road, in the presence of one of these damn memorials.

"Hey," Gabe said, standing. "You all right?"

She felt him touch her shoulder. Before she could turn and head back to the truck, he stepped closer and drew her into his embrace, pressed her tight against him. She could feel his hand rubbing circles against her back and the zipper of his jacket pressing into her chest. She buried her face into his collar and gave herself fully over to sobbing.

"It's okay," he kept saying. "Everything's going to be okay."

She tried to say something but it got stuck in her throat.

"Just let it out," he offered. "Sometimes it's best not to fight it."

After a while she slowly got control of herself and could breathe normally again. She pulled away and wiped her eyes with the back of her hand.

"Jesus," she said through her sniffles. "I feel so foolish."

"Don't worry about it. Here," he said. "Use this."

From his back pocket he produced the same rag he'd given her the night before to stop her nose from bleeding. She could see the darker spots of dried blood on it.

"Damn, do you ever wash this filthy thing?" she asked with a smile.

He grinned at her. "You have to do what you feel is right, Elizabeth. If it's important to you to go out there, then do it. Don't listen to me or anybody else."

"You really think so?" she said.

"Hell, yeah. I've done plenty of crazier things."

She laughed at this back-handed compliment. "So this sounds crazy to you?"

"I didn't mean it like that. I only meant you should do it if you think it'll give you some . . . whatever it is you're looking for. Answers. Closure. Peace of mind."

She stared at Gabe, who seemed lost in thought looking down at the cross. It appeared as if he was going to say something, then thought better of it.

"But if I did continue, I'd have to figure out how to get out there now," she said.

"I got an idea."

"Yeah?"

"Now just hear me out. I figure if you rent a car, it'll cost you what, seven, maybe eight hundred bucks. Maybe more with mileage. Plus you got to figure gas and car insurance. And with your luck around deer, you probably ought to get plenty of insurance," he said with a smile. "How about if I drive you?"

"You drive me?" she exclaimed.

"Why not?"

"I couldn't ask you to do that?"

"You're not asking. I'm offering."

"But what about your work? I thought you were so busy."

"Truth is, things have been a little slow lately. The economy and all."

"I couldn't let you drive me all the way out there."

"Why not?"

"I don't know. You hardly know me." What she was thinking was, I hardly know him.

"Besides I haven't taken a real vacation in years," he explained. "It'll be good to get away. And this way you'll have some company."

When she'd started out, company was the last thing she wanted. She wanted to be alone with her thoughts. Now, though, having someone to talk to didn't sound so bad.

"If it'll make you feel any better you can pick up my expenses. Food and gas."

Elizabeth thought about it for a moment, surprised she was even considering his offer. Finally, she said, "At least let me pay you something."

"All right. Let's say fifty a day."

"Let's make it a hundred. And I'll throw in the car."

"You already threw in the car," he reminded her, grinning so his buck tooth stuck out.

"What are you going to do about clothes and things?"

"I'm used to traveling light. If I need something, I'll pick it up. We got a deal then?" he asked, extending his hand.

Using the rag, she wiped her nose, which was still sore from the accident. Her entire crazy plan had become even crazier, she thought. But then she went ahead and took his hand.

"Deal," she said.

With that they got back in his truck and continued west.

Chapter 14

"What's the name of the town we're headed for?" Gabe asked.

"Marrizozo," Elizabeth replied, spelling it for him.

Gabe punched the name into his GPS on the dash.

"Says eleven hundred and twenty-two miles. Since we got a late start, I figure it'll take three days out and another two back. How long you planning on staying in this Marrizozo?"

"I don't know. A day maybe."

"So let's say six days."

"That means I'll owe you six hundred. I don't have that kind of cash on me though," Elizabeth confessed. "I could stop at an ATM."

"You worry too much. I know you're good for it."

"First thing, though, we have to stop in West Memphis."

"Why?"

"It's one of the places where my son stopped."

"Oh, that's right. You're following his trail. That may slow us down a bit."

"I'll pay you for your time."

By late afternoon they reached the Mississippi River, crossing it by way of a long, rusting metal bridge. Far below, the river slithered and undulated like a massive brown snake, its back writhing as it slid south under I-40. The heavy rains from two days before had swollen the river over its banks, and it carried a vast array of flotsam in its churning waters. Even from this far above, Elizabeth could see road signs and boards, fence posts, a blue tarp-like thing flapping up and down like a manta ray, part of a building's roof, the side of some unnameable animal bloated beyond recognition.

As she glanced over at Gabe, she happened to see the gold wedding band on his finger glimmer in the sunlight.

"So what happened with you and your wife?" she asked.

"She left for greener pastures?"

"With the proctologist?"

"Ah huh."

"You still miss her?"

"What makes you say that?"

"Well, you have pictures of her all around your place."

"Don't you think Picasso saved pictures of Marie-Thérèse even after they split up?" he said with a boyish grin.

"And you're still wearing your wedding ring."

He glanced at his hand. "I can't get it off," he said, straight-faced. "My fingers tend to swell up 'cause of all the work I do with my hands."

"You're a bad liar. You still care for her, don't you?"

"Is this your cross-examination mode?"

"Sorry. Didn't mean to get nosy."

"By the way, West Memphis is just on the other side of this bridge."

Elizabeth grabbed her notebook.

"We're looking for a restaurant called Lil' Sonny's."

She gave him the address and he entered it into the GPS.

"What do you hope to find there?"

"He spent a hundred and twelve dollars for lunch."

"Jesus," Gabe said, frowning. "He must've had a good appetite."

Right after they crossed the Mississippi, Gabe pulled off the highway and drove through a run-down section of the city. Every third store seemed closed, the windows boarded up, or with "for rent" signs in them. However, the pawn shops and bail bondsmen seemed to be doing a brisk business. Men, mostly African-American, hung out on the corners, drinking from bottles in paper bags. In one entryway Elizabeth spotted a man curled up, sleeping or dead, she couldn't tell.

"What was your son doing in this sort of place?" Gabe asked.

"I don't know," Elizabeth replied. But the question raised a red flag. What *was* Luke doing here, she wondered.

"There it is," Elizabeth said.

Lil' Sonny's, a rib joint, was in what appeared to be a converted gas station, with a large awning out front and an island where the pumps had once been. They got out and headed inside. Behind the grill was an obese black man wearing a filthy apron and a baseball cap that said "Razorbacks."

The waitress who seated them was a young black woman with cornrows. She led them into what had once been one of the bays of the garage, which still smelled vaguely of grease and where a dozen picnic tables were set up. They sat in the front, near a garage door that presumably pulled up during good weather so people could feel like they were eating outside. It was so bright Elizabeth had to squint to read the menu.

"Y'all be wanting something to drink?" the waitress asked.

"A Jack and Coke for me," Gabe said.

"Just water," added Elizabeth, holding her hand over her eyes.

"Here," Gabe said, offering her his hat. She hesitated, as much because it was so filthy as because she didn't want to deprive him of his hat. "Go on, take it. I don't need it."

She put the hat on, adjusted the Velcro closure in back.

In a few minutes the waitress returned with their drinks and took their orders. Gabe got the whole fried fish so Elizabeth decided to order that as well.

"You could bring me another Jack and Coke when you have a sec, sweetheart," Gabe said, smiling at her in a flirty sort of way.

He followed her swaying rear end as she walked away.

"She's young enough to be your daughter, for heaven's sake."

She'd said it as a joke but her comment seemed to sting Gabe. Frowning, he stared at Elizabeth for a moment. "What do you care?"

"I'm just making conversation."

Their meal came on red plastic trays, the sort they have in a grammar school lunchroom. Elizabeth had an entire fish placed in front of her. The thing was so big it covered the whole plate, with its tail hanging off one end, its head the other. It was deep fried, with the scales and fins and even the eyes still intact. Elizabeth cringed as she looked at the one glazed-over eye staring up at her.

"Don't mind how it looks," Gabe said. "Just dig in."

She didn't know how to start so he showed her, pulling the flesh off the fish with his fingers and dipping it into a tart lemony sauce on his tray.

"Damn, that's good," he said. "Go ahead and try it. But watch the bones."

To her surprise, she found the fish utterly delicious. Crisp on the outside, the flesh tender and sweet on the inside, with a hint of coriander and ginger. The meat fell right off the bones.

"Wow. It *is* good," she said.

"Your son knew where to eat. You just got to learn how to try new things, Elizabeth." He looked across at her. "Like what you're doing now."

"Eating fried fish?"

"I meant this trip of yours. Saying to hell with everybody. Throwing caution to the wind," he said with a dismissive wave of his hand.

"Is that what you think I'm doing? Throwing caution to the wind."

"Well, aren't you?" He sucked the grease off his fingers, slowly, one finger at a time. "It's just that you seem to me like somebody who's normally pretty cautious."

"Really?" she said, not sure she liked being called that.

"Somebody who always likes to play it safe. Keeps her cards close to the vest. Am I wrong?"

"You hardly know me," she said, taking a bite of her fish.

"I'm a pretty good judge of character. Mind if I ask you a question, Elizabeth?" he said.

"No," she replied, though she was already feeling a little apprehensive of what he might ask.

"Do you . . ." but he paused, reaching into his mouth and extracting a sliver of bone. He dropped it on his plate. "I told you, you gotta watch out for bones."

"Do I what?" she asked.

"Do you love your husband?"

She stared at him, frowning. "That's a little personal, isn't it?"

"Just asking."

"Of course, I love him," she said. "We've been married for twenty-six years."

The waitress happened to arrive then with Gabe's second drink. "Thank you, sweetheart?" he said, grinning at her.

"You going to be okay to drive?" Elizabeth asked.

"I'm just thirsty is all. I didn't ask how long you were married," he said to her. "I asked if you loved him."

"I'm not sure if that's any of your business," she replied indignantly.

"Don't go getting all huffy on me. Remember, it was all right for you to ask if I was still in love with my wife?" he said, with a wry smile.

Finally she replied, "Yes, I love him. Why do you ask?"

"I'm thinking you don't have a happy marriage."

"Based on what?"

"Just a feeling."

"Well, you're wrong. I mean, we've had some problems. Especially since the death of our son."

"I can imagine."

"No, you *can't*," Elizabeth said sharply. "You can't imagine what it's like. It changes everything. It's like the earth beneath you dropped away and you're falling. Only you never hit bottom."

"You ever cheat on your husband?"

Elizabeth almost choked on her food. She glared across the table at Gabe.

"Now what the hell would make you ask a question like that?" she exclaimed, but too quickly, with too much of a sense of indignation. It was an instinctive response, as if a doctor had struck her knee with a rubber mallet.

"It's just that you're a good-looking woman."

"What does that have to do with anything?"

"Your husband doesn't seem to appreciate you."

"Who said he doesn't appreciate me? My God! I can't believe you."

"Him letting you come out here all by yourself."

"I told you, he didn't know. Besides, he doesn't make decisions for me. We don't have that kind of marriage."

"I wouldn't let any wife of mine drive cross country all by herself."

"But you'd let her run off with another man?" By the startled expression on Gabe's face, she could see she'd gone too far. But he'd asked for it, hadn't he? "Listen, I'm sorry. Why don't we drop this whole conversation?"

They ate in silence for a while. Maybe she'd asked for it, getting into his private life the way she had earlier. Still, it was one thing for her to ask if he was still in love with his ex, quite another for him to bring up whether she'd cheated or not. That was a little too much. What the hell did he know about her marriage? What she felt? The twenty-six years that had bound her and Zack together? The memories they shared. The love for a child and the devastation that followed their losing that child. But she had to admit she was disconcerted by how close his comments had come to the truth, as if with those penetrating eyes of his he could see into her heart. Was that why she was so upset? At the same time, she also had to admit something to herself—she was annoyed at Zack, as well. Annoyed that he hadn't been another sort of man, the sort that *would* have appreciated her, that would have jumped in the car and sped after her as soon as he learned she'd left. The sort of man that would have kept her from seeking comfort in the arms of another to begin with. She had always blamed herself for the affair, had always assumed full responsibility for it. But *was* it all her fault? Didn't Zack own some of the blame? Maybe if he'd been more passionate, if he'd loved her more, *appreciated* her more, she wouldn't have had the affair. Maybe then she wouldn't have been with Peter that night.

"Listen, I have to hit the head," Gabe said, interrupting her thoughts.

He got up and walked toward the restrooms. While he was gone, Elizabeth now wondered if she'd made a terrible mistake in having Gabe drive her to New Mexico. She was already regretting the prospect of having to talk to him all that way, get into her life.

The waitress came over with the bill. As she took out her charge card, only then did Elizabeth remember why she'd come there in the first place.

"Oh, excuse me, miss," Elizabeth said to the waitress. She took out her phone and showed the woman the picture of Luke. "Do you recognize him?"

She stared at the picture, then at Elizabeth.

"He's my son. He came in here about a year ago. For lunch."

The woman shrugged her shoulders. "Cain't say I rec'nize him."

"He spent over a hundred dollars for lunch. He couldn't have eaten that much by himself."

The young woman shrugged. "Lemme go axe Sonny. Maybe he know."

The woman headed back toward the kitchen. While she waited, Elizabeth again wondered what her son had been doing here. A middle-class white kid from suburban Connecticut. Spending over a hundred dollars. Every possibility she could come up with only made her uneasy. In a minute the heavy-set black man behind the grill came shuffling up to her.

"LaVonda say you wantin' to know if your son came in here?" he asked.

"Yes, sir," she said, handing the man her cell phone with Luke's picture.

His hand was so huge that the phone was almost lost in the palm of it. He glanced at the photo, staring at it for a long while. Slowly, his soft brown eyes lit up with recognition. Then he smiled broadly. "I 'members him," the man said. "He come in and bought a mess of ribs and cornbread and beans and he brought it down the street."

"What for?"

"They's a bunch of folk hang out down there in the park. Your boy wanted to feed 'em."

"Feed them?"

"Uh huh."

"Why?

He shrugged his massive shoulders. "I reckon 'cuz they hungry," he said.

"What's the name of the park?"

"Franklin. It jess down the road a ways. Before you hit Broadway."

When Gabe returned he said, "Sorry about before."

"Forget it," she replied, without looking at him. "I probably deserved it. I shouldn't have gotten into your private life either. Let's just try to keep things on a professional basis."

"By the way, you find out what you came for?"

"In a way."

Once they got in the truck, she had him drive down the street toward Broadway. When she saw the park she had him pull over and stop. It was a small inner-city park, a few benches and picnic tables, a metal swingset, a couple of basketball hoops without nets. Standing around were a handful of people, mostly black. A small group of men lounged in a circle passing around a bottle in a paper bag. An old woman sat in a wheelchair waiting for a bus. A white guy with a camo jacket and baseball cap stood out at the road with a cardboard sign that said, *I used to be your neighbor.*

"What's here?" Gabe asked.

"Luke came here, too."

Elizabeth got out and headed into the park, with Gabe following along behind. She stopped several people and showed them the photo of Luke, asked if they remembered him bringing food here. They looked at it and shrugged or shook their heads. She was about to give up when she showed Luke's photo to an old black man with white hair, seated on one of the benches. He was holding a cigarette in one hand, a wooden cane in the other.

"He look familiar," the man said, knitting his brows.

"He brought some food here from Lil' Sonny's," Elizabeth offered, hoping to jar his memory. "You know, the barbecue place down the road."

"Not food," the man said. "He give me some cigarettes is what he give me. Who he anyway?"

"My son. Do you remember anything else about him?"

The man looked at the photo again, gathered his sunken mouth into a wrinkled ball.

"When I first laid eyes on him, I thought he a cop. About the only young white folks we get around here. But then he give me some cigarettes and he set a while and talked."

"Do you remember what you talked about?"

The man wagged his head. "Been a while. But I rec'leck he say God loves me."

"He said that?"

"Yes ma'am. And he give me a pack a cigarettes."

"Well, thank you," Elizabeth said.

Chapter 15

While Gabe chain-smoked, Elizabeth listened distractedly to the sound of the road sliding beneath them. She felt a dull headache swelling behind her eyes from the bright sunlight. Out the window the insipid landscape of eastern Arkansas swept by, endlessly flat fields where soybeans and cotton had been harvested and the dark soil turned over, and now lay exposed and barren as a vast lava flow. Gabe fiddled occasionally with the radio, trying to find something he liked, but mostly Elizabeth sensed it was just to cover the awkward silence that seemed to expand in the truck like an enormous balloon. Finally he mumbled a "damn it" and turned the radio off, and they continued on in this claustrophobic stillness for a while.

She tried to let the white noise of the highway lull her into a state of mental lassitude. But her mind kept returning to several troubling things. She thought of what her son had done—fed a bunch of poor people. It both surprised and relieved her, as well as made her proud of Luke. At his generosity, his compassion, even if he hardly showed the same sort of thoughtful feelings to his mother, and even if he had been generous with *her* money. She thought of all the times he had done similarly kind acts, often to complete strangers. With his father, he'd often helped out at the church. Collecting food and blankets for the poor. Going out to the Indian reservation in South Dakota. Dropping money in the cans of homeless people wherever he saw them. Then there was her conversation with Gabe and how he'd asked if she'd had an affair. How had he guessed it? Was there something stamped on her forehead, perhaps like the big red "A" carried around by Hester Prynne? Then she was embarrassed by how she'd tried to blame Zack for what had been *her* failing, *her* sin. Did she think that she could spin things in such a way that Zack was the guilty party simply because he wasn't the man she had wanted? Or because she had grown bored with their marriage. It was like a thief blaming the owner of something the thief had stolen simply because she coveted it. Zack had always been a good husband, a good father, a good *man*, someone tender and generous and loyal—yes, *loyal*—and she had, for her own selfish reasons, cheated on him. There was no way she could get out of her guilt, save perhaps by owning it.

"About before," she said after awhile, without looking over at Gabe. "I want to set the record straight. My husband's a good man."

"I don't doubt he is."

"No, I mean it. And he's had a rough go of it, too. With what happened to our son. With everything we've been through in the past year. With me especially."

Gabe looked over at her and gave her a mock salute. "Got it," he said.

"I just didn't want you to get the wrong impression."

"You don't have to explain anything to me. I shouldn't have opened my big mouth. I just thought we were talking. You know, like friends."

"But we're not friends. We hardly know each other."

"If you don't want to get into your personal life, that's fine by me. By the way, how's the nose?"

She was hardly aware of the pain now except for when she wrinkled her nose to squint into the bright sunlight. "Not bad. Can I have a cigarette?"

"You know they sell these things," he said.

He handed her the pack and the lighter. She took a cigarette, lit up, inhaled deeply, letting the smoke linger in her lungs for a moment. She felt some vague need to further explain things, to clarify what she meant, to present, if not quite the truth—whatever *that* was—at least a truer, or perhaps fairer, picture than the one she'd painted so far.

"I love my husband."

"I believe you."

"No, really. I do. It's just that it's complicated," she explained. Ahead on the highway she saw small pockets of shimmery air rising in ghostly columns above the asphalt. They looked like schools of tiny silver-scaled fish, undulating and writhing. "It was complicated before our son died and it's worse now."

"I know something about that."

She took a drag on her cigarette and stared out the window. Up ahead just off the highway, she saw another *descanso*. A plain white cross set above a steep gully. As they passed it she said, "Could you pull over?"

"Whatever you say."

Gabe slowed the truck and angled it over to the side of the highway. They got out and walked back along the shoulder of the road toward the cross. It was about two feet high, the white paint faded to gray. It didn't have any writing on it whatsoever and there was nothing on the ground around it. Just a stark cross marking the spot where someone had died, presumably having pitched over the edge and down into the stream some seventy feet below. Elizabeth could almost picture the car leaving the highway, flying over the edge of the gully, out into space for a moment. The person inside feeling that giddy, frightening sensation of weightlessness, momentarily throwing off the bounds of gravity and the demands of this mortal coil, becoming light as air.

"I don't get it," Gabe said. "Why would somebody go through the trouble of putting up a cross without writing anything on it."

"Maybe they didn't need to say anything. Maybe just putting it up was enough," Elizabeth said, looking down at the cross. For some reason, she thought of that rainy day along the side of the road when she'd met George Doucette, how he'd spoken to her about "regrets." In some ways that one word had prompted this entire journey.

"You were right before," she said.

"About what?"

"I'm ashamed to admit it but yes, I did have an affair."

"And?"

"And what?"

"What else?"

"What would you like to know?"

"How'd it happen?"

Elizabeth shrugged. "How does anything like that happen? You make a bad choice and then another one and another after that, and pretty soon you're in up to your neck. I guess I was bored with my marriage. And you were right, I didn't feel my husband appreciated me. I know that's just an excuse, but that's what I felt."

She went ahead and told him about Peter, not all of it, just the merest outline of the affair: how they met, how it unfolded, how it had lasted over a year. The thing she didn't tell him was that she was with Peter the night her son died. That part still seemed too intimate, too humiliating to share with someone she didn't even know. Then again, except for George Doucette, she hadn't told a soul any of this.

"How did it end?"

"I like to think I came to my senses and realized I loved my husband."

"Did he forgive you?" Gabe asked.

She thought of lying but then decided she'd come this far with the truth. What did it matter?

"I never told him. I just couldn't bring myself to confess what I'd done."

"Why?"

"Mostly I didn't want to hurt him. He'd been hurt enough with the loss of our son. If he found out that I'd been unfaithful, I don't know what it would have done to him."

"Did you ever think maybe it would've been better for him if you just told him the truth? For you, too. What do they say, the truth will set you free?"

"I'd thought of telling him. Many times. I just never found the courage to do it."

Gabe ran a hand along the angle of his unshaven jaw.

"Did your son know?"

"About the affair? I don't think so. Then again, there were times I suspected he knew something was up." She hesitated for a moment before adding, "He called me the night he died. He said he had something he wanted to talk about. Something important."

"What was it about?"

"That's the million dollar question. I was at a conference in Washington. I was busy and didn't take his call. I got it later on voicemail and when I finally called him back he didn't answer. Then in the middle of the night, I got another call. It was the police from Marrizozo, New Mexico."

"Jesus," Gabe said, drawing his mouth into a tight grimace. "That's awful."

"It was. Is."

"And you never found out what he wanted?"

"No. Sometimes I wonder if it had something to do with the affair. If he'd seen something. One of my emails or texts to Peter. Or some friend of a friend had seen us together and told Luke."

They stood there for a few seconds, then Gabe said, "We should probably get going."

"Wait." Elizabeth searched pockets. She found only some coins, a used Chapstick, a pen she'd taken from the last motel. Then she reached back into her hair and took out the scrunchie. She knelt down and put it at the base of the cross.

"What the hell is that for?" Gabe asked.

"I guess you're supposed to leave something at that these places. As a remembrance."

Gabe reached into his back pocket and removed the filthy oil rag.

"This is all I got."

"Leave it then."

So he placed that next to Elizabeth's scrunchie.

* * *

Just after sunset, they decided to stop for the night and pulled off the highway at a town whose name seemed to mock itself—New Hope. The place looked dismal, grim and pancake-flat, a two-stoplight farming town, with several enormous grain elevators near the railroad tracks and a main drag that was a couple of blocks long and ended abruptly in dun-colored prairie that stretched to the horizon. Elizabeth had Gabe stop at an ATM, where she withdrew some more cash. They found a Motel Six, and got two adjoining rooms on the second floor, reached by walking along an outside balcony. From up there, Elizabeth could see in the distance a large green water tower. In the growing twilight, with its enormous head and thin metal legs looking like tentacles, the tower resembled some War of the Worlds creature lumbering along the plains.

"Goodnight," she said. Before she shut her door, though, she called to him, "Thanks, Gabe."

"For what?"

"For agreeing to take me. And for listening."

"No biggie. Goodnight."

About a half hour later, she was brushing her teeth when she heard a knock.

"It's me," Gabe called through the door. She opened it to see him standing there, his face still damp and scrubbed pink from his having hastily shaved. He'd nicked himself along the angle of his jaw.

"Where did you get the razor?"

"Front office has complimentary guest packs."

He wasn't wearing his hat and his dark, thinning hair was slicked back over his skull. He had on the jacket with the name *Stu* stitched over the pocket.

"Listen, I'm going out to find a liquor store and grab a bite to eat. You need anything? Some food? Cigarettes, so you stop bumming me for one? Lipstick?"

"What would I need lipstick for?"

"I don't know. Don't women always need lipstick?" he said, grinning. "My Abby never went anywhere without lipstick. Said she didn't feel dressed without lipstick."

"*Your* Abby?"

"You know what I mean."

"How about a pack of Merits Light," Elizabeth replied. "Here, let me give you some money for your dinner."

"I got it."

"No. The deal was I'd pay your expenses. You're on your own for booze though."

"You want me to pick you up anything to drink?"

"I shouldn't."

She got her pocketbook and came back and handed him three crisp twenties, which he stuffed into his shirt pocket.

"You sure you're not hungry?" he asked.

She thought about it and decided that she might be hungry later, and of course then she'd be out of luck.

"All right. But I'm tired of greasy food. How about a Cobb salad?"

He glanced over his shoulder, at the town behind him. "This doesn't look like your Cobb salad sort of town, if you know what I mean."

"No, I guess not. A sandwich then. Turkey, if they have it."

While he was gone, she took a long, hot shower. The water felt delicious, and she let it massage the eye-strain headache she'd acquired from squinting into the sun all day. Afterwards, she lay down on the bed in her underwear. The mattress was lumpy and bowed toward the middle, and she couldn't help but imagine all the lonely bodies it had held in its sterile embrace. Only then did she realize that along with her sunglasses, she'd forgotten her pillow back at Gabe's place. Lying there looking up at the ceiling, she thought of the conversation she'd had with Gabe. About her affair. Why she'd cheated on her husband. She took out her phone and decided to call Zack.

"Hi. It's me," she said when he picked up.

"Oh," he replied, surprise registering in his voice, almost as if he'd been expecting someone else. "Where are you now?"

"Arkansas."

"I thought you'd be farther along."

"It's a big country," she explained. A foolish comment, but she didn't want to get into explaining to him why she hadn't made better progress. No need to tell him any of that.

"I just got in," he explained.

"Where were you?"

"I had a meeting at the church." He paused, then added, "You know the candlelight vigil we're planning for the green?"

"Yes."

"We now have the whole state involved," he explained, sounding proud.

"Wow."

"For anyone who's lost a child. We're going to call it 'An Evening of Remembrance.' If it goes well, we plan on making it part of a national re-membrance event. Having chapters all over the country. We're talking about one night in January when everybody who's lost a child gathers in their town square to light a candle and remember."

"Boy," she said, "you're really going big time with this."

Elizabeth tried to picture the entire town green of Garth's Point filled with grieving parents, all holding candles in the night. Then she thought of all the roadside memorials she'd seen coming across the country, and the thousands, perhaps tens of thousands she hadn't seen, and she tried to imag-ine a crowd that big, with all those parents and loved ones coming together and lighting candles, commiserating, offering up prayers. Such a concentra-tion of sadness, such a critical mass of grief. You could probably see the light from all those candles from the moon, she thought.

"It's amazing how many people have lost children just in Connecticut. Eighty-five last year alone."

"That is amazing," she said.

"And we thought we were all alone."

She felt like saying she still felt alone, that even knowing about all the other parents who'd suffered similar losses didn't lessen her own solitary grief. But instead she said, "You've really done a wonderful thing, Zack. I'm proud of you."

"Thanks. By the way, I'm making your favorite tonight," he offered. "Honey-glazed salmon with asparagus and hollandaise sauce."

It struck her as odd that he would go through the trouble of making a big meal, just for himself. If the tables were turned, she'd have come home from work and grabbed a spoon and filled up on peanut butter right out of the jar. Then again, that was Zack. He liked his routines. They defined and reassured him. Besides, he'd always enjoyed cooking. Even in the weeks after Luke died, he still went through the trouble of making regular meals, though neither of them had much of an appetite. She should have told Gabe about that, too, how that was something else she admired about Zack. The care, the attention to detail with which he prepared a meal. Feeding loved ones, she realized, was a gesture of love. She could remember when they were first dating how he would have her over for dinner in his little apartment down in The Village and make her something special. She, on the other hand, was like her mother; she could hardly be bothered with cooking, and when she did she slapped it together. "Slambo Bango," Luke used to joke about her cooking.

"Sounds wonderful," she replied.

"Wish you were here to enjoy it with me."

"I do, too, Zack," she said.

"Don't worry, I'll make it again."

"I'm sorry for leaving you like this." She paused, then added, "For everything."

"What everything?" Zack said.

"Just everything."

"We can sort it out when you come back." Then out of the blue, he added, "I love you."

She thought of saying one of several things: "I love you, too."; or "You deserve better than I can give you"; or, "Zack, I had an affair." Something. Anything. She thought about what Gabe had said, about the truth setting people free. Maybe he was right. Maybe the truth would set them free. Free to get on with their lives. Zack deserved some happiness, she felt. Deserved a woman who would want to make him happy, who would appreciate him for who he was, not hold it against him for who he wasn't. Not a woman so wrapped up in her own guilt, so enamored by grief. A woman less selfish than she. *Tell him*, she goaded herself. *Go on and tell him*. Yet she said nothing. Out of fear or selfishness or perhaps love—she wasn't sure.

"Oh. Guess who I ran into today?" Zack said. "Roxanne Pierson."

"Really."

"Yeah. In the Stop and Shop. She said you'd called TJ."

"I did, yes."

"Why?"

"To ask whether she and Luke were seeing each other that summer."

"Really? Why?"

"Because of what you said. Because I was curious."

"And were they?"

She considered telling him what TJ had said to her, about their son ceasing to be interested in women, that perhaps he was gay. But then she thought, why do that to him? Why make him share her pain and confusion regarding their son, about who and what he was? About what he had not wanted to share with them? What difference could it possibly make now? "She told me they weren't dating. That they were just friends."

"Just friends, huh?" Zack said. "I always liked her. She was a good kid."

"Yes, she was."

"Do you remember how they used to come over and watch TV and hold hands on the couch?"

"Yes."

"I could really see her with Luke. They were a good match."

"Evidently not so good really," Elizabeth offered flatly. "She's getting married, Zack."

"Really?" he said, trying to sound his usual upbeat self, but the disappointment managed to register in his voice. "To whom?"

"Somebody she met after Luke, I guess."

An audible groan slipped out from somewhere deep in his chest: *augh*. He didn't say anything for several seconds, then Elizabeth heard a noise that sounded as if he'd gotten something stuck in his throat and he was trying to clear it.

"Zack?"

"God, I miss him."

"I know you do, sweetheart," she tried to comfort. "I know."

"I shouldn't have agreed to his driving cross country."

"Don't blame yourself."

"But if I'd sided with you, maybe . . ."

"Don't do that, Zack. He was twenty-one. You were right—we really couldn't have stopped him."

"I didn't have to make it so easy though."

"It could've happened right here in town. Like with the Parsons boy. As you said, it was an accident." Funny, how she'd fought so long and so hard against it being just an accident. For her, there had to have been some meaning, some significance in his death. The arrogance which said that for *her* child, death couldn't simply be pointless. It had to have meaning, a reason, some greater purpose. "We couldn't protect him against everything."

"I know. But ever since you've been gone, I think about him all the time. I thought I'd gotten to a point where I could accept it. But now with you going out there, it's like it just happened. Like the grief is just starting all over again."

"I'm sorry. I didn't mean for that to happen."

"Who knows? Maybe it's for the best."

"Do you really think so?"

"Yes." She heard him take a breath and exhale. "Why didn't we talk more?"

"You mean, about Luke's death?"

"That. You and me. Everything," Zack replied.

The way he said *everything* suggested an expansive territory, their marriage as broad a topic as the country she'd just traversed.

"You're right. We should've talked more," Elizabeth said. "I'm sorry for that."

"It's my fault, too. I was just thinking about something the other day. Do you remember that time in Wales?"

"You mean when we lost him?"

"Yes. I hadn't thought about it in a long time." Zack's voice was thin and pained, just this side of cracking again. "And it turned out he was just fascinated with that toy plane in the gift shop. The Spitfire. Speaking of which, I went into his room the other night and it wasn't on the shelf."

"I took it," she replied.

"You took it?"

"Yes. I'm going to leave it out there. Where he died."

"Really?"

"Ah huh."

"That's a good idea," Zack said. "He'd like that."

"I don't know what he'd like. But it's what I'm going to do."

"Trust me. He'll be looking down and smiling at you when you put that there."

If only it was that easy, she thought. To Zack, Luke was still someplace where he could think and feel and react, where he was still very much the Luke they knew and loved, the one who confused and angered them, too. It was just that they couldn't see him. To Zack it was as if their son were in another room that they temporarily couldn't enter.

"I can't really picture him anywhere, Zack."

"What do you mean?"

"I'm not like you, I can't really buy into all that heaven business. I wish I could. It would make things a whole lot easier. But on the other hand, I can't bring myself to believe I'll never see him again. Talk to him. Hear his voice."

"Then just feel him in your heart, Elizabeth," he offered.

His comment was like something you would tell a frightened child, like one of those things she used to tell Luke when he was scared to go to bed at night. She was going to say something but decided not to. The cynic in her didn't want to permit herself the glittering but elusive hope of believing that Luke was *somewhere*, even if it were only in her heart. On the other hand she had to have something to hold onto. She couldn't just admit that her son had vanished into thin air.

"I worry about you," said Zack. "Driving all the way out there by yourself."

"I'll be all right. Really."

"I don't know what I'd do if anything were to happen to you."

"Zack . . ."

"Yeah."

She thought of telling him about the affair, coming clean. Just getting it all out for once. But she was interrupted by a loud rapping on the door.

"What's that?" Zack asked.

"Oh, I ordered room service," she lied.

"When you get back, think about coming to the candlelight vigil."

"I will. I'll think about it," Elizabeth offered. "Everything will be all right, Zack."

She didn't know why she'd said that, whom she was trying to cheer up, herself or Zack, or what she meant by saying that everything would be all right. How could *anything ever be all right again?*

The knocking came again, louder.

"You'd better go ahead and answer that," Zack said. "Just come home safely."

"Goodnight, Zack."

She quickly threw some clothes on and went to the door where she found Gabe standing there, holding a paper sack filled with food.

"They didn't have turkey so I got you chicken salad," he said.

He reached into the sack and pulled out a sandwich wrapped in butcher's paper and a Diet Coke. "And I got you these," he said, pulling from his jacket pocket a pair of sunglasses.

"Oh, thanks. Just what I needed."

He handed her some change, a few crumpled bills, and was about to turn around and head back to his room. Elizabeth was exhausted and didn't feel much like chatting, but she knew she wouldn't fall asleep right away after her conversation with Zack, and she wondered if company would be better than staring at the ceiling or watching some dopey TV show.

"You want to have dinner together?" she asked.

He stared at her for a moment, then said, "Sure. I'll be right back."

He returned with a plastic motel cup filled with ice. Elizabeth lay on the bed with her back propped up with pillows, while he occupied the only other chair in the room, at a small desk facing the window. From the sack he took out his sandwich and a bag of fries, as well as a pint of Jack Daniels, which he cracked open and poured some into his cup.

"You want some? Oh, I forgot, you're doing the wagon thing," he said. "How's that ride going anyway?"

"Bumpy. I was hitting the sauce a little too hard so I needed to slow down."

Gabe glanced at her, then took a long guzzle, as if rubbing it in.

"Don't we all. Your husband drink?"

"Occasionally. Why?"

"Stuart's a teetotaler."

"Stuart?" Elizabeth asked.

Gabe pointed at the name stitched on his jacket.

Elizabeth nodded, was about to take a bite of her sandwich, but she paused, looked back at Gabe. "He's the one your wife ran off with?"

Gabe wiped his mouth with a napkin and offered up a guilty smile as if he'd been caught in some lie. "I told you he used to work for me."

"Yeah, but you didn't tell me the two of them . . ."

Gabe shrugged. "He left the jacket behind."

"Geez. Why do you wear it then?"

"Why not? It's a perfectly good jacket. It seemed like I should get something back."

"Do your girls like him?"

"From the little I can pry out of Jo, she likes him okay. Says he tries hard."

He took a sip of his drink, winced, then downed the rest of it. "Stu and I went to school together. We weren't buddies or anything but we knew each other. He was divorced, living down at the Fairmont in town. So I reached out a helping hand. I gave him a job, let him sleep in the back room of the garage. What do they say about no good deed going unpunished?"

"Yeah, right."

"Stuart's a douchebag and all, but he's always been good to Jo. And Abby. I'm grateful to him for that."

"That's pretty magnanimous seeing as he stole your wife."

"He didn't steal her. It was more that I gave her to him."

"How do you figure that?"

"What do they say in court—'the whole truth and nothin' but.' I didn't tell you the whole story earlier. Ever hear of Ewing's sarcoma?"

"Sounds like some kind of cancer," Elizabeth offered.

"Ah huh. A pretty rare bone cancer."

Elizabeth thought of that drawing of his wife, the weariness in her eyes. "Your wife got sick?"

"No, not my wife. My daughter Kelly. She got it when she was a teen-ager."

"Oh, my God!" Elizabeth gasped. "Why didn't you tell me before?"

"It's not something I like to talk about."

Elizabeth thought then how he'd never really said much about his older daughter Kelly. How he'd mentioned that his younger one Jo lived with his ex, but he'd avoided saying anything about his other daughter. Elizabeth recalled, too, how when she'd said a person couldn't imagine what it was like to lose a child, he had said he could.

"Is she . . . I mean . . ."

He shook his head. "She passed away six years ago."

Elizabeth didn't know what to say. "Geez, Gabe. I'm so sorry."

"Abby never lost hope. She was a regular trooper through the whole thing. Going to the hospital. Doing research online. Finding the best doctors. Fighting for our kid."

He took another sip of his drink and looked over his shoulder toward the window. Elizabeth couldn't decide if he were looking out at the night or at his own reflection. He seemed suddenly tired, his eyes weary. It was the same look Elizabeth had noticed in the eyes of his wife in the sketch he'd done. She felt so shitty now for saying he couldn't possibly have understood what she was going through. He wrapped up what he hadn't eaten of his sandwich and tossed it into the waste basket under the table.

"The truth is, after our daughter got sick, it changed things between Abby and me. It just drained us. After she died, we didn't have anything left."

"It must've been awful."

"I wasn't always the best of husbands. Or fathers. I drank too much. That was my way of coping. And I was on the road a lot. I wasn't always there for her. Emotionally or otherwise. She had to do most of the heavy lifting on her own."

"You don't have to talk about any of this if you don't want to," she said, reminding him of what he'd said to her earlier that day.

"Like you with your husband, I just wanted to set the record straight. It wasn't all Abby's fault."

"And how did this Stuart figure in the picture?" Elizabeth asked.

"I hired him after Kelly got sick. I had my hands full and needed somebody to help out at the garage. He was a pretty fair mechanic. I let him stay in the room out in back of the garage until he could find something. Abby used to feel sorry for him, invite him over for dinner. Then when I'd be gone, out on the road, out at some bar, he used to keep her company. I guess they liked to play cards. That's what they called it anyway. You know, when the cat's away, the mice will play. But the plain truth is he was *there* for her and I wasn't."

"That's decent of you to say."

"Believe me, I wasn't so decent when I first found out about them. Truth is, I wanted to take a blowtorch to the guy's nuts. But then I realized that he was just giving her things I wasn't. Long and short of it, he was what Abby needed."

When he'd finished, he sat there for a moment staring down at a section of carpet. He removed his hat and ran his hand through his thinning hair.

"Well, that really put a damper on the evening."

"I'm sorry," Elizabeth said again.

"So like I told you, I do know what you're going through."

Both were silent for a while. Then Elizabeth offered, "So that's what I saw in your wife's eyes. That terrible sadness."

"I guess so."

"You really are talented, Gabe."

"You're just being sweet."

"No, it's true."

"Funny thing is Abby used to say the same thing. She was always supportive of me trying to make it as an artist. Before when you asked me what happened to my 'art career,'" he explained, making finger quotes around the words, "I said it was on account of my getting married. Since I'm 'fessing up all of a sudden, the truth is I was too damn gutless."

He downed the rest of his drink, tossed the cup in the garbage, and stood.

"Well, I should hit the road." He headed for the door, but paused there, his back to her. He seemed to be debating something with himself.

"Gabe?" she said.

"You were right. I do still love Abby. Always did, always will. Christ, we were high school sweethearts. Goodnight."

Elizabeth lay in bed for a long while, unable to sleep. She thought of all that Gabe had told her, about his child getting sick and how her death had affected his marriage. How he still loved his ex. Finally, around midnight she decided to call Zack.

"Did I wake you?" she asked.

"That's all right," he replied, his voice groggy with sleep.

"Sorry. There's something I needed to tell you, Zack."

"Can't it wait till you get home?"

"No, it can't. You know how earlier you said we should have talked more."

"Yes."

"You're right. We should have. There's so much I should've said. To Luke. To you."

"To me?"

"Yes. I should've told you I loved you, Zack."

"I know you do."

"But I should've told you. I don't know why I didn't. Sometimes life just gets away from us."

"Is that what you wanted to tell me?"

"That, too." She waited for a moment, working up the courage to say what she had to. "The night Luke died, I wasn't alone."

Her ear pressed against the cell phone was hot and throbbing, as if her eardrum would pop. Zack was silent on the other end.

"Did you hear what I said? I was with someone. Another man. I'm sorry."

There, she thought. It was out. And yet it hardly felt like freedom. It was just more guilt, from having wronged someone she cared very much for.

"Zack?"

"I know," he said.

"What?"

"I've known for a long time."

Elizabeth had no idea how to respond to this. Everything she had planned on saying just dissolved into nothing, became moot and pointless. Finally, she said, "If you knew, why didn't you say anything?"

"I don't know. I guess because I was afraid."

"Afraid?"

"Of losing you. Afraid, too, that if it were out in the open, I wouldn't be able to forgive you."

"Oh, Zack. I'm so sorry," she cried.

She waited for him to say something else, to forgive or curse her, or say he was going to leave her. But instead, he surprised her by asking, "Is it over?"

"Yes. It's been over for a long time."

"Did you love him?"

"No, Zack. I never loved him. I love you," she said. "Can you ever forgive me?"

Zack was silent for a long time. When he spoke again, he said only, "I don't know. It's asking a lot."

"I understand."

"Goodnight, Elizabeth."

"Goodnight."

Then he hung up and she was alone in the room.

Chapter 16

Elizabeth opened her eyes to see Luke sitting there, in the same chair that Gabe had been sitting in the previous night. Her son, though, was a little boy again, perhaps five, and he was in his pj's. His eyes were red and inflamed, as if he'd been crying.

Where did you go? he implored.
I was right here.
I didn't see you. I was afraid.
I'm sorry, sweetheart.
Don't leave me again.
I won't, sweetie. I promise.
Will you read me a story?
Of course. Do you want the one about the pig?

He got down off the chair and came running over and jumped into bed with Elizabeth. As he crawled into her arms, she could smell the warm, slightly sour fragrance of his scalp, feel the softness of the skin along his cheek. She began reading the book.
". . . for a pig is just downright supposed to be big."

* * *

In the shower the next morning, she thought about both conversations she'd had the previous evening. How Gabe had said his daughter had died. And how Zack had known all along about her affair. She'd thought about asking Zack how he'd learned about it or when, but those, she realized, were logistical questions and ultimately insignificant. Here she had been driving herself crazy with guilt and all the while he knew. *Did you love him?* Zack had asked.

After getting dressed, she headed over to Gabe's room. The morning was sunny with long shadows stretching across the flat earth. Gabe opened the door, rubbing his eyes, dressed only in his white BVDs. His naked chest was matted with gray hair and his arms and shoulders were muscular. His skinny legs were white as skin that had been covered with a bandage.

"Jesus," he said, squinting at her as if he'd just been released from solitary confinement. "Why so early?"

"It's almost eight. You okay?"

He looked hung over, his mouth slung open. "My alarm didn't go off."

"I'll be in the truck," she said.

"All right. Gimme ten."

In the motel lobby she paid the bill and bought a pack of cigarettes from the vending machine, then headed out to the truck. . . .She passed the time smoking and thinking about what Gabe had told her the night before. She felt sorry for him. He'd lost both his daughter and his wife. Maybe she would lose both as well. Perhaps Zack was packing his things at that very moment.

After a while she saw Gabe approaching the truck.

"You okay to drive?" she asked as he climbed in.

"Don't worry about me."

He pulled out of the motel, and they headed toward the highway. It was already getting hot, the air just above the asphalt wavering and bending in the heat. She was grateful for the sunglasses. They rode through Southwestern Arkansas, over lethargic, mud-brown rivers where Elizabeth imagined huge catfish floating in the depths. They passed long stretches of pine forests and open fields, some with cattle or horses grazing, others with oil derricks see-sawing up and down, metal rocking horses. Every once in a while, Elizabeth glanced over at Gabe. It seemed obvious to her that after their conversation the previous night he'd gone back to his room and tied one on. She couldn't stop thinking about her conversation with Zack the previous night. *I don't know*, he'd said. For some reason she pictured the soft flesh between Zack's thumb and forefinger. When they used to hold hands, say if they were at the movies or standing in line somewhere, she had liked to stroke that part of his hand. It used to feel so reassuring.

Mid-morning, Gabe pulled off the highway for gas and turned into the first convenience store they came upon.

"I'm gonna get something to eat," he said. "You want anything?"

"Just a coffee," she replied.

He headed into the convenience store. Gabe returned in a moment with two coffees and a breakfast burrito.

"You look tired," she said to him.

"I guess I had one too many last night."

"Was that on account of our conversation?"

"What did we talk about?" he asked, casting a blank look her way. She couldn't tell whether he was kidding or really couldn't remember.

"Your wife and daughter."

"Ex-wife," he corrected.

"Does she know you still love her?"

"What's done is done. Abby's happy now. And I'm happy for her."

"Are you?"

"Yeah. I am actually." Gabe glanced over at her. "Stu's a back-stabbing son of a bitch, but he's been decent with Abby and Jo. He's been there for them."

Elizabeth wondered if she would have the generosity to say that if Zack left her for another woman. She didn't think she could be so magnanimous.

"By the way, I told my husband last night," she said.

"You told him what?"

"About the affair."

Gabe looked over at her and wagged his head. "And how did that work out?"

She shrugged. "The funny thing is he said he already knew about it."

"No shit? Why didn't he say anything before?"

"I don't know."

He took a sip of his coffee. "So what's going to happen now?"

She pursed her lips and looked out the window. "I don't know."

"You want things to work out with him?"

"Of course. I love him."

"Did you tell him that?"

"Yes. But it's up to him."

"Why is it up to him?"

"Because I'm the one who cheated."

* * *

They drove hard through the rolling hills of western Arkansas, not even stopping for lunch; they reached Texarkana and the border of Texas by late afternoon. The heat was oppressive, heavy and damp, palpable as a sauna. His truck had air-conditioning but he preferred to drive with the windows down, said AC stuffed up his nose. This part of Texas surprised her. It was greener and more fertile than she'd imagined, with broad grasslands bisected by small creeks along which grew groves of cottonwoods and cedars.

Near dusk Gabe asked, "What do you say we call it a day?"

"Fine with me."

They got rooms at a Ramada Inn, a significant upgrade over the previous night's Motel Six. The bathroom was clean and the bed, a king, was firm and comfortable, and there were no cigarette burns on the nightstand either. They agreed to have a little time to get cleaned up and then to meet at seven for dinner. When Gabe showed up at her door an hour later, he surprised her. He was wearing a new shirt, a white button-down oxford matched with a stiff new pair of jeans. He wasn't wearing his baseball cap either or his greasy Stu jacket, and his hair was freshly washed and combed. She thought she smelled something like aftershave, too.

"Boy, look at you," she said.

"The other shirt was getting a little ripe," he joked. "So I went out and bought a couple of things. You ready?"

They decided to save time and have dinner at the hotel restaurant. The place was dimly lit with candles in small red jars on each table and a dance floor over at one end where no one was dancing. There was piped in music from the eighties, Prince and Madonna and Duran Duran. It wasn't very busy, just a handful of men bellied up to the bar, middle-aged guys in jeans and big straw cowboy hats. A busty woman with a smoker's laugh had drawn several of them like flies to flypaper. At the end of the bar, a guy in a business suit was talking to the bartender, a young blonde woman. Gabe and Elizabeth sat at a booth. The bartender, who also doubled as waitress, came over and gave them menus and took their drink orders. She was in her mid-thirties, with hair that she wore in a long braid that fell to her waist.

Gabe ordered the steak with a Jack and Coke, while Elizabeth had a salad and iced tea.

"How long have you been on the wagon?"

"A few weeks," she replied, though it seemed like months.

"Been there, done that. First couple of weeks are the hardest part."

When the bartender returned with their drinks, Elizabeth watched as Gabe knocked down his Jack and Coke in one motion, without coming up for air.

"After last night, maybe you ought to go a little easy on that."

"I'm not on the clock now," he explained. "And I'm not on that wagon either."

His phone rang then.

"Hi, sweetcakes," he said, his face suddenly brightening. *My daughter*, he mouthed the words to Elizabeth and pointed at the phone. "What's going on, sweetie? No, I don't have any plans for next summer. Amy? Yeah, I remember her. She's the fat one. You're right, I shouldn't have said that," he said, winking at Elizabeth. "I don't see why not. You'll have to work it out with her parents. But it's fine by me if you want to have her come and stay. Make sure you run it by your mother, too." There was a pause, then Gabe made a face. "*Yes*, you have to. . . Because she's the boss. I know she bugs you. But she's still your mother and you have to do what she says. No, you can't come and live with me. We've been over this before. Why? Because you can't, that's why. When you're older, maybe." He glanced over at Elizabeth and rolled his eyes, then smiled. Finally he said, "Sure thing. You take care, honey. Love ya."

When he got off the phone, he said, "Jo wants to bring a friend for next summer. I don't blame her. There's not a whole lot to do in town. When she was younger it was easy. I'd take her fishing. Or she'd help me in the shop. She knows her way around cars, that kid. Now she's older though, it's harder to keep her entertained."

"She wants to see her dad."

"I think she just wants to get away from her mother," Gabe said.

"They having problems?"

"Just the usual teenage stuff. Her mother won't let her wear a certain skirt to school. That sort of deal."

"I fought with my mother all the time. It was my dad I adored."

"I wouldn't go so far as Jo adoring me. But we get along pretty well."

When the waitress brought their food over, Gabe ordered another Jack and Coke.

"You sure you don't want a drink?" he said to Elizabeth.

"You wouldn't make a very good sponsor."

They dug into their food. Elizabeth found herself famished.

"Has there been anybody in your life since the divorce?" she asked.

He shrugged. "I've done the online dating thing. There was one gal I liked a lot. Carla."

"What happened?"

"She was," he explained, twirling his fork near his temple, "crazy as a bedbug."

"Men always say that."

"But this one was certifiable. Crazy Carla, I called her." He took a sip of his drink.

During dinner, Gabe had several more Jack and Cokes. Elizabeth found herself letting her guard down, talking and laughing easily with him, as if they were long-time friends instead of having met just two days before. The conversation centered mostly on his life. He told her funny stories about his dating experiences which Elizabeth laughed at. He related how he and Crazy Carla once got into a fight and she ended up locking him out of her house without his clothes or keys or cell phone, and he had to walk home naked several miles.

"I didn't have a stitch on. I'm talking my birthday suit. No underwear, shoes. Nothing. And it was January, too. Christ, I almost froze my balls off."

He talked some more about his daughters, too.

"That's Jo," he said handing Elizabeth a picture of his daughter on his cell phone. "That's her eighth-grade semi-formal."

"Boy, she's cute," Elizabeth offered.

"Luckily, they both got their looks from their mother. And their talent. Abby used to be a dancer in high school. She always had the two of them taking dance and voice lessons. Entered them into theater productions. Kel could sing like an angel." He took the phone back from Elizabeth and searched on it until he came to what he wanted. "That's Kelly in ninth grade. She played Laurey in *Oklahoma*," he said, handing the phone back to Elizabeth.

"She's gorgeous."

"Yeah, she was. Since she was a little girl, she was always talking about how she was going to head out to Hollywood. Become a movie star. That was her dream."

"How old was she when she died?"

"Seventeen. She'd have been twenty-two now."

"What Luke would have been." Elizabeth took her phone out, scrolled through until she got to a picture of Luke. "That's him there," she said, handing Gabe her phone.

"He's a good-looking boy. Must've had all the girls after him."

Elizabeth thought of what TJ had told her. "Actually, he had only one girlfriend growing up."

"Sounds like me. I married the first girl I slept with," he said with a laugh. "What did your boy want to be?"

Though it was the most ordinary of questions, it still took Elizabeth a little by surprise.

"I don't really know. When he was younger he talked about going to law school. Then again, that was mostly me trying to talk him into law school. What he ended up majoring in was theology."

"And I thought art was impractical. What the hell, was he going to be a preacher?"

Elizabeth shrugged. "I don't know."

"Was your family very religious?"

"Not really. My father was an old-school Irish Catholic. He used to take us to church when we were little. I don't go much any more though. In fact, not at all."

"So where did your son get his interest then?"

"Probably his father. Luke was always an introspective sort of kid."

"What was he doing on this trip?" Gabe asked.

"He told us he was visiting friends in San Francisco. And out of the blue I get a call from the New Mexico police saying he'd been in an accident."

"Couldn't the cops tell you anything more?"

She let out a high-pitched laugh. "They don't know their ass from their elbow. At first they said Luke had his seat belt on and then they said he didn't. They couldn't find his phone and when they finally did it'd been damaged beyond repair. I couldn't get any data off of it. Plus, I had asked several times about Luke's diary."

"His diary?"

"I'm pretty sure my son had his diary with him on the trip."

"And they couldn't find it?"

"I don't think they even looked."

"So that's why you're following his trail? To find out what he was up to."

"Something like that. But I also just want to see where he died."

"Why? Is it some kind of closure thing for you?"

"I suppose," replied Elizabeth, wiping the sweat off her glass. "Mostly I just want to offer a remembrance to Luke."

Gabe had two more Jack and Cokes and then for a nightcap a single shot of JD before they called it a night. He was weaving a little, unsteady as they headed up to their rooms. Once, she had to catch his elbow to keep him from stumbling up the stairs.

"You all right?" she asked.

"I'm just fuckin' great," he said.

When they reached her room, he said, "It was nice talking to you."

"Same here."

They stood there awkwardly for a moment. Finally Elizabeth stuck out her hand and said, "Well, goodnight, Gabe."

Instead of shaking her hand, he reached out and put his arms around her and hugged her.

"Thanks, Elizabeth."

"For what?"

"For listening to me."

"You're welcome."

That night as she lay in a tub of hot water, she heard, coming softly from the next room, a guitar being strummed. *Gabe*, she thought. She couldn't make out what he was playing but it was something unhurried and soulful. She lay there until the water started to get cold and then she added more hot. She thought of her conversation with Gabe, about what Luke had wanted to be in life. When her son was little he'd had the usual sort of career aspirations. Because of his interest in planes he'd wanted to be a pilot for the longest time, then a musician, and for a while he'd talked about being a lawyer, but again, that was mostly her influence. In college though, Elizabeth could never really say he had a passion for any vocation. When they talked about it he was vague, noncommittal. She could recall once at the dinner table with Zack and Luke, discussing what he was going to do, what he was going to *be*.

"I don't know," Luke had said.

"Well you need to start thinking about it!" Elizabeth exclaimed.

"I'll probably just go to grad school."

"Going to grad school isn't a career, Luke," she said.

"Don't worry. You won't have to pay for it."

"It's not that."

"I'll figure it out."

As she lay there she thought about that conversation she'd had with Sam Rosello, Luke's former roommate at college. How he'd said Luke was acting strange. Finally, she reached over the side of the tub and from her pants pocket extracted her cell phone. She got Sam's number and called.

"Hi, Sam. This is Elizabeth Gerlacher." When it seemed as if he didn't recognize the name, she added, "Luke's mom."

"Oh, yeah. Hi."

They made awkward small-talk for a while. Sam, it turned out, was living in Vermont and, not surprisingly, working as a ski instructor.

"When we spoke that other time, you said Luke was acting weird."

"Yeah. Sort of."

"Can you tell anything else, Sam?"

"He got all born-again on us."

"Born-again?"

"Super religious. He was always hanging out with Father Jerome. Helping him over at the abbey."

"You don't like Father Jerome?"

"No, it's not that. He's a good guy and everything. It's just after a while, Luke started wearing that crucifix. Acting different."

"Did he ever talk you about why he did that?"

"I don't know. I guess he was into all that stuff."

After Elizabeth hung up she thought of what Sam had told her. How Luke was born-again into all that religious stuff. How had she not seen that in him? Had he purposely gone out of his way to conceal it from Zack and her? And what need did it fill for her son? Was it something women couldn't provide for him? His friends? His own parents?

Chapter 17

The next morning Gabe was pretty quiet, while Elizabeth looked over her notebook plotting out where they would go next. As they drove west, the landscape of North Central Texas took on a remarkable clarity: white clouds hung against an achingly blue sky, a red barn blazing before dun-colored fields, Hereford cattle slouched against a backdrop of green pasture. She could smell the change, too, the air becoming thinner, more arid, hinting at the desert to come. Just past Dallas, she'd had Gabe get off the interstate and onto a narrow, two-lane state road that shot arrow-straight toward a low blue line of hills at the horizon.

"Where're we headed?" Gabe asked.

"A place called Ned's Landing."

"What's that?"

"An airplane museum. Luke stopped there and bought something."

Occasionally a semi traveling in the opposite direction would blow past them, sending a shudder through the small pickup, and now and then, the road funneled them through dusty, single-stoplight towns with bleak main streets that looked right out of Depression-era Hopper.

As they inched closer to New Mexico, Elizabeth was conscious of a tension growing in her, a vague unease in her stomach. It had to do with what lay ahead, she guessed. She tried to picture, really for the first time, what Marrizozo would look like, feel like. Would its stark ordinariness surprise her? Would it appear as clear and sharp as everything else now? She tried to conjure an image in her mind of the place, but all that came was an unforgiving landscape of cacti and tumbleweed, a land ruled by rattlesnake and scorpion and blistering heat. She recalled then what she'd read in the Bible that night in the motel room in Virginia; something about a desert, about a child growing up, waxing strong in spirit. She also wondered what she would feel when she saw the spot in the desert where her son had died. Would it be anything like what George Doucette had felt when he visited his wife's *descanso?* Would she feel closer to him there? Would she be granted her own resting place, a moment to recover her own strength? Or would it prove to be just a colossal let-down, the sort of empty sensation she felt when she went to Luke's grave?

"How long before we get to Marrizozo?" Elizabeth asked.

"I figure tomorrow afternoon some time," Gabe replied. Then, as if he'd been reading her thoughts, he said, "Try not to build it up too much."

"Build what up?"

"What you expect to happen out there? Just don't let your expectations run wild."

"I'm not really expecting much of anything," she said. But of course she was. She was expecting the world. That was the problem. Though she was too hard-headed to believe in all that supernatural stuff, she nonetheless expected the mystery and ambiguity of her son's death to be suddenly and irrefutably revealed, for clouds to part and bolts of ethereal light to descend, along with the singing of heavenly choirs, chubby little angels hovering about like in some painting by Raphael.

"Let me tell you a story," Gabe said.

"Does this one have a moral?"

"Just shut up and listen. About a year after Abby left me, she called out of the blue," Gabe began. "Said she wanted to meet. That she had something to tell me but she had to say it in person. So we agreed to meet at a restaurant halfway between where we lived. I got dressed up, shaved, put on cologne. All the way there, I kept telling myself that she was having second thoughts, that things with old Stu weren't working out and she wanted to try again to patch things up between us. I even practiced telling her I was sorry, that it was all my fault, that I loved her and would do anything to make it right, whatever she wanted. By the time I got there I had myself convinced that I'd have my wife and family back."

He paused dramatically to take a puff on his cigarette.

"And?" Elizabeth asked impatiently.

He chuckled cynically. "She wanted to tell me she was pregnant."

"Pregnant?"

"Ah huh. She didn't want me to find out through the grapevine that she and the proctologist were having a bambino together."

"So what's your point?"

"Well, my point is, you're better off keeping a lid on your expectations."

"Thanks for the words of wisdom."

"Do you always have to be such a wiseass?"

Around one o'clock they found the place called Ned's Landing. It was just south of Lubbock, way out in the middle of nowhere, an old airbase with an enormous metal hangar. Elizabeth and Gabe got out and headed inside. They found themselves in a small café and gift shop. Standing behind the counter was an old woman with a pinched face and silver hair done up in a bun.

"Would y'all care for tickets to the museum?" she asked.

"No," Elizabeth said, which seemed to disappoint the woman. "I spoke to a man a few days ago. About my son."

"That would probably be my husband. He's out in the museum now. I'll go get him."

The old woman headed out through a door at the back which had a sign over the window that said, *MUSEUM ENTRANCE*. Gabe followed her to the door and cupping his hands stared into the museum out back. Elizabeth glanced around the place. *He was here,* she thought. *Right here.* Not twenty-four hours before he died. She went over to the gift shop in one corner of the room. It offered shirts and caps and wind-breakers that had *Ned's Landing* printed on them. On one shelf were a number of tiny die-cast metal planes, like the one that Luke had bought. Elizabeth couldn't help but be reminded of that gift shop in Wales, where Luke had wandered off, enticed by that small British Spitfire.

When Gabe returned, he said to Elizabeth, "You should see what they got out back. All these cool World War II bombers and fighters. Your son was into planes?"

"When he was a little boy he collected them."

"My thing was cars. I used to have a nice collection of model cars."

After a while the woman returned accompanied by a thin old man, with rheumy blue eyes and one hand that trembled uncontrollably.

"Howdy," he said.

"I believe I spoke to you on the phone," Elizabeth began. "About my son. He stopped here and bought a model plane."

The man at first shook his head, his blue eyes looking confusedly at his wife. So Elizabeth got out her phone and showed both him and his wife the picture of Luke.

"Can't say I recall him," the husband said.

"Sure, you do, honey," she said. "Tall, good-looking young feller."

The man looked at his wife, his eyes clouded, still nothing registering. The wife smiled at Elizabeth and said, "He sometimes has trouble remembering things."

"I do not," he complained.

To her husband, the woman added, "Remember, the two of you talked about the P-51D we got out back."

Elizabeth reached into her pocketbook and took out Luke's model plane. "Is this what you talked about?"

Suddenly, a light went off in those pale blue eyes. He reached out with his trembling hand and took hold of the plane. Grinning a yellow-toothed grin, he said to Elizabeth, "That was *your* boy?"

"Yes."

"He knew his planes. I flew a Mustang in the Pacific Theater and he wanted to know all about it."

"Do you recall anything else about him?" Elizabeth asked.

The man looked to his wife again for help.

"Remember how polite he was, dear?" offered the wife.

"Oh, yes. That's true. He was a very a polite young man."

"Sometimes nowadays young people aren't so polite," his wife explained. "But your boy was a real gentleman."

Elizabeth had never heard Luke referred to as a gentleman before.

"Where you folks from?" the wife asked.

"Connecticut," replied Elizabeth.

"Is your boy here?" asked the old man, glancing over Elizabeth's shoulder, as if Luke were waiting in the car. She didn't want to bring up such sad news.

"No, he didn't come with us," she said, trading glances with Gabe. "Well, thank you so much."

"You sure you don't want to see the museum?" the old man asked. "We have some great planes."

"We have a long ways to drive," Gabe explained.

"Well, y'all take care," the wife said. "And come back and see us."

"Say hello to that boy of yours," the old man called after them.

* * *

About an hour before nightfall, they saw a sign along the road that said, "Welcome to New Mexico, Land of Enchantment." The landscape hardly looked enchanted, and it certainly didn't look like desert, at least not the sort Elizabeth had been expecting. More just rolling fields of dried grass with a few stunted cholla cactus cropping up here and there. Gabe told her that according to his GPS they were still more than two hundred miles from Marrizozo.

"Do you want to try making it?" Elizabeth asked.

Gabe looked over at her and shrugged. "If we're going to stop somewhere we'd better do it soon," he suggested. "There might not be a whole lot once it gets dark."

"Sounds good to me," Elizabeth replied.

"Roswell's an hour's drive. We can probably find something there."

"Okay." Then it dawned on her. "Isn't that the place—"

"Yeah, where all that alien stuff is," Gabe replied, rolling his eyes.

Roswell turned out to be equal to its reputation. It had a busy main drag and everywhere the UFO cottage industry was readily apparent. Places had names like the "Intergalactic Diner" or "Alien Realty" or "Lunar Laundromat." In most of the storefront windows the same scrawny, lime-green, big-headed, bug-eyed creature stared out at them, and all of the street lamps had the same creature's face painted on them. The Arby's and Wal-Mart had "Aliens Welcome" signs out front, and various businesses showed aliens promoting some sort of merchandise or other—aliens wearing cowboy hats or boots, playing a musical instrument, or in the Sleepy's, a green alien manikin dozing comfortably on a bed. Gabe and Elizabeth tried three different motels only to be told there were no vacancies. The clerk at the last one informed them that the town was in the midst of its annual UFO convention. Evidently alien nutjobs and conspiracy theorists, Star Trekkers and UFO aficionados from all over the country assembled there. Gabe and Elizabeth kept looking until they found a vacancy sign at a place called "The Star Ship Motel," a squat, adobe-style building whose outside walls were painted a matte black and overlaid with stars and planets and flying saucers of every shape and form.

After they checked in, they agreed to meet in half an hour for dinner. Later, as they walked along the main drag, the town buzzed with activity, the streets swarming with tourists in town for the convention. Elizabeth felt it was a cross between Halloween and Mardi Gras, with adults dressed up as Jedi Knights or Darth Vader or Chewbacca, others with their faces painted green or black or silver, some with bobbing antennae sticking out of their heads, others with Spock-like ears. They were laughing and some were drinking from bottles in paper bags.

"We forgot our costumes," Gabe said.

"It's kind of creepy."

"But fun, too."

"I suppose."

"Oh, just loosen up and enjoy it."

They stopped at a couple of restaurants only to be told it would be an hour or more wait. Along a side street, they happened upon a place called, "Casa de los Masciano," which had a sign out front with an alien wearing a sombrero and holding a margarita. Even this place was full. They had to settle for a table over near the kitchen doors. Their waitress, a tiny woman with sharp Native-American features, spoke such poor English Elizabeth resorted to speaking to her in Spanish. The woman reminded Elizabeth a little of Fabiana, and she made a note to herself to call the shelter and see how she was doing.

"*A Jack Daniels y Coca-Cola para mi amigo y una Coca-Cola light para mí, por favor*," Elizabeth said.

"*Sí, senora.*"

Elizabeth got a salad and a steak, while Gabe got the burrito grande with the works.

After a while the waitress brought their drinks over, along with a bowl of nachos and salsa. In the corner a jukebox was playing a Carrie Underwood song. A middle-aged couple danced in front of the jukebox, the only ones. Both were overweight but they seemed to know what they were doing, and were surprisingly light on their feet. The man spun the woman about in tight, skillful circles, and the two glided effortlessly across the dance floor as if they were skaters on ice.

"You like to dance?" Gabe asked.

"Not so much."

"I thought all women liked to dance. Abby loved to dance. She had all the moves, too. How about your husband?"

"More than I do."

"What's your husband's name again?"

"Zack."

"First thing you do when you get back is go out dancing with him."

"You think so?" Elizabeth said.

"It's fun. I wasn't much of a dancer but I loved being out there with Abby. Every guy in the place watching her."

As Elizabeth sipped her Coke, she eyed the two on the dance floor. There was an intimacy to the way they moved she found both erotic and yet vulnerable. She tried to remember the last time she'd danced with Zack. It was years ago, at some bar they'd both gotten a little drunk at. Zack asked her to dance but she refused, so he took her hand and pulled her out on the floor. There he put one arm on her back, with the other he took her hand and twirled her in slow circles. She remembered loving the feeling of being in his arms, slightly dizzy, slightly drunk. That night she could remember they went home and made love.

"Does the proctologist like to dance?" she asked.

"How the hell would I know?" Gabe said, batting the thought away with a flick of his hand. He polished off the rest of his drink. After a while the waitress came over with their food.

"Another one of these, *por favor*," Gabe said to the waitress, holding up his empty glass.

Elizabeth's steak was a bit tough. At one point she looked across at Gabe. He had his head down, eating with a single-mindedness of purpose, scooping up a forkful of burrito, then some beans and rice and guacamole, and washing it all down with gulps of Jack and Coke. She could imagine him eating like this when he was married and both his girls were alive, and he would come home from a long day of work, his wife and daughters around him at the dinner table, a regular, happy family. Like Zack and Luke and she had been. Before everything changed. Before the world turned dark and menacing. She was staring at him when he happened to look up.

"What?" he asked, wiping his mouth.

Instead of saying what she'd been thinking, she said, "Remember I told you the night my son died, I was away at a conference?"

"Yeah."

"I don't know why I didn't tell you before but I was with that man. Peter."

Gabe stopped chewing for a moment. "Oh, boy."

"Anyway, I didn't take Luke's call because I was with him," she explained.

Gabe raised his eyebrows. "Talk about bad timing."

"Actually, I was telling him it was over. That I couldn't see him anymore. That I loved my husband."

"So that was a good thing."

"Not so much a good thing as trying to make up for a bad thing."

"So let me guess—you blame yourself for your son's death?"

"Not his death exactly. But for not being there when he needed me."

"You know what your problem is, Elizabeth? You're way too hard on yourself."

"I was sleeping with another man when my son was killed."

"All right, I admit it was an unusual circumstance." Gabe put his fork down and stared at Elizabeth. "But number one," he said, counting on his fingers, "you couldn't possibly know it was your son calling. Number two, how were you supposed to know that he had something important to tell you? And three, and most importantly, how in God's name could you possibly know he'd get killed *that* night?" He held up three fingers in front of her, as if to prove his point. "I mean that's just bad karma."

"I thought bad karma comes from doing bad things."

"Listen, you need to let it go."

"I've tried."

"Try harder. I thought that's what this trip is all about? Letting things go. Getting some closure."

"The funny thing is, the last few days I've never thought more about Luke. Or that night. Or all the ways I failed him."

"Would you stop it? Guilt is easy," Gabe said.

"How do you figure that?"

"We just wallow in it like a pig in shit. We don't have to take responsibility. *Do* anything. Make changes. That's the hard part."

"And what about you?"

"What about me?"

"Aren't you wallowing in your own guilt?"

"Maybe I am a little. But the thing is, I don't have to make changes. Nobody's counting on me for anything."

"What about Jo?"

"Hell, she doesn't need me now."

"Sure she does. No matter how old a girl is, she always needs her dad. I still miss my father and he's been dead for almost twenty years."

He took another bite of his burrito and followed it with a big gulp of his drink.

"So tell me some more about this kid of yours."

"What would you like to know?"

"What sort of person was he?"

Elizabeth shrugged. "I guess he was like most twenty-one year-olds."

"Bullshit."

"Bullshit?"

"He was your kid and that means he wasn't like any other kid that ever walked God's green earth. And if he was anything like you, he must've been pretty special."

The question stumped her for a moment. After all, she'd never really had to describe her son to someone else. How many parents ever had to do such an exercise, define who their child was, to characterize what kind of human being he was? Not where he went to school or what grades he got or who his friends were or whether he played the guitar or was on the lacrosse team or who he dated, but to portray who he *was*, what made him tick, to describe his essence. What it was that made him different or unique from the billions of other children who had lived. To Elizabeth, her son had always been simply Luke. Her Lukey. It must have been similar to what Gabe had had to do when he sketched his family—to look at them objectively, carefully, their arms and hands, their mouths, those expressive eyes of theirs, and then to render them as truthfully as he could, not just the physical traits but who they *were*. And the more she thought about Gabe's question, the more she realized it was perhaps why people put up roadside crosses to mark where their children had died. Why they brought toys and keepsakes, pictures and baseball gloves and heaped them there. So as to define and remember who they were, as much for themselves as for the rest of the world.

"In most ways, at least the good ways, he took after my husband. He had an engineer's mind. He was good in math. He liked playing guitar," she said.

"Was he any good?"

"He was all right. I don't think he took it too seriously."

"That's not a bad thing necessarily. Too many kids are pushed too hard by their parents these days."

"I guess I was one of those pushy parents. Luke thought I was hard to please. That I was demanding."

"It was just because you wanted the best for him. Am I right?"

"That's what I told myself anyway."

"What else about your boy?"

"He liked to read. Always had his nose in a book. And he had this really incredible memory, too. He could recite things. Dialogue from movies. Songs. Lines of poetry. Used to write them down in his diary."

"And how would you know that?" Gabe said, grinning.

"I peeked sometimes. One time he wrote this line by Camus. I forget how it goes but something about how it's better to live your life as if there was a god and die and find out there wasn't rather than to live your life as if there wasn't only to die and find out there was."

"That's pretty deep."

She thought of that term Luke had written in his diary: *duc in altum*. She told him other things, too, about Luke. Things she'd almost forgotten. Things she couldn't say she'd ever really remembered in the first place. A funny thing began to happen as she spoke. The more she talked about her son, the more she seemed to remember about him. One memory conjured up another and another and so on. In some ways, it was like watching a film develop in a photographer's dark room—seeing Luke's features emerge from the blank paper, his nose and mouth and eyes take shape, arise out of the vagueness of her memory. She talked about how he had been a nervous child, anxious, easily upset by change. How he'd gone through a stage right after they'd moved to their lake house when he used to wet the bed for a while. She also told him how kind and generous and compassionate he could be. How even as a little boy, he always thought of the underdog, the downtrodden, the needy. How every night he'd insist that she read him the same story about the pig named Hamilton. Or how he liked collecting model planes. This led her to tell Gabe about the time they'd nearly lost him in Wales.

"The little stinker wandered off and scared us half to death," she said, laughing. "It was awful. Zack and I were running around crazy looking for him."

"Been there, done that," Gabe replied. "I remember Kelly pulling that stunt on us at the state fair once over in Nashville. Scared the living daylights out of us. What about that one girlfriend of his?"

"What about her?"

"Were they serious?"

She took a sip of her Coke. She thought again of what TJ had told her. Elizabeth felt that if she was trying to describe who her son really was, not who *she* wanted him to be or wanted others to believe him to be, wasn't that part of him, too? She felt she needed to be as faithful to Luke's memory as she could. Only in this way could she fully know her son.

"They broke up the fall before he died," she began.

"That's too bad. Why?"

"She thought . . . well, I don't really know how to say this. That Luke wasn't interested in women."

"What the hell's that supposed to mean? That he was gay?"

"She wasn't sure."

"Jesus. Why on earth would she tell you that?"

"It was sort of my fault. I called to ask why they'd split up. She didn't want to say it but I keep pushing her for an answer. And finally she told me it was because she thought he wasn't interested in women any more."

"Do you believe her?" Gabe asked.

Elizabeth shrugged. "I don't see why she would lie. She was always a good kid. And the thing is, I'm sure she really loved him."

"What do you think about your son? Do you think he was gay?"

"I frankly don't know. I guess there was always something about him, a part of him I didn't really know. Maybe didn't want to know. Or that *he* didn't want me to know. The funny thing is, after his girlfriend told me that, I began to wonder if *that* was what he wanted to tell me the night he died."

"That he was gay?"

"Or something."

"But why would he wait till he was halfway across the country to tell you that?"

"Maybe because he felt he couldn't tell me face to face. I guess I can be pretty intimidating."

"*You?*" Gabe said straight-faced.

"I think Luke felt I was too much of a perfectionist. That I expected him to be a certain way. Maybe that's what he wanted to tell me."

"Then again, maybe it was nothing important. Or maybe he just wanted to tell you he was thinking about you. That he loved you. Ever think of that?"

"You're sweet for saying that."

From his shirt pocket Gabe took out his little appointment book and a pen. "I just realized I don't even have a number where I could reach your husband. Just in case."

"Just in case what? Now you're creeping me out, Gabe."

"Relax."

She went ahead and gave him Zack's cell phone. From his address book he removed a card and slid it across the table. "Here's my card," he said. On it was written, *Gabe Tidrow, Towing and General Auto Repair. Free Estimates.*

"Now why would I need this?" she said.

"In case you're ever driving through Tennessee again and you run into a deer."

It had only been a couple of days but it seemed as if she'd known him much longer. Maybe it was the fact that they'd driven halfway across the country together, that they'd bonded during the long days on the road. Or that she'd shared so much with him, about her son, her husband, her private life, told him things she'd not told anyone before. Not Zack. Not George. Not anyone. Or maybe it was simply that they both shared the loss of children.

* * *

After dinner, they walked back to their motel. It was dark out now, decidedly cooler in the high desert night, making Elizabeth wish she'd brought along her sweatshirt. She felt goosebumps rippling the backs of her arms. The sky in the west was a lustrous Egyptian blue while straight overhead a million stars were scattered like grains of salt over a black canvas. They passed closed stores with more aliens staring out at them with their bug eyes. Across the street was a UFO museum with a marquee out front that suggested it had once been a movie theater.

"Look, it's still open," Gabe said. "Wanna go in?"

"I don't know."

"Oh, come on. It'll be fun."

Gabe paid and they went in and wandered around the place. It wasn't so much a museum, Elizabeth realized, as a carnival sideshow. The exhibits were all about supposed alien contact, with old, yellowed newspaper clippings on the walls from the 1950s about spaceship sightings, life on other planets, clandestine research facilities out in the desert, close encounters, hazy pictures of UFOs in the desert sky, and everywhere, little green men. In one exhibit, a sort of diorama, several mannequin doctors dressed up in white lab coats and masks were performing what appeared to be an autopsy on a green creature laid out on an operating table. The caption over the diorama said, "Proof positive of government cover-ups."

"That certainly convinces me," Gabe said.

Elizabeth laughed but felt a strange sensation in the pit of her stomach. Then she realized what it was. The dead alien reminded her a little of the time in the back room of Weldon's Funeral Home, seeing her son's body on the table. How his "remains" didn't look quite real, quite human. She turned and quickly left the room and headed out into the street.

"You okay?" Gabe asked when he'd caught up with her.

"Fine," she said.

As they headed back toward their motel, they passed a group of tipsy revelers dressed up as various figures from Star Wars—white-suited droids, an R2D2, a C3PO, Wookiees, Ewoks. They were yelling and laughing, sharing a bottle in a paper bag. Gabe stopped to stare at them while Elizabeth continued walking.

"Hey, what's the matter?" Gabe asked, grabbing her shoulder and stopping her.

"Just thinking."

"About what?"

"Luke."

"You mean about how he wasn't interested in women?"

"Not just that. Everything."

"You know, from all that you've told me, he seemed like a pretty neat kid."

"Yes, he was," she replied. "It's just that sometimes I feel I missed the boat with him."

"In what way?"

"Sometimes I don't feel that I really knew him. Who was he?"

"What parent knows everything about their kids? Hell, my Jo doesn't tell me or her mother half the shit she's up to. Otherwise we'd probably kill her." He laughed then, and Elizabeth followed suit. "But the important thing is you loved him, right?"

"I just hope he knew it."

"Of course, he did. Kids feel things even if they don't say anything."

Elizabeth looked at Gabe and shivered in the cool night air.

"You want my jacket?" he asked.

She tried to object but he wouldn't take no for an answer. He removed his coat—his ex-wife's husband's ex-coat—and draped it around her shoulders. They continued walking toward their motel.

"Gabe?"

"Yeah."

"What do you miss most about your daughter?" Elizabeth asked.

He didn't reply for a while. Then he said, "This is going to sound weird. Her feet."

"Her feet?"

"When she danced she used to get these really bad cramps in her feet. She'd like me to rub them, 'cause I have strong hands. I remember we'd be watching TV and I'd have her feet in my lap and I'd be rubbing her toes really hard. She'd squeal bloody murder sometimes, so I'd stop. But she'd always say, 'Do it some more, Dad. Please.' That's what I remember the most."

By then they'd reached the motel.

"Thanks for listening," Elizabeth said.

"You, too." As she turned toward her room, Gabe called after her, "You might want to give that husband of yours a call. He's probably worrying about you."

"You think so?"

"I would be."

Later, after she brushed her teeth and washed her face, she crawled into bed and called Zack.

"Hi," she said.

"Hi. Where are you now?"

"New Mexico."

"How far are you away from Marrizozo?"

"We should get there tomorrow." A slip of the tongue.

"We?"

She didn't want to have to get into what would be a long and convoluted explanation. She could do that later, in person. "I'm just so used to saying *we*."

"I know what you mean," he replied.

Neither said anything for a few seconds. Finally Elizabeth asked, "What do you think, Zack?"

"About what?" he asked. She could see he wasn't going to make it easy for her.

"About what I told you last night. I wouldn't blame you for leaving me."

"Is that what you want, Elizabeth?"

"No. No, I want us to stay married. I love you. I'm just saying I couldn't blame you."

"We can talk about it when you get home."

"What does that mean?"

"It means we can talk about it then. I have to be honest though. I'm hurt by what you did."

"I would be, too."

"What hurts even more is that you didn't tell me afterwards."

"I wanted to. I don't know why I didn't. I just want us to try again."

"I can't promise that. We'll just have to see."

"That's all I can expect."

"Goodnight, Elizabeth."

Chapter 18

The next morning, she met Gabe out at the truck. He was sitting on the hood reading a map and sipping a coffee.

"You want to grab a coffee or something before we hit the road?" he said, glancing up at her before returning his attention to the map. "Doesn't look like there's much till we hit Marrizozo."

"I'm not hungry," she said. "Let's just get going."

"Mind if I get something?"

After stopping at a McDonald's, they pulled out of the alien capital and headed west. The scenery changed rapidly. They passed through high, arid plains punctuated by dry creek beds and ocher-colored mesas, and in the distance, a thin, hazy-blue band of mountains. The farther west they traveled, the more mountainous and rugged the land became, with steep ravines and long, windy passes ascending the higher peaks. Elizabeth could feel the altitude change as a general light-headedness and a prickly, numbing feeling in her toes. She'd read somewhere that was a sign of altitude sickness.

An hour later, they were driving through a mountainous national forest, thickly wooded with ponderosa pine and aspen. For a while the road ascended a long, gradually undulating incline, generally following the contours of a river far below in the valley. A frail-looking guardrail was all that came between them and the steep abyss just to their right. Elizabeth, who had never liked heights, could feel herself tensing, the vertigo rising in her chest like a wave of hot sand. She tried to keep her eyes pointed directly forward.

They had nearly reached the summit when they saw them. At the edge of the road, in one of those scenic overlooks where tourists pull off to get out their cameras and snap pictures of "vistas" for future family albums, they stretched out in a long row, all glistening white, perfectly lined up side by side, like a papier-mâché cutout of little children holding hands. Elizabeth permitted herself a quick glance at the miniature crosses aligned just this side of the guard rail.

"Jesus," Gabe cried, slowing the truck. "Would you look at that?"

"Keep going," Elizabeth said.

"I want to see what it is."

He pulled the truck over into the turnoff.

"No. Please," she said, frightened of pausing so close to the edge of the cliff.

"I'll be right back. Wait here if you want."

Elizabeth watched Gabe get out and saunter up to the spectacle that was the crosses. She closed her eyes and felt her breath coming harder, her stomach knotting, the pulse in her neck going *dub-dub, dub-dub*. After a moment she opened her eyes, her gaze lighting once more on the crosses. As she stared at them, she wondered what had happened here. What unspeakable tragedy had occurred at this spot?

Finally, her curiosity got the better of her fear. She opened the door and got out and walked cautiously over to where Gabe was squatting before the crosses. She avoided looking over the edge. Gabe glanced up at her, then nodded toward the crosses.

"High school bus."

"What?"

"A bunch of kids traveling back from a basketball game went off the road right here," he explained like a park ranger at some Civil War battleground. "Fourteen kids were killed."

"Oh, my God," she sighed.

"And get this. They were from Marrizozo. Place we're headed to. Isn't that weird?"

All the crosses appeared identical and all were perfectly aligned facing east, toward the sunrise. In the middle of the line of crosses was a bronze plaque, heavily covered with verdigris. Elizabeth knelt beside Gabe to read what was written on it. The accident had happened here on a winter night back in January 1979. Many of the names were Hispanic. Some were girls' names, no doubt cheerleaders on the bus. Most, Elizabeth figured, would have been about her age now. Grown-ups with children of their own. Many of the crosses had mementos set before them—small crucifixes and rosary beads, plastic flowers or browned Christmas wreaths, toys and keepsakes, dolls and plastic super hero figurines. All of the crosses had laminated pictures of the dead children below their names, some showing young girls with Farrah Fawcett 'dos, the boys looking like Eric Estrada.

So many lost children, Elizabeth thought. So many grieving parents. How could one town have survived such a tragedy? But then she thought of what George Doucette had told her, how the spirits of the dead gave off that energy. Elizabeth could almost feel something here, something palpable, though she wasn't sure whether the dizzy, tingling sensation along the back of her scalp wasn't just vertigo or perhaps altitude sickness. She imagined the parents of the fourteen gathering in someone's living room and discussing plans, agreeing on putting up this memorial, donating money or time, arranging raffles at the high school and bake sales at the church, and then coming out here together on a certain day to dig the holes and put up the crosses, then light candles and pray, hold hands and cry. A vigil, like the one Zack was planning back home. People united in their suffering and in their love. She imagined the kids on that bus, moments before it pitched off the cliff, laughing and talking, the players going over the points they scored, the girls whispering about which boys they liked, some test they had the next day in school, their entire lives stretching out before them like an unchartered country. And then a momentary, dizzying flight into eternity.

As she stood there Elizabeth felt a sudden chill, a tingling between her shoulder blades. She shuddered as if a cool wind had just blown across her back.

"You ready?" Gabe asked.

"Yeah."

They got back in the truck and continued on.

* * *

Around noon, they came down out of the mountains. Below them lay a broad desert basin, flat and dun-colored, the air shimmering in the mid-day heat. Farther west another mountain range rose from the earth in purplish waves against crystalline blue skies. In the middle of the valley sat a small town, a handful of buildings congregated along a now-abandoned railroad track and a dry creek bed. As they approached, they passed a sign that said *Welcome to Marrizozo, Pop 978. Home of the Catamounts.*

As they entered the town, they drove past a convenience store, a service station, two adobe-style motels, a grocery store, a restaurant named The Fort, and a train station whose windows were long boarded up, and had peeling ads that said *Reagan/Bush '84.*

"So what's the plan?" Gabe asked.

She'd never really had a plan. A plan would've suggested she'd actually counted on getting here. It'd all been so much improvisation, done by the seat of her pants. When she'd left home several days ago, it was as if she just wanted to see how far she could get before her little game was up, and she admitted defeat, turned around, and headed home. Now that she was here though, she wasn't sure what came next.

"I guess we ought to start by finding out where the sheriff's office is."

Gabe made a U-turn and drove back to the convenience store.

"You want anything?" he asked.

"No, thanks."

Elizabeth got out to stretch. The back of her shirt was wet from her having been sitting for so long. Though fall, the day was warmish, with a lethargic heat rising from the asphalt. In front of the gas station she saw a curious thing: a statue of a donkey painted a bright blue with red spots all over it as if it had the measles. In a moment Gabe returned with a coffee and a pack of cigarettes.

"Sheriff's office is just down the street."

They pulled up before a one-story concrete structure that said, *Town Offices of Marrizozo, New Mexico.*

"You want me to come in with you?" Gabe asked.

"I probably should go by myself. Keep it simple."

"Sure."

Elizabeth got out and headed in. She spoke to the sheriff's secretary, a Mrs. McNanus said her name-plate, an older woman with straw-like blonde hair and frail, veiny hands.

"Is Sheriff Crowder in?"

"He's just heading out," the woman replied, her tone brusque, proprietary, as if she doled out the sheriff's time only grudgingly.

"I really need to speak him," Elizabeth pleaded.

Just then a tall, gristle-thin man in his sixties emerged from a back office.

"This woman's here to see you, Sheriff," the secretary said. The sheriff's silvery hair and pale blue eyes were in sharp contrast to the tanned and weathered features whose cragginess resembled the land Elizabeth had just passed through. He didn't wear a uniform, just a denim shirt, baggy jeans that hung on his thin frame, and a felt cowboy hat. The only way you could tell he was a police officer was by the big pearl-handled automatic pistol on his hip and the badge that said *Sheriff J. P. Crowder.*

Elizabeth introduced herself, handed him her business card. He gave the card a cursory glance. Her name didn't seem to register with him at all.

"You're a lawyer?" he asked.

"Yes. We've spoken before."

"We have?"

"About my son. Luke Gerlacher."

Recognition slowly came over the sheriff's face as his thin lips pursed into a grimace.

"Oh. *That* Gerlacher. What is it I can do for you, ma'am?" he asked, but his tone had suddenly turned defensive. "I'm running late to a dentist appointment. I got this darn toothache." He touched his jaw for added urgency.

"I just need a moment of your time, Sheriff," she explained.

"I told you everything I knew, ma'am. We sent you all of your son's personal effects. There's nothing else here."

"It's not about that. I just had a couple of questions."

He stood there for a moment, looking impatient, his mouth pinched.

"You really should get going, Sheriff," the secretary warned, giving Elizabeth a dirty look.

The sheriff removed his hat and ran his hand through his thick silvery hair.

"I guess I can spare five minutes. Whyn't you come in my office. Barb, call Dr. Peters and tell him I'm running a few minutes late."

"He ain't gonna like it."

"That's too bad."

The woman let out a sigh of annoyance but picked up the phone and called.

Elizabeth followed the sheriff into the sheriff's office where he offered her a chair while he sat behind his desk. He leaned back in his chair, put his hands behind his head, and placed his feet up on the desk. He wore pointy cowboy boots made out of some sort of exotic snake skin.

"I think you and me got off on the wrong foot, Mrs. Gerlacher," the sheriff began. "Let me start by offering my condolences for your loss."

"Thank you, Sheriff."

"Where is it you're coming from again?"

"Connecticut."

"That's a hike. You fly into Albuquerque?"

"No. I drove."

"The whole way?" When she nodded he puckered his thin lips and let out a dry whistle. "That *is* quite a hike. Now what is it I can do for you?"

"I want to see where my son died," Elizabeth said.

The sheriff stared across his desk at her, as if waiting for more information. "It was south of here. Down heading toward Tularosa, as best I recall."

"I'd like to see the spot."

"The spot, ma'am?"

"The scene of the accident."

The man frowned again, then put his feet down, leaned forward, and placed his elbows on the desk. "Can I ask what this is about, Mrs. Gerlacher?" His tone had shifted back to a cautionary formality.

"I just wanted to see where he died, Sheriff."

"I assure you we did everything possible to save your boy."

She realized then what he was thinking. That she, a lawyer, was here to cause him problems. To investigate her son's death, perhaps to find something wrong and bring some sort of negligence suit against the town or him or both. She could see the thought worrying his blue eyes.

"I'm sure you did all you could. I'm not looking to blame anybody, Sheriff. I'm just here as his mother. I simply want to see where he died."

"You came an awful long way just to do that. Can I ask you why?"

"I have my reasons. If you can just tell me where it is, I can be on my way."

"The problem is, you're talking about a whole lot of highway down there, and it all pretty much looks the same. If you're not familiar with it, it'd be like finding a needle in a haystack. Deputy Jimenez would be the one to talk to."

"Who is he?" Elizabeth said.

"He was the first responder that night. But he's out on patrol now. Won't be back till his shift ends at five. I could have him contact you when he gets in. Where you staying?"

"I don't know? I haven't decided yet."

"There's The Saguaro. Up toward the train station. Donna's rates are reasonable."

"My number's on the card, Sheriff," she replied, standing. Though she still resented the fact that he had stonewalled her, she extended her hand to shake. "Thank you, Sheriff."

"You're welcome, ma'am. Again, I'm sorry about your loss."

As she and Gabe drove back up the street, she related her conversation with the sheriff.

"So now what?" Gabe asked.

"I guess the deputy is going to call me later. Take me out to see where the accident happened."

"Did the sheriff find that diary you talked about?"

"No. He said they sent everything they had."

"What happened to your son's car?"

"I don't know," Elizabeth replied.

"I mean, was it totaled?"

"I think so. We got a check from the insurance company."

"Then it was probably sold to some junk yard for salvage. You should've asked where they towed it."

"Why?"

"You might be able to search it."

The thought of going through Luke's battered car, seeing the crumpled metal and shattered glass, maybe his dried blood, knowing this car had been, in effect, his coffin, chilled her.

"I'd rather not do that," she said. "Besides, it doesn't make any difference now, does it?"

"Just asking."

At the Saguaro Motel, Elizabeth got two rooms, side by side with an outdoor corridor. The motel had a little gift shop in the lobby that sold t-shirts with pictures of cacti and mountains printed on them, with the name of the motel across the front. Gabe bought a t-shirt.

"For Jo," he said. "She likes this sort of touristy crap."

"Listen, I'm a little beat," Elizabeth told him. "I think I'm going to take a nap."

"Okay. I'll check in with you later. I think I'll do a little exploring."

She lay down on the bed on top of the covers, and while she was exhausted her mind was too occupied to sleep right away. She felt on edge, anxious for some reason. Perhaps it was because she was so close to the emotional epicenter of what she'd come so far to see. How the end of her son's life had come here, *in this town,* and how he'd carried whatever secret he'd wanted to tell her to his grave. She thought about the question of whether or not he had been gay. How at the very least he'd had this entirely secretive life, a life apart from the one he'd presented to her and Zack. Yet didn't everyone have a secret life, she wondered. Didn't she? Or even Zack? Here he'd known about her affair all along yet hadn't said anything. Why? There were suddenly so many secrets, so many hidden parts to what she'd once thought to be her happy little family.

She dozed off finally and was awakened from jumbled dreams by a knock on the door. When she answered it, Gabe was slouching there.

"That deputy show up?" he asked.

"No. Not yet."

"You wanna grab a bite?"

"What time is it?"

"Almost six."

"Oh my God!" Without realizing it, she'd slept for almost four hours. "I don't want to miss him."

"He's got your number. Come on. There's a little place just a couple blocks down the street. I'm hungry."

"When aren't you hungry?"

"I have a fast metabolism."

"All right. Give me a minute to clean up."

As they walked down the main drag, Elizabeth felt the change in the weather. The heat of the day had quickly dissipated and the evening was cooler, with intimations of autumn. To the west, massive, dark-gray thunderheads had coalesced over the mountains like a shroud. In fact, it looked as if it was already raining there. Long bluish tails hung below the clouds, extending down to the high peaks. The air even smelled damp, and sweetly of creosote bush and chamisa. As they walked along Elizabeth noticed more statues of donkeys here and there: a bright pink one in front of the Marrizozo Hardware Store; another on the roof of a grocery, this one avocado green with red polka dots; a third, painted red, white, and blue, stood before a VFW Post. Another, in front of a small pharmacy, had a white nurse's cap stuck on its head.

"They got these damn things all over the town," Gabe explained. "I was told a local sculptor makes them. He uses the entire town as his gallery. Evidently, there's a little artists' quarter where a bunch of ex-hippies settled here back in the seventies. It's actually a cool little place."

"You could open a gallery here." She said it partly tongue-in-check. Gabe *humphed* sarcastically, as if she was making fun of him.

"No, I mean it."

"Who the hell would buy my work?"

"I would."

He rolled his eyes.

"You don't give yourself enough credit."

"Artists like me are a dime a dozen."

They ate at The Fort, a dark and, at first glance, rough-looking place. It was pretty crowded but then Elizabeth realized it was a Friday night. Men dressed in jeans and sweat-stained cowboy or baseball caps sat at the bar with brassy-voiced women, while families took up booths along the front wall. Most of the people seemed to know each other. They called out to one another from across the bar, conversations drifting and intermingling. People were laughing, having a good time. In the corner a young guy and girl were playing a game of pool. Elizabeth and Gabe went over and sat in a booth.

The waitress, a pretty brunette wearing a walking cast on her foot, hobbled over with some menus.

"What happened to you?" Gabe asked her.

"Long story," she replied, obviously tired of retelling it. "What can I get you to drink?"

Gabe got his usual J & C, and he was about to order a Diet Coke for Elizabeth when she said, "I think I'll have a scotch on the rocks."

Gabe looked at her, grinned, then spun one finger in the air. "*Woo-eee,*" he said. "I thought you're on the wagon?"

"I feel like celebrating."

"You sure about that?"

"Just one."

"Famous last words."

In a little while the waitress returned with their drinks. She told them the specials. There wasn't much to choose from on the menu so they played it safe and both ordered burgers and fries.

After she left, Gabe held up his glass. "To you," he said to Elizabeth.

She frowned. "Why are we toasting me?"

"Would you just relax for once and not over think every damn thing? I'm paying you a compliment. For coming all the way out here."

"Well, thanks."

The drink, her first in nearly three weeks, tasted both of victory and of defeat, a celebration of success and an acknowledgment of life's frailties. She'd set off expecting something, though she couldn't have said what that something was now, and she'd gotten both more and less than she'd anticipated. For each question that had been answered, it seemed two more had been placed in front of her. But one sip of her scotch made her relax a little.

"And to you," she offered. "For bringing me out here. For listening to me."

"No biggie."

"No, it was a biggie. You didn't have to do any of this. So thanks," she said.

Soon their food came and they settled into eating. Several times she checked her phone, just to make sure she hadn't missed the call from the deputy in the noisy bar.

"Any news yet?" Gabe asked.

"No. Maybe he stopped by the motel looking for me."

"He would've called."

"What if he doesn't remember where it happened?"

She felt that vague anxiety building again, now represented by a tightness in her chest. She thought of what the sheriff had said, that locating the spot would be like finding a needle in a haystack. What she worried about was that after all the trouble of getting here, she wouldn't be able to see where Luke had died. Then again, maybe what she worried about was that she *would* be able to see it. Maybe she was more afraid of going there, afraid of what she'd feel or, equally, of what she *wouldn't* feel.

"You're just one of those people that's not happy unless you're worrying about something," Gabe told her. "Just stop it."

Elizabeth's gaze happened to fall on the young couple playing pool. The guy was stocky and muscular, wore his jeans halfway down his butt so that when he bent over for a shot, the creamy-white top of his butt cheeks peeked out. The girl, with frizzy, reddish hair, was wide-hipped, and not particularly attractive. Still, there was something about them that made Elizabeth think of Luke and TJ when they were together. Perhaps it was how they were so tender with each other, so solicitous. When the girl took a shot the man would wrap his arms around her and help her steady her pool cue. Elizabeth thought of how she'd always imagined Luke and TJ getting married, having children, bringing the grandchildren over for holidays—the whole clichéd nine yards of married life. And yet if Luke had lived, perhaps he wouldn't have been getting married. He would have had some other sort of life, just not the one she'd imagined for him. After a while the couple finished the game and went over to a booth and sat down.

"Ever play?" Gabe asked, with a nod of his head toward the pool table.

"I'm not much of a pool player."

"Come on. It'll take your mind off things," he said. "Besides, I'll take it easy on you."

Even though she was terrible at pool, it turned out to be fun, and he was right—it distracted her for a while. She found herself laughing when she missed easy shots, once knocking the cue ball completely off the table and sending it skittering across the floor where some bearded guy in a cowboy hat picked it up for her and brought it over and handed it to her like it was some precious stone. "This is yours, I think, ma'am." And she whooped it up when she made one really difficult, insanely lucky shot. To which Gabe said, "So you're really a pool shark after all." There was something pleasurable about seeing the balls shooting over the wide, green surface, ricocheting off each other, making that sharp *ncckk* sound as they collided. The order, the re-assuring logic they seemed to represent. Gabe and Elizabeth played a couple games of eight ball. Without seeming to try, he beat her handily in the first one, then in the second he started to miss easy shots.

"You're doing that on purpose," she complained. "I don't want your pity."

"What pity? Just bad luck," he said.

"Well, you'd better bring your A-game, mister."

As she was lining up one shot, she felt the vibration of her cell phone in her jeans pocket. She removed her phone and saw the call wasn't from the deputy but from Joan.

She hesitated, then said to Gabe, "I'd better take this." She headed over to the women's room so she could hear. "Hi, Joan."

"Are you still on the road?" her friend asked.

"Yes."

There was a pause on the other end, one that Elizabeth knew wasn't good news. Then Joan said, "Listen, kiddo. I tried. Really I did. But Warren had had it. I'm sorry. He's offering you a good severance package though. You could try to fight it but if I were you I'd take it."

Instead of being upset with the news, Elizabeth felt oddly relieved.

"Elizabeth?" Joan asked.

"Yeah."

"Are you okay?"

"I'm fine."

"I tried. But he wasn't listening."

"I know you did. You're a good friend, Joan. It's not your fault."

"Let's talk when you get back, okay? I have some contacts you could try."

"Sure. Do me a favor? Don't say anything to Zack yet."

"Of course. Hang in there, kiddo."

After she hung up she headed back out into the restaurant, picked up her pool cue, and lined up her next shot.

"Something the matter?" Gabe asked.

Without looking at Gabe, she said, "I just got fired."

"Fired? Because you left?"

"It was a lot of things. But that was, as they say, the straw that broke the camel's back."

She struck the cue ball, which careened off the ball she was aiming at, and shot into a pocket.

"I should get fired more often," she cried.

"That sucks," Gabe offered. "What are you going to do now?"

She shrugged.

"I was thinking about making a change anyway."

"Change is good. Maybe I should make a change, too."

"What are you thinking?"

"Leaving Tennessee."

Gabe got on a hot streak and ran the table. After the last shot, they high-fived and then headed over and sat down in their booth. The waitress with the cast came up and asked if they wanted another round.

"I'd better not," said Elizabeth.

Gabe ordered another. "Did you talk to your husband?" he asked.

"Yeah."

"And?"

"He said we'll talk when I got home. He's angry and I can't really blame him."

"Well, that's a start, right? Talking."

Elizabeth nodded.

* * *

It was fully dark when they headed back to the motel. Though she'd managed to stick to the one-drink limit, she was still feeling a little woozy. She wasn't sure if it was the booze or the altitude. Marrizozo was mostly quiet and unlit, looking like a ghost town set amid the high desert.

"Goodnight, Gabe," she said.

"See you in the morning."

She was washing her face when she heard the knock on the door. A man in a uniform waited there. He appeared to be in his thirties, with a thick, squarish body and glistening black hair.

"Mrs. Gerlacher?" the officer said.

"Yes."

"I'm Deputy Jimenez. The chief said you were staying here. That you wanted to talk to me about your son's accident."

"Yes, I did. I was hoping you could show me where it happened."

"The accident site's way down towards Alamogordo."

"Could you take me there?"

"It's too late tonight. We'd never find it in the dark."

"Tomorrow?"

"I'll have to okay it with the Sheriff first. I'll call you in the morning."

Elizabeth nodded.

The man started to turn back to his police car.

"Oh, Officer Jimenez."

The man stopped and came back over.

"Yes, ma'am."

"Did my son say anything? I mean, did he have any last words?"

"No, ma'am. He was pretty much unresponsive when I got there."

"I see. Thank you."

Chapter 19

Luke sat in the corner of the small, ill-lit room. He looked the way he had when she'd last seen him, right before he left on his cross-country trip. Having recently shed the remnants of his boyish looks, he appeared every bit a man. Perhaps too thin. His face angular, with subtle shadows beneath his sharp cheeks. His jaw slightly unshaven. He looked almost ascetic.

Hi, mom.
How are you, sweetheart?
I've been waiting for you.
I know. I'm sorry it took me so long.
It's okay. But it's been lonely.
I would have gotten here sooner but . . .
It's all right. You're here now.
Is there anything you need?
He shook his head. I miss you.
I miss you, too, sweetheart.
I have to go soon, he said.
Make sure you eat enough. You're too thin.

She closed her eyes and nodded back off. When she woke again, it was already light out. On the opposite wall was a painting of the desert—a few cacti, mountains in the distance. It looked clumsily done, like it was painted by someone in a senior citizens' craft class. In a couple of hours the policeman would arrive and take her to the site of her son's death. Lying there, she felt the words float into her conscious mind: *Make sure you eat enough. You're too thin.* That's it, she thought. That's what she had said to her son, the last time she had laid eyes on him. He was getting into his car, about to take off on his cross-country trip. *Make sure you eat enough. You're too thin.*

Then she thought of George Doucette. He'd know what she was feeling. Besides, he was the one who put this crazy notion in her head to begin with. She grabbed her pocketbook, extracted her phone, and dialed his number. As it rang, she glanced at the alarm clock on the bedside table—it was a little after six, which would have made just after eight back in Connecticut. She was about to hang up when a voice said, "Yeah."

"It's me, George. Elizabeth Gerlacher. I'm the woman—"

"I know who you are." His voice sounded raspy with sleep but also slightly annoyed. "What the hell time is it?"

"I'm sorry. Did I wake you?"

"That's all right. How are you?" he asked.

"I'm fine," she replied. "I went out to New Mexico just like you suggested. As a matter of fact, I'm here right now."

"Good for you."

"Actually, that's why I'm calling. A police officer is going to take me out to the accident site this morning."

"What can I do for you, Elizabeth?"

"The thing is, I feel a little nervous."

"Of course, you are."

"I'm not sure what to do now. When I get there, I mean. To the place where he died."

"I think when you see it, you'll know what to do."

"I'm afraid though."

"Of what?"

"I can't really say."

"Something will come to you."

"Do you think I should pray?"

"You got to do what feels right for you. You already did the hard part, going out there. Tell him whatever's on your mind."

"Do you think that will do any good?"

"If you mean do I think he'll hear you, yes. I do. But whether you believe that or not, I can't say. You're his mother. You loved him. That's enough."

"Thank you, George. For everything."

"You take care of yourself."

After she hung up, she remembered the time when Luke was in fourth grade and one of his classmates' mothers had just died of breast cancer. Elizabeth was in the kitchen making Luke's lunch, while her son was seated behind her eating breakfast. "He won't be able to talk to her again?" he asked.

"Who, sweetie?"

"Todd. He won't be able to talk to his mother again, right?"

It was so very like Luke to ask something like that, something wise beyond his years.

"No, sweetie," she replied. "She's dead."

"And she won't be able to see him again?"

A truthful answer seemed to her too stark, too unremittingly pessimistic, especially for a nine-year-old.

"He'll see her again in heaven," she replied, though she didn't really believe in heaven. At least not in any simplistic notion of it. But it was like telling a child that Santa or the Easter Bunny existed. You didn't have to believe yourself to offer comfort to one who could use it. That's when Luke had said to her, "He won't have anybody to make his lunch now, Mom." So she had made a second lunch for his friend.

Was that what George Doucette had been doing with her, offering her comfort? She remembered the line George had said to her that first time and which she now knew by heart: *To give light to them that sit in darkness and in the shadow of death.* She hadn't a clue what it meant when he first told her. Just some Bible gibberish. Now, however, after having made this long journey, she felt she had some idea of what it was to sit in darkness, to wait in the shadow of death, and to yearn for light, to wait for it, even the frailest of light, hoping that it might, in some small way, relieve the darkness.

She got out her notebook and reviewed once more her notes on Luke's trip. She looked at the dots on the map, stared at them from various angles, hoping that now, after having followed in her son's footsteps, a comprehensible pattern might emerge at long last, a sense of order arising finally from the chaos surrounding Luke's death. Yet the dots remained obstinately meaningless, unconnected. They were like Braille to a sighted person. She was brought out of her reverie by the phone. It was Deputy Jimenez saying he'd be by around eight.

Elizabeth got up and dressed, threw on her St. Anselm sweatshirt, and left the room. She walked up the street to the convenience store. The day continued overcast with an autumnal coolness hanging in the air. Every sound seemed magnified in the high desert morning. Somewhere a bird cried, harshly, sounding like the swinging of a rusty hinge. She bought two coffees, and a pack of cigarettes. When she returned, she stood just outside her room, sipping her coffee and savoring the nicotine rush of the cigarette. Though it was a Saturday morning, the people of Marrizozo were busily making their way here and there—farmers in pickups, a milk truck en route to make deliveries, a semi loaded with chickens. A school bus filled with a football team going to a game somewhere. The town quietly, determinedly going about the serious business of living. She thought of that bus accident all those many years ago and how it must have shattered the peace of this small town. How for years no one could have run into another person without it coming up, without the tragedy making its way into every conversation, darkening every mood, infiltrating the town's consciousness. Everyone sitting in darkness waiting for light. Every time you saw someone in the grocery store, the post office, having a beer in The Fort, the deaths of those fourteen kids would have risen to the surface like poison leaching into the groundwater. And yet, here they were, getting up, going to work, somehow carrying on.

"Mornin'," Gabe said to her. He was hatless and his short hair stuck up at odd sleep-induced angles. The "Stu" jacket was zipped to his neck. He hopped from one foot to the next and rubbed his hands together. "Nippy out, huh?"

"I got you a coffee." She bent and picked up the coffee she'd set on the ground and handed it to Gabe.

"Thanks. You ready?" he asked.

"Ready?"

"For today."

"About as ready as I'll ever be."

A little after eight, Deputy Jimenez pulled into the parking lot of the motel in an SUV with *Marrizozo Sheriff's Department* painted on the side.

"Sorry. I had to bring my kids to my ex's," he explained.

"So you got one of those, too?" Gabe joked.

"She's not so bad, really," the deputy replied.

Elizabeth got in up front while Gabe sat in the back. They drove south through town, passing a Pizza Hut, a grocery store, a small adobe-style Catholic church on a side street, and a half dozen more of those gaudily painted donkeys.

They continued on south of town. They passed several abandoned houses, an out-of-business gas station, and an empty motel as well as a sprawling junkyard where cars extended far out into the desert, some dating back to the forties.

From the backseat, Gabe asked the deputy, "Would you know where her son's car was towed?"

"I sure wouldn't," the man replied.

While Gabe and the deputy carried on a conversation, Elizabeth stared out the window at the passing landscape. Its repetitive sameness reminded her of the background of one of those Wile E. Coyote cartoons.

"How big is the town?" Gabe inquired.

"About nine hundred. In its heyday Marrizozo used to be a lot bigger. Nearly double that."

"A regular metropolis," joked Gabe.

"People used to come here to see where the bomb exploded."

"What bomb?" Gabe asked.

"The first atomic bomb."

"Really. I didn't know that."

"It was just down in Alamagordo a ways," the deputy said, pointing a finger down the road. "We used to get lots of tourists. But then I-Forty went through north of here and that was all she wrote. We've had a little comeback in recent years. A lot of artists and whatnot."

"I imagine a place like this draws its whatnots," said Gabe.

The farther south they went the fewer signs there were of a human hand. With the exception of barbed wire fencing and the occasional cattle stile, the countryside around Marrizozo was a vast brown stretch of mountain and desert; it looked like a sea-bed devoid of water. The land extended on either side of the road flat and desolate, covered with spindly buffalo grass and sage brush, stunted pinyon pine. Occasionally a boulder or rock formation would break the monotony, but otherwise the reddish-brown earth ran uninterrupted all the way to mountains in the west.

"We're supposed to get some rain," the deputy offered to Elizabeth.

"Really?"

"We sure could use it."

Though the deputy wasn't handsome, Elizabeth thought he had a nice smile. A friendly, eager-to-please expression on his broad, dark face.

"How old are your kids, officer?" Elizabeth inquired of him.

"My daughter is five. The little one, a boy, just turned three."

"Those are good ages," Gabe commented from the back.

"My son just learned the word 'no,'" Deputy Jimenez said with a laugh. "Everything's no."

The deputy asked Elizabeth about the long drive from Connecticut, and he offered how the farthest east he'd been was Fort Dix, New Jersey when he was in the service. But soon the conversation ran out of steam under the relentless onslaught of the withering landscape shooting by along the roadside.

The desert seemed to lull them, make them lethargic. Elizabeth felt herself yawning. Maybe it had that effect on people passing through its repetitious expansiveness, she thought. Perhaps that's what had happened to her son, lulled him into a tragic sleep, one from which he would never wake. She thought of the dream of Luke telling her that he'd been waiting for her. It was just a stupid dream but she couldn't help but appreciate the symbolism of it.

They'd been driving for half an hour when the deputy took his foot off the gas. He began to look out his driver's side window at the opposite side of the road.

"Happened over there in the northbound lane. Somewhere," Deputy Jimenez said, as if he himself didn't feel very confident of actually finding the spot.

"Which way was he headed?" Elizabeth asked.

"South."

"But wasn't there some confusion about which way he was headed?"

"No, ma'am. It was clear from the skid marks he was headed south toward Alamagordo."

"Oh."

"We're getting close now." He looked over at Elizabeth. "What was he doing in Marrizozo anyway?"

"He was driving out to the west coast. I guess he wanted to see some of the country."

"We don't get that many visitors down here," the deputy said. "People passing through usually don't get off the interstate."

"Except the whatnots," Gabe said. Elizabeth turned to look at him and he grinned, foolishly.

Looking out on the desiccated landscape, Elizabeth thought, *Of all the places to die, why here, for heaven's sake?*

They continued on, with the deputy now and then slowing almost to a stop, inspecting a section of desert that looked indistinguishable from every other section, frowning, before shaking his head and driving on. After a while, though, he came to a complete stop, surveyed a stretch of land the way one might a piece of property he was interested in buying and building a home on. Finally, he exclaimed, "Here we go. See that cattle stile. It was just past that a little ways."

The deputy swung the SUV in a wide U-turn and pulled off onto the shoulder of the northbound lane. He shut the motor off and got out. Gabe and Elizabeth followed suit.

As they headed off the road and out into the desert a ways, Deputy Jimenez said, "Keep an eye out for snakes."

"Snakes?" said Gabe, his eyes scanning the ground.

"The chief would have my neck if somebody was to get bit."

Elizabeth turned and looked at Gabe. He had stopped in his tracks.

"Jesus. I hate snakes."

"You could wait in the car if you want," she told him.

"No. But I should get hazardous duty pay for this," he said, as he stared almost comically at the ground around him.

The deputy wandered around for a while, walking this way and that, scrutinizing the ground with the intensity of a dowser hunting for water. He stopped finally, glanced around.

"Here?" Elizabeth said.

Deputy Jimenez screwed up his mouth, then shook his head. "Naw. This doesn't look right somehow."

He walked farther along, heading north, parallel to the road, scanning the ground. At one point he stopped abruptly, turned around and started walking back the other way, almost bumping into Elizabeth. At last, the deputy held up his hand for them to stop. He stared pensively at the earth in front of him, then he lifted his head and glanced around him.

"Here," he said.

"*Here?*" Elizabeth repeated.

"Ah huh."

"Are you sure?"

"Yes, ma'am. See that rock over there near the road," he explained. "I remember that. The car went off the road just before that."

To Elizabeth, however, this piece of earth seemed no different, seemed as devoid of human connection as everything else around them. She gazed at the baked dirt, the scattered clumps of buffalo grass sprouting from it. If there had been an accident here, the desert had certainly covered up its tracks. Elizabeth tried to will herself to feel something, a tremor of emotion. As she had with all the other roadside memorials she'd stopped at, she tried to picture her son's last moments on earth—what it had been like for him, what he was thinking, was he afraid, in pain, had he called out for her?

Elizabeth took out her phone, with the thought of calling Zack, telling him she'd found the place where their son had passed on. But she didn't have any reception way out here.

"Where was he exactly when you found him?" Elizabeth inquired.

"It was almost dark by the time I arrived on the scene. The vehicle was over there a ways," explained Deputy Jimenez, pointing at a section of ground about thirty feet away. "The car had flipped over a couple of times. Your son had been thrown from it. He'd be right about here, ma'am. Close as I can figure anyway." The deputy extended both hands toward the ground, fingers straight out.

"And he wasn't conscious when you arrived?" Elizabeth asked.

"No, ma'am. He didn't appear to be. He seemed . . ." He hesitated, searching for the right words. "At peace."

"At peace?"

"What I'm trying to say is he didn't look like he was in any pain."

"Was he on his back or face down?"

She happened to glance at Gabe. He gave her a look of warning, as if to say, *Enough. Just leave it be.* But she couldn't leave it be. She'd come too far to leave things be.

"I'm pretty sure he was lying on his back."

"Were his eyes closed?"

"To tell you the truth, I don't remember, ma'am. It's been a while."

"Do you recall anything else about that night, Deputy?" she asked.

The deputy took off his hat and ran a hand through his shiny black hair. He had the beginnings of a bald spot at the back of his head. She imagined he was probably in his early thirties. Had grown up here, had known those kids on the bus who'd perished.

"Nothing I can think of, ma'am. Sorry."

Gabe said to the deputy, "How about if we give her a few moments alone?"

"No, I think I'm all set," Elizabeth said.

"You sure?" Gabe asked, raising his eyebrows. "You came a long ways for this."

"Thank you, Deputy," she said. "But we can leave now."

They headed back toward the SUV. Before she got in, Elizabeth turned and reviewed the spot again, trying to burn it into her memory. For good measure, she pulled off her St. Anselm sweatshirt and walked back and draped it over the rock.

"Are you going to leave that?" Gabe asked when she got back into the cruiser.

"Yes."

As they drove back to town, Elizabeth gazed out the window. Staring at the passing landscape, she tried to imagine her son looking out at the same desert scene, tried to imagine what he'd been thinking, where his head was in those last moments. Was he happy? Was he looking forward to getting home? To his last year of college? She wondered what he'd have done when he graduated? What sort of career would he have pursued? What sort of *life*. In short, had he lived, she wondered what would have become of her precious little boy.

It was a little before noon when they got back to the motel. Elizabeth thanked the deputy again.

"Please accept my sympathies, ma'am," he said, touching the brim of his hat before pulling out.

"You okay?" Gabe asked, putting a hand on her back.

"Yeah."

"You sure? You look like there's something wrong."

"What could be wrong?" she said, forcing a smile.

"You know what I mean. If we get started, we could probably reach Albuquerque in time to get you a flight back home."

"I'm not done here yet."

"What?"

"There's something else I need to do. If you have to get back I can manage on my own from here."

"I'm not in a big rush to get back. I just thought you were done."

"I want to put up some kind of memorial."

"I was wondering about that," Gabe said. Then quickly shifting into his problem-solving mode, he added, "Okay, then we'll need some stuff."

They drove over to the hardware store, where they purchased a ten-foot piece of one-by-four pressure-treated pine, the straightest and least knotty one Gabe could pick out, a box of wood screws, a small can of primer, another of high-gloss white, as well as sandpaper and a paint brush. Elizabeth was going to buy a hammer and saw and shovel, but Gabe told her he had those things in the back of his truck.

"And we'll need some Quikcrete if you want the thing to last."

He also bought a gallon jug of water, and they brought all the materials back to the motel and headed over to Elizabeth's room.

"We'll need some newspaper," he said. He left and returned in a moment with a copy of the *Albuquerque Journal*.

"You owe me a buck for this."

"Put it on my tab," she replied.

"Don't worry. It's all up here," he said, tapping his temple.

Using the chair as a sawhorse, Gabe cut two pieces from the length of pine, a longer vertical section about five feet and a horizontal one about two feet, and using the screws assembled them at right angles. Elizabeth then sanded the rough-sawed edges, and spread newspapers on the floor. Gabe shook the can of primer and opened it with a bottle opener he had in his pocket.

"Shouldn't we crack some windows before we start painting?" Elizabeth said.

"Why, afraid of getting high on the fumes?" Gabe kidded. But then he opened the window and the door a few inches.

"Make sure you cover the screwheads real good or they'll rust and then you'll have a mess on your hands," Gabe offered.

"I wouldn't want that."

As she worked, she thought of all the crosses she'd seen, all the parents and loved ones who'd spent time making similar memorials. She thought, too, of what George had told her about knowing what to do when she got out there, of what she'd say, and whether or not her son would be able to hear her.

It was the middle of the afternoon by the time she'd finished priming the cross. While it dried, they decided to head out and get something to eat. A light rain had started, so they drove instead of walking. They stopped at the convenience store near the old train station, where Gabe got a sandwich and a bottle of Coke, while she purchased a yogurt, a bruised-looking apple, and a bottle of low-fat milk. Elizabeth vowed to eat better when this was all over, stop smoking, get back into running, take better care of herself. Suddenly her future, which had once seemed a pointless wasteland as barren as the desert surrounding her, now appeared as a distant but very reachable probability. Life would go on, she now knew, and she'd have to be in shape for it. It wouldn't be easy and she would need to be strong and well conditioned to make it. They sat in the truck and ate facing west toward the purplish mountains. She watched droplets of rain land on the windshield, become swollen, then suddenly seem to burst and run down at odd angles.

Gabe glanced over at her. "Not a bad little place," he said.

"I suppose it has its upside."

"I was thinking about what you said."

"What's that?"

"How I could open a gallery here."

"Are you kidding?"

"No, I'm serious. Sort of. Nothing big-time. Just some little place where I could paint in my spare time. I could always do towing or mechanic work to make ends meet. There's nothing really holding me in Tennessee."

"What about your daughter? You'd be pretty far away from her."

"She could be bored out of her mind here just as well as in Tennessee."

"Do you think she'd like it?"

"She might. Who knows, if she gets really fed up with her mother she might just come and live with me."

"Is that a possibility?"

"I'd have to check with my attorney."

"I might be able to help you in that respect."

He glanced over at her and grinned. "Oh, I forgot, you're a lawyer."

When they'd finished eating, they headed back to the motel and Elizabeth put a finish coat on the cross. She propped it upright against the chair so that the paint wouldn't stick to the newspaper. The white gloss shone like a baby's first tooth, and the room smelled heavily of latex and sawdust.

Gabe stood, hands on his hips. "I'm thinking maybe you might want to go back down there by yourself."

"You don't want to come?"

"It's not that. I'd be glad to help out but I figure you might want some time alone. To be with your son."

She considered it for a moment. "Maybe you're right."

"Here's the keys," he offered, then he turned and headed for the door. "I'll be putzing around here. Take your time." As she climbed into the truck he added, "Go easy on the water."

"What?"

"With the concrete. Don't put in too much. Or it'll be like soup."

* * *

She was staring out at the mountains in the distance, her mind abuzz with a dozen different things, when her phone rang.

"Is this Mrs. Gerlacher?" asked a young girl's voice, frail and feathery. Elizabeth didn't recognize the number or the voice.

"It is," replied Elizabeth. "Who's this?"

"Nadine."

Elizabeth still couldn't place the name. "Who?"

"I'm the waitress. You gave me your card."

"Oh, right. Right."

"I wanted to thank you for the tip."

"Don't worry about it."

"No, that was really nice of you."

"Hope it helps."

"You said to call if I had a question?"

"Of course."

"If I don't get married to Howard, does he still get to have any say in Amber Moon's life?"

"In most states, the unmarried mother is presumed to have the right to custody of children born out of wedlock."

"So that jerk can't butt in?"

"Not unless he could prove that you're an unfit mother."

"And I won't be, believe me."

"If he gives you any problems, you contact me again. All right?"

"I will."

"When are you due?"

"March twelfth."

"You take care of this baby, Nadine."

"I will."

"Love it fiercely. Do you understand? Fiercely."

"Oh, I will. Don't you worry. Thanks again, Mrs. Gerlacher."

Elizabeth drove south until she spotted the St. Anselm sweatshirt draped like a flag of surrender over the rock. The rain had darkened the light gray cloth almost to black. She swung the truck across the road as the deputy had and pulled off onto the shoulder and then climbed out. The rain had lessened to a fine mist, and a soft wind swept across the valley from west to east. From the back of the truck, she grabbed the cross and the shovel and the gallon of water, and she headed out into the desert a short ways.

Elizabeth glanced around, wondering where the spot should be. Finally she decided one was as good as another. She lay the cross on the ground to get her bearings, then positioned the shovel where the bottom of the cross ended and drove the blade into the dirt with a vigorous kick of the heel of her sneaker. The ground was hard, obdurate, resentful of being disturbed, and she had to fight it. She worked diligently, lifting up shovelful after shovelful of the sienna-colored soil and placing it neatly in a pile beside the hole. There were small stones and pale grub-like looking things and light-brown, horn-shaped pieces that looked like roots, as well as rocks as big as a human heart. The metal made a nerve-grating sound as it rooted around in the hole, occasionally scraping a large rock. When she met the resistance of one, she felt it up in her shoulders and her neck. Once she had to get on her hands and knees and dig around one bone-white rock and with her hands jimmy it out and lift it and drop it on the pile of dirt. She fell to digging again, all the more fiercely now, almost maniacally, so as not to be dissuaded from her task. Soon she felt flushed from her labors, and the sweat began dripping off her face and down the center of her spine. Her hands became sore, then raw, and finally the beginnings of blisters formed on her palms and along the loose flesh between thumb and forefinger.

Slow down, Elizabeth told herself. What's the big rush? She had plenty of time. In fact, all the time in the world. She picked up the gallon of water and drank some. Then she went back to work again, this time more slowly, more methodically, pacing herself.

After working steadily for perhaps an hour, she felt the hole was deep enough. She headed back to the truck and struggled lifting the heavy, un-wieldy bag of Quikcrete. She almost wished that Gabe had come along with her, the thing was so weighty. Nonetheless, she managed somehow to lug it over to the hole and drop it nearby with a sigh of relief. She had no idea what she was doing, not the slightest, but she went ahead anyway and emptied the bag of concrete in the hole and then started pouring in water, a little bit at a time, as Gabe had advised. She mixed it using the shovel. When the con-crete was the consistency of cake batter, she picked up the cross and slowly sunk it into the gray muck, moving it back and forth until it had settled on the bottom. With one hand she held the cross erect, while with the other she selected various stones from the pile of dirt she'd dug up, and wedged them around the wood to buttress it. Once the cross was straight and firmly propped up, she began pushing the remaining dirt back in, using nothing but her bare hands. She smoothed the dirt and tamped it down, the way she used to when planting flowers in her garden. Finished, she used some water to rinse the dirt and concrete from her hands, and having worked up a powerful thirst, she took another long and greedy swig, the water shooting past her mouth and down her cheeks and spilling onto her chest.

There, she thought, standing back and reviewing her work. The cross was straight and solidly fixed to the earth. It looked substantial and permanent, as if it would last many freezing winters as well as blistering hot summers. However, something, she soon realized, was missing. When she realized what it was, she went back to the truck and searched around in the console for something to write with. She found a blue Sharpie and tested it on her palm to make sure it would write. When she returned to the cross, she knelt down and wrote, *Luke James Gerlacher, July 16, 1992–August 12, 2013* on the horizontal part of the cross. Above that she scrawled, *We miss you, sweetheart, Love always, Mom and Dad.*

Twilight was coming on fast now, the sun having slipped down behind the western mountains and she felt the chill of night in her wet shoulders. From down the road, she heard someone approaching. A battered truck with a faulty muffler, the noise reverberating across the flat expanse of desert. She watched it pass, the bearded driver, who wore a straw cowboy hat, staring at her, probably wondering what the hell this woman was doing out here. Perhaps he assumed she was an archaeologist out on a dig or an engineer searching for oil. Elizabeth then recalled that moment—not so long ago, though it now seemed like an eternity—when she'd passed by George Doucette at his wife's memorial and she'd wondered the same thing. She wondered again why she had stopped, and, too, what would have happened if she hadn't. Would she even be here? It was a question that didn't seem all that relevant now.

For a moment she knelt looking at the cross, staring at the name and dates she'd written on it. It made Elizabeth think of the many others she'd come across in the past few weeks. But unlike those, this *descanso* was her son's. And unlike earlier with the deputy, now she *did* feel something. She couldn't say what exactly but something. An amorphous but tangible sensation, something as light as feather brushing against her face. It made her shudder, and the back of her throat go dry. Perhaps it had to do with the fact that she had dug the hole and erected the cross with her own two hands. Or maybe it had to do with the effort it had taken to come all this way. To be with her son.

It was only then that she remembered the model planes she'd brought from home. She went back to the truck and got them from her pocketbook, and returned and knelt on the ground; she set the Mustang and the Spitfire at the base of the cross, on top of the newly disturbed soil, at right angles to each other. The Spitfire brought back a tangled nexus of memories. Before this moment, she couldn't recall that time in Wales without it conjuring primarily a terrifying moment, a moment of grotesque vulnerability, of confusion and fear and chaos. Now, though, she saw the other side of what that toy represented: those additional fifteen years she'd had her son appeared as a gift, a wondrous and precious gift. She'd had fifteen years to be able to watch Luke grow up, become a man, in all of his complexity and in all of his mystery. Fifteen more years to love him. For that she was grateful, and her tears now were not tears of sadness but rather of joy and of gratitude.

She ran her fingers over her son's name on the cross. "Luke," she whispered, remembering the moment she'd first called him by his name when the nurse had laid him in her arms in the hospital. She tried to still her mind, tried, as George had told her, to clear out all of the noise, all of the confusion and regrets, all the guilt and doubt and anger, all of the recent stuff, too, that roiled in her brain, to empty it, and simply let herself feel whatever it was she was meant to feel in this moment.

"Sweetheart," she said finally. "I'm here. Mommy's right here."

She closed her eyes then. She wasn't sure *where* her son was, couldn't picture a specific place or a context, in fact, couldn't envision him in *any* sort of setting. But she felt him nonetheless. Felt him close by, a palpable, physical sensation. She felt him below her navel, in the space that was her womb, as she had for those nine months. She felt him in the beating of her heart, felt him in her bones and coursing through her blood. She felt him in her fingertips as she touched his soft skin, and in her nipples as she nursed his small mouth. And she felt him with each breath she took, and in each exhalation. He was there suddenly, so close now she could almost feel his warm, living breath against her ear. *Luke, honey. I'm here. I'm right here.* She waited, concentrating on detecting the slightest sound, but the only noise she heard was the desert rain, striking the earth as a gentle whisper. Beyond that there was only this infinite silence.

After a while she rose, walked back to the truck, and got in. As she pulled onto the blacktop, she glanced back briefly, the white cross set against the harsh, endless landscape. It seemed so frail a thing, as did her gesture. She wondered if others who'd lost loved ones would stop and read the inscription, perhaps leave something, a stone or some memento of their own dead. She didn't think she'd ever get back here again and that made her a little sad.

Please watch over my son, she prayed as she drove away.

Chapter 20

Elizabeth got back to the hotel well after dark. She was tired, not just from digging but from the past several days. She took a long, hot shower, washing away the desert soil and the sweat and the concrete from beneath her nails. As she lounged under the water, she thought about what it had cost her to come here—her car, her job, perhaps her marriage, as well as a certain image she had coveted of Luke. Maybe her own self-image. Was it all worth it, she wondered. She wasn't sure. She couldn't help feeling something almost anticlimactic. When she got out, she toweled off and blow-dried her hair. She would have loved a drink but she thought she'd better not. She knew how easy it had been to cover up her pain with booze. Perhaps she felt the pain more acutely now that she was sober. She got dressed and sat on the bed. She looked up flights out of Albuquerque. Finally, she called Father Paul.

"Hey, stranger," he said to her.

"Is your offer still available?" she asked.

"My offer?" he repeated, surprised. "Yes, it is."

"I'll take it."

"Don't you want to know the details first?"

"We can talk about that later."

"When can you start?"

"Is right away okay?"

"Won't you need to give your law firm some notice?"

"No," she said with a bitter snort. Then she added, "On second thought, I might need a week before I can start. There are some things I need to sort out at home."

"Is everything all right, Elizabeth?"

"Yeah. I guess. Zack and I need some time alone."

"Do you want to talk about it?"

"No. But thanks."

"Sure. I'll get the paperwork ready then."

She was about to hang up when she said, "Paul."

"Yeah."

"How's Fabiana?"

"She's fine. She asks after you."

"Tell her to hang in there."

"I will."

No sooner had she hung up than a knock interrupted her thoughts. Opening the door, she saw Gabe standing there. He was wearing a new straw cowboy hat.

"How'd it go?" he asked.

"Good." Then she added, "Hard."

"You knew it was going to be hard."

"Ah huh. Where did you get the hat?"

"This store a couple of blocks over. And get this. The woman who makes 'em is from Knoxville. She's cute. About thirty."

She was going to say something when she saw he was holding an object in his hand down by his thigh. "What's that?" she asked.

"I got a surprise for you."

He extended his arm toward her, in his hand a small dark book. Part of her brain recognized it immediately, but another part thought, *No freakin' way*.

"Where . . ." she began.

"After you left, I went over to the sheriff's office and asked where they'd towed your son's car. It turned out to be that junkyard we passed just south of here. Sheriff Crowder even gave me a lift. He's not such a bad dude after all."

"My God, Gabe! Where did you find it?"

"It was wedged down between the driver's seat and the console. I don't even think they looked. Here," he said.

She hesitated. "I . . . I don't know what to say," she exclaimed, finally accepting the book. She thought she'd never see it again.

"Listen, you're probably going to want some time to read it. Besides, I got some stuff to do."

"Stuff?"

"I'm meeting a realtor for a beer."

"Really?"

"Thought it wouldn't hurt to check out what houses cost. We heading home tomorrow?"

"I guess so. I'm finished here. There's a six-fifteen flight out of Albuquerque to New York." Then she reached out and hugged him. "I can't thank you enough."

"Don't worry about it. Besides, you're paying me. How about if I pick you up for breakfast and we can hit the road."

After he left, Elizabeth went over and sat on the bed. She lit a cigarette and for a long while didn't open the book, just held it in her hands. She touched the gold embossed initials, the ones she'd had engraved: *LJG*. She was anxious, almost afraid to open it, of what it might contain. For a moment she actually wondered if it might be better if she didn't read it, just threw it away and closed the door on that part of her life. But, of course, she knew she wouldn't do that. *Couldn't* do that. When she finally did open it, she was struck by Luke's familiar handwriting, the looping *j*s and *p*s, the crabbed *a*s, her son evident in every word and letter. Though she was tempted to skip to the end, she began at the beginning, taking her time, savoring it, letting his words reverberate in her mind. She could almost hear his voice behind them. Mostly he wrote about the same prosaic concerns she'd already read about: school assignments or errands to complete or upcoming events or reminders to himself. Once he mentioned TJ; he wrote a note to himself to send her a certain picture. Nothing seemed out of the ordinary, and yet, reading Luke's words was enough of a make Elizabeth almost light-headed with joy.

It was in the last few months of the diary that she came across that word again: *discernment*. In one entry, her son had written, *Father J says confusion is normal . . . He recommends a few weeks of discernment.* Elizabeth assumed Father J was Father Jerome from St. Anselm, but she hadn't a clue what this was referring to. Discernment? Confusion? She herself was confused. She continued reading. A few pages from the end she came upon an address. It was for a place called Blessed Mother of the Redeemer Monastery, in Silver City, New Mexico.

The name struck her as familiar. Where had she heard it before? What did it mean? Then all at once it came to her; it was where Luke had ordered some coffee for Father Jerome. She decided finally to call Father Jerome, see if he knew anything about this. She dialed the main St. Anselm number and was transferred to his office. He wasn't in so she left a message. "Hi, Father Jerome. This is Elizabeth Gerlacher, Luke's mom. Could you call me when you get a chance?"

She read on but the diary didn't end so much as simply stop. In fact, in mid-sentence. Luke's last words were *Will have to . . .* But his thought was left unfinished. It somehow seemed a metaphor for his life. She lay on the bed with the diary for a long time, thinking, remembering.

She must have dozed off for she was awakened by her phone. She found the diary on the bed beside her.

"Is this Mrs. Gerlacher?" asked a man's voice.

"Yes, it is."

"This is Father Jerome. From St. A's."

"Oh, hello, Father," she said.

"How are you doing, Mrs. Gerlacher?"

"Better."

"Luke's death was such shock to all of us. He was such a brilliant student." There was silence on the other end for several seconds. Then Father Jerome said, "I couldn't help feeling a little responsible."

It was what he'd said at the grave site. She didn't understand it then, nor did she now.

"You had nothing to do with Luke's accident."

"But in a way I feel I did."

"How?"

"I was the one who put him in touch with Brother Vincent."

"Who's Brother Vincent?" Elizabeth asked.

"He's an old friend from my seminary days. Now he's the spiritual director at the monastery down in Silver City."

Elizabeth paused before asking, "I'm not following any of this, Father."

"I see. I take it, you didn't know?"

"Know what?"

Elizabeth heard Father Jerome sigh deeply.

"Luke was supposed to tell you. He promised he would. I told him it would be better for everybody if he told his parents."

Elizabeth was starting to get a bad feeling about this. "Tell us what?" she cried.

"Luke wanted to spend some time at the monastery down there."

"Why?"

"He was thinking about joining the Benedictines."

For a moment, Elizabeth was rendered speechless. Only a frail laugh escaped her throat. "My son wanted to become . . . a *monk*?" she said. "You're kidding me?"

"No, actually he was pretty serious. He'd been thinking about it for some time. He used to come in my office and talk to me. We used to pray together about it."

"A monk?" Elizabeth repeated.

"Yes. I thought you and your husband knew, Mrs. Gerlacher. That's why I didn't mention anything at the funeral. I'm so sorry."

"He didn't say a thing to us. We just thought . . . that he was acting odd. A monk?"

"He'd been in touch with Brother Vincent. He was going to stay there for a few weeks. Like a retreat."

She recalled then the word she'd come across in the diary. "Discernment. Is that what it means?" Elizabeth asked.

"Yes. It's a short stay at a monastery. A retreat that a young man goes away on to see if it's the right fit for him."

"Luke had mentioned that word in his diary. So *that's* why he was headed down to New Mexico?"

"Yes. He was going to the Blessed Mother of the Redeemer monastery. Brother Vincent was going to be his spiritual advisor."

Elizabeth's head was swirling. Even more than it had when she'd spoken to TJ. She had more questions but instead she only said, "Thank you, Father Jerome," and hung up.

She sat there, trying to wrap her mind around what she'd just learned: that her son had wanted to become a monk. It was preposterous. Her son, a monk! Yet in some strange way it made perfect sense. Everything, in fact, seemed to make sense now. That's why he had grown so distant, so secretive. Why he'd drifted away from his friends. Why he'd lost interest in women. She had just begun to accept the fact that Luke might have been gay, and now she found herself having to adjust to the equally alien notion that he was going to be a monk. My God! That's why he'd seemed in his own little world. He'd been slowly retreating from this world to prepare himself for another. Was *that* what Luke had wanted to tell her that night? That he was going to join a monastery? She wanted to laugh out loud at the strangeness of it all.

She called Zack and told him everything. When she finished, he was silent.

"Isn't that just the weirdest thing?" Elizabeth said.

"I suppose."

"You don't seem that shocked."

"I guess I'm not."

"Did you . . . did you know anything about this?" She thought then of how the two of them, Zack and Luke, that night at the dinner table had been in such subtle agreement on his making this trip.

"No. Not really."

"What does that mean, 'not really'?"

"I mean, Luke never came out and said anything to me. But in a way it doesn't surprise me that sort of life would suit him."

"What sort of life?"

"A life of contemplation. The life of a monk."

"You saw that in him?"

"In some ways."

"Why didn't you say anything to me?"

"I had nothing to go on, Elizabeth. He never said anything to me either. It's just a feeling I had. The way he acted in church sometimes."

"Why do you think Luke didn't tell us?"

"I don't know."

"Do you think that he was afraid to? That we'd be disappointed?"

"Maybe. Are you coming home now?"

"Yes." She paused, then said, "Zack."

"Yes."

"I just want you to know that whatever happens, whatever you decide, I'm sorry. For everything."

The only thing he said was, "I know."

Chapter 21

The next morning, Elizabeth waited for Gabe to stop by. When he didn't show up by eight, she went over to his room and knocked. There was no answer. Scanning the parking lot, she didn't see his truck so she returned to her room and waited. She finally grabbed her phone, looked up his number on the business card he'd given her, and called. No answer there either. She picked up Luke's diary and began skimming through it again. Her son's voice behind the words soothed her, seemed so recognizable and familiar; yet at the same time the writing appeared so inaccessible, so alien to her ear now. Luke had wanted to become a monk. How could such a thing have happened right under her nose, as it were? In some ways, she'd almost have preferred that he had been gay. At least then, had he lived, Luke would still have occupied the same world she did; he'd still have been her son, someone who would have been a part of her life, even if that life had been different from what she had once imagined. But *this* life? He might as well have been serving life in prison. It seemed so strange to her, so other worldly. A life of contemplation, Zack had called it. What had led her son down this path? It almost seemed that for every answer she'd managed to glean from this trip, a dozen new questions were spawned.

Around ten thirty, Gabe finally returned.

"Where the hell were you?" Elizabeth asked, annoyance leaching into her voice.

"Met with my realtor again," he said, rubbing his hands together.

"*Your* realtor?"

"We looked at a couple of houses."

"Really?"

"Yes. You ready? We should be able to make Albuquerque by five."

"There's something else I have to do," Elizabeth told him.

"Now what?"

"I need to visit one more place. I Googled it. It's about a four hours' drive."

"What place?"

"A monastery."

"A monastery? What on earth for?"

"I'll explain in the truck."

They stopped and filled up with gas, got coffees and a breakfast sandwich for Gabe. The weather continued cool, with a light drizzle leaking out of a leaden sky. On the GPS, Elizabeth punched in the address in Silver City, and they headed south out of Marrizozo. As they drove along, she told Gabe what she'd found in the diary and from her conversation with Father Jerome. When she'd finished, he looked over at her with that dopey grin on his un-shaven face. He looked youthful, buoyant, his face seeming to glow with the promise of something, like a child on the first day of school.

"You're shitting me?" he said.

"Evidently that's why he came down here. He was planning on going to that monastery for some sort of retreat. To see if he liked it."

"Jesus. A monk? And he never told you guys anything about it?"

"Nothing. Not a word."

"And I thought my family had its secrets."

Elizabeth took a sip of her coffee and stared out the window. The truck's wipers made a dull *klick-klack, klick-klack* as they swept the water away. In the distance the gray mountains looked like giant sleeping elephants, their sides furrowed and rough-textured.

"So what do you hope to learn at this monastery?"

"I want to talk to Brother Vincent. He's the one my son was in contact with."

"Do you think he can tell you anything you don't already know?"

She shrugged.

They'd been driving for a while when Gabe cried, "Is that it?"

Elizabeth followed where he was pointing out the driver's window, at the cross she'd put up for her son the previous day. With all the new develop-ments since last night, she'd almost forgotten about it.

"Yes."

"You did a halfway decent job," Gabe offered.

During the ride, Gabe chattered on about this one house he was consid-ering, just outside of town, that had a barn where he could park his wrecker and work on cars.

"And there's an attic up above the barn I could convert to a little studio. And it's all dirt cheap. I have enough to put down a deposit to hold it until I tie up things back east."

"Aren't you moving a little fast?" Elizabeth warned him.

"You got to strike while the iron's hot."

"I'm just saying you don't want to go off half-cocked."

Gabe glanced over at her. "Look who's talking. Miss Half-cocked herself."

She glanced over at him. "I don't mean to sound negative. It actually sounds like a good idea. It really does."

The rain stopped by mid-afternoon, about the time they arrived in Silver City, a small town pressed up against the mountains. The clouds slowly parted and the sun broke through just above the high peaks, sending gaudy slivers of pale light cascading down them. They followed the GPS north, heading up into the Gila National Forest. Here the mountains were thickly covered by pine and pinyon and juniper, and in the distance jagged peaks rose sharply toward a now bluish-gray sky. The scene looked like something out of a painting by Thomas Moran, all that daring light and high dramatic cliffs. After a while they came upon a sign that said **Blessed Mother of the Redeemer Monastery**. They turned onto a narrow dirt road that wound its way up a canyon, until they saw a group of tawny-colored adobe structures set amid the forest, their roofs covered with bright Spanish tiles. In the center of the monastery rose a tall bell tower.

They pulled up in front and parked in a paved circle before the bell tower. Across the road from the monastery the land fell away abruptly, so that above the greenish-blue tree tops a vista continued all the way to the valley miles below.

"Should I come along?" Gabe asked.

"I don't see why not."

They headed through an arched entryway and started down an outdoor colonnade when they came upon a man in a dark habit. He was kneeling on his hands and knees scrubbing the floor.

"Excuse me," said Elizabeth.

The man glanced up at them. He wore thick, smudged glasses and his pinkish head was shaved except for a narrow rim of hair around his skull like a crown. The bald part was shiny with sweat.

"I'm afraid, you're early for Mass," he replied, smiling from his knees. At first glance he looked older, but the more Elizabeth stared at him the more she realized he was only in his late-twenties. The severity of the haircut and roughness of the habit made him look older.

"Actually, I'm looking for a Brother Vincent."

"Oh. He's probably in the barn now. We're awaiting the arrival of a new calf." He said it as if he were an expectant father.

When he didn't make a move, Elizabeth said, "I wonder if I might speak to him?"

The monk stood finally and dried his hands on a rag. "I'll tell him you're here," he said and headed off down the hall.

"Boy, it's quiet," Gabe said, glancing around the place, his voice echoing down the otherwise silent hallway.

The first monk returned in a few minutes accompanied by another, this one a tall, heavy-set man also wearing a dark habit. His head was similarly shaved but without the crown of hair.

"Hello, I'm Brother Vincent," he said. Elizabeth extended her hand to shake, but the man didn't reciprocate. He said with a smile, "I've been working in the barn, I'm afraid. Brother Thomas here said you wanted to speak to me."

Brother Vincent was in his fifties, with sleepy brown eyes, a dark beard peppered with gray, and the concentrated look of a professor grading papers. His shaven head exhibited every little bump and recess of his skull.

"My son, Luke Gerlacher, was scheduled to come here for a retreat."

"Ah, yes, Luke," Brother Vincent said, nodding gravely. "We were all so upset to hear about the accident. My deepest sympathies, Mr. and Mrs. Gerlacher," he said, looking from Elizabeth to Gabe.

It didn't seem the right moment for Elizabeth to correct him. Instead she said, "I wonder if I could ask you a few questions."

His eyes suggested a certain surprise but he said, "Why, of course. Let's go someplace where we can talk."

He led them down the hall and into a small room that appeared to be some sort of library. The ceiling was supported by rough-hewn logs, the walls decorated with framed pictures of religious figures, most with luminous rings of halos around their heads. Half a dozen shelves were lined with worn, leather-bound books, while against one wall stood an old wooden card catalogue, the sort Elizabeth had had back in grammar school. They sat at a square oak table.

"This is our library," Brother Vincent explained. "May I offer you some refreshments? Tea, coffee? We make our own coffee."

"No, thank you," Elizabeth said.

The monk placed his elbows on the table, folded his fleshy hands, and rested his bearded chin on them. Emanating from the man was the sweetish odor of hay and grain, as well as the slightly sour pong of manure.

"Again, let me say just how saddened I was at the news of your son's death," the man said.

"Thank you," Elizabeth said.

"In my conversations with him he sounded so excited to be joining us."

"Really?" commented Elizabeth.

"Very much so. He seemed like such a fine young man." Brother Vincent paused for a moment, seeming to search for the right words. "So grounded."

"Grounded?" Elizabeth asked.

"He seemed as if he knew exactly what he wanted to do with his life. I think he would have made a wonderful addition to our community."

To Elizabeth, it seemed as if the man was talking about someone else, certainly not Luke. She hadn't seen those attributes in her son—grounded, knowing exactly what he wanted to do in life. Yet if one thing had become painfully obvious during her trip, it was the fact that she hadn't seen a great deal in her son that others apparently saw.

"The thing is, Brother Vincent," Elizabeth began, "my son hadn't told us about any of this. I mean, about wanting to come here."

"He didn't?"

"No."

"Ah," he said, stroking his beard as you would a cat.

"Is that, well, normal? For a young man not to say anything to his parents?"

"It happens," Brother Vincent replied, nodding.

"It just seems to me such an enormous decision for someone that age to make on his own. Without telling his family."

"You're right. It's the biggest decision a person can make. To enter a religious order. In my experience, though, sometimes a young man isn't quite ready."

"But I thought you said my son knew exactly what he wanted to do."

"He did. What I meant was he wasn't ready to tell his parents. Sometimes a young man might be afraid to disappoint his family."

"Disappoint?" Elizabeth asked.

"Some parents don't understand such a choice. They might feel short-changed."

"In what way?"

"That they won't have a daughter-in-law. Grandchildren. That their son can't just drop by for Sunday dinners. What they see as a 'normal life,'" he said, making quotes around the words with thick fingers that had tufts of dark hair along the knuckles. "So on occasion a young man will come to us without informing his parents."

Elizabeth thought how she would, indeed, have felt cheated, had her son entered the monastic life. But now, she realized how much she'd have preferred that to him being gone. She would have gladly accepted the smallest piece of her son now.

"Did he tell you why, Brother Vincent? I mean, why he wanted to become a monk."

The man looked from Gabe to Elizabeth, smiling as if he were going to tell them they had just won some sort of prize. "He hoped to deepen his relationship with God."

Elizabeth didn't quite know what to say. She didn't even go to church and here her son had wanted this deep relationship with something she wasn't sure she even believed in.

"Frankly, Brother Vincent, I find this all hard to fathom. I mean," she began, glancing around the room, "why would my son choose *this* when he could have had . . ."

"A wife and family? A good job? Golf on the weekends?" Brother Vincent said in a slightly bemused tone.

"Well, yes."

The man nodded sympathetically. "No, I understand what you're saying, Mrs. Gerlacher. I really do. This is a strange way of life for most people to understand. A difficult way of life. Why someone would give up all *that*," he said, waving his hand toward the outside world before he settled it onto the table before them, "for *this*."

Elizabeth thought of the Blake poem she had read in Luke's diary: *To see a world in a grain of sand and heaven in a wild flower.* Was this place the grain of sand for Luke?

"May I make a suggestion?" the monk offered. "Perhaps I could show you around a little bit. It might give you a better sense of what your son was hoping to find here.

"I don't know if we have time," Elizabeth said, looking at Gabe. In fact, she wasn't sure she wanted to stay. To learn more about this place. There was this unformed urge in her to run, to get out of here and leave it all behind.

"We got time," Gabe said.

"Well, okay, then," she said, acquiescing.

Brother Vincent stood and led them out of the room and down the hall. As they walked along he explained about the place and the life of the monastery.

"*Ora et labora*," he said. "Prayer and work. That's the Benedictine motto. We have our *horarum*, or the daily schedule, which is filled with work and prayer, as well as time for quiet reflection. We feel that in organizing our life carefully we can live closer to God."

As he spoke, Elizabeth glanced around at the place. She tried to picture her son here, in this place, this life, one so far removed from that he had known with her and Zack.

"This is our kitchen," Brother Vincent explained, indicating a room where three men in the same dark habits stood at a butcher block table cutting up vegetables. They looked up in unison at the visitors and smiled. Their smiles, Elizabeth noted, appeared both genuine as well as a little bit unnatural, as if they were high on some sort of drug. After that Brother Vincent showed them the laundry room where a single young man, hardly out of his teens, stood ironing clothes, steam rising up around him. His pink face was soft, almost unformed, his cheeks flushed from the heat. Over his habit he wore a kind of black apron.

"That's Llywelyn. He's our new postulant from Wales."

"What's a postulant?" Elizabeth asked.

"Sort of like a monk in training."

"Is that what my son would have been?"

"Yes. If he had decided to join us."

"He'd have been ironing clothes?"

Brother Vincent chuckled softly, a playful glimmer momentarily sliding into his somber dark eyes. "We all take turns sharing in the work needed to run our home. We feel work brings us closer to God. Your son would have taken turns doing necessary chores. We serve each other, as in any family."

"How long would he have been a postulant?"

"Usually several months. Until he was ready to move on to the novitiate stage. That usually lasts for a year, or until a candidate is ready to make his temporary vows."

"Then he would have been a monk?"

"If we felt he was ready to progress to that stage. And if he desired to continue."

Elizabeth looked at the monk ironing clothes and tried to imagine Luke in his place. It occurred to her then that the young man was from Wales, where she had first lost Luke. It seemed somehow significant, a symbol of something, though of what she wasn't quite sure.

They continued on into a beautiful garden cloister that smelled richly of basil and mint and some other herb Elizabeth couldn't name. Another monk was on his knees working the soil with a trowel. After that Brother Vincent showed them the refectory where the monks ate together, followed by the chapel, the infirmary, and then into the gift shop which smelled heavily of coffee. "We buy the beans from all over the world and make our own coffee. It's one of our few cash crops."

"So it's all right to make money?" Gabe asked.

"We try to be self-sufficient but we still need to buy some things."

Next they were shown into a building with a central hallway off of which was a series of small, shadowy rooms. Brother Vincent opened the door to one and invited them to peer in. "This is Brother Anthony's room," he explained. The bed, shoved against one wall, was narrow and low, more just a cot covered by a woolen blanket that had been pulled military-taut at the edges, and a thin lumpy pillow. Beside the bed stood a night table on which sat a lamp and a framed photograph showing a family, a single cane-back chair, and a small three-drawer bureau. There was no mirror in the room, Elizabeth noticed. On the wall over the head of the bed hung a crucifix carved of some dark wood.

"These are our cells," Brother Vincent said.

"Cells?" Gabe replied, glancing at Elizabeth.

"I know it sounds like a prison," Brother Vincent replied, smiling again. "On the contrary, we feel that the simplicity of our rooms gives us the quiet and privacy needed for contemplation. For growing closer to God."

Staring into the dark, stuffy chamber, Elizabeth felt it was so unlike Luke's bright, airy room at home, a room that had expansive views of the lake, a room that, when Luke was little, she had taken great pains to make cheery and homey, welcoming and embracing. Nothing like this dark and sinister-looking cell.

As if reading her mind, Brother Vincent offered, "We try to simplify the external, so that we may live abundant spiritual lives. Thoreau said that for the person who simplifies his life, solitude won't seem like solitude, nor poverty as poverty. Too much in our lives comes between us and what's really important."

"So this was important to my son?" Elizabeth said.

"Very much so," he replied. "For those who come here, peace and quietude are essential to spiritual growth. Socrates warned of the barrenness of a busy life. Come," he instructed.

He showed them into a barn made of sheet metal, where half a dozen cows in stanchions stood eating from a trough.

"We do all our own milking. Make our own cheese," the monk explained. "It's one of our few luxuries."

In one stall Elizabeth saw a newborn calf feeding from her mother's teat.

"That's our latest addition," the man said, leaning an elbow on the gate of the stall. "Sarah," he said.

"Brother Vincent," Elizabeth began, "if my son had come here, would I ever have been able to see him?"

"Yes, of course. Not right away. But later on, after he took his vows. In fact, many of our brothers take their vacations to see family. And we do have internet. Some even use Skype."

"Could I have come to visit him here?"

"Yes. We do permit visiting periods. My own mother who's in her seventies came just last year to visit me." He looked directly at Elizabeth. "As in any other marriage, you don't really lose a son."

Elizabeth stared into the stall at the newborn calf which appeared to be trying to perpetrate some sort of violence upon its mother's body. The animal pulled viciously on the teat, jerking its head and sucking savagely to draw life from its mother.

"I'd like to show you something," Brother Vincent said after a while.

He led them back into the main building and down the hall of the monks' personal rooms. He entered one which turned out to be a little larger than the other rooms but just as spartan. It appeared to be an office, with a desk at the far end and two folding chairs in front of it. On one wall Elizabeth noticed what seemed to be a schedule of the weekly duties for the monks.

"Please, sit," he said. He went over to a wooden file cabinet and opened a drawer. He put on a pair of reading glasses and searched for a moment. When he found what he was looking for, he walked over to Elizabeth.

"I wouldn't normally do this," he said. "I regard such a thing as private. Like a confession. But under the circumstances, I think it would be appropriate to give this to you."

Brother Vincent handed Elizabeth a piece of paper. She glanced at it. It was a letter, she realized, handwritten on yellow legal paper. As soon as she saw the handwriting, she recognized it as that of her son.

"We corresponded a little," the monk explained. "Our postulants often have questions."

> *August 5, 2013*
>
> *Dear Brother Vincent,*
>
> *I'm looking forward to meeting you. I should be arriving sometime on August 13th, if all goes well. I thank you for your kind letter and for answering my many questions. I appreciate your advice. I hope that I didn't sound uncommitted or indecisive, because I am not. As you warned me though, discernment is a big step. Venturing into the unknown, leaving all that one knows and loves. Yet it is not so much for me that I'm concerned as it is for my parents. I don't think they have a clue as to my intended vocation. It's mostly my fault for keeping this decision from them. This will be especially hard on my mother. She will, I fear, take this personally, that I'm somehow abandoning the life she wanted for me or even that I'm abandoning her. Of course, this couldn't be further from the truth. Still, I will need to find a way to tell her that my choice is not one of leaving her but of moving toward God, of getting her to understand that I don't love her any less because of this.*
>
> *I want to thank you again for all your help. One last question—does it get cold there in the mountains? Should I bring a winter coat?*
>
> *Ut in omnibus glorificetur Deus,*
Luke Gerlacher

When Elizabeth finished reading, she thought, *So that's what he wanted to tell her.* That he was coming here. That he knew it would be hard for her to understand. That he loved her. Tears, hot and abundant, sprang effortlessly to her eyes. Gabe reached into his back pocket and handed her one of those smelly rags of his. Elizabeth gave him a look, then smiled through the tears.

"Your son," Brother Vincent said, "was mature for his years."

"More so than I ever knew," Elizabeth replied, wiping her eyes.

"You must have been very proud of him."

She thought for a moment, then replied, "Yes. I am."

As she sat there holding Luke's letter, a memory came to her. In it Luke was a little boy, perhaps four or five. They were at a park somewhere, just the two of them. It was cold out, early spring, the trees bare and gray. She was at the foot of a metal slide and her son was at the top, about to come roaring down. *Be careful*, she'd warned. *I'm not a baby*, he insisted. Yet she recalled the look in his eyes, a hesitant, apprehensive expression. *Will you catch me?* he asked. *Of course.* She remembered him holding on for a while more, building up his courage. Then finally, letting go and with a triumphant *whooo* flying down toward her waiting arms.

Brother Vincent escorted them out of his office and toward the chapel. The day had turned bright, even warmish, with sharp blue skies stretching to the horizon. Steam rose up off the pavement in front of the monastery, and wafted skyward.

"It's beautiful here," Elizabeth said. "And so peaceful."

"Yes, it is," Brother Vincent said. "I hope that gives you a better sense of who we are, Mrs. Gerlacher."

"Do you think he would have been happy here?"

"I don't know if 'happy' is the word to describe our lives here. It's certainly not an easy life. Perhaps 'fulfillment,'" he said, using the finger quotes again, "is a better word."

Though the idea of Luke finding his home here, so far from her and from the world she knew, from the world he had lived in, made her a little sad, she welcomed the thought that her son would have fit in, found his place, his niche. Found fulfillment. She glanced out over the trees to the valley below. In the distance there were more mountains and beyond that still more, stretching as far as the eye could see. She imagined her son waking to that every morning, being surrounded by the pure silence and assured brotherhood of these men.

"Mrs. Gerlacher," Brother Vincent said to her, "Would you like to join me in lighting a candle for Luke?"

She hesitated for just a moment, then said, "Yes, I would."

"Do you mind if I light one, too?" Gabe asked. "For my daughter."

"Of course," the monk said, as he led them into the chapel.

As she entered the chapel, Elizabeth was struck by a single sensation: the profound silence of the place. She wasn't sure if she had ever encountered such perfect stillness in her life.

About the Author
Michael C. White

MICHAEL C. WHITE is the author of six previous novels: *Beautiful Assassin* (Harper Collins, 2010), which won the 2011 Connecticut Book Award for Fiction; *Soul Catcher*, which was a *Booksense* and *Historical Novels Review* selection, as well as a finalist for the Connecticut Book Award; *A Brother's Blood*, a *New York Times Book Review* Notable Book and a Barnes and Noble Discover Great New Writers nominee; *The Blind Side of the Heart*, an  Alternate Book-of-the-Month Club selection; *A Dream of Wolves*, which received starred reviews from *Booklist* and *Publisher's Weekly*; and *The Garden of Martyrs*, also a Connecticut Book Award finalist.

A collection of his short stories, *Marked Men*, was published by the University of Missouri Press. He has also published over 50 short stories in national magazines and journals, and has won the *Advocate Newspapers* Fiction Award and been nominated for both a National Magazine Award and a Pushcart.

He was the founding editor of the yearly fiction anthology *American Fiction* as well as *Dogwood*. He is the founder and director of Fairfield University's low-residency MFA Creative Writing Program.